PRECIOUS CARGO

PRECIOUS CARGO

PETER LUTHER

y **L***olfa*

To Donna

First impression: 2010

© Peter Luther & Y Lolfa Cyf., 2010

Cover design: Y Lolfa

The publisher acknowledges the support of the Welsh Books Council

ISBN: 9781847711984

Printed on acid-free and partly recycled paper
and published and bound in Wales by
Y Lolfa Cyf., Talybont, Ceredigion SY24 5HE
e-mail ylolfa@ylolfa.com
website www.ylolfa.com
tel 01970 832 304
fax 832 782

The Imagined Child

ALEX'S HUSBAND, USUALLY suspicious of everything but his own capable hands, didn't care that this supposed fertility clinic, Precious Cargo, was unlisted. He didn't even mind that its hand-delivered card had fixed an appointment which required no confirmation. All that he saw was the promise, etched in copperplate and framed in gold:

We promise you a son. We name him Theo.

"Theo," he had whispered, a light switching on in his eyes.

Theo was a special name: *their* name if they were to have a boy. With the patience and efficiency of people accustomed to disappointment it had been chosen with great care, so Alex couldn't understand why he didn't share both her indignation and her concern. These people must have hacked into her e-mails, or spoken to their friends and family; they should call the police, speak to the regulatory body...

Instead here they were, seated in a wood-panelled office with a damp hum of sandalwood, two framed certificates positioned strategically in their direct view. One recorded Precious Cargo's charitable status, the other the medical qualification of Dr Lauren Mays, obstetrician.

This doctor was sitting to their left, at a writing bureau decorated with ancient Egyptian figures in the style of 1920s art deco. She was a heavy, middle-aged woman, proudly filling a pink trouser suit with fur collar and cuffs, her thin hair a bare wisp of curls that endless cycles had reduced to a pale veal colour.

"Lloyd and Alex Morrow," she said at length in a quiet drone, her lips barely moving. Her foundation was thickly applied, a creamy white mask. As if taking care the mask didn't crack, she slowly looked up from her file. "You're very beautiful," she remarked to Alex.

"Thank you," Alex said uncomfortably, her hand going to the tummy that had expanded considerably over the past few years. It had been a long time since anyone had given her such a compliment and she looked away, unsure what to do with it. Her attention was caught by the busy walls with their many framed black and white photographs, which she soon realised were of the same family: mother, father and a boy and girl who might have been twins; the children at their studies with grave masks of concentration; grimly playing with their toys as the father looked on; the four of them standing on a pier with forlorn faces and holiday hats; sitting stiffly at the dinner table in prayer. Alex stopped at the one old photograph that was out of place in this homage to family: a posed photograph of a young woman she believed she recognised, though she couldn't quite place her.

"Marie Stopes," Dr Mays muttered, without looking up. "Once the most famous woman alive."

Alex nodded thoughtfully.

"We've been pregnant before," Lloyd declared, growing impatient with the doctor's leisurely stroll through their thick file. "Had an ectopic five years ago, Alex lost one of her tubes." He lifted his chin and took a long breath through his nose. "I still blame the doctors for not spotting that. We should have sued."

"You have some faith in litigation, Mr Morrow?" the doctor asked the file.

He licked his lower lip, a habit he had acquired a few years ago, about the same time as the red veins had appeared around his close-set eyes. "Lawyers and quack doctors," he muttered contemptuously. "Anyway, what I mean is that I know we can get pregnant, but we went for IVF just in case because the clock's against us, what with Alex being thirty-eight and all. But we've had eleven attempts and eleven no shows. Eleven, and we don't even get to first base. Not even to first fucking base."

"We had a hair test last year and it showed that Lloyd's zinc deficient," Alex added hastily, with a smile of apology for her husband's language. The smile didn't come naturally: she had a drained appearance, accentuated by pale skin and black hair, which she kept short and easy these days, lending some truth to her mother-in-law's description of her 'washed out and lazy' look. "We're told low zinc can be a cause of infertility. Lloyd's taking supplements."

Lloyd fingered the zinc band on his right wrist, bent out wide so it could fit. "The doctors say that we should just be patient," he muttered. "They say the missing tube isn't important, that there's nothing wrong with us. Nothing wrong at all." An eye narrowed. "Is that what *you* think?"

The doctor ran a suspicious finger down a page of the file.

"Is there something you've seen? Something in the file?" Alex ventured uneasily. "Something the other doctors have missed?"

"The file tells me you should be pregnant," the doctor replied, her tone carrying no reassurance. "Something's in these pages, Mrs Morrow, in all these tests and checklists;

something hidden, something patient … smothering every one of your lost and helpless eggs."

A bubble of surprise popped silently.

"It must be the zinc, right?" Alex said uneasily, the illusion finding a foothold in her paranoia. A vicious wheel turned in her imagination as she saw the assassin, the baby killer, at work. In that unforgiving place in her subconscious where there was only truth and reality, she knew that whatever was going wrong, it wasn't a deficiency in zinc.

"Tell me how you know the name of our son," Alex asked, an edge of defiance concealing her disquiet.

"We know the name of your son because his life is pre-ordained," the doctor answered. She paused, slowly and carefully turning a page as if she were pulling away the shroud of an ancient corpse. "Do you believe that? That life is pre-ordained?"

"Yes," Lloyd said immediately.

Dr Mays had arched pencil lines for eyebrows, which she now raised. "Mrs Morrow?"

"No," Alex replied calmly, folding her arms as she marshalled her courage. "No, I don't believe it. And I asked you how you know the name of our son."

The doctor looked up, her pencil-ringed eyes pinning Alex as she delivered a flat monologue. "But you *do* believe it, don't you, Mrs Morrow? And you *know*, don't you? In spite of all the reassurances from your doctors, herbalists and dieticians, and for all your reflexology and acupuncture, you *know*. After sex, as you lie back, feeling your ovaries hardening. With every period that comes with the inevitability of death. With every egg on the end of a plastic tube, which your body rejects as if they were germs. With every tick of the calendar, with every folic acid tablet, with every prick of the needle,

8

you *know* … you know that your failed pregnancy was your one chance to be a mother and that you will never, ever, conceive again."

The door of the office opened with the return of the young Latin-looking nurse who had ushered them in, his white linen uniform tight around his wide midriff. He handed Lloyd an envelope, which he accepted uncertainly, still dazed by the doctor's words. The paper was of the same emblazoned gold as their appointment card, but a number was embossed in the top right corner. The number was 113.

"What did you say?" Alex gasped.

The doctor's expression darkened momentarily.

"I said: *with every prick of the needle.*"

Alex made to answer but closed her eyes instead, as if her jaw muscles moved her eyelids. Her mind became a tiny picture of the doctor at her bureau, looking up and uttering those words:

With every prick of the needle…

The picture flashed and increased in size, then again and again, as if through the shutter of a zoom lens. The doctor, captured and frozen, appeared to look at her with hatred.

"What is this?" Lloyd asked, holding the envelope with both hands. He noticed its window, which felt like glass but moved like plastic and was misted with condensation, as if something was breathing inside.

"You came to us because we promised you a child," Dr Mays said, regarding Lloyd's rapt demeanour with some satisfaction. "You're very privileged, because we select only two families every year. We'll be giving you the names of the families that we've helped already, when you need proof of the miracle we offer. You will meet the children of Precious Cargo."

"Lloyd, I want to go home," Alex muttered, her folded arms now a protective wrap, her hands reaching her shoulders. She was still recovering from the doctor's verbal assault, almost an incantation predicting her infertility, and in a fleeting moment of horror she imagined that something was in her mind, buried deep, somewhere dirty, like a tapeworm's egg waiting to hatch. She wanted to scratch her brain.

"What's in the envelope?" Lloyd asked, ignoring her.

"Your son," the doctor replied.

"Lloyd, we're *leaving*," Alex insisted, turning to him.

He looked up from the envelope with a sly grin. "What do we have to do?"

The nurse lowered his head in a solemn gesture of respect; the doctor considered Lloyd awhile with a thoughtful air.

She allowed herself a small, reluctant smile. "Something so*, so* simple…"

★

The kitchen table was heavy unpainted oak and bore the faint, careless scars of children. This was where they cut up their Halloween masks, Easter bunnies and Christmas cards, pressed too hard with their pencils or had mishaps with their food. It was a busy, working table where the family ate and played, and was at the very heart of her dream.

She knew her children were there because she heard them, albeit in faint echoes, and sometimes caught a glimpse of their hands. The youngest cried when the table was needed for tea and had to be cleared, when the oldest liked to help by stirring the custard and pouring the squash.

Then the table's scars were smooth and stained, for her children's hands were bigger. The oldest was in university, home for the summer holiday and moaning about the accommodation and the course work. The youngest was in love for the first time, moody and hypersensitive. The table was still the place where they all met amid the chatter and challenge of the house; to occasional tantrums, minor tragedies and laughter.

Alex saw this table as clearly as she saw anything, but she didn't see her children. Even her dream betrayed her as she struggled in vain to see their faces, to hear their voices clearly, even to detect their sex. They remained, simply *oldest* and *youngest*.

You know, don't you? that doctor had said. *You know that you will never, ever, conceive again...*

She blinked away the doctor's words, spoken just before she had stormed out of the office in astonishment and outrage. The memory of her passage through the clinic was boxed away in a dreamlike haze.

Down to the reception lit only by its computers, the rolling red globs of the screensavers casting tall walking shadows on the faded floral wallpaper. She imagined them flicking off, furtively putting the area into darkness, as she hurried down the stairs.

Towards the two Chesterfield armchairs where they had waited, the nylon carpet balding and a strong air freshener only partially disguising the air of damp and neglect.

Past the nurse, who with dancing fingers reminded them not to open the envelope: not unless they were accepting their help.

"We don't *want* your help!" she screamed, only later realising that the nurse hadn't spoken, that his mouth was closed tight in his sweating, cherubic face. He had signed his statement with his hands and she had read it precisely; or at least she'd imagined she had.

She stopped and turned in frustration; Lloyd was lagging behind.

"But you *will* open it," Dr Mays had called from the stairs. She was carrying an intricately carved golden egg on a stand of four legs, each leg ending in an animal's claw. "You'll open it because your son's name is not only written on the card..." and she had tapped the lid, which was a diamond-studded pelican feeding its young, "...it is written *here*."

Then out, scrambling into the car and racing off as Lloyd was finding his seatbelt. Down the hill towards the market town of Brecon and coming to a braking halt on the small bridge overlooking the canal basin, where she attempted to rip the gold appointment card. It had resisted her shaking hands. She remembered Lloyd snatching it from her and throwing it into the water.

She had cried in spite of herself on their journey through the Brecon Beacons, muttering self-rebukes at being so desperate as to have allowed herself to be conned and spooked by some religious cranks. When they joined the motorway, she took an angry breath and let the tears dry on her cheek.

Lloyd offered no opinion on the episode, maintaining a look of puzzled concentration, his eyes occasionally going to the wing mirror. Shortly, he smiled, as if to acknowledge her distress for the first time, and suggested they turn off at a services.

"I think that's him," he murmured as he squeezed his six foot three inches frame between the coffee shop's fixed metal table and seat. His second latte had the aroma of brandy, courtesy of his hip flask.

"Who?" Alex asked, pretending not to notice the smell of alcohol. She looked over his shoulder to see a large man in an overcoat seated at the opposite end of the coffee shop, dipping a tea bag on a string into a mug. His face could barely be made out in an expanse of hair and beard which looked as if it had never seen a comb.

"He's been following us on the motorway," Lloyd said. "I noticed his four-by-four parked on the road opposite the clinic then picked him up again on the A470." He took a sip of his coffee and thoughtfully licked his lower lip. "We lost him in the car park but that's got to be him." The coffee shop was empty except for two families and a young couple wrapped up in each other.

Alex was alarmed. "Do you think he works for that clinic? For those people?"

"Maybe." Lloyd tapped his mug absently and took out the envelope that his wife thought had been left behind at the clinic, but had actually found its way into his coat pocket. He concealed his surprise as he noticed a splash of colour in the top right-hand corner of the misted window. It was the colour of pale skin; it resembled the corner of an ear.

He made to break the envelope seal.

"Lloyd what are you doing?" She reached for the envelope but he held it away from her.

"It might tell us what's going on. Maybe it contains a warning about that guy over there or something. I don't know."

"Lloyd, I don't want you to open it. I mean it."

He shrugged. "If it contains the same old nonsense then I'll just throw it away." He carefully unsealed a corner of the envelope. The seal came away easily without tearing the paper, which felt very strong, and the glue glistened with the smell of soap and baby oil. His nostrils flared with pleasure.

"Lloyd, no! They told us…"

"Told us what?" he murmured, savouring the smell. The seal was almost broken.

"Told us that if we opened the envelope we were accepting their help."

"We haven't signed anything, Allie. Christ, you're the lawyer…"

"I don't care, that's what they said. They told us we couldn't open it."

"But they're nut jobs, religious freaks – you said so yourself!"

"I know, but…"

"I'm going to open it."

"Lloyd, please…"

"Your wife is right, Mr Morrow."

The bearded man in an overcoat was standing over them. They hadn't heard him approach.

"Who the fuck are you?" Lloyd snapped.

"You're wife is right," the man repeated, unperturbed by this response.

"And who asked *you* to butt in?" Lloyd barked.

The man was looking at the envelope. "This … *thing* is a contract. That's why they put you on notice. There are rules, you see … rules they have to follow. Listen to your wife, Mr Morrow. Throw the envelope away. Throw it away now."

"What's in it?" Alex whispered.

He turned to her with small dark eyes. When he answered, his words had a lyrical beat. "A dream for one of you, ruin for the other, depending on which of you is faithful." With his North Wales accent the word *faithful* was created in the throat rather than on the tongue, the emphasis on the first syllable.

"Who are you?" Lloyd repeated.

"My name is Tristyn Honeyman. I'm a minister."

Lloyd eyed him up and down. "You're a churchman?"

"Without a parish for some time now," Honeyman admitted.

"Mr Honeyman…" Alex began.

"Just Honeyman."

She stalled, uncertain. "How do you know our name?"

He didn't reply.

"And why are you following us?" Lloyd demanded.

Honeyman returned to the envelope. "I was following you to warn you, Mr Morrow. Seal it back up now. Seal it up and throw it away."

"Shouldn't we just destroy it?" Alex asked.

Honeyman shook his head, a shift of his moustache registering his decision not to elaborate on his answer.

Lloyd resealed the envelope, thinking that he didn't want to open it anyway, not in front of this stranger. The glue angrily burned his thumb as it sucked up the paper. "You've got a fucking cheek," he muttered bitterly, licking his thumb. "One big fucking cheek, whatever your name is."

"Lloyd!" Alex exclaimed in a whisper. "He's a minister."

"Yeah? Who says? More like a fucking stalker, if you ask me." His voice was booming as he allowed himself to get angry. One of the parents on the other tables glanced over disapprovingly.

Honeyman breathed deeply through his nose then closed his eyes, as if he had ingested the words and was harmlessly dissolving them. "Use whatever language you will, Mr Morrow. Just throw away the envelope and let your life go on."

Lloyd presented a finger.

"Your wife understands," Honeyman persisted. "Look at her."

Alex was trembling. "Do it, Lloyd. I'm frightened."

"You're kidding me!" Lloyd exclaimed in disbelief.

"I mean it. I don't like it and I'm frightened." Her

expression was insistent. "The thing gives me the creeps."

Lloyd narrowed one eye, thinking quickly. He didn't want to admit it but he realised he had lost his nerve, he wasn't ready to open the envelope. In fact, his impetuosity in ripping it open just now was making his head spin. He squeezed out of the bench and strolled over to a flip top bin near the tills. "Don't know what all the fuss is about..." he grumbled, knocking the lid open by bashing the pedal with his foot then kicking the bin for good measure. He returned glumly to his seat. "Happy now?" he growled.

Alex looked at him for a few moments before returning to the stranger. "Who were those people?" she asked. "In the clinic I mean?"

"Never mind, let it go," Honeyman said softly.

"No, I want to know! You can't just come and say things like this to us without a word of explanation."

Honeyman gave a dissatisfied grumble that acknowledged her position. "Please understand that I can't tell you, Mrs Morrow. To even give you the simplest, the briefest of explanations would contaminate you. Would bring you within their reach." He glanced at the pedal bin. "Just know that you've had a lucky escape."

"Who are they?" she persisted. "What do they want? There was this thing they told us to do, they said it was a prayer..."

But Honeyman was already walking away, moving quickly and nimbly for a man of his age and in spite of some stiffness in his right leg.

"Lloyd, go after him. Talk to him." She looked at her husband in exasperation. "Lloyd? Can't you hear me?"

Lloyd couldn't hear her; he was considering his shovel-like hands, the fingers outstretched. It was the strangest thing, but as he had walked to the pedal bin he had felt the envelope's pulse in its corners: the faint rumour of a heartbeat.

The veins in his fingertips carried the memory.

As he lay in bed that night he still felt the envelope, as an amputee feels a lost limb.

With the heavy blinds drawn the bedroom was pitch black and he squeezed his sightless eyes shut then opened them. This ritual allowed the face of the little boy to find its shape and form in the darkness, the face he had seen every night for over two years.

"Prancer and Vixen," Alex murmured, asleep with her back to him.

The face, originally appearing within an opaque mist of uncertainty, had gradually emerged. It was of a lad about three years old, with chalk-white hair combed down to his eyebrows and blue, watery eyes. His ears stuck out. The tip of one those ears particularly interested Lloyd this evening as he struggled to recall the splash of colour in the window of the envelope.

"Donner and Blitzen…"

"Theo," he moaned loudly.

He held his breath at his blunder, waiting for Alex's breathing to settle in the hope he hadn't woken her. Aside from the few moonstruck days every month when they felt obliged to have sex, their bodies had formed moulds in the mattress that ensured they never touched.

"Comet and Cupid…" she announced with a troubled voice.

He made out the faint outline of the wardrobe. It contained his coat with the pocket that held the envelope he had pretended to throw away at the service station. He frowned, wondering at the number, 113, impressed in the top right-hand corner. Perhaps it was the number of the building, though the lonely road on the Brecon mountain hadn't seemed long enough. Perhaps it was its charity licence or something. He licked his lower lip, putting these questions aside as irrelevant; far more important was how and when he should open the envelope.

It needed to be done with care, he realised; with appropriate mental preparation. He was conscious of the beginning of a torment, of a longing to see inside the envelope that at some point would become unbearable, but for the moment it felt warm in his chest, like a good brandy. The promise of his son.

He settled back and a sigh of pleasure rocked the bed. Alex whimpered as she plummeted deeper into her dream.

"Alex?" he whispered, but when she didn't answer his eyes returned to the ceiling. He wondered if other parents were lucky enough to know their child even before that child was born. Perhaps it was a secret kept by parents since time began.

We *are* going to have a boy, he had assured his wife as he hugged her on the bridge overlooking the Brecon canal, and they watched the appointment card float away. In that moment of tenderness he experienced a rare moment of empathetic sadness for his wife, understanding that she lacked something that he now took for granted. He indeed had a faith, but not just any old faith: something ethereal or theoretical. It was real. It was *visual*.

His son had been born inside his head more than two years ago, had been raised in his imagination, and he *was* called Theo.

11

Faithful

"I ALWAYS KNEW what my little girl would look like," said the mother, her damp hair stuck to her forehead with the stress of the day. "Even before she was born, I saw her. I saw her eyes … her sweet, sweet smile."

There were enough pews for about a hundred people in the small chapel in Talybont, if the congregation was crammed in tightly enough and they shared the hymnbooks as on this cold morning. There was a gentle murmur of agreement, no one suspecting that the grieving parent was speaking literally.

The coffin had been put in the ground a week before – a private ceremony with the parents heavily medicated – and for this special remembrance service the focus of attention was a large photograph, framed in flowers, on the altar. It showed a sixteen-year-old girl with flaxen braided hair. Her name was Jemima Matthews and she was, by any objective standard, strikingly beautiful.

Many in the congregation were considering the photograph as the mother spoke. The child's resemblance to her mother was evident in the oval shape of the eyes, with the nose and hair belonging to her ashen-faced father seated in the first pew, although neither parent could ever have been regarded as handsome. In their youth they might have been described respectively as 'a little plain' and 'somewhat insipid', and those descriptions would have been on the generous side.

Those pondering the odd turn of the gene barrel reproached themselves for being so diverted at such a time, but that very human failing of valuing a thing by its outward appearance made the loss of the Matthews' only child seem all the more acute. The doctors were mystified, they were told: she had just gone to bed one night … and died. Her heart had stopped.

Linda Matthews was making a valiant attempt at her daughter's eulogy; her voice was shaking but she was yet to stumble. She appeared to be holding something tightly in her right fist, as if for support. It was too small to see and many let their curiosity end there, supposing it was either medication or something of Jemima's. Her sisters had urged her not to say anything, that it would be too hard, but as she had stepped up to the podium her blood mercifully turned to ice and everything she wanted to say was being said.

How she had cheered her daughter on at the swimming pools, tennis courts and running tracks, and that moment of revelation when Jemmy had discovered the parallel bars and through gymnastics had finally harnessed all her athletic talent and energy. How they both dreamed, together and inseparable, with the world at her feet…

A trace of resentment gradually spread across the faces of many of the Matthews family, annoyed that the woman was making no mention of Ray's contribution to the girl's upbringing. They had little doubt that Jemmy's death would bring an end to this marriage, and good riddance to it, many thought: Ray and Linda were so estranged that they didn't even hate each any more. The seating arrangements in the chapel had split naturally: Ray was in a separate pew from his wife and the Matthews and Mitchell families were on separate sides of the chapel, just as they had been when the couple were married here a quarter of a century ago.

Ray had declined to speak, but was taking the chance to visit his private memories and relive his secret relationship with his daughter.

The times she came to him tearfully under the weight of her mother's ambition and together they made their doomed plots of rebellion, away from his wife's twitching ears and ... that *thing*; the monstrosity that ruled Jemmy's life.

He pictured a sort of wooden rocking horse in the shape of a giraffe, with stripes scored roughly on its back and a neck that had been shortened for practical purposes, giving the animal a deformed appearance. Further liberties with realism were taken with the wide laughing eyes and a smile carved with such care it created exquisite shadows down the long, equine head.

Ray pictured Jemmy as a toddler pushing curiously at the slatted base and making the animal rock. When it rocked it went on and on, the head seeming to shake with excitement.

As a little girl, furiously riding it in the middle of the night, his wife closing down his protests with hissed whispers.

As a teenager, performing handstands on its back, mounting and dismounting over the head, her weary body perfectly toned from a lifetime of intense, relentless training.

And in this last year, abandoning it; left redundant in a corner of the bedroom, the creature appearing to deteriorate visibly. His wife hysterical as Jemmy announced she didn't want to carry on with the gymnastics anymore, that she didn't have the heart for it; blaming her husband for never giving her support and encouragement, her screams so loud the neighbours banged the walls.

"Is there someone … a boy perhaps?" he had asked his daughter when they were alone.

"Oh Dad, of course there's a boy. And I love him, I do. I wish I didn't, but I can't help it, I can't…"

Linda stumbled and another murmur, this time a mix of relief and sympathy, rose from the congregation as everyone anticipated the tears. But she had stopped because she had noticed three people enter the chapel. They stood at the entrance, perhaps because the pews seemed rather full, or possibly because they had no wish to go beyond the baptism font and stacked prayer books that guarded the aisle. Linda mastered her surprise, looking down at her notes and pretending to read, then shook her head and quickly returned to her pew. After a few moments of whispered confusion her place was taken by Jemmy's gym teacher with a prepared speech about how the extraordinary young girl could easily have been in the Welsh squad and made her country proud at the 2012 Olympics. His words of regret and sorrow were entirely genuine; it was a professional as well as a personal tragedy for the man who had coached her for the last five years.

Ray had recognised his wife's moment of hesitation and looked around. He saw Dr Lauren Mays, dressed in a black velvet trouser suit, and her new young assistant, the rotund Roman DeMarco, also in a black suit. Between them was a slender sixteen-year-old boy, showing no apparent embarrassment as both his escorts placed a supportive hand on his shoulder.

Out of the corner of his eye, Ray noticed his wife

give a warning twitch of her head; he turned back round, reasoning that Jemmy wouldn't have wanted him to interrupt her sports teacher. He cursed his cowardliness, wondering if he would ever have the strength to redeem himself.

There was a modest reception planned and most of the mourners made their way to their cars in what had turned out to be a miserably wet February day. The road running through the village overlooked the sheep fields and the graveyard. It was narrow and there would be a period of chaos while cars reversed to the horns of those blocked in.

The three visitors remained at the entrance of the chapel as people drifted past, a few wondering who the unlikely looking family were. Linda Matthews, head down until it was necessary for her to look up, offered them a long blink in greeting.

"My heart is broken," Dr Mays remarked, her perennial blank demeanour suitably tempered with regret. Roman concurred with a palm on his chest.

Linda motioned to her two sisters at her side to go on. She offered a nod of acknowledgement to the boy standing between the two visitors, only a twitch of her mouth betraying her thoughts, her right hand still making a protective fist. The tall young man, Carl Tyrone, returned a smile of sympathy but his expression was reserved and cautious.

"I hope you don't think I'm intruding, Mrs Matthews," he said. He had gaunt but extremely handsome features: a poet's face, his father liked to boast to anyone who would listen.

Dr Mays took a tighter grip of his shoulder. "Linda doesn't think that at all, my Little Lord B." She had coined the name years ago before he acquired his height: the B stood for *Byron*. "It is wholly fitting that you're here. My Graceful Athlete would have paid *her* respects too…"

Linda managed a nod and a smile to some curious onlookers passing by. "I hear you're a writer," she mumbled to Carl. The words would have been comical for their understatement to anyone who knew her history; she had followed Carl Tyrone's life with a fanatical interest. It hadn't begun with the moment he had discovered his flare for literature in a school writing competition at the age of twelve, or even at age seven when his teacher realised his spelling was always perfect, but with his second birthday party, when she had gate crashed his Aberystwyth home posing as a friend of a friend of a friend. She had received a stern warning from the old man who was then the senior Trustee as a result of that adventure, her insatiable curiosity subsequently taking more clandestine forms.

"Hopefully," Carl answered breezily. "I've had some interest from a publisher in London. My father's very excited about it."

"Novels?" she asked, in a hollow voice.

"Yes, I think so." His heavy lidded eyes went to the ceiling as he inhaled the promise of his future success. "Fiction is where the nation's psyche will be brought into sharp focus in the early twenty-first century. I think we're seeing a rebirth in creative escapism, now that popular broadcasting has found itself incapable of any further deconstructionist self-parody."

Linda nodded, then shook her head in admission that she didn't have a clue what he was talking about. "Well good luck," she said quietly.

"Thank you, Linda," Dr Mays purred. "You know how much that means to us. To our work. These times … well, they are never easy."

Roman agreed with the twirl of a forefinger. Linda's expression looked pained with concentration as she followed the movement of his hand; she felt she understood what he was signing.

I am new to Precious Cargo but already I feel the weight of its sorrow…

"What are *they* doing here?" Ray snarled, coming up behind his wife. "They weren't invited."

"Raymond, shut up!" Linda whispered.

Dr Mays stepped in front of Carl, who had backed away nervously. Ray Matthews was a slight man with a bend in his spine, but his expression was fierce.

"Remember who they are," his wife hissed directly in her husband's ear.

He paused. "What do you want?" he asked breathlessly.

"To pay our respects," the doctor said, removing with a fingertip a glob of mascara that had collected in the corner of her eye. "But also to reclaim what is ours." She considered her fingertip with dull curiosity. "The baptism gift has been part of your life for sixteen years; I'm sure you wish to be free of it."

A shadow passed across Linda's face. "You want it back? You never said that you'd want it back."

The doctor took her left hand and squeezed it reassuringly. "It has no meaning for you now."

"It has … sentimental value," Linda remarked faintly, retrieving her left hand.

"It has no value at all," the doctor returned. "None, now that my Graceful Athlete is gone…"

"Raymond, say something," she said helplessly.

In spite of his hatred for the giraffe, Ray didn't like the idea of the Trustees taking it back at their whim; Jemmy's toy was as much a monument to their grief as the gravestone at the bottom of the road. "Why do you want it?" he asked suspiciously.

Roman answered with a raised hand, that this was not a matter for debate. His lips were closed tightly in anger.

"Do you want ... everything?" Linda asked.

Dr Mays glanced at her clenched right fist and slowly shook her head. "We wouldn't be so cruel," she said.

Ray noticed the look, then his wife's hand. "What if I refuse?" he asked. His wife stiffened in horror.

Dr Mays slowly and thoughtfully ran two long fingernails down her cheek, leaving smeared gashes. "Do you imagine you no longer need our goodwill, Mr Matthews?" she hissed, her eyes narrowing with sudden ferocity.

Ray hesitated, in the scratched make-up seeing two wounds slashed across his daughter's beautiful, serene face. He shook his head, his resolve weakening, and barged past them in frustration.

"You can have the giraffe, of course," Linda spluttered. "Yes, and the egg too," she added, reading Roman's crooked thumb and forefinger. She paused. "Lauren, my little girl ... she will be safe, won't she?"

The doctor gave a sigh of exasperation. "Linda, our promises were made long ago, were they not?"

There was a short, uncomfortable silence. "When my first novel is published," Carl declared at last, "I'll go to the grave and read it to Jemmy. So that she knows it wasn't in vain. So that I can comfort her, and you."

Dr Mays gave the boy's waist a strong, protective hug

with a heavy velvet arm. "My Little Lord B," she said with rare affection. "You're such a sweet, talented boy."

"Yes," Linda heard herself saying, "he'll go far, I'm sure."

Honeyman was waiting at the door of his Land Rover, parked in a lay-by opposite the two neighbouring local pubs that competed for the thirst of the village. He dared a discreet wave as he saw Ray Matthews walking in his direction, a solitary figure in the grey drizzle.

"I'm sorry, Ray," Honeyman said, wrapping his overcoat tightly around him.

"The Trustees are here," Ray muttered. "They didn't come to the funeral, so I thought, I hoped…" He caught his breath, struggling with lifelong asthma which had become chronic in the last year. "Anyway, they'll be coming out soon. Get going, or they'll see you." He was referring not only to the Trustees of Precious Cargo but to his wife also.

"They always see me," Honeyman remarked sadly, "though they pretend not to."

"That's right, they've got nothing to worry about with you, have they? You're next to useless really, aren't you?"

"I failed you," Honeyman agreed gently, content to be the lightening rod for the man's anger.

"Do you even have the slightest…" and he puffed on his inhaler "…*slightest* idea how to stop them?" He wanted to swear but two meetings with the minister in the snug of the Black Lion across the road – the first a surprise encounter ending with his rebuffing the minister, the second called at Ray's own instigation when it was all too late – had taught him to modify his language.

"All I can do is watch and wait. And have faith that the way will be shown."

"Bull*shit*. My daughter is dead."

"Yes. Yes she is."

Ray's recently acquired stoop betrayed his exhaustion. "It's not your fault," he said to the ground. "It's my bitch of a wife's fault, and mine too for not standing up to her … all those years ago." He took a long embittered breath which seemed to scrape through his throat like jagged glass. "They want the baptism gift back. Jemmy's giraffe."

"Yes," Honeyman remarked thoughtfully.

"Should I give it to them?"

"You have no choice, Ray. Your daughter's gone. The toy remaining in her bedroom would be as inappropriate as anything could be."

"Then I'll destroy it. Anything, to stop *them* having it."

Honeyman popped two sticks of chewing gum in his mouth, wishing once more that he had met Ray Matthews earlier, that he'd had more time to gain his confidence. "Have you ever touched the giraffe?" he asked.

Ray hesitated, recalling that Honeyman had said something like that before in the snug of the pub. His mind had discarded it as impossible but now, in his grief, he found a dark hidden door of understanding.

The giraffe had been delivered by the Trustees sixteen years ago, carried by Lauren Mays, then a stunning woman in her early thirties who seemed unable to speak, and her counterpart, a loquacious old man with a badly fitting red wig. He had too many memories of the abomination that ruled his daughter's bedroom, but he couldn't for the life of him recall one occasion when he had actually touched it.

He groaned, wishing he had never met the minister, that

his mind hadn't been opened: that he could have sat through that ceremony believing they were a normal family whose daughter had died of natural causes.

"If you had touched it," Honeyman said, "you would know you couldn't possibly destroy it." A shift in his huge moustache indicated that he was smiling ruefully. "But this is all hypothetical, for only the Trustees, the child and the faithful parent can touch the baptism gift. You couldn't hold it any more than you could take hold of the shoulders of Julius Caesar."

Ray was nodding as he spoke, his expression hardening. "Somehow ... *somehow* ... I'll find a way of hurting them."

And there's something that I can touch, he thought.

Something of hers.

He pictured his wife and his mind's eye located her right fist.

"They're coming," Honeyman said. He quickly got into his Land Rover and by the time he pulled the door shut he was already reversing. He dared a quick wave at the childless father left behind on the pavement, who mouthed a question:

Where will you go?

Honeyman read his lips and shrugged amiably, but as he reversed to the end of the road he glanced up at the mountain that overlooked the chapel and its graveyard. A section of trees on the bleak crest would provide some good cover.

He shivered and shrivelled into his overcoat as he imagined the wind and the cold already in his bones.

Longer term his destination was uncertain, but he knew where he would be tonight.

The team of men arrived around 1 am. One guard was posted at each end of the road while the rest waited in the graveyard, their high-powered pocket torches glinting off secreted hand shovels.

The men in the graveyard waited until they were satisfied there was no one in the vicinity; standing motionless as gargoyles until a silent message activated them and they fell to their knees and worked furiously.

The trees had seemed far more densely packed from the road and when Honeyman had set up his high-powered telescopic camera that evening he was concerned at the lack of cover. The darkness came quickly, however, the bright moon obscured by black clouds that hung overhead like ragged curtains; he viewed the scene with a measure of confidence, clicking his camera as the faces came into view. He didn't recognise any of these men.

For cataloguing purposes he decided to take a photograph of the gravestone where the men were working. He brought the inscription in the marble into focus ... *Jemima Matthews, beloved daughter* ... then clicked. His telescope returned to the team of men on their hands and knees, shovelling out the earth.

He froze. One of the men had stopped and was looking directly at him. No, not at him, just past him. Honeyman held his breath, knowing it would be a mistake to move away from the telescope even though every primal instinct inside him told him to hide. His breath stayed in his chest until one of the man's colleagues roughly punched him on the shoulder to tell him to return to work.

Barely five minutes had passed before they were making their way out of the graveyard and jumping into the back of a moving van. Within moments, they were gone.

Readjusting his focus, Honeyman attempted to make out the ground near the grave, now black through the absence of the torches. Gradually he found what he was looking for and clicked: a deep but narrow rectangular trench adjoining Jemmy's grave. The sides of the trench were smooth; the men had been careful to pat down the earth as they dug and the earth had been collected in a large heap nearby, one large shovel having been left behind.

He switched his view to one end of the road, then the other, then returned to the trench and waited. Eventually, with a dissatisfied grumble he sat back and reached for his flask of tea. He was unscrewing the lid as he heard the smooth rumble of a vehicle approaching; he returned the flask to his bag with both excitement and regret and put his right eye to the telescope.

The Trustees' transport had arrived. He had seen it before: it was a hotchpotch of many different vehicles but it resembled a limousine with a four-by-four suspension and it was painted gold; a close examination revealed small ornamental animals' feet over the sidelights. It reminded him of the gold pelican eggs the temple distributed: exact imitations of one of the famous Russian Fabergé eggs. This was Precious Cargo's motif, an appropriate symbol for fertility and the rearing of children, for the Trustees were concerned with both.

The headlights provided a soft beacon of light as Lauren Mays and Roman DeMarco opened the hatchback. The young assistant was puffing, holding something spherical under a cloth. The cloth was discarded to reveal one of the eggs; it was upside down with its animal claw legs facing upwards. Such was Honeyman's knowledge of this artefact that it was immediately recognisable even in this poor light.

"Ah, what have you got there?" Honeyman whispered questioningly. "Now what have you got there?"

A twitch of surprise registered in his eyebrows as the egg

31

was turned the correct way up. The pelican feeding her young couldn't be seen: the lid was missing. He switched to the faces of the Trustees. The doctor was muttering to the trench. The nurse was silent, his head bowed.

"Empty," Honeyman muttered, looking up thoughtfully. He was convinced he knew what these eggs contained when the child was alive: Fabergé eggs revealed a 'surprise', and the 'surprise' with this particular egg was a display of miniatures painted by Johannes Zehngraf, an accomplished nineteenth-century portrait painter. He had seen examples of his work; not realistic exactly, for they were obviously oil paintings, but eerily lifelike, carrying the personalities of their subjects.

Returning to the telescope, the trench was no more than a dark shadow. He found the Trustees, now walking back to the grave. They were carrying something big and heavy, about five feet in length, covered with a blanket. Maybe it was just that the doctor and nurse were cold but it seemed to be twitching in their hands as they carried it between them, each effortlessly holding on to its base with one hand, the doctor slowly shaking her head as they walked. Occasionally they had to reposition their hands as the blanket moved. The doctor was talking continuously; the lack of response in the glistening face of the nurse indicated that the words were not intended for him.

"Frightened, are you?" Honeyman whispered under his breath to the object under the blanket. "Frightened…?" he repeated thoughtfully.

The Trustees stopped and the blanket came off to reveal the giraffe. It was placed directly into the trench.

As the nurse made to pick up the shovel, the doctor stopped him with a raised hand. She reached down to grab the toy, lifting it up to reposition it in the earth, as if she feared that it wasn't quite comfortable. The giraffe's head was given a moment of freedom as its body tilted, briefly peeking above ground, to be caught by Honeyman with a click of his camera.

It was also the moment that the moon chose to escape from behind the clouds.

The head was black with something rotten growing from inside, draining the wood of its life and energy; the face was wretched, with closed eyes and open mouth, as if on the brink of a scream. It resembled a pagan totem from some horrific sacrificial ceremony, its look of despair the harbinger to some unimaginable cruelty.

Honeyman recoiled from the telescope, fearing that the moonlit image would be stamped on his subconscious forever, such was the impression of abject misery. He collected his composure as the moon passed back behind the clouds and he returned, cautiously, to the telescope.

The toy couldn't be seen. The young man had taken up the shovel and was raking in the earth.

A pregnant Madonna

"GRADE ONE EGGS," Judy said, with mock severity. "We need as many of those silly grade ones as we can get." The brisk, open-faced nurse experienced every failed Morrow pregnancy as if it were her own: during the last treatment session she had admitted that she had never seen a couple so deserving but so unlucky.

That was just to keep them coming back and forking out the cash, Lloyd had remarked bitterly. He barely managed to conceal his contempt for Millennium Fertility's nurse these days, nor the physician with the African accent whom he suspected was from some backward state where they had the gun crime and AIDS.

Alex sat up and returned from behind the screen where she had been scanned. "We always get a lot of eggs, Judy," she remarked, buttoning her trousers.

Judy ran a pencil along her calendar. "The more the better. We'll blast the Puregon at four hundred millimetres right from the beginning. Just like last time, okay?"

"And the time before that," Lloyd murmured from the armchair at the foot of the bed.

Judy briefly considered Alex's husband – she always thought of him simply as *Alex's husband* – then returned to her patient. "I know our problem seems to be the egg holding on after implantation but the more eggs we have, the more chance we have of getting good cell division. At least we're getting the best possible start."

"Absolutely," Alex said, throwing a warning look at Lloyd, who narrowed one eye in wry amusement.

"It would help if you don't drink," Judy said, carefully directing the statement at both of them. "I mean, cut it out completely, at least for a few weeks. Booze will reduce your chances of catching." Behind the mints she had detected the trace of alcohol on the man's breath; it was easy to pick up, it being so rare for her clients to be drinkers, spending their life as they did on a merry-go-round of planned abstinence.

"I gave up completely the second and third time," Lloyd protested, "and a fat lot of good it did." He produced his wrist. "Now I'm wearing this damn zinc band. What more do you want?"

"Lloyd always gives up three days before egg retrieval," Alex explained, inwardly shuddering as she pictured another seventy-two hours of her husband climbing the walls. With a blink she banished her concerns over her husband's drinking: one problem at a time.

Judy nodded, hiding her dissatisfaction, and picked up her chart. She placed it on her desk and brought her hands together in a slow clapping motion, her habit when she gave important instructions. "Your period's in two weeks' time, so come back on the first day for another scan so we can check your lining. Start with the Puregon on the second day. We'll get it ordered today. It's a tight timetable but we'll make it."

As she marked up the dates she wondered about the short notice. After their last session the Morrows had planned to wait until the spring before their next attempt, to at least get some sort of holiday under their belt and to allow Alex to recover from the steroids and drugs. Something must have happened to bring the schedule forward. And from Alex's look of eager anticipation when they arrived, and the sullen face of her husband, she guessed it was *her* idea.

"It will have to be week Friday. I know that's cutting it fine but your periods have always been on the nail, haven't they? The drugs will arrive on the second day of your cycle but if they're late just keep them in the fridge and we'll start next month." She brought her hands together once more as she turned to Alex. "I'm afraid I can't give you a time when they'll deliver, just that it will be in the afternoon."

Alex looked questioningly at Lloyd, aware that he spent most of the time in his diving store reading sporting magazines.

"Don't look at me, I'm busy," he said moodily. He shrugged. "Mam can be there. She won't mind."

Judy nodded and scribbled something in her notes. She waited for the question.

"What's going wrong, Judy?" Alex asked. "Why don't we get a break?"

Lloyd looked down, his cynical expression fading as he touched his zinc band. He pictured his rugby club and the friends he no longer saw because he couldn't bear to hear them talking about their sons. How they took them to the club matches on Saturdays and explained the line-out strategy; gave them pep talks about the school team over burgers and Nintendos.

Passing compliments to each other on how smart their boys were; no, no, *your* kid's going to be the high-flier with those sort of marks, without a doubt...

A smile in the shower room as they guiltily caught his eye, then with rough towelling asking him what he had planned for his holidays...

"I don't know my darling," Judy replied.

It was true: she didn't know. This was a couple who didn't even need IVF; on paper there wasn't a single medical problem they could identify. She felt a twinge of guilt; the Morrows were some £40,000 poorer and had suffered eleven bereavements for their time here. It wasn't a statistic destined for Millennium Fertility's CV.

She closed her file with a smile of encouragement.

The Morrows were subdued as they returned to their terraced house, weary with the argument that had erupted as soon as they got into their car. Once again, the cause of the row was Precious Cargo; it was becoming a daily routine.

Lloyd leant down to hug his dog, Sheba, the German Shepherd who came bounding out of the kitchen. His expression softened as he stroked her. Sheba was virtually blind with cataracts but knew her master's smell, immediately finding his legs and growling with contentment as her ears were tickled.

"I can't believe we're still discussing those people," Alex muttered, to close off the argument.

"All I said was that at least they didn't give us a big fancy bill. Not like Millennium Fucking Fertility."

"Precious Cargo are charlatans, Lloyd."

"Why? Because they work for *free*?" He gave Sheba a rough hug. "Perhaps you've been a lawyer so long you've grown cynical. Maybe you've forgotten there are people out there who aren't just in it for the cash."

"That's not fair. Judy really cares. They all do."

"Right." He made to say something else but stopped, his tongue finding his lower lip. The pause became a silence.

These Precious Cargo arguments were different from all

the others, Alex had begun to realise. Lloyd always whined and moaned when he wanted something, never letting up, but now he seemed ready to make a strategic retreat, as some wily QC knows when to withdraw from an unhelpful witness and bank his winnings. She was detecting some satisfaction in his demeanour when the arguments ended, as if he was confident of final victory.

"I'm worried about us," she admitted. And when she received no response added, with a touch of melodrama, "This is destroying us".

Lloyd shrugged as if she had remarked that they were low on tea bags. "Good girl," he murmured to Sheba. "You're a good girl, aren't you?"

"Why don't we adopt?"

"No way," he snapped.

"Why not?" A shard of pain splintered her eyes; her hand went to her forehead.

"The kid wouldn't have our genes. Don't tell me it wouldn't bother you that it wouldn't be our genes."

"What's so special about our genes?" she murmured, her hand still at her forehead. She looked reproachfully at the ceiling, to that section that was the floor of the box room. "We just want a family, that's all. We'd love the child the same, whatever."

"Maybe we would, and maybe we wouldn't. Maybe when the kid turned sixteen he'd want to find his real parents."

"How do you know it would be a *he*?"

"It'll be a boy," he said, patting the dog's back to signal that she'd had enough. He got up as Sheba plodded back into the kitchen to the thick rug where she spent most of her time. "You okay?" he asked, noticing Alex's hand on her forehead.

"Just a headache. I think I'll go and lie down for a bit."

As she went up the stairs she had the notion that Lloyd had walked disinterestedly into the kitchen, then left the house through the back door. She reached the box room, planning to go through the ritual that would bring the pain an end. Then, over the constant throb of her headache she imagined that she heard galloping hooves.

She opened the door. The room was empty except for a side table with a candle, which she lit once a year to mourn the child they had lost five years ago.

There were two posters on the walls. On her left was a print of the *Madonna del Parto* by the fifteenth-century painter Piero della Francesa. To her knowledge, and to the knowledge of the friend who had recommended it to her, it was unique in being the only Renaissance picture of a heavily pregnant Madonna. Notwithstanding the presence of two angels in the wings the Madonna looked uncomfortable and fatigued, seemingly more concerned with backache than with the notion of the immaculate conception.

Alex had been told that this picture had magical qualities, that every woman who treasured it became pregnant. She had a smaller print by her bed, which she touched every morning, and a laminated card that she kept in her purse.

The other poster, which was so large that it almost completely swallowed up the facing wall, had been put up by Lloyd over two years ago. She didn't know where he had found it but it had some sticky-back plastic that was so stubborn the poster had been literally sucked onto the wall, and was now bonded so tight it would take bowls of soapy water and a patient razor to peel it off. A rough corner, where some paper was nibbled away, was evidence that the project had been started and abandoned.

She hated this poster. It was a highly realistic painting of Santa's sleigh and reindeer but at the time she had complained to Lloyd that there was no Rudolph; that children loved Rudolph. He answered that it was based on the 1832 poem *The Night before Christmas* when there were only eight reindeers.

These eight reindeers were heavily muscled and galloped through the air with fierce expressions, coming towards the line of vision with as much enthusiasm and violence as the famous painting of the charge of the Scots Greys. At the bottom of the poster was the inscription: *"Now Dasher! Now Dancer! Now, Prancer and Vixen! On, Comet! On, Cupid! On, Donner and Blitzen!"*

As part of the ritual she read the inscription with dreary eyes. The poster was entitled *A Visit from St Nick* but St Nicholas, his face hidden in the red, fur-lined hood, seemed a little too thin and rakish to be Santa Claus. He was also cracking a long and evil-looking whip.

She shook her head wearily. When the baby was born she would scrape it off the wall even if it took her a year. Until then, it could stay; she was too tired to be bothered with it now.

With a measure of relief she gently shut the door. She believed the ritual to ease her headache involved the Pregnant Madonna, that the painting had a calming effect: anyway, her headache was retreating, though still heavy in her mind, and she felt like lying down. In the past she had occasionally suffered from migraines but they were arriving with a vengeance since their visit to the Brecon clinic, and always when they argued.

From the garden shed, Lloyd noticed the top of her head in the bedroom window and waited until she disappeared from view. He drained his bottle of Budweiser with a final swig, confident that he could now drink in peace, then collected a replacement from the portable fridge at his feet, his favourite possession. It was an awkward crouch, his drinking position, for the shed was cluttered with his diving repairs: empty air tanks, masks which needed realigning, dry suits with tears in the rubber, all of which he had brought home from the store with the intention of reconditioning and selling them.

The repairs were his excuse for privacy on the weekends until he emerged at 6 pm and casually announced it was time for a drink. He wasn't aware that Alex had as much need of the pretence as he did, nodding with mute understanding when he muttered something about *going to see if I can get some of that stuff fixed,* then later pretending not to notice the stale lager on his breath.

He glanced up at the bedroom window once more then reached over to a compressor tank, pulled it out from under some old clothes and unclipped it. The bottom of the tank screwed out where it had been neatly sheared; holding his breath, as if he was handling a bomb, he took out Precious Cargo's envelope.

It was still sealed, its incarceration having caused it to lose none of its lustre, though it pulsed gratefully in his hands with its sudden, if temporary freedom. The plastic window showed only white paper through the condensation, and with a frown he shook it until a splash of colour, which he believed was the lobe of an ear under a brush of white-blond hair, appeared in its corner.

He settled back contentedly, pulling his legs up towards his chest, and swigged his lager. He would study the envelope for the next three hours, wondering about the thrill if he had the courage to open it, while the eye in the mist window would acknowledge his attention with silent understanding. His perfect drinking companion.

He smiled, imagining some future time, with money and no cares, when he was on his charter yacht swigging a cold beer with his son and First Mate, Theo Morrow. Theo was only twelve and had trouble pulling at a rope, unaware that his father was holding its end to help when it was necessary.

"Take the starboard line first, check the wind," Lloyd muttered. "That's it, wrap it round. Don't let it get tangled with your feet. Feet! Watch your feet!"

Lloyd stopped himself, remembering he was alone and speaking to an envelope. A glance up at the house confirmed that the bedroom light was still off and he returned gloomily to his drink and his dream.

She wasn't on the yacht. No, no, no. That trip was reserved for father and son.

★

In anticipation of Valentine's Day the Morrows' valentine cards were placed dutifully on the kitchen fridge.

These were the same durable cards they had exchanged in the first year of their marriage and were pulled out each year as both a raised finger to the commercialism of the day and as a lovers' foible. This in any event was their reasoning, although this year, and probably the one before, the convention was welcomed as a timesaving exercise that spared them an embarrassing pretence at romance.

Alex was nevertheless determined to make an effort this year, having booked a table at *Le Gallois*, a glorious French restaurant where, on their first date seven years ago, Lloyd had excitedly told her about his plans to set up a diving instruction franchise. The business plan was riddled with inconsistencies, her analytical mind ripping it apart behind her wine while the little girl in her was mesmerized by his passionate descriptions of exotic fish and pearl fishing.

Was it his dreams, or his jaw line and his shoulders, that had caused her to fall in love? Applying her lipstick for the first time in weeks, pursing her lips in the dressing table mirror, she supposed it was irrelevant: she was married to the man and that was that. Whether it was a good decision or bad, whether it had been out of love or lust, whether it would prove to be a mistake or a triumph, was a matter for the secret historians who analyse lives after they are done.

"Shut up, shut up," she told her paranoia and concentrated on her mascara. Her large brown eyes with their long lashes responded well to make-up; Lloyd insisted it was her eyes that had wowed him the first night, that and an hourglass figure that was as hot as hell.

She sighed. Four years of steroids, combined with a lack of exercise due to the treatment, made it seem a hundred years ago.

You're very beautiful...

The doctor's remark was so complimentary because it wasn't a compliment at all, more a disinterested statement of fact. Whenever the bizarrely dressed obstetrician surfaced in her memory Alex quickly removed her with a shake of the head, but this time the doctor found her way in just long enough to revisit that speech, sounding like a curse.

You know you will never, ever, conceive again.

Alex's lipstick stopped in mid air, as she considered the doctor's promise of a son.

"No, no, no," she whispered, shaking her head. "People aren't pre-ordained. People are just born. They're just born."

She closed her eyes to find the oak kitchen table, in the hope she might see the faces of her children. Still they eluded her.

"No matter," she declared, getting up from the dressing table and slipping into her heels. She was wearing her short black dress with her sexiest underwear and all her best jewellery had come out for the occasion. She sprayed on her expensive Silver Rain perfume, an airmailed birthday present from her father, popping the metal raindrop into her most petite and impractical of handbags. "Lloyd, I'm ready," she called downstairs. He was already in his suit when she got home; he told her she should take her time, have a long bath and stuff. They had even kissed.

"Sex tonight," she had whispered. "Get it while you can."

She made a quiet entrance at the door of the front room, her arms slightly raised for perfect poise as she presented her ensemble.

"Hello, Valentine," she said.

He didn't have anything to say. He was snoring on the settee, a brandy bottle nearby.

I V

Birthmark

S HELBY WIGHT WAS a Valentine's Day baby, which allowed her delighted father to joke that he was able to get away with giving his wife Margie just the one bunch of flowers.

In fact, Margie's private hospital room was decorated with flowers, all of them roses in exquisite bouquets, each card handwritten. Henry Wight was a wealthy man who adored his wife.

They had married at the age of sixteen and even by the frail standards of puppy love the omens weren't favourable: he was dyslexic and only interested in cars; she had dropped out of school to look after her clinically depressed mother. They began with a small rented garage in Tiger Bay, the docklands of Cardiff; while he was fixing the cars, she ran the accounts and discovered that she not only had a head for business but a flair for marketing. Within five years there were three garages and a roadside territory agreement with the RAC. Within ten years, *Wights* was the biggest haulage company in South Wales, slicing through the competition with the efficiency systems Margie had devised and with the network of contacts she had nurtured. Henry now sat on several government committees; he already had his CBE and it was rumoured that for his services to the transport industry the knighthood was on the horizon.

It was a fairytale story, or would have been if they had been able to produce an heir for their hand-built fortune, the one thing that eluded them. Margie was now fifty years of age and her friends whispered the baby was a miracle, sure that she had mentioned starting the menopause.

Margie disliked the term 'miracle', jumping severely on anyone who let the word slip out. She did like the idea of Shelby being a Valentine's Day baby, however, because of the brown birthmark near the left corner of her mouth, which she thought looked like a heart. Henry remarked it was more of a pimple but didn't argue when she reminded him that Cindy Crawford had one just like it and it certainly hadn't done *her* any harm.

The Wights were restless by nature, moving home regularly; for the last two years they had lived in a townhouse overlooking Penarth Marina, which Henry had fallen in love with because it had a private berth for his twenty-foot Trader. *We can save on the harbour fees!* he reasoned when the house became available. Margie agreed, provided the house was completely redecorated and furnished to fit its maritime theme, a task that had occupied her for six months and put a six-figure dent in their bank balance. Now that Shelby was born, Margie had decided that they would be moving again because they needed a house with a garden. The matter was beyond discussion.

Beyond discussion.

Margie had discovered that phrase when she had dealt with her first irate customer some thirty years ago, while Henry hid in the back room wiping the grease off his hands. It marked the end to any debate.

"So you're moving?" Dr Mays asked wistfully as she looked out at the harbour from the ground-floor kitchen, the masts of the schooners rattling with a light breeze.

Margie followed the doctor's gaze. "This isn't a family home, Lauren. It's a home for either a well-heeled young couple or a retirement couple."

"And we're not ready to retire just yet," Henry declared, emptying a bottle of Krug into four large crystal flutes. He was as portly as his wife was thin, although they both had skin made a little leathery from too many suntans.

The doctor gave the briefest acknowledgement of thanks as she was handed the champagne. She watched as the champagne was handed to Roman, who was seated at the table and dressed conservatively in grey jeans and a baggy white shirt. Today was Shelby's baptism but the Trustees had given notice at the last moment that they would be visiting, when of course no one else could be present. Henry had muttered that it was impossible, that it was far too late to cancel the party they had arranged: almost everyone had confirmed, he growled, producing the pile of RSVP cards. Margie told him to shut up and passed him one of their two duplicate phone books, telling him to start with the As while she worked backwards from the Ys. The caterers could deliver the food to the Salvation Army.

"There's nowhere for children to play," Margie clarified, raising her flute politely in a toast to the Trustees. She sipped the champagne cautiously, knowing her visitors wouldn't drink any of it.

Roman tapped the table with a fingernail to attract their attention, then indicated the common at the rear of the house.

"It's not very safe," Margie replied uncomfortably. "Travellers set down there sometimes."

"Oh, not for years now, Margie..." Henry said. He sipped his champagne as he glimpsed the flash in her eyes.

"It's not my business of course..." Dr Mays said, her attention drifting back towards the view.

"What?" Margie asked.

Dr Mays didn't respond.

"What, Lauren? Tell me," Margie insisted, a trace of panic in her tone.

The doctor turned to her with a distracted air, pausing a few moments before speaking. "My apologies, your view was enthralling me. I think this is a charming place to raise a child." She glanced once more at the harbour. "Yes, I can imagine the tinkle of the masts in the night and the walks along the sea down to the barrage; the parties on the deck in the summer."

Henry chuckled as he refilled his glass. "I'm afraid my wife has made up her mind, doctor," he said. He couldn't quite get his head around calling the old bat by her first name, and still had to suppress a smirk whenever he saw what she was wearing – today, a tight outfit in black leather with red stripes and a high collar.

In fact, now he thought about it, the doctor had never invited him to call her by her first name, as she had done early on with Margie. He considered his champagne. He hadn't once crossed swords with the odd-looking woman, having simply followed Margie's lead from the outset, but for the first time he imagined the prospect and didn't care for it.

"We like our families to have ... roots," the doctor remarked. "It's none of our business, of course, but families shouldn't move from the houses they love. This is Shelby's home; the first thing she'll see when her eyes focus."

Henry chuckled once more at the futility of argument,

while Margie looked from nurse to doctor. "Penarth does have good schools," she conceded.

"And an excellent GP's surgery, I'm told," the doctor added.

"Yes, yes you're right," Margie agreed. "I'd forgotten about that." She turned to Henry and said, "We'll stay." Henry choked and spat out his champagne. Ignoring his mishap, Margie turned to Dr Mays. "We'll stay," she repeated calmly, a wave of relief crossing her face as she saw the doctor turn with a look of delighted surprise.

A few moments of silence ticked past.

"Well I think it's time to see your little treasure," Dr Mays suggested. "We've brought a gift for her baptism. Something very special."

Margie considered the object on the table covered with a lint cloth. It was about two foot high, some kind of square frame device that had rattled when the nurse carried it in. She swallowed, summoning her courage. "The other family … do you know…?" She shook off Henry's hand on her arm.

"Know?" Dr Mays asked gently.

Margie put in place a blank expression. "Do you know who the other family will be?"

"Yes, we've found them," came the reply.

Margie nodded, desperately attempting to maintain her demeanour of mild disinterest.

"Margie…" Henry warned.

"I'm just interested," Margie snapped.

"They live in North Cardiff, at the Caerphilly Crossroads," the doctor answered. "Their name is Morrow."

"Morrow," Margie repeated distastefully. "At the crossroads," she added, finding the location description more to her taste than the name. She reached for the champagne and poured the last few drops into the doctor's flute, though the doctor was yet to touch it. "What does she do, this woman by the crossroads?"

"She's a lawyer."

Margie's face was all confusion. "A lawyer? But I thought...?"

"They're on hard times," the doctor clarified. "He has debts. She's a solicitor, but in a small practice."

"A solicitor," Margie remarked, cheering up, having pictured some highflying barrister type. "Oh, solicitors are ten a penny. We've got a few of those working for us, haven't we Henry? Part of our support staff, you know. Lots of them looking for jobs, what with the credit crunch." She took a reflective sip of champagne. "Does this woman have time to follow a career and raise a child?"

"A good question," Dr Mays agreed.

"You're locked in a room with a snake, a scorpion and a lawyer," Henry said, his hands becoming animated. "You've got a gun but only two bullets. What do you do?"

Dr Mays considered him with an odd expression, as if this were the rude and unexpected interruption of a stranger. Then she raised her pencil eyebrows, inviting him to continue.

"Shoot the lawyer," Henry declared happily, motioning with his forefinger to imitate the gun, "then shoot him again."

The silence was palpable. Margie finished her champagne, privately approving of the advice.

The brown birthmark above the baby's mouth caused much interest among the army of visitors that flocked past the cot, Shelby's expression veering between disinterested flatulence and irritation as she was poked and tickled. Dr Mays had an animated face as she leant towards the baby, her eyes blazing with excitement, her neutral mask only reappearing as she turned away. She noticed the gold pelican egg occupying pride of place on a wall shelf near the cot and nodded approvingly, then beckoned for Roman to enter with the covered object in both arms. He stopped in the middle of the room, looked around carefully, then placed it down gently on a low table against the wall. Henry appeared at the door, reluctant to come in.

"Lauren, what is it?" Margie asked, looking at the object.

"Shelby's baptism gift, from Precious Cargo," Dr Mays replied.

"You didn't need to," Margie murmured. "You've already been so kind, what with the lovely Fabergé egg."

"And she's got loads of toys already," Henry agreed cautiously. "Cupboards crammed full of them."

But not like this, Mr Wight, not like this, Roman appeared to say with a flamboyant tap of his fingers on the cloth. He lifted the lint cloth to reveal four rows of painted squares on an elegant wooden frame.

"It's an alphabet abacus," Dr Mays said.

"Oh, it's beautiful," Margie sighed. She nodded to herself as a moment of understanding passed across her face. Both Trustees waited, studying her reaction, then Roman turned the Aa block. It presented a picture of an anchor.

⚓	Bb	Cc	Dd	Ee	Ff	Gg
Hh	Ii	Jj	Kk	Ll	Mn	Nn
Oo	Pp	Qq	Rr	Ss	Tt	Uu
Vv	Ww	Xx	Yy	Zz	!	👁

"Lauren, it's charming," Margie purred, kneeling down to the toy and turning over the Gg to find a gate, then the Pp to find a pirate. She jumped back as the Dd turned round by itself, to display a dog.

"It's clockwork," the doctor explained. Roman's fingers tapped out a ticking movement against the air. "See the eye down here? That means the random mechanism is on. Swivel the eye off, and it goes to sleep. It's handmade and very special." Roman turned the eye and the letters in the abacus clicked back into place.

Aa	Bb	Cc	Dd	Ee	Ff	Gg
Hh	Ii	Jj	Kk	Ll	Mn	Nn
Oo	Pp	Qq	Rr	Ss	Tt	Uu
Vv	Ww	Xx	Yy	Zz	!	

"It's really quite instructional…" Margie began, then paused, noticing that the eye had silently swivelled back to its open setting, on its own accord.

"The mechanism is noise sensitive and reacts to voices," the doctor explained. Roman tilted his head and put two palms against his cheek. "It sleeps when the baby sleeps." Margie opened her mouth in quiet amazement, then again nodded slowly.

"We set great store by subliminal learning, Margie," Dr Mays said. "I predict that Shelby will be the first in her nursery to read."

"She will," Margie agreed.

Henry tutted quietly from somewhere in the background.

Dr Mays' expression hardened a moment, but otherwise she ignored him. "In fact, I believe this is the perfect gift for little Shelby Wight: my Lady of Letters." She briefly closed her eyes, her mouth tight with quiet resolve.

"Lady of Letters," Margie whispered, liking the name and chuckling when the Bb square turned and became a bee. "Buzz buzz," she said, then came across the exclamation mark, turning it to find its reverse held a question mark. Her forehead creased as she fleetingly pondered the appropriateness of such a symbol on a toy abacus, then she got up and returned to the cot. Having examined the toy, she felt satisfied that there was no need to look at it again. In fact, it would be *better* if she never looked at it again: it was Shelby's toy, after all. The Trustees followed her, both observing the cot from a small distance as the mother crouched over and cooed, "You can see me, yes, you can, can't you?"

Henry was waiting for the next click of the machine with a suspicious fascination. It came with the Ss block, to present a shell.

"Shelby," Margie purred. "It's Mummy. Mummy's here."

Another click of the machine, and the question mark became an exclamation mark.

Bee … shell… Henry thought.

The three symbols now rotated once, with no purpose other than to stretch their muscles, as an eye blinks or a mouth yawns. Then they rotated without stopping, first the shell, then the bee, then the exclamation mark, spinning in unison before falling rigidly into place one by one.

"Shelby!" Margie said. "Mummy's here."

Her husband soundlessly repeated the name, *Shelby*, his expression one of acute confusion. Soon, he put his hands in his pockets defiantly. "It's very kind of you," he said to the room, "but I really don't think we've got space in the bedroom for such a large toy."

Margie looked at him briefly. "Tommyrot," she said merrily.

"Margie, I mean it," he said, stuffing his hands deeper into his pockets. "And if it doesn't come from a reputable manufacturer then we don't know it's safe." His eyes twitched as the shell and the bee clicked abruptly back to Ss and Bb.

"Safe? Henry, what are you wittering on about?" Margie's playful tone contained a shard of irritation.

"There's a machine inside this thing," he replied. "Moving parts. Moving parts and little fingers?"

"We're keeping it," Margie said, straightening up with a stern face. "It's beyond discussion."

Roman tapped his watch to indicate they should go.

"You don't care for our gift, Mr Wight?" Dr Mays inquired coldly.

"Can't say that I do," he muttered quietly, something else bothering him. The simplistic artwork sketched in black and white didn't seem appropriate to a children's toy: the pictures weren't happy.

"We love it, Lauren," Margie said, "and it's staying." Her eyes angrily locked on Henry as she led the Trustees out of the bedroom.

"Bring the egg," Henry heard the doctor mutter. Margie trotted back into the bedroom, took the egg from its shelf, then hurried out.

Henry watched her go, but didn't follow.

He was unable to move: something was pressing down on his shoulders. If he had to describe it, the thing that had suddenly assaulted him, the closest he could come would be to say that it was like a dark mood, but so oppressive it had a density; a weight. His legs felt as if they were made of paper as he fought the urge to slump to his knees. The abacus seemed quite different now that he was alone with it, for every letter block he read was a needle in his brain, a moment of agony as he scanned each one in turn.

Qq ... quill quiver...

Rr ... razor rub...

Ss ... scissor shear

With a groan he was on his knees, and the pain receded. The force on his shoulders was gone, replaced by a nausea of fear in his stomach. The machine in the abacus turned the Ll block, to show a lorry, then the Kk, to show a king.

"Lorry king," Henry muttered.

That's me, he realised.

The blocks spun again, the lorry, then the king, clicking firmly into place.

"Yes?" he said, accepting his appellation.

The abacus retrieved the lorry and the king as deftly

as a poker ace collects cards. It waited, only the letters on display.

"Yes?" he repeated.

Still the abacus waited.

"I'm not afraid of you," he muttered.

The abacus answered.

Henry would never tell his wife what he saw: the image that ensured he would never dare confront his daughter's abacus again. It would be the first secret he had ever kept from her.

"Are you sure you don't want some more champagne?" Margie asked as the Trustees made ready to leave, her eyes darting irritably towards the ceiling as she wondered what was keeping her husband.

"Your hospitality is exemplary, as always," Dr Mays assured her.

Margie breathed an audible sigh of relief. "Was everything else…?"

"The room is perfect," the doctor confirmed.

"I'm sorry about Henry," Margie said nervously. "You won't … you won't…"

"Mr Wight does not even factor into our calculations. You're the only parent that counts, Margie, the only parent that can make a difference." The doctor paused meaningfully. "You must remain faithful."

Margie nodded furiously.

Dr Mays nodded too and took her hand reassuringly; Margie did her best to conceal a shudder. The doctor picked up the egg from the dining table. It was open. "Margie, we need the picture now," she said.

Margie hesitated, pretending not to understand.

"The picture of the three-year-old," the doctor clarified with a stone face. "We did discuss this…"

"Oh yes, of course," Margie murmured. She reluctantly went to a locked kitchen drawer where the gold window envelope was secreted, took out a piece of paper and unfolded it. It appeared to be a miniature oil painting, a highly realistic portrait of a little girl. A lavish gold frame was also painted, with a crest at its top and carved cord ropes at its bottom, as if it were used to hanging on the wall of a royal gallery.

Margie looked at the doctor's outstretched hand and her face dropped with melancholic longing as she passed her the painting. There was a turn of ruthlessness in the doctor's eyes as she folded it until it was nothing but a small square, then placed it inside the egg. She snapped the lid shut.

"Can I still look at it?" Margie asked. "Perhaps take it out from time to time?"

In answer, the doctor offered her the egg. Margie took it eagerly and twisted the lock. She frowned and tried again, then again. The strong teeth levers didn't seem to be connecting.

"It's locked now," the doctor explained. "It's locked to keep the painting safe. You want it to be safe, don't you?"

Margie nodded uncertainly.

"Only your child can open the egg now. Only my Lady of Letters. No one else, and even then only when the egg is ready to be observed."

Margie had tested the egg's lock on several occasions and always found it easy to open. Inside, she had examined the supple belt that folded out and held small glass compartments, all empty: frames awaiting their photographs. She had counted the compartments and there were eighty-eight. Now, as she tried without success to negotiate the lock, she knew the doctor spoke the truth. Something about the egg itself made her realise it too. It seemed different: no longer a fanciful trinket, but powerful, inscrutable and full of rage; a prison fortress. She whimpered and brought a hand to her mouth.

"All is as it should be," Dr Mays said patiently.

Margie nodded, willing herself to be calm, and wondering whether some malicious destiny had seen fit to detain Henry upstairs. The loss of the painting distressed her beyond all measure for it was of the face of a little girl, about three years old with auburn locks and the most wonderful hazel eyes.

The little girl had a small brown birthmark above the left corner of her mouth.

V

The prick of the needle

L LOYD WAS SHELTERING in the entrance of the university hospital's swimming pool, immersed in his body-length cagoule, when Alex rang him to say the drugs had arrived. The wind was howling, the rain falling at a steep angle, and he had to shout as he reminded her to thank his mother for taking the delivery. When she asked where he was and why he was standing outside, he replied that he was working then abruptly terminated the connection.

He gave scuba diving lessons, with a sideline in selling diving equipment, but the cheap unit he rented was on an industrial estate miles from the sea and he had no passing trade. It was part of his weekly routine to visit the university pool, the place where he gave his novice lessons, to check that his handwritten adverts were still on the notice board.

A particularly heavy blast of rain drenched his face but he was damned if he would go back inside and wait under the curious stares of the students who used the pool on weekday afternoons. He hated students and so wanted to make it appear as if he were waiting for someone who hadn't turned up. Perhaps it was a party of fucking bookworms who had bottled out of the dive just because he insisted they buy his equipment, that they couldn't use their own no matter how fancy it was and how much *Daddy* had paid for it. Like those arseholes last year, who bounced their cheques then sent him a solicitor's letter inviting him to sue.

The thought of solicitors had him reaching under the plastic sheets of his waterproofing to find his hip flask, reasoning that it was cold enough to justify a nip of brandy, even though he was driving.

The Rémy Martin was glorious in his throat, and he pressed the hip flask to his lips a little longer than planned. Savouring the taste on his lower lip with his tongue, he was returning the flask to his trouser pocket when he noticed a plump, middle-aged woman approaching from the rise of the car park. She was holding a very large umbrella directly above her head, which was fixed almost immovably, notwithstanding the wind. Such was the rigid precision with which the umbrella was held that she almost created her own dry vacuum in the storm.

She stopped in front of him, offering a leather-gloved hand. He stepped back in surprise, seeing that it was the obstetrician from Precious Cargo.

"Hello again," Dr Mays said.

Lloyd wiped his hand thoroughly on his cagoule and took her hand. The grip was exceptionally firm; under the brown leather it felt as if her fingers were made of iron.

"We like to keep in close contact with our families," the doctor said by way of explanation.

He nodded in confusion. "Where is…?"

"My nurse? He's in the car. I thought the two of us could take this opportunity to get to know each other a little better." The vague twitch of a smile acknowledged her intent. "Are you here on business, Lloyd? I can call you Lloyd, can't I?"

He shrugged with embarrassment, feeling oddly shy and nervous in front of her. "Business is a bit slow," he conceded.

The umbrella was still rigid above her head, held in her left hand. She moved it towards him, without moving closer herself, just the left arm and umbrella extending in a horizontal plane. The rain now began to splatter on the shoulders of her suede raincoat and her sacrifice made it seem an almost intimate gesture. He instinctively bowed his head a little towards her. The air under the umbrella carried her perfume, which was sweet and fresh.

"Business slow? Why is that?" she asked.

He swallowed uncomfortably, noticing the stretch lines and cracks in her make-up. On the forehead, where it wasn't caked on but spread thinly, the foundation had a grey-red tint from the skin. "I had a lawsuit two years ago. It's the lawyers who ruined me."

"Lawyers?"

"This kid in this group I was teaching, it was an intermediary rescue course, he ascended too quickly and bashed into someone swimming on the surface. Broke her nose and cheekbone. I'd told the kid about the five-point plan for ascending, but the lawyers said I shouldn't have let him go up at all until I knew the area was clear." He wrapped his cagoule around him and winced at unpleasant memories. He had left out the essential detail raised in the first allegation on the court papers:

Conducting a rescue course while under the influence of alcohol...

"Weren't you insured?" she asked.

He shrugged. The insurers had repudiated his policy on the grounds of intoxication and Alex had told him he couldn't challenge it. "My wife settled the case early on, and pretty cheap, all told." He paused. "What did for me was the admission. The diving community is a bunch of chattering girls: they all knew about the accident, all across the country in a matter of months. I *told* my wife we should have fought it. I tried to hammer it into her thick skull that no one would trust me if we didn't fight it." He reached into his cagoule and his hip flask was out before he realised his mistake. Unsure what to do, he offered the flask lamely to the doctor, who declined it with good humour.

"I used to be in AA myself," the doctor remarked quietly. She paused with old memories. "But then … alcohol was the least of my vices…"

"I'm not in AA," he returned defensively. "Just like a drink, that's all. And it's cold."

She considered the swimming pool beyond the glass doors. "Would you like to be free of it?"

"Free of what?"

With a sudden movement she brought down the umbrella, her wispy hair immediately flattening wet against her skull, and motioned Lloyd through the automatic doors. They walked, sodden and dripping, towards the swimming pool, leaving muddy footprints on the tiles.

"Ignore him," she said, referring to the lifeguard at the far end who was waving them back. They came to a stop at the water's edge, the smell of chlorine in their nostrils.

Lloyd shook his head with disbelief. "What are we doing?" he muttered.

"Look at the water," she whispered. "Look at it. No … look at it properly, as if you're seeing it for the first time. Try to understand its structure. Imagine its weight."

He was glaring at the water, his tongue welded to his lower lip. The chlorine air was washing his thoughts, rinsing and cleaning them.

"Don't be alarmed," she said. "In our society we call this

gift *the prayers that are keys*; think of it simply as a form of hypnosis if that comforts you."

"Hypnosis, yeah," he croaked. "I've heard of that." He was fighting the urge to jump in: he wanted to drink all the water in the swimming pool and on the earth, all the pure, clear, alcohol-free liquid. He glanced furtively at the doctor, her head was bowed and her eyes closed, then looked up at the lifeguard; he was considering them carefully but had obviously decided not to enforce the rules on this occasion. The pool had emptied in the ten minutes or so the two odd strangers had spent staring into the water.

Lloyd smiled, both confused and ecstatic, then turned and followed the woman out of the doors and back into the rain. The umbrella was up once more, as solid as a roof, the rain banging uselessly above them.

"Who are you?" he murmured.

"Lloyd, you mustn't be complacent," she said, ignoring the question. "Two years ago we planted something in your imagination: your son, Theo. The only child you're destined to have. But in the end the choice is yours: he can stay in your imagination, or he can be born. You know what you have to do."

"We're … we're trying for IVF," he said weakly. "We've got one more shot at it. Alex wants one more shot."

The doctor offered her gloved hand in farewell. Lloyd took it and shuddered inwardly at the touch of the hard leather.

"I think you'll find that your wife has had enough of needles," she said in parting.

In a crouch over her dressing table, the table lamp on, it was the work of fifteen minutes to prepare the evening injection with the Puregon Pen: a measuring needle designed so not a drop of the highly expensive drug would be wasted. It came with a DVD that demonstrated the complicated procedure for ensuring the exact dosage be administered, but after eleven sessions – eleven fortnights of priming and injecting – Alex could arm the pen with her eyes shut.

She always injected alone because Lloyd hated needles. She wasn't crazy about them herself, but had discovered a clever trick: each needle was given a name.

It was important to her method that she didn't become lazy with the name selection; each needle had a new one. She had begun with names of every pet cat and rabbit she'd heard of, then moved on to dogs. As each needle was disposable she had long exhausted these categories.

"Name," she whispered wearily to herself as she removed the plastic cap to reveal the needle for this, her first injection. As part of her mantra when she began a session, she reminded herself that the needle was extraordinarily thin, that there was merely the sensation of being scratched; Judy had once filled the pen with water and used it on herself to demonstrate how painless it was.

"I'll call you Freckles," Alex said, a name she had given to a large mottled spider that had once parked itself in an inaccessible corner, the naming trick helping her to overcome another of her fears. She swivelled the pen until the tiniest drop of Puregon appeared at the needle point.

Now she rubbed her flesh at a plump part of the left side of her stomach, her right side sore from repeated use. This was an act of desperation: she had always been paranoid about her left side, believing it contained some stubborn gristle, so against advice she had only injected in the right. "Freckles, you're going to be soft and gentle," she whispered, "like a puppy's kiss."

In answer, the needle gleamed excitedly, the follicle-stimulating drug glistening at its point like saliva. She held it to her stomach, to the left virginal muscle, and forced herself to relax.

"Just a tickle, that's all it is," she murmured, and pushed the needle in. She winced with uncertainty. It felt a little different this time, more of a numbing sensation than a scratch. She waited a moment then proceeded to the next stage, twisting the end of the pen to inject the drug. The numbness intensified, sending a weary signal to her brain which forced her to close her eyes.

A furious Dr Lauren Mays looked up at her from her writing bureau. The ancient Egyptian figures were wearing white surgeon masks and carrying needles bigger than they were.

With every prick of the needle, the doctor declared.

The numbness retreated and the pain arrived.

Alex's jaw sagged as she opened her eyes. She knew that she had to leave the needle in the flesh for a couple of seconds but the pain was awful and … and wrong, somehow. It was dirty and alien, like an insect's sting. She pulled the needle out with a gasp and fought back the tears. A white pimple had appeared at the point of entry. It was tender to the touch.

She staggered downstairs and went to the kitchen to return the drugs to the fridge. She appeared at the door of the living room with tears in her eyes.

"You alright?" Lloyd asked from the settee.

Cristabella, a thin and immaculately dressed woman with an erect posture was seated next to him, balancing herself so as not to fall into the depression caused by her son's bulk. Her head swivelled towards the door like a gun turret.

"That's it," Alex said.

"What's wrong?" Lloyd asked, considering getting up but deciding he was too comfortable.

"It hurts, Lloyd," she said, the tears welling up.

"Oh come on," he muttered with the beginnings of a smirk, returning to the television.

"I'm telling you it hurts. I've stuck so many needles in me they're starting to really hurt. I'm not doing this again. If this one fails, we can adopt or do nothing, I don't care, but this is the last time."

Cristabella was a handsome woman in late middle age who had carefully addressed the problem of time with cosmetics, diet and exercise, although she also believed in sparing her skin through a minimum of exertion in her face. Her expression was typically deadpan as she considered the problem of her highly strung daughter-in-law. "Alex," she said, "it's completely understandable that you're feeling sensitive."

Alex hesitated, uncertainly.

"Having children *is* stressful," Cristabella explained. "I know. Oh, I remember…"

"*What* do you know, exactly?" Alex snapped. "You haven't been through this, have you?" She put a hand to her mouth, then ran upstairs, sobbing. Lloyd now got up with a scowl of anger and alarm, his mother maintaining her composure notwithstanding the sudden spring of the cushion under her bottom.

"Alex, come down here and apologise to my mother!"

Alex didn't reply. She had locked herself in the bathroom to monopolise the toilet for an hour as a form of defiance before going back down to face her mother-in-law. She sat on the lowered toilet seat, nursing her bruised stomach and wondering if the pain and the grief were worth it.

She squeezed her eyes shut to see her oak kitchen table; her children's faces were still lost to her.

It was late morning by the time Alex got to work on Monday, having waited an hour in Millennium Fertility for a free slot. In response to her episode with the needle, Judy had once more happily injected herself with water to assure her how harmless it was.

It must be something psychological, Judy had suggested. An extreme phobia, perhaps. She would arrange for her to speak to someone...

Beere & Co's receptionist and only secretary Harriet, flustered at having to hold the fort for over two hours, hurriedly told her that she had someone waiting in the interview room. She had told the man that Mr Beere was not back from his ski holiday until tomorrow, but he'd said that he wanted to speak to Alex Morrow. He said he'd come concerning a contract. Harriet showed her pad where she had written down the word: *contract*.

"A contract?" Alex asked, glancing at the closed door of the interview room, a small partitioned affair with fabricated panels and a large window. The blinds were drawn. "Did he say what it was about?"

The thin, freckled girl shook her head. "I told him you were out, but he said he'd wait. I've made him a cup of tea."

"Good girl." Alex picked up a pad of paper and took her pen from her inside jacket, Harriet returning to her computer with relief. As Alex opened the interview room door, the large man seated inside turned to look at her. Containing her surprise, she stepped in and closed the door behind her. Aware of the thin partition wall she decided to speak quietly.

"Mr...?" she struggled.

"Honeyman," he said. "Just Honeyman." His woollen overcoat had been folded neatly on the floor to reveal a white collarless shirt under a green velvet waistcoat. A shift of his beard suggested a smile as he carefully placed the empty teacup and saucer on the table. She noticed that he didn't fully stretch his arm but carefully moved the limb at an angle, like a lever with fixed joints; he had a tendon problem, she suspected.

She took the seat opposite him with a neutral expression. "I take it you're not here concerning contracts."

"Oh but I am," he replied gently. "I confess that I often create deceptions to get myself through doors, but on this occasion I spoke the truth. I speak of contracts made with the soul, Mrs Morrow."

"I see," she muttered, with a resigned sigh. She wrote his name on her notepad, and then the date, the routine of her job increasing her feeling of security. "Well, I'm surprised you're here. At our last meeting you seemed in a great hurry to leave."

"It's with the greatest sadness that I'm imposing myself on you again." He considered her notepad with a raise of his eyebrows as she wrote down his words.

"Really? Why is that?"

"Your husband didn't give up the envelope from Precious Cargo, Mrs Morrow. The gold envelope," he clarified, "the one with their number."

She blinked, concealing her surprise. "You were there, in the service station, when he threw it away. He threw it in the bin."

"So I believed." He sighed as she returned to her notes. "In recent days … you must have noticed a change in him." Her pen froze. "He *is* changing," he continued. "Someone very powerful has visited him."

"Someone…? Who?"

Honeyman's small dark eyes became pinpoints of concern. "Your chance of escape is narrowing. The coven has you in their sights now, you see."

"The coven…? Mr … Honeyman, what on God's earth are you talking about?"

From a front pocket in his waistcoat he took out sticks of spearmint and peppermint chewing gum, which he unwrapped carefully before popping them in his mouth. He chewed thoughtfully for a few moments. "You must be very confused," he continued.

"We're in agreement on that, at least." She put down her pen, abandoning the idea of recording this conversation for the police. "The first thing I know is that we get this appointment card from these people, and they know the name of our … of our child." She was reluctant to give the name to the man. "The name we'd both agreed on…"

"They sent you something long before that."

She frowned. "What? What else have they sent us?"

He shifted uncomfortably in his seat.

"What else have they sent us?" she demanded.

"I don't know, Mrs Morrow, but they would have sent you *something*. About two years ago I would guess, or a little more. They bring baptism gifts, you see, and these gifts are very important to them. Very, very important. But they need to prepare the ground beforehand, just as John the Baptist prepared the ground for Christ."

Alex shook her head in bewilderment. One of her hands

went to the underside of the table, where there was an alarm button connected to the local police station. Beere & Co was primarily a criminal practice with more than its usual share of sociopaths.

"John the Baptist was a miracle birth," Honeyman continued. "His mother was barren. And his father was struck dumb, just as you will be struck dumb, for there can only be one faithful parent, as it was with the crime upon which this temple was founded. Yes, it is a temple, Mrs Morrow, a place of worship, and the doctor and the nurse you met are its servants, its Trustees. The temple mocks the miracle birth of the Baptist. You and the others are merely pawns; victims of their mockery."

Alex's finger had found the alarm button.

"Don't push the alarm. You have nothing to fear from me and I promise to leave when you tell me to leave." His voice was soft and reassuring and he waited until her hand returned cautiously to the desk. "Just remember my words, to ponder them in your own time."

"Who are Precious Cargo? What do they want?"

"They want you to have a child. In that, they speak the truth and they'll deliver on their promise. I'm ... I'm aware of the thing they've asked you and your husband to do, to achieve it. A man in Talybont ... a very unhappy man ... explained it to me."

Her eyes narrowed.

Honeyman repositioned his gum in his mouth. "They'll not lie to you. They can't, you see, there are rules they have to follow. But they won't tell you *everything*. Not immediately at any rate. They'll lead you down their road until there's no turning back. I..." and he faltered, "...I have knowledge which you'll acquire, but when it is all too late."

"Knowledge of what?"

"A birth. And a death."

She waited, her expression urging him to continue.

"Last month I observed a funeral," he said. "The funeral of a sixteen-year-old girl. A very beautiful, very talented girl. A sixteen-year-old boy, equally gifted, was present at her remembrance service."

"Who were they?"

"They were children born through Precious Cargo."

She thought about this. "So they *aren't* charlatans," she muttered to herself.

"Aren't you hearing me? It was a funeral."

She was silent for a moment as she attempted to digest this last piece of information: that Precious Cargo gave children. Children! And no more needles...

"Mrs Morrow?"

She blinked and refocused on Honeyman. "A funeral, I see. That's very sad. What did the girl die of?"

He shrugged unhappily.

"Was there foul play? Did she have some disease? A genetic disease, perhaps? Is that what's worrying you: something passed on by their treatment?" She waited. "What did the girl die of?" she repeated.

"She just died," he conceded unhappily. "Do you believe these people would gift you a child if there wasn't a price to be paid?"

"What price?" she asked, but with no imperative in her tone. She didn't expect an answer, the question was simply fired back automatically.

"I also mentioned a birth," he said carefully, aware from her tone that he had limited time remaining. "There's a couple who Precious Cargo have helped, who had a baby girl last month. It's always one boy and one girl, each year, you see. You were promised a boy, were you not?"

"Been checking my e-mails too, have you?" she asked, starting to get angry. "I know that's how those people created that appointment card. I'm looking into that, by the way. I *will* go to the police."

"The mother of this child has already taken a great interest in both of you," he explained, unperturbed. "As your husband will become obsessed with *her*, in time. The mother I speak of is both capable and determined; she already understands what's at stake."

Alex folded her arms. "I think it's time for you to go," she said.

Honeyman nodded and stood up, leaving a small white business card on the table. "Ring me when you're ready. You need me now, I'm afraid. Believe me when I say that I hoped our meeting in the service station would be the last."

She stood up and opened the door. "Well, we'll let *this* one be the last," she said sternly.

He hesitated. "The in vitro fertilisation which you're starting…" he began.

"What about it?" she snapped.

He shook his head.

"What about it?" she repeated, louder, so that Harriet's ginger bob popped up from behind her computer.

"It'll fail," he whispered sadly.

"What do you mean?"

"It'll fail. They'll do everything in their power to see that it fails; more than that, they'll see to it that you never contemplate it again."

The blister on her stomach took this opportunity to smart, as if it had been roasting in the sun. A gasp of pain escaped her.

"What's the matter?" he asked with concern, pausing as he put on his overcoat with stiff arms.

She was still holding the door open, but looking down. "Just go," she murmured.

The blister raged for almost an hour after the minister had left, as if in punishment for sitting across the table from him. When it finally released her she took a deep breath of deliverance and the moment was long and delicious, such was the misery that had preceded it. As she sat in a state of blessed release she remembered that the Puregon pen awaited her this evening.

I'll call you Cheddar with Marmite, she thought wretchedly, suspecting that it didn't matter what she called the damn needle, it would still be agony.

She winced, her suspicion being confirmed by a final snarl of her blister as the hieroglyphics on the writing bureau flashed behind her eyes.

There were apparently no reindeers in Alex's dreams that night; instead she seemed to be whimpering about Egyptians, clutching pitifully at her stomach as she turned in her sleep. She whispered in protest as Lloyd carefully got out of bed and tiptoed out of the bedroom.

He held his breath as he made his way through the hall to make sure that Sheba didn't wake until he was in the kitchen. As the dog looked up, his hand quickly reached for her muzzle. He shushed and stroked her, until her white rheumy eyes closed.

He counted four heartbeats, holding his breath once more, and he was in the garden shed, his eyes on the bedroom window. He was poised to bolt back into the kitchen if the light went on, ready with the excuse that he thought Sheba was in trouble.

She had noticed tonight, for the first time, that he wasn't drinking. His explanation that the IVF would have a better chance of success if he stayed off the sauce didn't really seem to satisfy her.

Let her be suspicious then, he thought, thinking that when the IVF was over he would simply explain that he realised he liked being teetotal. In truth, ever since he had looked into that swimming pool he couldn't face drinking anything but water; even the thought of tea or coffee made him nauseous.

He was unscrewing the compressor tank. His heavy-duty diving torch was nearby on the floor, covered with towels to absorb the beam.

The envelope slid out of the tank and fell onto the floor.

He waited, controlling his excitement, then smiled.

He was ready. He didn't need any more time.

As the envelope opened, gracefully and easily, he was reminded of his first sexual fumble as a teenager. He smelt his fingers, remembering the smell of baby oil in the service station, then ran a thumb along the seal with a reflective shake of his head. This time it seemed like a normal envelope.

The piece of paper inside slipped out, unfolding quickly in his hands, leaving no crease. It was an oil painting of a face set within an ornate frame with cord ropes at the base. And in the crest at the top, faintly impressed so that it could only be made out by its shadow, was the number 113. At the bottom of the painting was a small squiggle of a signature: *Zehngraf*.

Lloyd groaned with pleasure. Whatever all this ornate dressing was, whatever it meant, was irrelevant. It didn't matter that the face was a painting either, albeit such a perfect likeness that it could have been a photograph if it weren't for the rough texture of the paint.

The face was all that mattered: the three-year-old boy

from his dreams, conjured from the darkness. It was his son.

"Theo," he said, his face contorting with emotion as he held the picture to his chest.

For the moment he didn't notice the two other faces that had spilled out of the envelope: these were photographs of a little boy and girl, with scribbled instructions on the back. The scribble named the three-year-olds as *the boy by the sea* and *the girl on the hill*.

The boy by the sea

A STRONG WIND was pursuing the people carrier down the coast road as it headed towards the Mumbles, giving the sea a treacherous energy. Alex spotted the islands' lighthouse, a thin stick shadow in the distant gloom.

"You didn't used to dive here, did you?" she asked.

"Nah, currents too strong," Lloyd answered. "Know this bit of coast pretty well, though. The Mumbles Mile. Used to work on the lifeboats down here when I was a kid." He slowed down as they arrived at the mile-long stretch of houses that overlooked the mud and sand of Swansea Bay.

"This is a treat," she said again, referring to his offer to chauffeur her to find some sea air. "Nice to be driven for a change."

The reference to him driving was all she felt she could say about his sobriety: the drink problem had never been formally acknowledged, so it seemed inappropriate to discuss its abrupt resolution.

She sighed to herself: in the same vein there had been no discussion over her appointment with the psychiatrist yesterday and she wondered if their lack of communication on difficult issues was intuitive or simply convenient. She put the question aside, thinking that at least the psychiatrist had sorted out her needle phobia: he had explained that her reaction to the needle was a form of psychosomatic stigmata because she blamed herself for her failure to conceive. The explanation had hit a logical bullseye in her subconscious; the injections yesterday evening had been blissfully painless.

She looked out of the window and smiled. It was such a relief; Lloyd's drinking and her phobia both cured in a matter of days. It was a miracle.

"Are we going anywhere in particular?" she asked. "To the pier?" The long Victorian pier was now coming into view, its perished wood old and grey in the mist sitting on the water.

"You'll see."

He turned sharply right into a narrow side street, then left into another street, then left again, this time up a fierce incline, calling on all the car's horsepower. He brought the vehicle to a halt two thirds of the way up the hill. "We're here," he said, pulling the handbrake out full. They were parked outside a small terraced house.

"What's going on?" she said, noticing the curtain twitch in the window of the front room directly facing them. The house looked poorly maintained from the patchwork pebble dash exterior.

"Just some people I want you to meet," he replied thoughtfully, his finger tapping the steering wheel.

"People?" She glanced again at the window; the garish floral curtains were drawn and motionless. "What people?"

"They're just going to offer us some advice on treatment and stuff."

"What kind of advice? Lloyd, what's going on?"

He didn't answer, but got out of the car and waited. Conscious of the twitch of the curtain, she got out too, following him in confusion as he walked to the front door and rang the bell. The door was opened almost immediately, in spite of her suspicion that the doorbell was faulty and hadn't rung.

"Hello! Hello!" a large black woman declared to the ceiling as she beckoned them through into the tiny hall and then into the front room with the drawn curtains. The woman padded quickly to the settee where she punched two of the cushions in rapid succession, as an invitation for them to sit down. From the armchair on the opposite side of the room a man, ebony black and equally rotund, looked up from his newspaper. He left this until the Morrows took their places on the settee, as if he was in denial over this intrusion into his home and wished to delay acknowledging his visitors until the very last second.

"This is Mr and Mrs Tyde," Lloyd said.

"He's Jerry, I'm Mercedes," the woman said as she glided around the room, taking the opportunity to straighten a picture on the wall – a sentimental painting of a little girl with a huge tear in her eye – and then adjust two of the many miniature china animals on her mantelpiece. She looked at neither painting nor miniatures as they were moved, perhaps touching them just to bring them to the attention of her visitors; she was yet to make eye contact with the Morrows. They could have assumed she was blind if she hadn't suddenly flashed a glance at her husband. "Put the paper down, Jerry," she said in a hushed tone.

Jerry complied, folding the newspaper carefully and placing it on his swollen knees. Alex was struck by a contradiction in his demeanour: his fingers were restless notwithstanding an agreeable smile bolted in place during the meeting.

"So you and Lloyd know each other...?" Alex inquired with a puzzled air.

Mercedes examined the cushions of the available armchair,

plumped them up, then sat down to a creak of protest from the chair. "Friends?" she asked, examining the mantelpiece.

"Alex doesn't know," Lloyd remarked uncomfortably. He made a point of ignoring the brief but deliberate switch of Jerry's eyes to Alex, then back to him.

"*What* don't I know?" Alex asked impatiently.

"We're parents," Mercedes said to her mantelpiece. "Precious Cargo parents."

Alex stiffened.

"Hear them out," Lloyd muttered.

"Is that why you brought me here?" Alex asked angrily.

"Yeah, but hear them out," he repeated in a louder, warning voice. "There's another family I want you to meet too."

Mercedes' expression darkened as he said this, then she remembered herself and found her amiable, busy demeanour. "If you're looking for proof, then we're it," she said, now to the wall.

"Proof? What do you mean?" Alex asked.

"Our boy, Franklyn, is proof," Mercedes answered.

"How old is he?" Lloyd inquired, anxious to give the conversation a momentum that would stop his wife getting up and leaving.

"He'll be sixteen in a few months time. Important birthday, sixteen," Mercedes added, after a pause. Her husband's eyes switched to her for the first time.

Alex shook her head, slowly and thoughtfully. "You can't be more than early forties. If your boy is sixteen, then the two of you must have been in your twenties, maybe even mid-twenties, when he was born."

"I was twenty-four," Mercedes confirmed. "Twenty-four, fresh off the tree with all in front of me."

Alex folded her arms and sat back to announce the end of the discussion. To her, infertility concerned people in their thirties and forties.

"We couldn't have children, Mrs Morrow," Mercedes said.

"Well, clearly you could," Alex remarked irritably.

From under her chair Mercedes produced a ream of photocopied papers held together with a bulldog clip. She weighed it in her hands, as if this was evidence of its worth, then passed it to Alex. "Look at those, when you get home. Show them to a doctor, if you like. They're our clinical notes, going back twenty years, explaining why we couldn't have children. Doctors said they'd never seen such a hopeless case, what with my *polycystic* ovaries." The word 'polycystic' was awkward on her tongue, a scientific name memorised many years gone. "Made cysts in my ovaries. They told us to give up. Give up, give up, they said."

"But you didn't?" Lloyd asked with a nod of encouragement.

Mercedes pursed her lips defiantly, briefly making eye contact with the Morrows before looking away again. "How could I? I saw my boy, saw my little Franklyn, even before he was born."

Alex was flicking through the photocopied notes, reading the doctors' comments with a bemused frown. The important text was marked with circles and many exclamation marks in red marker pen.

Patient informed that infertility obstacles amount to sterility...

Patient refuses to adopt, counselling recommended...

"You'll see our blood tests in there," Mercedes said, "in case you're thinking Franklyn wasn't ours."

"I'm not thinking that at all," Alex said defensively, deciding it was time to put the materials down. She sensed that the woman resented the invasion into her medical history, even though she'd offered her notes to be read. She was attempting to conceal this conflict but failing dismally.

"We may not have much. I stack shelves and Jerry mops toilets, but the boy is ours."

"Yes, yes, I'm sure," Alex said.

"What do *you* do?" Jerry asked Lloyd, speaking for the first time. Unlike his wife, he had a faint Caribbean accent.

"I'm in sports," Lloyd answered. "Diving, mainly."

Jerry uttered a short chuckle, a *hmmph!* that was rolled around in his cheeks. "Don't think your child will be sporty."

"I'm sorry?" Lloyd muttered.

"They find their own talents. Our boy Franklyn, he's musical, and Mercedes ain't got a musical bone in her body. Hmmph! Thinks a middle eight is a bingo number."

"Shut up, Jerry."

"Bothered her mightily over the years, the fact that she was tone deaf. What with her wanting to do everything she could to clear his path."

"Jerry, be quiet now!" Mercedes snapped. And as if her husband were a robot that had run to the end of its battery life, his smile slipped back into place and he went quiet.

Alex was considering Mercedes, fancying that the woman was glaring right back at her from some secret window in her mind, even though her eyes were elsewhere. "Mrs Tyde, let me get this straight. You couldn't have children and so you went to Precious Cargo?"

"That's right."

"And they helped you?"

"With a miracle," Mercedes confirmed.

Alex nodded slowly. "I'm sure it must have seemed that way…"

"I can tell *you* that, that it was a miracle," Mercedes explained, suddenly a little concerned over her use of the word. "I never told no one else." Her eyes checked the corners of the room as if she were fearful of hidden cameras.

"And what did they do for you?" Alex asked.

"*They* didn't do nuthin', Mrs Morrow. They just explained what *we* needed to do."

"I see." Alex gathered her thoughts with a raise of her eyebrows. "So what is it that *you* did, that made this miracle possible?"

"We prayed." Mercedes paused. "You know the prayer. You know the one."

Alex's expression darkened.

"Don't be afraid, Mrs Morrow. The prayer's a gift. It's holy dust. Don't you believe in the power of prayer?"

"I believe in prayer," Alex agreed cautiously.

"Then believe this. You'll have the miracle too."

There was a brief silence, interrupted only by the uncomfortable rustle of Jerry's newspaper on his legs as he shifted position.

"We didn't believe it either," Mercedes said. "We were sent to visit families, just like you."

Alex glanced at Lloyd, who shrugged in response. He hadn't told her he had kept Precious Cargo's envelope, nor had he mentioned that the Trustees had visited him at his diving store and given him the telephone numbers of the two families they needed to approach. When he had telephoned it was clear they were expecting his call.

"Come and meet our boy," Mercedes said, getting up and beckoning Jerry up also. "He's in his bedroom."

"That really isn't necessary," Alex said. "I wouldn't want to disturb him."

"Yeah, I hated strangers coming into my bedroom when I was a teenager," Lloyd agreed. "Can't you just call him down?" Noticing Alex's disapproving look, he added, "Just to make sure he isn't deformed."

It was a joke that Mercedes didn't appreciate, her eyes widening momentarily as she helplessly revealed her pique, but Jerry found his closed-mouthed chuckle as he got to his feet. Lloyd considered the two parents, who had at least forty stone between them, and imagined what young Franklyn would look like. Probably vegetating upstairs, chocolate wrappers on the floor and a TV dinner balanced on the rise of his stomach.

Well, my son will be fit, he secretly resolved.

Theo won't be no slob, no fat lazy bookworm. He'll be a sportsman, an athlete, like me. Bronzed and lean from working on our boat...

"You must forgive my husband's sense of humour, Mrs Tyde," Alex said, "although I think he's right when he says that fifteen-year-old boys don't like to have their bedrooms invaded."

"Franklyn won't mind. He wants to meet you."

Alex shook her head. "We're happy just to..."

"But you gotta see his *bedroom*," Mercedes insisted. She struggled to make full eye contact, managing a few seconds before looking away. "It's necessary, yes *necessary* for me to show you..."

Alex cleared her throat uncomfortably. "Necessary?" she inquired.

Mercedes nodded cautiously, unsure how to respond and choosing instead to quickly reposition some of her china animals. Alex thought that from the moment she opened the front door there was something of a rehearsed air about her, but she was now on uncertain ground, unsure what to do if they refused to follow her.

"Perhaps the kid's in bed or something, and can't come down," Lloyd whispered to Alex.

Probably having trouble getting up, because he's so fat. What sort of kid stays in his bedroom on a Saturday...?

A sudden movement of Mercedes' hand suggested that she'd read Lloyd's thoughts from his expression. "Come and meet my boy," she said, her resolve returning and with just the trace of a challenge in her tone.

The young man rose smoothly from his seated position on the bed in precise time with the opening of the door. His mother, who had been constantly calling his name on her heavy hike up the stairs, didn't feel the need to knock.

"My boy, Franklyn," she said proudly, throwing an irritated glance at her husband; he was wheezing halfway up the stairs and had decided to stop there. It was a very small house and Lloyd and Alex were squeezed behind her on the landing.

"Hello Franklyn," Alex said, finding a line of vision to the right of Mercedes' bulky shoulder, and swallowing her surprise. She noticed Lloyd mouth a silent *fuck me*.

"Frank," the slender fifteen-year-old boy said, with a cautious smile. The fingers of a long hand were at his chin, a barrier for his shyness or perhaps as some kind of pose: it was difficult to determine whether he was aware of how beautiful he was. Lloyd registered the heavy eyelids of his mother, and Alex the long jaw line of his father, both hunting down such details as they had never seen a child so unlike his parents.

"Come in! Come in!" Mercedes said, moving aside to usher the visitors past, aware that if she entered the room as well the space would be swallowed up. In acknowledgement of the physics of the situation, Franklyn climbed back onto his single bed and folded his legs under him in a yoga position.

"Outdoor type, are you?" Lloyd asked, noticing a large poster of someone running almost horizontally against a wall. The caption read *L'Art de Displacement*.

Franklyn shyly ran a hand across his razored hair. "Free running," he said.

"You do any?"

The boy's hand moved to his elbow to cover a large red graze. "My mum don't approve," he said.

"No I don't," Mercedes confirmed from the door. "Running over roofs and over walls. Those kids he runs with are crazy."

"Good to have an interest in sport though," Lloyd suggested, coming to his defence. "Builds up a competitive spirit."

"There ain't no competition," Franklyn said immediately. "None at all. Everyone does their own thing." He shook his head anxiously. "No one loses, see. No one loses at all." The sudden, insistent outburst produced a moment of awkwardness and the Morrows, embarrassed, each found somewhere to look.

"And you're a musician," Alex remarked, registering the electric guitar and a clarinet resting against the wall.

"Yeah," Franklyn answered. "I play seventeen instruments…"

"And…" Mercedes urged.

"And I compose, a bit," he added uncomfortably. He indicated a handwritten music score on the windowsill behind his bed, the only place he would be able to write in the cramped space.

"It ain't finished yet," his mother said, disapproval in her tone.

"So you want to be a composer?" Alex asked. It was rare that she took to someone as quickly as she had taken to young Frank Tyde, thinking of him now as *Frank* if only to put herself in opposition to his mother. She wanted to bundle him up in her arms and rescue him.

"Yes, yes, a composer," Mercedes confirmed from the landing. "He writes beautifully. His teacher's amazed at what he does. I've heard the school band play some of the things he's written, though they don't play in tune…"

"Composition is what I'm meant to do with my life," Franklyn muttered gloomily. The words prompted an involuntary glance to his left, and Lloyd and Alex registered the gold pelican egg on the top of the wardrobe.

"The doctor was holding one of those in the clinic," Lloyd murmured, with a curious smile at the boy's statement concerning his future. "What is it?"

"That's from Precious Cargo," Mercedes said. "They always give a gold egg to the parents. A gift … when they conceive."

Alex glanced at her, surprised at the choice of word … *conceive*. She pictured Dr Mays waiting by the marital bed looking at her watch, her fat nurse ready with the egg, waiting for the doctor to declare *Conception!*

Mercedes noticed the look but didn't acknowledge it. Her eyes stayed on her son, her mind willing him on.

"And what's that?" Lloyd asked, looking at a small low table at the foot of the bed.

"That's Franklyn's baptism gift," Mercedes answered.

"That's from Precious Cargo too."

Lloyd knelt down to examine it. Shortly, he chuckled.

It seemed to be a toy. Three figures with carved wooden faces and jointed limbs stood on a stage dotted with yellow stars. The stage read *The Dead Pharaohs*.

"There's a mechanism inside the stage platform," Franklyn whispered. "Clockwork, I think. I don't really know."

"Is it a glam rock band?" Lloyd asked in delight. The three puppet figures, all about six inches tall, were dressed in red jumpsuits, gold lightening strikes down their sides. The singer guitarist, who he saw from an inscription at his feet was called *Izzy Sphinx,* had a wig of huge multicoloured curls which produced a startling contrast to his rudimentary features. The singer was looking up with unfinished eyes, as if he was trying to remember his words.

"His head moves to the microphone when he sings," Franklyn explained.

"He moves?" Lloyd asked excitedly.

"Each of them has a move." Franklyn gestured to the bass player to Izzy Sphinx's right; the musician was po-faced with a basin haircut, his booted right foot raised slightly. "Nile Rivers taps his foot when he plays."

"Nile Rivers, I like it," Lloyd said, absurdly pleased. Alex cleared her throat impatiently.

"Rivers is okay," Franklyn confirmed. "He's my friend."

"And who's the other guy?" Lloyd asked, thinking that *friend* was an odd description.

Franklyn didn't answer.

Lloyd stretched to examine the bald drummer seated behind a bass drum, a drumstick poised over the snare drum. The drummer had a fierce expression, the lines in the wood of his face made with jagged cuts.

"He looks like he means business," Lloyd remarked. Leaning further forward he read the drummer's name, "Sandy Tombes," then sat back to admire the ensemble. "That's one unusual toy."

"Very unusual," Alex agreed distastefully, surprised at her husband's interest in the thing.

"They look a bit past it though," Lloyd mused, equally curious at his own fascination. Somehow, ridiculously, he felt as if he were meeting some long-lost relative or making a new friend with whom he had everything in common.

"Yeah, they've aged in the last few years," Franklyn agreed, his fingers going unhappily to his chin. "Especially in the last year."

Lloyd smiled at what he perceived to be a joke.

"Sphinx stutters now," Franklyn said. "He never used to."

"It must be the mechanism winding down, I suppose," Lloyd remarked. "It's incredible that it still works." He nodded, approvingly. "Good to see a toy that's handmade for a change, what with all the plastic tat they churn out."

Unusual for a fifteen-year-old boy to have a toy at all, Alex was thinking. She could see no other toys or puppets in the room: the free running and the electric guitar suggested older interests.

"Touch the stage," Franklyn suggested to Lloyd. "They'll play for you."

"Yeah?"

"The mechanism's touch sensitive."

Lloyd pressed the platform, snatching his finger back as he felt the hollow wood vibrate. Nile Rivers' right boot started tapping the stage to a bass riff reminiscent of *The Gene Genie* although the first three notes were slightly out of time. It was a thin ringing sound, as if made by the twang of an elastic band, but much louder than it should have been. The volume seemed to be coming from somewhere else, as if there were a real rock band playing across the street.

"That's brilliant!" Lloyd declared in a loud voice. He looked up with embarrassment, realising that the sound had no volume after all. "Try it, Allie," he suggested quietly. Alex shrugged, leaned down and slowly reached out in the direction of the small stage. "Go on, it won't bite," Lloyd murmured.

Alex's mind went blank for a split second. She was standing up once more, her hand at her mouth. The hand hadn't touched the stage.

"Is it only the bass that plays?" Lloyd asked.

"It ain't finished yet," Franklyn said, having observed Alex's failed attempt at touching the stage with cautious interest.

"Franklyn always plays along to the bass," Mercedes called. "Has done since he was a child. The toy made him want his instruments, that's why we saved for them. Saved and saved. The bass man taught him to play."

Lloyd was about to say something, but stopped as Sphinx's head moved slowly to the microphone to say in a deep, neutral monotone, with the same far away volume of the bass:

C-cool.

The singer's head returned to its upward position, prompting the abrupt end of the bass in mid bar. Rivers' boot returned to its poised position.

"Cool. Brilliant," Lloyd murmured, after a time.

"Sphinx thinks you're okay," Franklyn remarked. Lloyd nodded with a face of mock seriousness, as if the singer's statement had indeed been intended for him.

"Well, we really should go," Alex said. "Sorry we bothered you, Frank, and thank you for showing us your room."

"That's okay, Mrs...?"

"Morrow. But call me Alex, okay?"

"Okay."

An impulse made her offer her hand, which Franklyn considered for a moment before he shook it. This form of social etiquette was something new to him, his grip awkward and slight, and Lloyd stood up with a tut, disapproving of her adult formality. She was unable to hide a blush of embarrassment; later she would realise that she simply wanted to touch the boy, as if the pressing of their flesh would create a promise they would see each other again. Something in his demeanour made her concerned for him; made her believe he was in danger.

"Anyway, we'll be off," she said, casting a final glance at the puppet toy as she turned. Perhaps it was the bad acoustics within the small room but she could have sworn that neither the bass nor the words came from within the concealed platform stage, where the mechanism and voice box were stored. Rather, they seemed to emanate from the wooden puppets themselves.

The Morrows were almost through the front door when Franklyn appeared at the turn of the stairs; Alex stopped and looked round, even though he had moved into position silently. With his hand again at his long chin he cut a reflective, philosophical figure.

"Will you be seeing the girl on the hill?" he asked cautiously.

Alex smiled. "The girl on the hill? Who's she?" She again felt a protective twinge in her stomach.

"That's Gracie Barrett-Danes," Lloyd murmured. "The Barrett-Danes are another family in Swansea. Precious Cargo family," he added, under his breath.

"Franklyn, go back to your room," Mercedes called, attempting a nonchalant tone. Franklyn nodded and turned.

"Do you know Gracie, Frank?" Alex asked, annoyed at his mother's dismissal. "Is she your friend?"

"I'm not really meant to know her. But I've seen her a few times. She's really pretty."

"Ah, like that, is it?" Lloyd said.

"No, no, nothing like that," Mercedes answered, her eyes furious behind her smile.

"But he do like the ladies, don't you Frank?" his father called from the front room, having decided to return to find his newspaper.

"Yes, he likes them," his mother muttered bitterly. "He likes the running, and he likes the girls."

"How do you know this girl, Gracie?" Alex inquired, anxious to keep the discussion going. She didn't want the boy to return to that bedroom: something was waiting for him in there, a presence glowering at him across the landing.

"She's always been there," he answered.

Alex frowned. "Really? Are you related?"

The boy shook his head. "You'll like her," he said sadly. "She's smarter than me."

"Franklyn! Back to your room!" Mercedes spluttered, reaching for the front door and opening it wide, as far as it would go. The Morrows took the hint and left. "Goodbye, Goodbye!" Mercedes called to them as they went to their car. She attempted to affect a laughing, sophisticated attitude, as if she had just hosted a sedate and completely successful dinner party. As the front door closed, she turned angrily to the stairs but, finding her son had returned to his bedroom, decided to make the front room her first place of retribution.

The snare drum was sounding as Franklyn closed his bedroom door behind him. He dutifully walked to the bed and sat down on the mattress, his legs together, a fist nestling his chin as he watched The Dead Pharaohs. Tombes was banging the snare drum at two-second intervals with a moveable joint in his wrist, each whack heavier than the last. Franklyn shuddered with each beat until at last Sphinx turned to the microphone and in his flat, toneless baritone, which defied laws of space and volume, declared:

H-hippy spit.

Franklyn gasped, his eyes instinctively going to the egg.

A final snap of the snare drum ended the torment. With a fear so old and familiar that it was fused into his DNA, his hands went helplessly to his crotch as he wet himself.

VII

Bruised

I F LLOYD COULD escape to his shed, Alex decided, then she could escape too.

She was seated on her mother-in-law's upstairs toilet, the seat down. Cristabella's bathroom, bleach clean as always, the air heavy with too much air freshener, was often her temporary refuge during these Sunday lunches. Today she needed solitude more than ever as she attempted to come to terms with her stomach pain.

So the psychiatrist hadn't cured her phobia after all: their Friday session had just given her one night's reprieve. The cure had seemed so complete that on her return from Swansea she had taken up the needles with a carefree disregard, and the agony, when the pain broke through the numbness, was worse than ever, steeled as it was with surprise. It was as if the injections were playing with her, as if they understood her psychology.

A perfunctory rap at the door made her look up.

"Allie, you okay?" Lloyd muttered from the landing.

"I'm on the loo, Lloyd."

"I know, but are you okay?

"I'm fine. I won't be long."

"Mam says she's ready to carve the beef."

"I'll be down in a minute."

There was a pause. She could sense him still at the door, could almost hear his mind turning.

"Little Tasha's a sweety, isn't she?" he said, in a voice that was notably cold given his choice of words. Tasha was the two-year-old of his niece, Cerys, and she was now sitting on the carpet of the lounge under the eyes of her adoring family, examining and discarding the countless toys that were offered to her. Cerys' mother, Lloyd's older sister Bethan, lived in the Midlands and this was her daughter's first visit since the birth.

"She's lovely," Alex agreed with a half-smile as she looked down at her knees. She closed her eyes and once more searched for her oak kitchen table, hoping to see the busy hands and hear the young voices at the hub of her home.

Tasha will be a mother before me, she realised. *That little baby is nearer to motherhood than I am.*

"Come on Allie!"

She stood up and pulled the flush. She had merely required the toilet as a seat but nevertheless at the sink rebelliously washed her hands with Cristabella's expensive Molton Brown handwash, using far more than Cristabella would have approved of. Lloyd called again, from halfway down the stairs, and she reached for a towel, her mind in a whirr.

They want you to have a child … and they'll deliver on their promise…

She shook her head to banish the minister's words and walked towards the stairs, her stomach muscles hard with protest. Last night she had shown her bruises to Lloyd, but rather than display his usual squeamishness when it came to the injections he had smiled and kissed her stomach, saying that she was very brave. That it would all be over soon.

"I'm coming," she called as she made her way down the stairs, hearing Lloyd's summons once more. One hand found the balustrade, the other her stomach, pressing the ache away with her palm.

Cristabella had stationed herself, as usual, in the centre of her immaculate kitchen, supervising her two children who had offered to help bring out the meal. A vaguely hostile stance suggested that she didn't care for the interference: Lloyd was carving the beef, his sister Bethan shuffling the roast potatoes in the baking tray. A sly morsel which found its way into Bethan's mouth had her considering the stove with disapproval.

"Mam, have you salted these?" she asked.

"Salt's bad for you," Cristabella replied.

"I know, but a little…"

"You can always add it afterwards."

Bethan shook her head. "It's not the same."

"Nonsense."

Bethan flashed a weary smile at Lloyd, who smirked back.

"Bethan's roasts are lovely, Mam," Lloyd remarked. "All the best restaurants use a little salt in their cooking…"

"Now don't you start with your nonsense too. If it was up to me I'd ban salt altogether, along with all the other junk the supermarkets churn out." Cristabella now found an activity in draining the greens, a hand occasionally going to her waspish waist; a reminder to her overweight daughter of the benefits a spartan lifestyle could bring.

Bethan, looking harassed, stirred the gravy. "Could you save the water from the greens, Mam?" she asked, but saw that the green water had already gone down the sink. With a sigh she accepted the water that Lloyd passed her in a filter jug; he was still sporting his smirk – she couldn't remember seeing him this happy in a long, long while – and crumbled the Oxo cubes into the pan with regret. At least she could put some red wine in the gravy; she poured herself a glass of Rioja in readiness and gestured with the bottle to her brother. He shook his head quickly.

"No wine in the gravy, Bethan," her mother warned.

"Oh, Mother!"

Bethan turned to the sink, ready now to make a stand, but saw Alex in the doorway: she looked awful, her face drawn and completely drained of colour.

"You okay, sweetie?" Bethan asked, hiding her concern.

"Oh, I'm fine," Alex replied. "The injections are hurting a bit this time, that's all."

Bethan nodded, her mind locked in indecision. Should she ask about the IVF treatment, or stay quiet? She had to balance the danger of appearing disinterested against the risk of prying: it was a never-ending dilemma. She had paced her house when her daughter became pregnant, then again when her granddaughter was born, debating whether she should ring Alex and tell her the news. She wondered now what Alex was really thinking when the family had flocked around little Tasha this morning, as if she were a messenger from God; her own daughter Cerys looking on with a trace of sympathy as Alex tried to bond with the baby. Tasha would forget her almost immediately when they returned home: babies had a cruel honesty concerning the people who were important to them.

Does she hate us, secretly? Bethan wondered.

"I was just about to have an argument with Mam about putting wine in the gravy," Bethan remarked, deciding that food was as good an antidote as any to an uncomfortable silence. "Gives it body, don't you think? And this is that nice M&S Rioja too."

"No wine," Cristabella repeated, turning from the sink and making a very obvious face of surprise as she saw Alex clutching her stomach. "You need to speak to those doctors of yours. You shouldn't be having this sort of trouble."

Alex shook her head. "It's just that it's been so many times," she muttered.

"How many times now, sweetie?" Bethan dared.

"This will be the twelfth," Alex answered, in a voice that was barely audible.

"And Allie only takes a few months off in between," Lloyd explained. "So there's no holiday, or break or anything. It's no wonder she's sore."

"Well, time is against her," Cristabella remarked.

Bethan counted to three in her head. "You've got all the time in the world," she declared, readying her bottle of wine to pour it into the pan.

"Bethan, no," Cristabella said.

"Mam, it's just a little…"

"Alex can't have it," Cristabella said. "Don't you understand? She can't have alcohol while she's on her protocol."

Bethan, looking devastated, put the bottle down as if it was cursed. "Oh God, I'm so sorry…"

Alex was shaking her head good-humouredly. "Bethan, a little wine in the gravy is fine, just fine. Mam's being a bit over-protective, I think."

"Are you sure?" Bethan asked, with relief. Alex smiled back at her.

"Actually, I'd rather you didn't put any in."

It was Lloyd who had spoken. He shrugged as he finished carving the meat, a little embarrassed at having to make the announcement. "I'll taste it even if you put a small drop in," he admitted. "Won't be able to have any."

"My, you have given up the pop, haven't you?" Bethan said incredulously. Cristabella made to say something but decided against it. Instead, she looked at her son thoughtfully.

97

Lloyd shrugged once more, but didn't answer. He heard Sheba bark and immediately left the beef to hurry out into the hall, grateful for the excuse to leave.

"Don't let the dog near the baby!" Cristabella called, as he passed Cerys coming in to the kitchen.

"It's alright Gran, it's my fault," Cerys said. "Sheba's on the mat in the hall, sleeping. I couldn't resist a cuddle."

"She doesn't know your smell," Cristabella huffed, "and the poor thing's almost blind. Of course she'll bark."

"I know, Gran, I'm sorry. I just couldn't help it. She just looked so cute lying there."

Alex considered the pretty nineteen-year-old and wondered if she had stroked the dog as an attempt to reciprocate her affection for the baby. With this reflection packed away in her bag of apparent slights, which she would contemplate with self-disgust when depression took her, she noted that Cerys had fully recovered her figure after her pregnancy. Did she even remotely realise how lucky she was?

A dark shadow briefly passed across Alex's face as she reproached herself for being so unfair and so bitter.

"I'm praying for you, Aunt Alex," Cerys declared, her expression open. Bethan cleared her throat in embarrassment.

"Why thank you, Cerys," Alex replied.

"I've been praying for you for the last four years," Cerys clarified. "Ever since you started."

Alex nodded. "Well, my dear, judging on results, all I can say is that you clearly don't stand in well with the Lord."

Cerys' eyes widened momentarily in surprise, before she broke into a smirk. She gave Alex a hug, which Alex accepted gratefully; Cerys had always been her favourite person in the

Morrow family but that didn't make the young woman's happiness any easier to bear.

"You'll get there, I know you will," Cerys whispered.

"No you don't," Alex replied quietly, wincing as the girl pressed too close to her stomach.

"Let's eat," Bethan said, having finished the gravy. Lloyd returned from the hall and took the two dishes of vegetables his mother indicated, while Cerys made for the beef and Yorkshire puddings. Alex walked towards the stove but Cristabella waved a disapproving finger.

"Mam, I can carry the roasters at least," Alex said wearily.

"Just go into the dining room and sit down," Cristabella ordered, waving a hand that purported to dismiss her. Alex nodded, waited for the others to leave and followed them out into the hall. Sheba, her eyes encrusted with rheumy white cataracts, was lying on the mat by the front door, awake but docile. The sight of the animal, combined with the smell of the roast beef, created a sentimental wave of rustic homeliness; once more the oak kitchen table loomed in her imagination.

No, Cerys, you don't know. No one *knows…*

She paused, recalling the promise on the appointment card from Precious Cargo that suggested quite the opposite.

We promise you a son. We name him Theo.

A chill travelled quickly down her spine as she considered the brash conceit behind the statement. Then she reflected on Mercedes Tyde, the woman with the ovarian cysts, who had insisted her son was a miracle.

"A miracle," Alex muttered. She shook her head and walked through to the dining room.

"So who are the Barrett-Danes?" Alex called from the bedroom that evening. She was sitting at her dressing table in her underwear, an anti-septic swab near her bellybutton.

The Suprefact needle and the Puregon pen were primed and positioned, both carefully checked for air bubbles, the plastic handles depressed until the fluid had dribbled at the needle point. The sharp instruments glistened as they waited.

Name us, Alex! Name us!

She wondered which one would sting this evening. It was only ever one, something that she had learnt on her second evening when the Puregon pen had been a mere twitch of the skin, to be followed by what felt like a knife thrust from the thinner but longer needle of the Suprefact. Of her seven sessions so far the pain was tipped four to two in favour of the Puregon, with one no show. And maybe it was the bruising and hard skin, but she was sure the injections were becoming increasingly painful.

Tweedledum and Tweedledee...

Naming the needles didn't help any more. Nausea crept up her throat: the odds told her that tonight it would be the Suprefact that hurt.

"That's the other family I found," Lloyd called from downstairs. "For references and stuff."

She nodded. She wasn't angry, she merely wanted to talk, to delay the inevitable. "The family Frank mentioned when we were leaving?"

"Think so, yeah."

"Where did you find these families?"

There was a pause.

"On the internet," he replied cautiously.

"No you didn't. I looked myself."

"You must have googled the wrong key word."

"There's not a single reference on the web…"

"Course there is. They're a registered charity."

She ran a caring palm over her stomach, remembering something the minister had said in her office concerning the gold envelope. "Lloyd, you did throw that envelope away, didn't you?"

"You saw me throw it away. What's wrong with you?"

She cast a furtive glance at the mirror, ashamed that she could take the word of a religious nut over that of her own husband. "So why are you looking for testimonials?" she asked. Her tone wasn't confrontational. "What good will it do?"

"Just in case the IVF doesn't work," he replied in a distant, muted voice. Sheba's low contented growls told her he was in the kitchen.

"If this session doesn't work then we'll try again in the summer," she called. "Why does this have to be our last time? It isn't twelve tries and you're out."

"It's costing us a fortune."

"So? We're not going on holiday or anything, are we?"

And it's my money, she thought.

"Fine, fine. You're the one who made a scene after that first injection, saying it was the last time. You're the one pumping up on steroids. You're the one who has to take that last big needle: you know, the one you hate so much. What is it? The Pregnell?"

The Pregnell! She had completely forgotten about the Pregnell, the drug that was injected exactly thirty-six hours before egg retrieval to loosen the eggs in their follicles and allow them to be collected. The Pregnell needed a long, thick needle because it had to burrow into the heavy muscle of the thigh; it was worse, far worse, than all the Puregon and

Suprefact injections put together. The face in her mirror had a hangdog expression.

The long silence was interrupted only by the occasional whelp of pleasure from the dog.

"Are you done yet?" he called.

She reached quickly for the Suprefact. Closing her eyes with morbid acceptance, as if she was playing Russian roulette, she removed the swab, pressed the needle into her stomach and pushed the syringe.

She uttered a whimper of relief. It didn't hurt.

There, it should have been the Suprefact tonight, on law of averages. It won't be the Puregon twice in a row.

With a nervous smile she put a swab on another part of her stomach. She took the Puregon pen and pressed the needle in.

Just Tweedledum and Tweedledee…

There was no numbness, the needle cold inside her flesh. She paused, her imagination as receptive as the sensors in her skin, then her free hand went to the screw at the rear of the pen, which she turned clockwise to push in the fluid. She imagined it creaking with medieval cruelty.

"It won't hurt, it won't…" she whispered, as the image of Dr Mays, looking up from her Egyptian bureau, shuttered in her mind.

With every prick of the needle…

Downstairs, Sheba jumped on hearing the high-pitched scream, the cataracts having accentuated her hearing and age making any sudden noise a terror.

"There, there," Lloyd whispered, tickling her throat. "Don't listen to Mummy, she's just being silly." He patted the dog thoughtfully, believing he could hear Alex sobbing piteously upstairs. "Silly Mummy," he said quietly to his dog, with the faintest of smiles.

Alex squeezed her eyes tightly shut as the pain constricted the muscles of her stomach, then opened them with a fragile intake of breath. It was Monday morning and she was sorting through her post, passing the cramps off as a bad case of indigestion when Harriet asked her what was wrong.

"Harriet, what exactly did this man want?" she asked, considering a scribbled name and telephone number. She didn't recognise the dialling code.

"I didn't speak to him," Harriet replied from the small kitchen with the kettle that generally occupied an hour of her time during the morning. "The message was on the answer phone. I think he rang on the weekend. Might have been Sunday 'cos it was the last message and Mr Beere had Rumney Police Station ring him Sunday morning with that little monster Gary Holmes who's being joyriding again. I spoke to his parents this morning, they're in a right state and…"

"But did he say what it was about?" Alex pressed.

"I can't remember."

Alex groaned, then smiled as Harriet appeared with her coffee.

"Would you like to listen to the message?" Harriet asked, taking Alex's silence as criticism. "I haven't deleted them. I never delete them until you tell me to."

Alex offered the young woman an appreciative murmur as she sipped the coffee, detecting a trace of distress in her tone. "I know you don't, Harriet. And that's a good idea."

The message was short and abrupt, the man speaking in a flat, subdued voice. He said, "This is a message for Alex Morrow. My name is Ray Matthews and I'm the father of Jemima Matthews. I have something for you." He gave a telephone number, asking her to ring it immediately.

"Goodbye," he said as an afterthought, then ended the call.

Alex played the message again, this time checking that the number had been written down correctly. She punched up a page on the web and saw that the dialling code was for Aberystwyth, Mid Wales, then sat back with a frown. Why would anyone introduce themselves as the *father* of someone, unless the child was the subject of the message? She was prepared to offer five to one odds that when Mrs Holmes had rung the office this morning the first thing she would have sobbed was that she was the mother of Gary Holmes.

The telephone number put her through to a solicitor's office in Aberystwyth, and on giving her name she was immediately transferred to a man who announced he was dealing with the estate of Ray Matthews, who had committed suicide over the weekend. Stabbed himself, the probate lawyer explained: they found him by his daughter's grave.

"His daughter...?" Alex asked breathlessly, her mind in a whirl.

"The daughter died a few weeks ago."

There was a pause.

"Oh I see..." Alex said. "Is that why...?"

"Probably," the lawyer answered sadly. "His wife's in a bad way too. There's talk of her being sectioned."

"Oh dear. Were they very close?"

"Presumably, although I'm hearing conflicting reports from the family. Maybe it's delayed shock over the daughter that's sent her over the edge." The lawyer cleared his throat, to acknowledge that he was perhaps being too free with his information and opinions.

"How is it that you've been instructed so quickly?" Alex asked at length, her surprise having turned into confusion.

Why had Mr Matthews introduced himself in his capacity as a father if his daughter was dead?

The lawyer's response was rapid, suggesting that she wasn't the first caller this morning to ask that question. Mr Matthews had contacted him last week, giving sealed envelopes for members of his family and friends in the event of his death, explaining that he was ill. He had then left a message on their answer phone on the weekend to say that he would be committing suicide and that friends and family would be ringing the office this morning.

"So ... I have an envelope?" Alex asked.

"That's correct."

"But I didn't know him."

The lawyer didn't answer.

"Look, I really don't understand ... don't understand what's going on," Alex managed, the worst cramp seizure of the day suddenly hitting her in mid sentence.

"Mrs Morrow, you really know as much as I do. I've got an envelope that the late Mr Matthews tasked me with delivering to you. Now that you've called, I'll be arranging to courier it to your office today."

"Courier it? Can't you just post it?"

"No, Mr Matthews' instructions were explicit when it came to *this* envelope." A pause reinforced the point. "The envelope is to be either collected or couriered and no one else can see it. It's presently in our safe, in fact. Mr Matthews made us lock it away and confirm that you'd be the only person who knew about it."

Alex shook her head, unable to make sense out of any of this. A man who lived miles away, whom she had never met, had contacted her about his dead daughter, on the day of his suicide. Now he had left her something that was so secret he had ensured it was locked in a safe. "What's in the envelope?" she asked warily.

"I have absolutely no idea, Mrs Morrow."

When it arrived by courier later that day, she saw it was in fact a small padded envelope, addressed to her, care of her office. Inside, there was no letter or note. There was just a small key ring with a wooden ornament, a curious thing fashioned smoothly out of a single block of wood, scored with stripes on its flanks and a smile on its tiny but exquisitely carved head. The ring passed between the slats of the curved base attached to its legs. It was an interesting trick and she wasn't sure how it had been done, because the ring was a solid circle.

She turned the ornament over in her hand. It was heavier than it looked, and felt expensive.

It was a giraffe.

VIII

The girl on the hill

T HE BARRETT-DANES LIVED in an eight-bedroom residence with elevated views of the Gower peninsula. The house was hidden behind a row of well-appointed sycamores, although Franklyn had discovered that if he climbed to the fifth branch of the huge oak that ruled the trees in the leafy avenue, a break in the sycamores allowed a clear view of a second-floor window. Through this window, he sometimes glimpsed the head and shoulders of a girl.

He had only come face to face with the girl on two occasions. The first time was by accident when he was eight; they had knocked into each other in a playground. Even now he could clearly recall the impact, the flush of her skin and her tiny bones, but the meeting was really between the parents. Realising who he was, her father was as anxious to withdraw from the surprise encounter as his mother: two enemy soldiers suddenly thrown into close confrontation. Unprepared and frightened, they had backed away.

The second time was almost two years ago, this time by design and very much their own affair. He had waited for her outside the private school she attended and she had been content to hear him out as he pleaded with her, for it was his intrusion, not hers: his mistake, her victory. That night Tombes had banged his snare incessantly, for far longer than normal prescribed punishment. It was the rap of desperation, for after that day nothing seemed to go right. He found himself distracted, preferring the graze of stone on his palms and the thud in his trainers to his music and composition.

From the branch of the tree he glimpsed a quick shadow behind the glass. He smiled as he pictured her face; the face that was constantly before him in his imagination, which would be before him at his death.

The girl was part of him and she had risen as he had fallen, as if they were seated opposite each other on a see saw. That time in the playground she had seemed nervous and tongue tied, but outside her school he could see she was finding her magisterial confidence. After that meeting, her ascent was dramatic: two years on she was a princess in her tower; even to assume he could ever have competed with her was a presumption.

He leaned into the foliage as she came suddenly to the window and looked out, then angrily pulled the curtains shut.

"Hey! Hey you! Come down from there!" came a loud voice from a distance.

The voice belonged to a man standing in the porch of the house. Franklyn recognised him instantly: it was the girl's father.

"Come down goddam it or I'll torch the bloody tree with you in it!" the man called.

Franklyn nimbly negotiated the tree, swinging and then jumping from the branches to make an effortless landing. He offered the man a cautious look, the best form of apology he could manage in the circumstances, then made for the ridge of the steep wood that would take him skidding down into the town, avoiding the road. He stopped just as he arrived at the last paving stone before the ridge; memory telling him how far he could go before he fell backwards.

"If I see you out there again I'll…" But the man in the porch was suddenly distracted, standing on tiptoe in order to get a better view of the road, where a car was coming up the rise of the hill. The man quickly returned into the house and shut the door.

Franklyn briefly followed his view, catching a glimpse of an old people carrier before he disappeared down the slope.

Gracie Barrett-Danes remained behind the curtain awhile, her eyes closed as she saw herself watching the boy by the sea. She opened them when she heard the approach of a vehicle on the forecourt, followed by the sound of footsteps on the gravel. Her telephone rang, the irregular buzz telling her it was an internal call.

"They're here, Gracie," her father said quietly. "I'll be in the international room. Just come down when you're ready."

She terminated the connection without a word and checked her appearance in one of her standing mirrors. Her extensive art deco bedroom contained a dressing room with a cosmopolitan array of outfits, her father having taken her to the Milan fashion shows since she was twelve, but today she decided that simple would be better. She had tried to explain to her father that their wealth might work against them in impressing the Morrows, that the couple's sympathy would inevitably lie with the poorer family, but he didn't agree: money and status could never be considered a drawback, he argued.

Gracie considered her reflection in the mirror. *No, I'll stay in my jeans,* she decided, aware that her father still considered that natural laws and life experience were relevant when it came to the workings of Precious Cargo. She trotted to her changing room and selected one of her plainer tops, something very girly with a heart of sequins near the collar. Her auburn hair, so shiny it was almost copper-coloured, was tied back severely in Spanish equestrian style but she now removed the bands and hooks, letting her hair tumble around her neck. She blinked with agreement, thinking that the style went with her top. Normally she wore minimal make-up, no more than a little eyeliner, but she decided to plump up her lips with a cherry lipstick. A girl her age would wear lipstick.

She moved to the rug that had been carefully positioned to allow her to see her reflection in three of her bedroom mirrors, turning as she did so. It had been remarked that the severity of her demeanour was studied, that with just a smile she could easily be one of those supermodels, with her long bones and those wondrous green eyes and their incredible lashes. Some friends of her parents had even dared to call her stunningly beautiful, to the indignation of her father who had the monopoly on compliments for his daughter.

She *was* beautiful, she decided, as she finished her circle. It was an observation made completely outside her store of vanity; it was merely a fact, a detail she needed to be aware of. Physical appeal had its uses, she supposed, even behind the scenes in the bloody arena of politics and international affairs.

Spin doctor! her father would announce proudly. *What father could boast that his teenage daughter wants to be a* spin doctor?

It was a description she disliked: it had connotations with the British government and her path lay far beyond the United Kingdom. She preferred the term *political attaché*.

She heard the doorbell and as naturally as she breathed air she turned towards the friend she always consulted before leaving the bedroom.

"Well, they're here," she whispered.

She was addressing an Edwardian-style doll's house. The house was some five feet tall and occupied the wall facing her bed, which it claimed as its own, nothing else being allowed there except for the gold pelican egg just in reach inside a feature alcove. At least a third of the wooden house was its base, the place she called *the servants' quarters* which was hidden from view; some windows on the facia gave the impression of service below stairs, but the glass was smeared and opaque.

The servants' quarters was in fact the storage compartment for countless figurines accessed via a trap door, the square hole just big enough to allow in Gracie's tiny hand and stick-thin forearm. The room above, where this trap door was found, was proudly revealed when the walls of the doll's house were opened. The room took up the entire ground floor and was perhaps a ballroom, or some sort of public reception: she called it *the gallery* for it was very grand, with gold leaf wallpaper and floor-to-ceiling arched windows rising from the floor in green and blue Venetian-style glass. A chandelier hung at the centre of its ceiling, the diamonds so brilliant they caught the light and cast a faint yellow spotlight on the marble-effect floor.

In this spotlight was a figurine about two inches tall. It resembled her, or at least as well as it could do with the china features smoothed to a bare representation of a face. The figurines gave suggestions through key signals: this figurine had bright red hair tied tightly back, with hands behind its back, one hand thoughtfully nursing the index finger of the other as was her habit; she was doing it now. It was the sixth figurine of herself she had found in *the servants' quarters*, arriving when she became a teenager. She would change less dramatically as an adult and she suspected there were no more than another twenty or so Gracies buried in the bowels of the house.

Standing in the wings, beyond the glittering windows and out of the spotlight, were two more figurines. One was her father with his salt-and-pepper hair, one hand on his hip, the other pointing in an instructive manner. The second figurine was a wide-shouldered young man with a colourful bow tie and painted red cheeks: this was Jake, a school friend who, to the consternation of her father, had taken to visiting her in the last year. Jake didn't have red cheeks, but sometimes the figurines found a motif to identify the person and to exaggerate a characteristic: the rosy face was undoubtedly a reference to Jake's shyness. The doll's house recorded all her visitors and was happy to accommodate him in *the gallery*, the place of friends and safety. She in her turn was prepared to admit him as a guest. This would have been unthinkable if the house hadn't approved.

The flicker of a bemused smile crossed her face as she thought of Jake. She wasn't sure why the house approved of him so, given that he was neither smart nor talented.

With the slightest finger of pressure she released the spring on the trap door and reached down into *the servants' quarters*. She had no idea how many china figurines were in there but they were many ranks deep, like a mass grave, and with the doll's house more than four feet wide there had to be thousands of them. She brought out two new figures. The first was a tall, athletic-looking man with an excited face and a red nose. She frowned as she wondered what the redness signified.

Alcoholic, she decided.

The second figurine was of a woman with bleached white skin and short black hair. She looked ill and unhappy.

Gracie nodded. *The man is the faithful parent*, she thought, although logic gave her this information anyway given that she had met Margie Wight, the other faithful parent.

On the first floor of the doll's house, occupying two thirds of its length, was *the library*. Here, the ribs of books, each an intricately worked leather binder, occupied a dozen shelves. All visitors went to *the library* for vetting purposes as a kind of quarantine. She slid the man with the red nose along the polished parquet floor and a book clicked and popped out slightly from its bookcase. She examined its rib with a tilt of her head and saw that it was *Plays Pleasant* by Bernard Shaw. This was the book of playful artifice: the man was concealing something behind a carefree demeanour.

She pondered this information and supposed this was a typical message for a faithful parent at this stage in the cycle. He was secretly in contact with the Trustees and his wife had been brought here by guile. The man was not useful or capable, otherwise the house would have emphasised his talents rather than highlight a weakness, in this case his alcoholism, and it would have shown her more books. He needed as much help as possible.

She had never understood how the books worked on her subconscious. They begun speaking to her when she was very young, long before she got round to reading and researching all of the real books to understand their significance: it was simply the way the house had always talked to her, something that made perfect sense.

She dropped him back through the hole, hearing it land with a clunk in *the servants' quarters*, and clicked the book back into the bookcase. She needn't try to impress the faithful parent; the purpose of this meeting was to win round the reluctant, sceptical parent. She thoughtfully held the female figurine between two fingers for a moment in expectation, then slid it across the floor of *the library*.

She frowned. Nothing had happened.

She repeated the motion, sliding the figurine across the floor and back again, but no books were activated.

Her stomach fluttered. If the doll's house could not read the visitor then there were only two possibilities. She placed the figure in *the gallery*, but the light of the chandelier immediately dimmed. She snatched it up again quickly.

There was only one room left, and the figurine of the ill-looking woman settled there without protest. This room adjoined *the library* and it was completely bare, the walls were made of dark stone and exuded a damp air. If the front walls of the doll's house were to be closed, this room would have no windows.

For this reason she called it *the room with no windows*, and it was the room of danger and warning. The woman shared the room with another figurine: a slender young black man.

This figurine was Franklyn Tyde, and he had also had six representations during her life; they had always been kept in *the room with no windows*. His most recent incarnation was the figurine that had been uncovered after he approached her two years ago. The electric guitar his figurine always carried was only barely on show under one folded arm, his free hand going to his chin, his eyes widening in terror. The doll's house had a triumphal radiance as she mentally transferred the look of horror in the smooth china face to the face of the boy who watched her window from the tree in the road. She now saw his flesh behind the emblematic representation of his figurine and a moment of empathic sympathy made her eyes flicker. The reaction was noted as being most unwelcome by a momentary dulling of the light in the chandelier.

She stepped away quickly. "Remember the woman is dangerous," she said to herself, her hands going behind her back, the right hand massaging her left index finger. "I can't be blamed for that. I can only do my best with the information I'm given."

She smiled to bolster her confidence. There were points and prizes riding on this meeting, the visits of the new families an essential service that the Trustees expected them to perform both efficiently and diplomatically. She imagined the flustered woman by the sea, over-rehearsed and obsessive, and her son, shell-shocked and directionless, and wondered how they had scored.

I pretend to be surprised as I walk down into the hall. Father rises from his armchair in the international room as he sees me pass the double doors, and beckons me in. I am going for a walk: I will take my bag. I will need some coaxing to speak to these strangers, because I am only fifteen and can't be troubled with such things.

She walked into her dressing room and returned with a utilitarian bag slung over her shoulder.

Father will say that they have come for a reference from Precious Cargo. It will be necessary that they see my bedroom: see the egg and the baptism gift.

She took hold of the outside walls and closed up the house. There was no lock to the walls but she would decline to open it, saying it was private.

I must remember that the visitors will be in a state of disbelief. After all, Father may be an energetic seventy-three-year-old but Mother is seventy and the visitors will have done their sums. My existence will be more puzzling to them than all the doctors' reports they were given by the family by the sea. It is important that no lies are told: it is better to make a mistake than to lie. If they ask how it was possible, we say that it was through prayer. That it was a miracle.

She drew the entire, closed-up doll's house into her vision. Her thoughts shuffled into order as she considered the room she called *the roof attic*, set in the roof of tiny tiles. As with *the servants' quarters* it was a part of the house that was always closed. One small window was to be found in the centre of the roof, smeared and opaque as with the windows in the basement, but with one difference.

A light was on inside.

"That's one smart kid," Lloyd remarked to the steering wheel as he sharply turned the car in the forecourt.

"Hmmm," Alex agreed. They both raised a hand and smiled as they drove past the Barrett-Danes family standing on the porch and waving. They had stayed an hour and Miles Barrett-Danes had been the most attentive of hosts, effortlessly leading the conversation. He was a man who could talk on any subject, and after ascertaining the occupations of his guests had recounted an extraordinary anecdote about when, as a young man, he was sued by a South American government for salvaging some Spanish artefacts from a shipwreck. He casually recited the court reference, for in passing the find onto the British Museum he had created some new maritime precedent.

Lloyd was fascinated with both the story and the huge room, elaborately decorated with artefacts from around the world, from African tribal masks to Japanese screens and Siberian furs, all adding to the exotic flavour of the host. His wife, Anthea, had looked on silently with precise posture, nervous hands and a permanent smile.

"How would you like to have a kid like that?" Lloyd added, waving one final time before hitting the stretch of the gravel drive.

"Not sure really," Alex answered distantly.

"What are you talking about? She was lovely. Charming..."

"Yes, yes she was."

The girl had appeared at the double doors, stopping uncertainly before her father had jumped up and beckoned her in. She shyly took a position on the large armrest of her father's sofa, as if to signal that she was only temporarily in the room, but had gradually relaxed into conversation. Out of the corner of her eye Alex had noticed Lloyd's face light up when he saw her and, with a sure and intimate knowledge of his body and his passions, she had felt his pulse quicken as the girl walked towards them with her small quick strides. Perhaps it was that which made her prefer her dear, lovely Frank, or perhaps it was something else: the feeling that the girl was a little wary of her. Alex thought hard as they made eye contact.

It's not that she doesn't like me ... it's something deeper than that ... she views me as dangerous...

"Talk about confident," Lloyd continued. "She seemed to know as much about the law as you do."

"Probably more," Alex muttered, recalling the conversation on recent legislation that provided a *desirable activity* defence for accidents during outdoor activities. Gracie had mentioned she had started a lobby group in school to reinstate the summer outing to the Brecon Beacons, cancelled two years ago after a parent sued because of an accident.

"Good for you," Lloyd had declared. "The nanny state's getting to the stage that everyone's going to be afraid to take a bit of fresh air in case they catch a cold."

"Quite so," Miles agreed. He was a tall, handsome man with small interrogative eyes and minimal wrinkles for a man of his age.

Alex remarked that the desirable activity defence was yet to be tested in the higher courts and no one was sure of the level of protection it would offer to schools. Gracie agreed but cited half a dozen cases yet to be reported on a national level, which she had used to focus the pressure lobby in the press. She added that the legal precedents to date didn't remove the need for a risk assessment, but protected schools against pupils hurting themselves through simple mischance. Specifically, on the basis of the recorded cases, mischance included tripping over tree roots, falling from slides, and aggressive actions of other children. She had devised the risk assessment for the school from Health & Safety Executive extracts, which the local paper had published alongside the article. The article had caused the school to change its policy.

Miles sat back proudly as his daughter had recounted this episode in a neutral, newsreader's voice, his wife shaking her head in amused disbelief.

"So you want to be a lawyer?" Alex asked with a smile.

Gracie shook her head with a serious face. "No, I'd rather *make* law than interpret it."

As they prepared to leave, Lloyd fawningly praising the house and thanking the family for their time, Alex had shuffled through her handbag. She had briefly brought out her keys; she didn't need them, for Lloyd insisted on driving these days, but she wanted an activity while her husband played the sycophant. She flashed a smile at Anthea, the woman appearing just as anxious for the staged meeting to end. Both she and her husband had made a point of declaring their ages early on: her husband very casually and in the context of the Spanish salvage story, she more clumsily, by tagging her own year count onto his. She had visibly relaxed after doing so, as if a necessary and unpleasant task had been performed.

When the Morrows protested that they both looked ten years younger, the Barrett-Danes returned with greater force that their declarations were totally accurate. This swift exchange pre-empted any discussion on the bona fides of Precious Cargo and the whole thing struck Alex as a little absurd, in spite of the natural grace of the host: a game of adult Punch and Judy.

The keys were jangling in her hand, and only now she remembered that she had attached the giraffe key ring to her own keys. The girl was looking at the giraffe; her father had stopped talking and was looking at it too. It was as if she had brought a gun out of her handbag. For the first time she saw that Miles was lost for words, raising a finger uncertainly, then putting it away with an inquiring glance at his daughter. Alex hastily returned the keys to her handbag, declaring that she had just remembered that her husband was driving. Lloyd looked over and tutted his confirmation, having completed his eye tour of the room.

"Wouldn't you like to have a kid like that?" Lloyd repeated as they returned to the main road.

"Lloyd, I'd like to have a kid, full stop. The kid doesn't have to be a genius."

"Sure. I'm just saying."

She looked at him. "What *are* you saying?"

He threw her a smile.

"Lloyd?"

"I'm just saying that Precious Cargo can't be all that bad. And at least we know that whatever their technique is, that it actually works."

"Technique ... technique! Lloyd, we know exactly what their *technique* is and it's not exactly scientific, is it?"

"It works, that's all that matters."

"We don't know that."

"We've seen two families, Allie. How many will it take to convince you?"

"Two families who got lucky. They wouldn't show us their failures, would they?"

"Oh come on…"

"No, *you* come on. Explain to me how prayers are going to get me pregnant."

There was a long silence. "You're a fine one to talk," he muttered eventually. "You're the one who's always touching that pregnant Madonna picture. And you're not even Catholic."

"That's different," Alex said, on less certain ground.

"Different? How?"

"The picture's good luck, that's all. Nothing wrong with good luck. I don't pass people on the stairs either, or walk under ladders. But the point is I don't plan my fertility treatment around a Renaissance painting."

Lloyd narrowed one eye. "Maybe you should. We might have more success."

"What does *that* mean?"

He tapped the steering wheel thoughtfully. His speech had been prepared some time ago but he needed to make it sound as natural as possible by throwing in the occasional pause, even the odd irritated glance at inconsiderate drivers, for good measure.

"I'm not going to go all religious on you," he said. "I believe in God as well as the next man, no more, no less, but I've seen a few things in the last few days, well, that have made me think. We place too much faith in science, if you ask me. Anyway, no one really knows how the body works. Maybe there's something in it. Prayer, I mean. I'm not saying there's a divine being up there waiting for the phone to ring, but maybe, just maybe, what goes on up here…" and he tapped his head "…is directly linked to what goes on down there…" and he tapped his chest. "Psychosomatic or something, I'm not sure if that's the right word, but you believe it will happen, so it does. These people we've visited believed that a prayer would give them a child, and against all the odds. Well, we've seen the result, haven't we?"

She was considering him with alarm. "It's not just *any* prayer," she murmured.

"I know."

He was attempting to control his breathing, looking in his wing mirror with a yawn to give the impression that this was a casual, throwaway conversation. With controlled excitement he sensed that she was close.

"You honestly believe that?" she asked.

His expression darkened. "I believe we have a son. Theo, our son. I believe that one hundred per cent, and I'd do anything, *anything* to find him."

She looked away, watching the road. Put like that, it didn't seem so wrong. And there was something to be said for the power of the mind; after all, the needles weren't meant to hurt, but they did. The agony was in her imagination, some phobia she must have developed after years of sticking syringes into her flesh, but it was no less real for all that.

"We finish the IVF first," she said quietly. "Then we'll talk about it."

"Really?"

"I'm not saying I'm agreeing, Lloyd. Just that we'll talk about it."

"Sure." His delight showed only briefly in another swift tap of his fingers on the steering wheel.

"We give it one more shot," she said firmly. "There's no reason why it shouldn't work this time."

"Absolutely. One more shot. Look, I've given up the booze, like the doctors advised, haven't I?" He bit his lip as a warning to himself not to say anything more.

"Yes, you've been marvellous," she admitted. Her expression was troubled. "We've got a good chance this time, I think."

She was lying. The night before she had flushed her measures of Suprefact and Puregon down the toilet, rather than face the needles.

Lady of letters

"HOW DID YOU get our address?" Margie Wight muttered as she studied the business card. She silently repeated the name and job description with an expression that suggested both were incomprehensible.

Tristyn Honeyman
Freelance journalist

"This is a remarkable view," Honeyman said from the doorstep, a slow emphasis on the *mark* in remarkable. He leaned slightly to her left to take a peek at the large semi-circular window that framed the harbour, holding a patient but bemused expression at being made to wait at the door.

"I asked you how you got our address," Margie repeated, handing back the card. She glanced suspiciously at the reporter's expanse of hair, while studiously avoiding his dark, intense stare.

"But your husband, Henry, said I should call," he remarked.

"And how do you know Henry?"

Honeyman grumbled. "He hasn't told you, has he? Well, this is embarrassing. I asked him if he'd care to do a feature on your new baby, given that you're both local celebrities."

"How are *we* local celebrities?"

"Not in the sense of all that glitz, perhaps, but *Wights* is the biggest haulage company in South Wales, employs more than a thousand people and has founded three charitable trusts. Your husband sits on government transport committees and is marked for a knighthood." He coughed a short laugh. "But my research on a human level tells me you're the major driving force behind it all. What's that saying? Behind every successful man you'll find a good woman."

Margie replied with a distrustful sneer, having always been completely impervious to flattery. "I don't like uninvited visitors," she remarked. Her finger indicated the doormat. "Wait there." Her mobile was held open in her palm and she waited as it rang, the silence that was building a matter of no concern to her. She was ringing her husband, and no matter where he was or what he was doing he would find a way of answering. He never turned his mobile off; if he was in an important meeting it would be on vibrate and he would find an excuse to leave.

"Please, take your time," Honeyman said, reassessing his strategy. Henry Wight had been putty in his hands, preening with the notion of *an heir to the throne* article replete with a photograph on the deck with his yacht in the background; his wife was a very different proposition.

Margie's attention remained on the mobile, but Honeyman noticed that in her free hand she was turning and squeezing a white fluffy cube. Its sides showed either an *S is for Shakespeare*, with a sketch representation of the bearded scribe, or *S is for Shelby*, with a cartoon face of a smiling little girl.

"You're hoping your daughter will be a dramatist?" he inquired, thinking that 'sea' or 'ship' would have been a more suitable image than 'Shakespeare' for a baby's toy.

"That was a present," Margie returned, putting the white cube quickly inside her trouser pocket. She looked at the mobile with even more insistence than before, until eventually it was answered. The heavy breaths on the other line suggested that Henry had been hurrying.

"Everything okay?" he gasped. "I was in the middle of..."

"Henry, I have a reporter here." She again required sight of the card with identification, reading the name with a frown. "Honeyman. Tristyn Honeyman."

"Just Honeyman."

"He says he's here at your invitation," Margie continued, studiously ignoring the qualification but pausing long enough to register that she didn't care for it. "Something about a feature he wants to sell to the newspapers."

Henry was mumbling, uncomfortable to have to admit that he had spoken to someone in private regarding the baby, his mind conditioned to deny anything that might conceivably be the cause of *Margie displeasure.*

"A reporter?" he stumbled. "I ... I really can't remember. Someone might have contacted me..."

"Hello Henry!" Honeyman called to the mobile.

"Oh, hello," came the miserable response. "I thought you were going to telephone?"

Honeyman took out a small leather-bound notebook, producing a charcoal pencil from its rib. "The photographs will be taken by a professional, of course, but I thought that if I could just cover a few key points in advance I could send you the draft feature, to help you make up your mind." He paused. "Perhaps if I could just ask you a few questions; and if you could quickly introduce me to your baby?"

"Margie, it will be something nice for the scrapbook," Henry suggested, gathering his courage. "Shelby will read it one day."

Margie softened somewhat at the notion of something that might please Shelby, even if it were years in the future. Reluctantly, she beckoned Honeyman inside the house, snapping the mobile shut without announcing her decision to Henry; the uncertainty he would carry for the rest of the day would be his punishment for making a unilateral decision that affected their home and daughter. "You'll have to be quick and very quiet. Shelby's sleeping. Fifteen minutes."

"Fifteen minutes it is," he agreed. "But before we go up, I'd just like to ask how you're coping?" He wrote something in the notebook to lend some credence to the question as he walked with a slight limp past the stairs to the double doors of the lounge.

"Why should I be having trouble coping?" she asked, her eyes following the reporter. She took her fluffy cube out of her pocket and squeezed it.

"Oh, because it's your first," he answered, following her hand. "It's a question all first-time mothers are asked, is it not?"

Margie nodded slowly, but her expression darkened momentarily as a camera in her head snapped the reporter for future study. "We're fine. Shelby has everything she needs."

"I'm sure she has," he remarked, with a brief admiring glance into the lounge. The furniture was baroque and the oil paintings – arresting seascapes in stormy grey – were original works. "Your husband tells me that Shelby was a Valentine's Day baby?" he asked the lounge.

"Yes," she confirmed wearily.

"You must be overjoyed."

"Of course."

"Are you planning to have more?"

There was a moment of hesitation. "More? No, I don't think so."

Honeyman nodded, still admiring the lounge. "I don't have children myself, but I can imagine how exciting it must be."

"Yes, I recommend it."

"No family at all, anymore," he continued, but to himself. "Except my Heavenly Family, of course."

She didn't answer, completely disinterested in the reporter's family, heavenly or otherwise.

"And would you recommend the fertility clinic too?"

When she didn't respond, he turned back round, his pencil poised over his notebook.

"What makes you think there was a fertility clinic involved?" she asked acidly.

"I'm sorry, I assumed…"

"Assumed?"

"Well, without being indelicate, you married in your teens. I find it hard to imagine that you'd have *chosen* to wait this long before having children."

Margie acknowledged the unassailable logic within the reporter's assessment with a crease of the brown, leathery skin around her eyes.

"I don't mean to pry," he said, "but I thought you might like to give this fertility centre a mention in the article. Or anyone else you think deserves an acknowledgement."

"I've nothing to say on the subject."

"Let me see," he pondered, ignoring the response. "*She's a little miracle*, declares the delighted Mrs Wight. After more than thirty years…"

"Mr Honeyman," Margie snapped, "Shelby is *not* a miracle baby. If you refer to her as such, I will sue you as well as your paper. Do you understand? The subject is beyond discussion."

Honeyman affected confusion, making a deliberate show of moving his pencil a distance from his notepad, as a marked gunman moves his hand from his holster. "You don't think of your child as a miracle?"

"No."

"Are not *all* babies miracles?" he asked with a shift of his moustache. "That's the sense in which I meant it. Why, what did you think I meant?"

She regarded the pencil's cautious return to the orbit of the notebook and she frowned, noticing the number 113 written faintly on its cover.

A Mozart string quartet was playing in the baby's bedroom, orchestrated through four speakers.

Honeyman lingered on the threshold, unsure what to make of this development. Inside, he saw the cot under a window. The window was open just enough to flutter the white linen drapes.

"You like chamber music?" he asked.

"I like ... some pieces..." Margie said cautiously. "I'm not particularly knowledgeable."

"Me neither," he lied, having immediately recognised the stirring fourth movement of Mozart's K421. "This is Vivaldi, isn't it?"

"I think so, yes. A friend of mine put it together. It's on a loop."

"Really? Why?"

"Classical is the only music it likes."

"*It?*"

Margie started. "Shelby, the baby," she muttered by way of correction. "We decided music would be good for her. Henry read this article on subliminal learning."

Honeyman nodded, not believing her. He couldn't imagine Henry Wight getting any of his ideas through on the rhythm of the house without his wife's full approval, especially over something that concerned their daughter.

"Shall we go in?" she asked. "I did say I only had a few minutes."

"You did indeed." Again he observed the squeeze of her hand. "But I'm fascinated by your Shakespeare dice. Is it Shelby's?"

"It's mine," came the flat response.

"Was I correct when I suggested you wanted your daughter to be a dramatist?"

Margie's mind was elsewhere, her brain working furiously. "Shelby will be a writer one day. A famous novelist, perhaps ... possibly an acclaimed critic ... a great lady of letters." The words had a rehearsed monotony, the prediction uttered on so many occasions that all the juice had been squeezed out of it.

"And S is her letter; it stands for Shelby, and for Shakespeare," he remarked. "Where did you get it?"

She was startled by the question. It was inappropriate to raise any question on her Shelby cube. "I ... I don't remember..." she muttered.

"How long have you had it?"

Her confusion increased, as she realised she didn't have answers to these questions.

He offered a large open palm. "May I see it?"

Instinctively, she shook her head.

"Why not?" he asked, with a curious smile.

She hesitated, unsure what to do.

"Mrs Wight?"

She quickly handed it over and his hand closed on the

cube, squeezing it into a tiny ball. His eyes glazed over as he staggered slightly.

There was a long pause. "No ... S is for *shell*..." he murmured eventually in a faraway voice. The cube sprung effortless back into its shape as it was released.

Margie retrieved it, having recovered from her disorientation and at last realising who this man was: the one Lauren had warned her about. The cube, however, was soft and relaxing, telling her that she should admit the visitor to the bedroom.

"Shall we?" she asked coldly, indicating the open door.

Honeyman hesitated, suddenly concerned at what lay beyond the threshold. Within the music he detected an atmosphere, which he would later translate simply as a *mood*; an infection so morose it hung in the air like poison gas.

With an uncertain breath, he stepped inside.

A wooden block turned.

An eye opened.

★

Honeyman's churches measured the distance of his wandering, as water holes are left to be found by desert travellers. There was a time when churches were forbidden to him; it seemed long ago now, that dark age from which he had been miraculously delivered.

His stopping point in Cardiff was an evangelical church in the centre of the city, where the large congregation joyously sang Wesleyan hymns to the huge organ pipes and listened reverently to the passionate call of its pastor. Here, amid the message of sin and redemption, the cares of the world were set down as slight and unnecessary, the tears and agonies of children.

Honeyman's place was at the back, near the door. His present accomodation was a studio flat in Brecon in clear view of Precious Cargo, but the Morrows and the Wights had temporarily diverted him to the capital where he had been forced to make further demands on his dwindling savings to establish another digs. And so, he had found another church.

He nodded to acknowledge the people in the pew in front and he wondered if he should shortly move on. This was a sociable church: he had already received invitations to tea from the ushers, who engaged him with conversations designed to elicit his identity. He never lied about his name – among his many deceptions it was the one truth he was always determined to preserve – but he dared not give it out to churchmen, who would recognise it instantly. As he stood up with the rest of the congregation to the insistent note of the organ, he bitterly lamented his nomadic, outlawed existence.

"Our God is gracious nor will leave the desolate to mourn," he sang resolutely in his resounding bass, his eyes raised to the high roof rafters. Still, he had a more pressing worry: how to break into the temple before yet another sixteen-year-old died.

The ache in his joints went beyond tiredness. The horrendous experience with Shelby Wight's abacus had told him that confronting the guardians was a mistake: they were too powerful. Ray Matthews had introduced him briefly to the giraffe, but by that time it was wretched and disinterested, the battle already lost.

He shuddered as he recalled his glimpse of the abacus in the bedroom, turning slowly and gleefully in its cloud of despair.

Something wrong, *Baptist*? Margie Wight had sneered.

And he had run, his legs working with adrenalin and instinct. The abacus had been on the verge of telling him something.

It had a message for him...

He lifted his voice. No, he would try a different strategy now: he'd attempt to visit the children in school, perhaps. A faithful parent combined with a guardian was an impossible obstacle; he should have realised that the moment he held that fluffy letter cube.

S is for Shelby...

He made to sit down, believing that the hymn was over, then realised another verse had started. Something had stalled in his brain.

Yes, the Shakespeare cube. The memory had almost been lost to him; it was so intense his mind had attempted to eradicate it.

He saw it now, replaying the scene in his mind. His hand was squeezing the cube and he saw the turn of the blocks of a white alphabet abacus.

P ... T...

He saw a pirate and a set of teeth

H ... M...

then a halo and a man.

Then the S became a shell, and he realised that the cube in his hand belonged to the turning blocks in his mind.

"No, S is for *shell*," he had murmured.

With sudden insight he understood that the thing in his hand was called a *character,* and it had imagined the abacus.

It had *imagined* the abacus!

His eyes widened. Something had snapped, a barrier that he had been struggling to breach but which had also protected him. This forbidden knowledge came at a price, said the memory of the cube.

You have gone too far now, Baptist…

You have trespassed…

His mouth voicelessly worded the hymn, his eyes a silent frenzy of panic as he heard the chimes of tiny bells. The bells were from a music box he had been shown when he had stumbled across the coven's first holy place, a derelict house that was once the home of a Victorian scientist. The Trustee of that temple, a beautiful woman called Sorrel Page, presented him with the music box to punish what she described as his *trespass*.

In his head the chimes tapped out with tiny bells the tune to *Silent Night*: the chime curse he believed had been lifted forever when Sorrel Page's temple fell. He knew what this meant and he pressed his lips tightly together in terror.

A ball tightened in his stomach and he longed to sit down, for the hymn to end; he dared not even pretend to sing. Though it was difficult to see in the dense mass of his moustache and beard his mouth was tightly shut, braced as the words threatened to emerge from his throat.

The hymn had ended, the closing chords of the organ fading with the shuffle of people returning to their seats. He collected his overcoat and asked the lady next to him if she would kindly let him pass, because he had to leave. The chimes of *Silent Night* sounded in his brain

all is calm, all is…

and the words came out, loudly, as:

"Move you pissy cunt."

He barged past the horrified woman and hurried along the pew, his head down, then past the astonished glare of the usher at the door who snatched the hymn book from his hand. Outside the church, resting against its yellowing stone, his body rocked with a beat of shock. He stumbled away, beyond the building's boundary, not stopping until it was out of view.

X

Arena

"ROME WAS A city of winners and losers. Success and failure were part of its mythology, the DNA that informed its eventual route to empire."

Gracie was standing at the head of the class recounting her experiences of her recent holiday in Rome. St Joseph's, a private school built on traditions that may well have emulated the aspirations of the eternal city, had a longstanding tradition of making its pupils offer this verbal postcard on their return. It worked: the children started plaguing their parents to take them somewhere new rather than have to attempt yet another speech on the timeshare in Tenerife.

This was the first day for Gracie's form teacher, one Mr John, who was sitting to the side of the classroom and nodding thoughtfully. He had been warned about Gracie Barrett-Danes: his new colleagues had explained in humorous but totally serious terms that she could make the most experienced teacher look like a rookie. *Troublemaker, is she?* he had asked, rising to the challenge, only to be told she was no such thing. She just seemed to have knowledge … far too much of it. It went way beyond being a precocious bookworm; nothing and no one seemed to faze her.

"Myth said that Romulus and Remus founded Rome," Gracie continued, "and there was never such an apocryphal tale of winners and losers as those two brothers."

"Which brings us to that famous statue," Mr John interjected, "the one of the she-wolf suckling Romulus and Remus. Do you know who built that…?"

"It's Etruscan," Gracie said quietly, without looking at the teacher.

"Yes … that's correct," Mr John remarked, changing his position from thoughtful crouch to dissatisfied stretch. "Well done. Many people assume it's Roman."

Gracie allowed a good few seconds to pass after the interruption before she continued. The doll's house had presented Mr John's figurine this morning and it was almost featureless, notwithstanding that her new form teacher had a very prominent nose and chin. He prompted the click of only a single book from *the library*: *The Count of Monte Cristo* by Dumas, the book of banishment. Mr John had nothing to contribute to her development and would soon be sacked by St Joseph's.

"The brothers each stood on one of Rome's seven hills," she explained. "Romulus took the Palatine, Remus the Aventine, agreeing that wherever the crows circled they would build the city. The crows circled the Palatine and from that time on the Palatine was the hill of the elite, the Aventine of the poor. Success or failure was in the very earth under their feet."

It's yours, Gracie. From here, you will rule the world…

Her father had gripped her by the shoulders on the Palatine as they looked over the ruins of the imperial city and imagined they felt the surge of destiny. For her it was not in the sins and achievements of an ancient civilisation but in the tingle of her father's fingers, the survival instinct energised by the urgent love of a strong parent.

Don't worry, Daddy. All is well. All is well…

But if I were to lose you...

With a gasp of anguish her father took from his jacket his constant companion, a child's crayon drawing of a house, and held it to his chest for comfort as an addict takes his fix. She had never asked what it was, aware that it was something private, just as her doll's house was private to her. The Precious Cargo gifts were not to be shared.

She took a moment to consider the small class. Jake, a good-looking, athletic young man was completely attentive, understanding very little of what she was saying, his awe-based infatuation finding a look of thoughtful astonishment. Her attention momentarily settled briefly on two girls at the back, who last term had been her enemies. They were bored but not making eye contact. The fat one with the ringlets was a lesbian but wasn't aware of it yet, while her sullen friend had some embarrassing tattoos she was desperately trying to conceal from her parents. Gracie had been given their figurines on the morning they planned to flush her head down the toilet after gym as a good prank; they quickly changed their minds as she told them a few home truths which she offered to share with their parents. A few more revelations had the two girls fighting each other in a screaming frenzy that required the gym teacher's assistance to pull them apart.

Everything was peaceful now, Gracie considered; everything was good. It hadn't always been that way: the years between eleven and fourteen had been the hardest, when the boy by the sea had gone from success to success, culminating in his admission to the Royal College of Music. They were dark years, her father mortified that she seemed unable to discover any kind of creative or physical talent, notwithstanding the number of clubs and societies he arranged for her to patronise. She would never make an artist, scientist or athlete, but her doll's house was encouraging her to read. She read biographies in particular, from ancient kings to modern-day politicians and in the cataloguing of information she realised that she did indeed have a talent: the ability to collate and use information. And with that logic jump made, she became aware of her intelligence, the shy friend that had been stalking her all her life. Understanding who she was at last, she found that all her instincts were sharpened.

That's why the doll's house has a library, she realised. *It could have chosen any number of methods to warn me of people's agendas, but the house wants me to read, read, read...*

She was now recounting her impressions of the Colosseum, with an emphasis on the more subtle details such as the private toilet facilities within the senatorial section. Her hand behind her back tightened on the index finger it was holding when she saw the large bearded man pass by the glass classroom door, accompanied by two police officers. They would have been called by her father and were escorting him off the premises.

She didn't pause in her lecture, though her mind went elsewhere. The man was posing as a journalist, here to do a feature about her astonishing success in lobbying the local council, and to learn of her plans once she had received the straight A grades her school confidently expected of her. The story had evidently fooled the headmistress, who allowed him to wait in the common room until the mid-morning break. Gracie had smiled and told the headmistress she would look forward to meeting him, then rang her father to say there was an enemy in the school.

For she had taken two figurines from *the servants' quarters* this morning and the second, a large, bearded man with a bible protruding from a pocket of his overcoat, had defied analysis within *the library*. The figurine had instead found its place in *the room with no windows*.

Honeyman glanced through the glass and with a punch of surprise made a brief eye contact.

The Baptist, Gracie thought, unsure where this name came from. The name was revealed as the image of his figurine reared up in her memory, the shadows in the corners of *the room with no windows* darkening with malice around it. She hesitated; for the first time in her life the doll's house appeared as a wild and dangerous animal, rather than the friend she had always known it to be. A loving watchdog that had suddenly bared its teeth.

"Sir! Sir!"

One of the boys had his hand up with a mischievous grin. Mr John checked his desk diagram to discover the boy's name.

"Ansari, is it?"

"Yes Sir."

"Well, what is it?"

"Have you seen that film, *Gladiator,* Sir?"

Mr John gave a tedious sigh. "Yes, we've all seen the film, Ansari."

"Is it true about the thumbs up and the down, Sir? That thumbs down meant death?" The young man turned to his classmates and made a face of agony as he put his thumb down.

"Yes, well done," the teacher groaned. "I see we've found our comedian."

"Actually, it's not true," Gracie said quietly. She looked at the teacher and brought her hands out from behind her back. "Well it's true about the thumbs up and thumbs down, but Hollywood got it the wrong way round and it's just stuck.

Thumbs down meant *life*." She demonstrated carefully with her right hand. "It was a symbol for *put your sword down*. It was thumbs up that was *death*. It meant *stick it up him*." She glanced around the room, a smile arriving as she sensed the scepticism, her eyes eventually settling on her teacher. "I can show you the historical records if you want."

Some of the pupils looked inquiringly at Mr John for confirmation and he cleared his throat, not prepared to gamble that the young woman might be right. "Yes, I was just about to explain that to Ansari here. It's a common mistake, perpetuated by Hollywood, as Barrett-Danes has explained."

Gracie was back in the Colosseum with her father, looking down at where the gladiators would have fought to the death. It had occurred to her then that she and the boy by the sea were also facing each other on the sand, the stakes no less deadly, no less final. She had taken her father's arm and squeezed it in terror despite her confidence about the outcome; it hadn't occurred to her that there could be mercy or reprieve.

She wondered if she was wrong.

Whether it was thumbs up or thumbs down … life was given, even in that terrible place, the bloody arena.

Couldn't the loser in the battle between the sea and the hill also be spared?

"I can't tell you how disappointed I am, Franklyn."

"I know, Mrs Winters. Sorry, Mrs Winters."

Franklyn was sitting in the small office of his music tutor, the stern-faced Hilary Winters, who until a few years ago was being told by her better-paid contemporaries that she was wasting her time looking for talent in a comprehensive like Glamorgan House. That was until she found Franklyn Tyde, a nine-year-old violinist who could play entire concertos from memory and had a very promising bent for composition. Energised by her discovery she had completely forgotten that she was approaching retirement and with the passion of a missionary had immersed herself in his life and arranged for his school-funded tuition. By the time he was ten, she had helped him become one of the three hundred Saturday students trained in the Royal College of Music, Kensington. The tutors agreed that proficient as Franklyn was on just about any type of instrument, his real future lay in composition. His exciting variations on Schubert's chamber music had found their way up to the director, who was considering a scholarship.

Mercedes Tyde meanwhile collected every scrap of material available on the Royal College of Music, regaling her neighbours with its history and the alumni who had passed through its doors, most of whom she managed to memorise. All the Lloyd Webbers you know, and that Sir Thomas Allen, the singer…

Then something happened. A few years ago, after Franklyn had launched into his first major classical composition, Hilary Winters started receiving excuses from her protégé. The piece wasn't ready because he needed to think about the theme; his homework was getting in the way; it was too noisy at home. Before long he started skipping his Saturdays in Kensington, until his place expired. Around this time she heard that he had injured himself running over buildings. She spoke to some of the girls who knew him, all of whom were clearly infatuated with him, and they said that Frank slipped deliberately just to have the pain, that they had seen him run a hundred times and he never lost his footing by mistake: never ever. After the injury, which put him briefly into hospital, his musical output plummeted. The last six months had been almost completely non-productive; it was as if he was deliberately pushing the self-destruct button.

"I know you think you've got all your life in front of you, Franklyn," she murmured with a look of mild outrage, "but you don't know how important these years are." Her voice took on a cautiously hopeful tone. "It's not too late to press your cause again with Kensington."

Franklyn shook his head. "I can't do it, Mrs Winters," he said, looking down at his hands. "Whatever talent I had … it's gone. It's just … gone."

"You can never lose your talent, Franklyn. Discipline and self-belief are the things you've lost." She blinked twice, her expression one of mild shock. "You were the most promising, most gifted child I ever knew. What happened to you? What went wrong?"

He shook his head once more. He had told himself it was the exhilaration of the free running, but he was deceiving himself. Deep down he knew he needed to rebel against The Dead Pharaohs. Perhaps he had just wanted to reassure himself that he could do it, that he could be free if he wanted to be, but that small tug of rebellion had been enough to break the cycle. Now he could spend hours looking helplessly at his unfinished composition, wondering whether he really did have any talent, or if it had been The Dead Pharaohs all along. When he put that question to Sphinx the answer was returned immediately, and in the negative.

B-bum note.

He was wrong then: the talent *did* belong to him. Perhaps he was so conditioned to being guided that when he rebelled something had switched off in his head: something to do with trust or faith, something essential to his development. Anyway, it was all too late now. His years of dedication

142

might have still counted, he might still have made up for lost ground, if an irrational impulse when he came out of hospital hadn't made him break the most cardinal of rules: he made contact with the girl on the hill, showing her his wounds as if they were marks of his freedom.

Look what I've done, just to escape them. Free running. There ain't no winners or losers. Run with me, we belong to each other. Run with me...

After that, there was no way back. Now he spent his Saturdays watching her forlornly from a tree; Kensington belonged to a different life.

"So what will you do?" Mrs Winters asked.

"I've applied to Point Blank. They're in London too."

"Hoxton," she clarified, with a sigh. "Don't they train DJs?"

"Not just DJs, Mrs Winters. It's modern music training."

"Modern music," she scoffed, then bit her tongue. He was so beautiful, her protégé: she was aware that girls in the school had taken music just so they could be near him, which could hardly have helped his concentration. Perhaps he'd come back to her in a few years time. Perhaps it wasn't too late.

As if he read her thoughts, he offered her a sad shake of his head.

Mrs Winters considered him awhile, before tapping his hand and getting up. "There's someone waiting for you in the concert hall," she announced sullenly. She checked her watch, it was almost four. "You'd better hurry. I've kept you longer than I thought."

"Waiting for me? Who's waiting for me?"

"A reporter." The music teacher raised her eyebrows. "He's doing an article on talented teenagers. He asked for you." As she opened the door she looked out of her window to observe the playground. In a bitter moment of reflection the empty concrete space seemed to be a symbol for all the regrets of a career where she had sacrificed more than just money, upon the dream of turning some deprived, written-off kid into a great artist. "Perhaps you can explain to him what you can't explain to me."

"Yes, Mrs Winters." He left the room experiencing only a twinge of discomfort over the teacher's mood; he was wondering why an adult would visit him at school. There had been no call to the house, no letter, as he would have expected. As he walked perplexed down the corridor he didn't see the two girls from his form who sang hello to him, then giggled to each other.

The school bell would shortly ring and the concert hall was empty except for a large man in a green waistcoat, tapping out a note on the upright piano at the front of the stage. The hall was full of leaden echoes, the repeated note bouncing along the wooden floor like a submarine's radar. The man studied him awhile with a curious shift of his huge moustache as he approached, then stepped respectfully away from the piano, taking his folded overcoat from the top of the instrument and putting it on the floor.

"I hear that you're a musician?" the man asked in a rich voice of greeting, thinking that the photograph in his file didn't do the handsome young man justice: perhaps it was the boy's body language that was part of charisma. Franklyn didn't answer, but put a hand to his chin in a shy, defensive posture. "I was hoping you could spare me a few minutes, my boy. My name is Honeyman." He offered him a business card, which Franklyn took and put in his pocket, without looking at it. "I'm a journalist doing a piece on talented children in this area." He glanced at the upright. "Do you play the piano?"

Franklyn nodded. "Ain't got one at home, no room, but I played the school piano for about six months a few years back because I hoped it'd throw up some writing ideas." He shrugged, as if to say that it hadn't worked out that way.

"Yes, your music teacher mentioned that you stopped playing at the end of last year. I can't see any guitars or violins lying around. Perhaps you could play something on the piano for me? I'll promise to mention that you're new to it."

Franklyn considered him uneasily for a few moments then sat down at the piano, stretching his fingers. "Anything in particular?" he asked.

"Well, my wife always loved Chopin. But you wouldn't know either of his two piano concertos yet. Something more intermediary, let's see…"

"The concerto in E minor okay?" Franklyn asked, then proceeded to play. Honeyman stepped away in surprise, for the piece was rendered almost perfectly. He watched the boy's long, graceful fingers with fascination, only the odd clunky key in need of tuning, and the bad acoustics of the hall, stopping him from believing he was at his home in Flint, in his library den with his headphones on. A tear started in his eye, which he dabbed away irritably as the boy came to the slow section that his wife had particularly loved.

Noticing the tear, Franklyn stopped playing, embarrassed. "My mum makes tea for five. I've gotta go soon."

"Yes, yes of course," Honeyman said, annoyed that the rendition had found such an unexpected weak point in his composure. "That was astounding," he said, with a long emphasis on the adjective. "You know that, don't you?"

Franklyn shrugged.

Honeyman sighed. "Your music teacher is a very fine lady. She tells me that you had a place in the Royal College of Music. That you've let it go. Why?" He glanced around the hall, the lack of décor and the antiquated equipment stark reminders of the music budget for Glamorgan House. "Don't you want to escape, to leave this place? Musicians of your calibre are well paid, they travel the world…"

"I can't be a musician," he muttered.

Honeyman gave a short grunt. "Why not?"

Franklyn was still looking at the keys. "I've always been able to play … able to play anything. As long as I can remember, it just came natural."

"But … that's good…"

"I can't be a musician," he repeated. "Playing is easy. That's a gift, something I was given, without any effort from me … so it wouldn't be fair for me to succeed with that…"

"Fair? What are you talking about?"

"But writing is difficult," Franklyn continued, ignoring the question, "something I have to work at. Really *work* at. Something which I would have got right if I'd had the patience … put in the time, the effort. That's why I know it's what the Pharaohs wanted for me."

Honeyman held his breath. "The Pharaohs…?" he ventured.

"I know you don't understand," Franklyn murmured, his eyes forlornly on the keys. "You *couldn't* understand." He wanted to say more, but shook his head instead.

Honeyman took careful stock of the situation, keeping his tone neutral so as not to startle him. "That girl would understand, wouldn't she? The one in the expensive house overlooking the city: Gracie Barrett-Danes."

Franklyn looked up, his face suddenly a mask of stress and

anxiety. "You ain't here for no news feature, are you?"

Honeyman considered the boy awhile, then winked apologetically.

"You're investigating the temple, ain't you?"

"The *temple*?"

Franklyn corrected himself quickly. "The clinic … Precious Cargo…"

"I know that you were a Precious Cargo baby," Honeyman said gently. "I know a great deal, my boy, and I understand your troubles."

Franklyn returned fearfully to the keys. "You're *the Baptist,* ain't you?" he muttered. "Sphinx warned me about you."

"Sphinx?"

Franklyn was silent awhile. "You think you can help me?" he asked the keys suspiciously.

"I can try. Your baptism gift: help me to examine it … to speak to it."

Franklyn found a look of baffled outrage.

"Someone your age shouldn't have such worries," Honeyman said. "A fifteen-year-old shouldn't…"

"Fifteen? You think I'm fifteen? You're wrong, minister man. I'm a slave." The boy smiled bitterly. "I ain't got no right to be alive."

The downward thrust of his moustache signalled Honeyman's anger. "Never believe that," he whispered furiously. "Never! Every soul is God's creation."

Franklyn didn't answer, instead studying the keys in a quizzical fashion. Shortly, his expression changed, his features distorting with exertion as he struggled to speak.

"Help me," he whispered, in the smallest of voices.

Honeyman held out his hand. "Yes, of course I'll help you. But you have to tell me…"

Franklyn grunted with surprise and embarrassment, as he noticed the wet patch that had appeared at his crotch, soaking the piano seat. He moaned, the energy draining from his face.

"It doesn't matter," Honeyman whispered, seeing his distress, then stepped back as Franklyn's hands returned to the piano and once again he began to play. This time his palms were pounding the keys furiously, creating explosions of discordant noise. Honeyman shook his head with resignation, putting his hands to the hair over his ears to shut out the cacophony.

Franklyn stopped abruptly to the angry echoes in the hall, attempting to repair themselves after the trauma.

Honeyman was shaking slightly from the episode. As Franklyn looked up, peering just over his shoulder, his eyes appeared sightless. "Let me help you," Honeyman said, with a twinge of panic. Had the boy gone into shock? Perhaps it was some sort of epileptic fit. Should he call someone?

"H–hippy spit," Franklyn remarked in a dead baritone, then jumped up from his chair and with his hands over his crotch ran out of the hall.

XI

Sixteen

FRANKLYN WAS STILL running as he neared his house, slowing down only through exhaustion as he left the Mumbles Mile for the steep roads that led home. He collapsed a little distance from the door, wheezing but relieved.

Sphinx was out of his head.

If he thought about it, and he didn't care to, he could probably count a dozen occasions during his lifetime when Sphinx had invaded his mind. The first time was when he was six and had ripped up some musical scores his mother had bought him in a temper, but as he got older he found that the invasions were not so much a means of correction – it was Tombes who delivered punishment detail; rather, it was a means of regaining control, as a driving instructor will rapidly brake and pull on the steering wheel in a moment of crisis.

He heard his mother call to him from the front room as he came through the front door. His parents were waiting for him patiently, an instrument case on the floor in front or them.

"We've a present for you, Franklyn," Mercedes declared. Jerry managed a smile to acknowledge the moment, then relapsed into his attitude of apathetic disapproval.

"A present?" Franklyn asked, in confusion.

"Birthday present," his mother answered.

"But I ain't sixteen until May."

Mercedes' eyes were ablaze. "It's *her* birthday tomorrow."

Franklyn was all too aware of this fact. He shrugged in inquiry.

"So we thought you could have a birthday too," Mercedes explained. "We could bring it forward, so you won't feel left out." Her voice was shaking. "Bring it forward, so you're sixteen too."

"Happy birthday son," Jerry muttered, nodding to the case. "Your mother's got some crazy notion about you becoming sixteen. I tell her everyone's got to grow up."

"Shut up Jerry," she said quietly. "I'm not fretted at all about him being sixteen. He'll be seventeen too."

Franklyn had opened the felt-lined case to find a gleaming new alto saxophone. He lifted it out reverently. "This is a Boosey and Hawkes," he whispered. "It must have cost you a bomb."

"We got good credit," Mercedes remarked, ignoring her husband's groan.

"You shouldn't have, Mum. I've got more than enough things to play already."

"But you like the clarinet," she remarked. "You always say the clarinet's your favourite. And the man in the music shop said the saxophone is the … is the same *relation*."

"It's the same *family*, woman," Jerry corrected her.

"Woodwind," Franklyn confirmed, detaching the wooden reed from the mouthpiece and damping it on both sides with his tongue. His heart filled with passion as he absorbed the saxophone in his imagination, as he always did when he encountered a new instrument. He saw the finger buttons connecting the pads that would press the notes, saw the different combination of buttons and thumb levers that would take it through the octave range. He felt his lower lip on the reed squeezing out the sound, his tongue darting to its tip for the staccato.

"Play something for us son," his father urged. His parents knew he would be a little hesitant with a new instrument, managing only a basic series of notes at first and requiring a few weeks before becoming proficient, but Mercedes had been talking all day about the sax being 'related' to the clarinet: that he would probably play it as if he had been playing for years.

"You're going to do great things with the sax, I just know it," Mercedes declared to the ceiling, tapping her knees with excitement. "I've bought these books on the great sax players. Lots of proud black men. Jazz, that's it, that's what you need, not this old white man concerto trash."

"Mum, the thing I'm working on don't really need a sax. It's sort of orchestral…"

"Jazz, it's jazz!" Mercedes insisted, her eyes wide and scouring the room. "The sax will make it all good again. You'll see, you'll see. The horn will bring everything back. Bring it back, bring it all back."

There was a moment of silence. "Play something son," Jerry said uncomfortably. "It'll mean a lot to your mother."

Franklyn placed the strap of his instrument over his head then let his fingers find their allotted places; they always knew what they were looking for, he simply had to relax. He took a breath and rubbed his lower gum with his tongue. Woodwind required strong lip muscles: the clarinet had the same type of reed and used the same muscle group, but he would need a little more breath for this bigger instrument. He closed his eyes to imagine Rivers' tapping foot, to find the rolling bass that would guide him like a metronome.

He blew, but no sound came out; he smiled apologetically

and massaged his lips with his tongue. He blew harder, and the saxophone squeaked. With a harder breath again, the effort showing in his eyes, the saxophone belched three discordant notes. He looked at the instrument in alarm.

"I'm going to have to practice," he murmured, attempting a relaxed manner. He unhooked it and put it back in the case.

"Franklyn?" his mother whispered.

Franklyn carefully closed and locked the case. "Thanks for my present," he said quietly, trotting upstairs with it under his arm. Such was the delicacy with which he had handled the crisis that his mother's wailing didn't begin until he was at the door of his bedroom.

Sitting on his bed, the saxophone case on the floor, he tapped the stage platform of The Dead Pharaohs. There was no response.

"Play for me," he muttered, making to touch the stage again, but at the last moment pulling his hand back in horror. The bass player's right leg was still raised, ready to tap along to the beat, but the boot was missing, the leg ending in a stump. Perhaps it wasn't a stump, perhaps the boot was simply detached, although he was sure that where the leg ended he could detect a darker shade of red in the jumpsuit.

"How's this happened?" he whispered, tears streaming down his face as he touched the stage. Sphinx turned to the microphone and answered in his monotone.

The H-haight-Ashbury.

The Haight-Ashbury. It was Sphinx's term for the girl on the hill: Franklyn was never quite sure why Sphinx used the famous San Francisco location from the Summer of Love to identify her, but he suspected that Sphinx liked the sound of the word *hate* in conjunction with a phrase that signified free love. Sphinx was restricted to dialogue suggested by his form, that of an aging rocker, but he had a keen sense of irony.

"What about her?" Franklyn asked uncomfortably.

Ch-chick's overage.

She's sixteen now...

Tombes gave a quick rap of the snare.

C-curtain's coming down.

...and we can't help you anymore.

Miles Barrett-Danes had been planning his daughter's sixteenth birthday for two years and even his enormous house was today stretched to use every available corner and table. Such was the invitation list that portaloos had been placed in the gardens, although the top tier of guests had discreetly been given their own keys to the upstairs bathrooms.

These selected few were generally the local politicians and members of the media, although he had added some of Gracie's teachers to the list, as well as the celebrities he had enlisted for the corporate hospitality. There was a famous rock keyboard player who would be arriving to do a musical turn later on and an ex-racing driver was presently doing the rounds among the floating canapés and champagne.

Only one guest was a teenager. This was Jake Cassidy, invited only at Gracie's insistence. Squeezed into a hired tuxedo he had spent a miserable hour alone by the piano, broken only by five gruelling minutes when Miles had grilled him on his career plans, and the odd awkward exchange with passing guests who felt sorry for him. There was only one all too brief and blissful moment when Gracie had come over and spoken to him.

She was wearing a radiant silk gown that shimmered as she patrolled the house introducing herself to her guests. Her father had singled out several people for her particular attention beforehand and as he proudly observed her working the room, with the skill and delicacy of an experienced diplomat, he felt a sudden tug at his chest.

He mumbled his apologies and broke away, his head bowed with his forefinger on his forehead. He walked quickly through the kitchen, where he waved away an inquiring look from his wife and hurried out into the back garden, around the swimming pool and up the steps, past the landscaped rockery stream, then up to the gazebo. At this point in the schedule of the day the dining pavilion in the back garden was reserved solely for the catering staff, the rear entrances guarded by bouncers discreetly posing as guests. He was alone.

He sat down on the circular seat of the gazebo, drawing its canvas curtains. He knew the twinge in his chest wasn't anything that concerned his health, his doctor having recently remarked that he was the fittest and healthiest septuagenarian he had ever seen. The sharp, sudden pain had come before, when he was so bursting with love and pride for his daughter that he was overcome with a feeling of worthlessness because, no matter how hard he tried, he was unable to protect her. He took out his crayon drawing of the house and smoothed it out on the table. When in the past he had been observed studying it he explained it was one of Gracie's drawings, but that was a lie. It had first come into his possession three years before she was born, when he had begun to dream the impossible dream that he might after all have a child. When he had begun to see her face.

He let out a long, baleful moan. His hands ran over the drawing that refused to perish or even fade with the years, the blues, greens and reds of the walls, roof and windows still crumbly and glistening as if the crayon was newly applied. The drawing brought back an unpleasant and frightening memory: the time when he had lost the wonderful painting of a three-year-old Gracie, the one with her red curls, the painting he had nurtured in the envelope given to him by Precious Cargo before she was born.

He still remembered the liver spots on the fingers of the old man, then the senior Trustee, as the painting was folded, then folded again.

The old man placing it inside the Fabergé egg.

The lid closing.

Closed.

Locked.

The old man telling him that the lock was unassailable.

It was terrible … terrible…

The crayon drawing of the house issued him with a warning reminder whenever he chose to look at it: remember the agony of losing that painting, which was just a painting; imagine the agony of actually losing your child.

"Daddy?"

He quickly collected up his drawing and stuffed it into his jacket, knowing that the crumple creases would never show, then found a serious expression as his daughter sat next to him. "Just catching a breath of fresh air," he said.

She smiled, remembering once playing word games in this gazebo; all her family and relatives sitting round after a winter barbeque, being warmed by oil lanterns. "Hot work," she agreed.

He looked at the table and pulled at one of his fingers, making a special effort not to look at her just yet in case he should lose his composure. "Have you spoken to the people I mentioned?" he asked.

"I've said hello to all of them."

"See if you can talk to them over lunch. I've arranged the tables so they're all in earshot. I thought the chairman of that travel company might come in useful and you'll be surprised what a local councillor can do for you, if you know the right buttons to push."

"I'm sure you're right Daddy."

He recognised the hesitant tone. "But?"

Her face was impassive. "I thought I should spend a little more time with that nice woman in commodities. The one who came with Arnold Moss."

"Jan Spedding?" he asked after a time, as he mentally scanned his guest list.

"Jan, that's right."

He waved his hand dismissively. "Oh, she's just Arnold's assistant. I think Arnold asked for her to come so he could have a free drive home." He grunted a laugh. "He pays a small fortune for that berth in Majorca and he's too mean to order a taxi."

"She's important."

He frowned. "Important? How?"

"I don't know yet, but I suspect she won't be Arnold's assistant for very long. She's moving abroad and I think my future's connected with hers. She's smart, and she's ambitious."

"Really?" he inquired, looking squarely at her, his curiosity and appetite for a business opportunity having conquered his malaise.

She gave a small nod. "Looks unassuming, doesn't she? But she's already devised the technological infrastructure for a central European commodity market that can rationalise prices twice as fast and ten times cheaper. She's probably been eating up Arnold's contacts. He doesn't know it yet, but by Christmas she'll have taken half his business to Brussels."

Her father looked away in astonishment. "Poor Arnold," he said, with a dry smirk.

"She still has a lot of networking she needs to do, and I think she's going to need to meet a lot of politicians. MEPs especially."

"MEPs," he murmured approvingly, thinking that this rather put his offering of local councillors and ex-mayors in the shade. He didn't think of querying his daughter's character assessment of the quiet and demure Jan Spedding; his daughter had an unerring sixth sense when it came to people.

"That's the foothold into Europe we were looking for," she whispered, with a glance behind her. "I think when the time is right she'll offer me a summer placement."

He nodded thoughtfully, already thinking of inventive ways of investing some money into this new relationship, and of how he could engage the Spedding woman later today without making it seem obvious. "Shame Lauren couldn't be here to see this," he remarked bitterly. Dr Lauren Mays and her new assistant had been at the very top of his invitation list.

"You knew she wouldn't come. She wouldn't mix with our people, would she?"

He frowned. "But it's your sixteenth. I thought she might make an exception, given that you're doing so well." He briefly closed his eyes. "We *are* doing well, aren't we?"

She placed her hand reassuringly on his. "We couldn't be doing better."

In that brief moment of silence they shared the glimpse of paradise; that place in the future where there was no uncertainty, no fear. He returned to the present with a dissatisfied air. "That Lauren ... Dr Mays..." he muttered as they stood up. "Gracie, any idea what her agenda is? Or that..." and he bit his lip "...that new assistant of hers." He didn't like the look of Roman DeMarco but wouldn't dare criticise the Trustees even in private. At the very least, it would be bad luck.

Gracie slowly shook her head. Her doll's house had never even offered figurines for any of Trustees, let alone attempted to analyse them: she suspected that the servants of Precious Cargo were beyond the house's reach. "Daddy, it doesn't make any difference whether the Trustees are here or not. Aunt Lauren won't decide ... what happens."

"Then who will?" he returned irritably.

She chose not to answer. To tell him that the answer lay in the temple's Fabergé eggs would only have confused and distressed him. "The Baptist is outside," she said to change the subject. "He's parked across the street, watching the guests arrive."

Miles became angry. "What? Outside? Today? I don't care if it *is* a weekend, I'll get him locked up, he's in breach of that injunction I slapped on him."

"You know you can't do that. Aunt Lauren was very clear on the subject. The Baptist isn't allowed to speak to me, but apart from that you can't interfere."

He silently swore with frustration. "Bet he hasn't come anywhere near the school though," he growled.

"No, no he hasn't," Gracie replied sweetly.

"I was allowed to sort him out *there* at least."

She offered her arm. Her father took it and they walked back to the house.

From his Land Rover, a flask of tea at his side, Honeyman had observed every guest that arrived at the Barrett-Danes house. He suspected they were friends and business colleagues of the father, noting only one obvious candidate as a friend of Gracie's: a nervous youth in a badly fitting tuxedo, whose embarrassment would no doubt heighten when he realised it wasn't a black tie affair.

As he was refilling his plastic cup there was a rough rap on his window and he turned to see a dishevelled Franklyn Tyde leaning down and looking at him. Eagerly winding the window down, Honeyman smelt the alcohol on his breath.

"Franklyn...?"

"It's her birthday," Franklyn slurred, the reek of cheap cider wafting its way into the vehicle. Honeyman grunted in response as Franklyn looked up at the house, almost losing his balance in the process, then returned to the window. "I can't play no more, did ya know that?"

"Can't play? What do you mean?"

"Thought it was just the sax, but I can't play nuthin' ... nuthin' ... I've forgotten how..."

Honeyman nodded, urging him to continue.

"The Dead Pharaohs ... that's my baptism gift see, it's like a puppet pop group ... but it's all broken. Bass player's lost his boot. And he needs his boot to help me play. So I can't play. It was them all along ... never me ... never me..."

"Why has this happened, Franklyn? Is it because Gracie's sixteen?"

Franklyn closed his eyes to consider his queasy stomach.

When he opened them he looked sick. "She's sixteen now," he slurred. "So everything's breaking down. Pharaohs ... giving up."

Honeyman swigged his tea so to replace the lid on the flask. "Let me help you, Franklyn. Let me speak to these ... these Dead Pharaohs."

"They won't speak to you. You're the minister man, the Baptist, I've been told about you. Uh huh. I've probably lost another year just for speaking to you."

Honeyman frowned. "Lost a year? What do you mean?"

Franklyn closed his eyes again and didn't answer.

"Only one parent from Precious Cargo has spoken to me so far," Honeyman said cautiously, "and then far too late. He wasn't the faithful parent anyway, so he couldn't tell me that much. I need the help of a faithful parent, which I suspect is impossible, or one of the children." He paused. "Franklyn, tell me what's inside your egg. I know it has something to do with Zehngraf paintings, but what do the paintings show?"

Franklyn opened his eyes and pushed himself away from the bonnet with his hands. He was slight and the vehicle barely shuddered. "What's in the egg?" he asked, repeating the minister's question.

"Tell me, my boy."

"Death ... *my* death," he said, then stumbled away.

★

Gracie waited patiently, her eyes half open, until the attic light in the doll's house went out. With a sigh of relief and exhaustion at the end of this important day she cast aside the large pillow that had kept her raised and closed her eyes.

Across the city, Franklyn lay on his side listening to the distant crash of the waves. The Pharaohs were taking a long time this night and he was bone tired, his face raw with his tears.

"Please..." he murmured. "I'm sorry, I'm sorry..."

The three puppet rock stars that were The Dead Pharaohs chose that moment to bow. A joint in their waist clicked and released their torsos; they hung forward at an angle, as if stricken.

Franklyn was asleep almost immediately afterwards: his mind conditioned to await this click of their bodies.

In Cardiff, on the marina, a baby was returned lovingly to its cot, contented and sleepy. The eye in the alphabet abacus slowly turned and went from open to closed, ready to turn once more if the baby awoke.

There would be no sleep for the animal buried next to a grave in Talybont. From the block of wood that was its throat, it attempted a muffled, frenzied howl, struggling in the earth to be heard.

XII

The light in the darkness

ALEX STAYED ON the couch awhile considering the news. It was bad, of course, but not nearly as bad as she was expecting.

"I'm sorry, my darling," Judy said, glaring at the scan as if it was the monitor's fault.

"One's better than nothing, though," Alex suggested.

"True enough. And it is a beauty: as big as Christmas." Judy's expression softened as she considered the solitary white splash on the screen that was Alex's follicle. "It only takes one follicle to make an egg, and it only takes one egg to make a baby." She sighed. "But I was hoping for more. With all the Puregon you're taking, we should have had more."

"I'm sorry, Judy," Alex muttered guiltily, sitting up and getting dressed.

"Not your fault, my darling." The nurse brought her hands together decisively. "Oh well, we can only play the cards as they're dealt. We have the option of stopping now and going on to a new cycle of drugs next month. I know you'll have to buy the drugs package again but it's still cheaper than paying for egg retrieval, just to find you've got no eggs."

"But I've got a follicle," Alex said in weak protest. Having discarded the drugs before the end of the cycle she had expected nothing but a few failed speck attempts at follicles; she was, after all, pre-menopausal.

"Yes, but who knows whether it holds an egg or not? And anyway we need to implant *two* eggs to give you a realistic chance."

Alex shrugged wearily. "I've had two eggs before, for all the good it's done." She was thoughtful for a few moments. "I can't go through this again, Judy," she said quietly, with the weight of exhaustion. "This is the last time, in fact. Whether it works or not, this is the last time." She took a breath that was heavy with tears.

"What did the psychiatrist say?" Judy asked gently. "Did he get a handle on this needle phobia of yours?"

"He said it's just my body's way of telling me it has to stop. I suppose the whole thing ... the whole IVF thing ... has become just like one huge monster in my head. It rules my life ... it takes my years, months, days weeks and hours. It's all I do, all I think about. After four years I feel that it's all I am. It takes everything and gives me nothing. I hate it. I *hate* it."

Judy nodded in resignation, but inwardly she felt relief. Everyone had their breaking point and Alex Morrow had stoically endured far longer than most. "How are your bruises?" she asked.

"Better, thank you," Alex replied, looking at her knees. "But I couldn't bear any more needles."

"Just one more, my darling." From the fridge Judy produced a small case with two bottles of solution and two needles, one of which was thick and very long. The smaller needle was for mixing the solutions, the second for injecting the thigh thirty-six hours before egg retrieval. This injection would loosen the eggs in their follicles, allowing them to be collected. Alex felt her thigh tingle with horror: this one couldn't be sidestepped.

"I've booked you in for nine am Thursday morning," Judy

said. "That means it's essential you inject nine pm Tuesday evening." She chuckled. "What am I saying? You know the score by now."

Alex nodded mournfully.

Judy snapped the case shut. "Is that husband of yours looking after you?"

"He's been marvellous. Given up drinking."

"That's good," Judy remarked, pleasantly surprised.

"I haven't seen him this energised for years, Judy. He's convinced we're going to have a baby."

"Good. Excellent."

"A son, in fact."

"Okay…"

Alex rubbed her right thigh. "Tuesday night…" she muttered.

"I'll have everything crossed. One follicle or not, this time it will work. You'll see."

Alex considered the scan monitor once more to find her follicle. Even to her untrained eye it did seem big: round and bursting with protein, a single light in the night sky, a sun radiating energy. Surely, it held an egg…

She pictured her oak kitchen table. Her line of vision travelled along the grooves of the wood until she located one of the hands of her children. She froze with surprise.

"You okay, my darling?"

She was travelling up the child's arm. To the child's shoulder. To the neck.

"Alex?"

In her mind she stepped back, to take in the scene. That wonderfully glorious scene of her kitchen table where her children played, talked and ate; the picture of a family. Her family.

But there was a difference. There was only one child that she could see, whose hands visited the table, and the child was most definitely a boy.

We promise you son. We name him Theo.

She shuddered, finding the image horrific: the boy's face was obscured, but in the shadow she made out the shape of a scream.

"Alex?" the nurse repeated.

Alex shook her head to dispel the image. Shortly her eyes focussed on Judy.

"This is it," Alex declared, her expression a mix of determination and fear. "If the IVF fails, that's the end of the road. Nothing else … *nothing*." She took a breath. "I don't want to be a mother if this is the price."

Her announcement that she would have nothing to do with Precious Cargo, that it would be the IVF or bust, had Lloyd wandering to his shed without protest. It was her decision; he wasn't going to argue with her any more.

That evening, the migraine started. By the time Lloyd emerged from the shed Alex was curled up on the settee, the television on as a distraction, and she wearily shook her head when he asked if she was coming to tea with his mother. Once more he didn't protest; she frowned when the door didn't slam.

Sure she could hear the sound of hooves, she turned up the television and watched with a hangdog expression. As she flicked her remote all that was offered up was babies: celebrities pregnant again; discount family holidays; the perfect cereal for those energetic kids, served up with endless sunshine reflecting through the kitchen window of a domestic paradise…

She turned the television back down and glanced sourly at her ceiling.

"Shut up," she muttered, for no reason she could understand identifying her stress headaches more and more directly with the reindeer poster in the room above. She closed her eyes, supposing she should be grateful for small mercies; the headache had at least allowed her to escape the ordeal of supper with her mother-in-law. Anyway, Lloyd probably preferred visiting Mother Morrow alone so they could happily debate her shortcomings as a wife and prospective mother.

"Oh shut up," she repeated, but this time to herself as reproof of her paranoia. She again stabbed at the remote control. The television was now virtually mute and she lay for a moment as if in space, feeling impossibly alone. It was a wonderful moment of martyrdom as the throbbing pain warped her isolation through the moving shapes of the television and sent her tumbling through the ether. She had no weight, her existence so meaningless, her ambitions so irrelevant that gravity didn't recognise her body.

Perhaps it was good, just to be dust.

Perhaps the pain would go, if she would just submit.

She blinked, relief surging through her as the throbbing momentarily subsided, as if in confirmation of her inquiry.

She took a breath, then attempted to eject from her mind some difficult information.

A strange meeting with a minister at her office, when he said something about children dying. Yes, that memory was spongy with pain, and should be forgotten.

She sighed as the vice loosened.

Some things from that conversation with the minister remained, but they had no sharp edges. A boy and a girl are born each year to Precious Cargo, he had said: they would deliver on their promise.

She took a deeper breath, then exhaled. No, that information was safe; welcome even, if the barometer of her headache was any measure. The minister had merely confirmed what they had subsequently gleaned from the families in Swansea.

She looked up at the ceiling once more; the reindeers were distant but stamping threateningly. Most importantly, she needed to expel that image from Judy's office; the one of the boy frozen in the scream. She nodded slowly.

Yes, he was forgotten.

The heavy blinds were drawn but it was still early when Lloyd finally crept into bed, the mattress shaking with his weight in spite of his attempt to hold his breath.

Out of the darkness, her hand softly found his shoulder.

"Headache still bad?" he asked cautiously.

"A little," she lied.

He grunted as he turned over to lie away from her, feigning disappointment.

"Sorry," she muttered. "Perhaps in the morning…"

He didn't answer. She turned over too.

"Lloyd, I didn't mean what I said earlier. About if the IVF fails, I mean." She waited. "We'll talk about those people in Brecon, okay? Like we agreed."

"Okay," he murmured at last, without emotion, and she wondered whether he was just tired of arguing or whether he knew she would come round anyway. As he switched off his sidelight she chewed over her words awhile, conscious that her olive branch had failed to animate him; these days Lloyd hated talking when the lights were off, even though he always took a long time to get off to sleep.

"Lloyd…?" she ventured.

"Alex, I'm trying to sleep."

"Where did you get that poster from? The one in the box room, I mean."

It was the first time she had asked this question. She had regarded the poster with bemusement when she had come home at Christmas two years ago to find it in the room once decorated for the baby they had lost. She hadn't liked it, but hadn't questioned him: if finding some obscure poster in readiness for their next child was his form of mourning ritual, then so be it. After all, she lit candles.

Perhaps she didn't understand her husband as well as she had believed. Their gradual breakdown in communication had in some way served to increase the power of the poster, as if it were a symbol of their estrangement.

"What, the Rudolph poster?" he muttered.

"Rudolph's not in it. It's from *The Night before Christmas*, and I think the Santa's horrible. I've seen friendlier reindeers, too."

"Rubbish."

"Lloyd, if it scares me, it's certainly going to scare a baby."

"Rubbish."

"I mean it, Lloyd. I want it taken down."

He didn't reply.

"Anyway, where did you get it?" she repeated. She had searched the web and hadn't been able to find anything remotely similar.

"The same place you got your *Pregnant Madonna*," he said, with a dark chuckle.

"What, online?" she asked, but from his tone suspecting that he meant something very different, something philosophical. She sighed and closed her eyes, knowing it was useless trying to talk to him when he was in this mood.

He was staring into the darkness, searching his memories, but for the life of him he couldn't remember where he had found the damn thing. It troubled him: he must have been drunk when he picked it up but he had the vague notion that he didn't have that kind of thirst back then.

No, I must have been drunk ... must have been drunk when I bought it and when I put it up...

His memory found the moment when the wall was bare, then the moment when the reindeer poster was up, but some kind of fault line divided the two time zones. He turned irritably onto his back and stared into the darkness, waiting for his son to appear.

Lloyd was dreary with sleep when he crept into the box room. He didn't dare risk an electric light in case he woke Alex, so he lit the candle that she kept in here. He had spent half the night concentrating, trying without success to remember the poster coming into his possession.

There were no windows in the box room and he picked up the saucer on which the candle had been waxed and moved it carefully around the room. The fragile light crossed the face of the pregnant Madonna, then found the sleigh and the reindeers. With a morbid fascination he studied the reindeers' heads, one by one considering their furious and frantic expressions, then turned to St Nick, his face hidden in the hood. The light followed the trajectory of his whip.

He stepped back, holding the candle before him, as close to the poster as he was able.

Perhaps this is a test, he thought. Something Lauren Mays had devised to ensure that he was ... what was the word she used...? Yes, *faithful*.

"I'm the faithful parent," he muttered. "Help me remember."

In answer the darkness intensified, deepening beyond black, so that it almost had density. Only the candle flame was visible, unaccountably finding a brilliance that allowed it to be seen even though it was unable to breach the darkness. He gasped as something unlocked in his brain, the candle flame trembling as he struggled to hold the saucer steady.

The poster had been left in his store one day... No, not just any day, it was Christmas Eve: he was in a mood because Alex had told him to put some decorations up, then no one had come in to appreciate them. Another waste of money...

He shook his head, trying to concentrate.

The poster came with a note that he simply had to put it on his wall for his son to be born. Well, he had thought that Alex had a lucky poster, so why shouldn't he?

No, it wasn't a note. Someone was there, explaining this to him. Perhaps it was Lauren Mays herself. Another lever in his memory turned and he was sure that he saw her across the counter, explaining that she was gifting him with one of *the prayers that are keys* to make him forget, just as it would help him remember, when he was ready.

He had gone straight home and unrolled the poster. It had sucked itself on to the wall, in perfect alignment to the ceiling.

In the flicker of the candle light, he gasped as a final lever unlocked the memory.

The poster he had put up then didn't show a sleigh and reindeers at all: it was simply black, with shadows of varying intensities creating an effect similar to a tunnel, lost in endless distance. He felt as if he could put his hand through the wall. He tried it, moving closer, his hand outstretched...

Then he was unconscious for a time. Perhaps he fainted. Yes, he must have fainted.

When he awoke, the tunnel was gone. The poster had become, and would remain, *The Night before Christmas*.

★

The sandalwood office was empty, the framed photographs silently replaying a family life for no one to see. This family was called Sobarth, the father having once ruled the house from his beloved writing bureau; it was often his whim to make his daughter name all its Egyptian symbols, as a test of memory and study.

On the floor but shortly to be stored away, sat an intricate metal toy.

It was a sleigh, made of silver and pulled by eight iron-grey reindeers, their necks and backs jointed to enable them to gallop. Straddling the sleigh was a lead figure dressed in red and white, his face concealed under his hood. In his right hand he held a whip which trailed in the air behind him. It was so thin it must have been made of a specially reinforced steel.

It sat underneath a portrait photograph of the head of the family, who scowled his approval.

XIII

The 31st portrait

*T*HE BAPTIST HAS *held a* character, Roman signed to Dr Mays. They were in Precious Cargo's gold limousine just coming in to Swansea, the doctor at the wheel. *Is there to be such an easy punishment for his trespass?*

"The coven has its own plans for him, Mr DeMarco."

But I've seen the records, Veneration. Shouldn't we avenge the martyrdoms? The desecration of our sacraments?

"Enough."

The young man nodded, taking no offence: neither Trustee knew the other in private life but in the service of a temple the elder Trustee's authority was absolute. He would obey her in anything without question; if she wanted him sexually, he would offer himself gratefully and freely.

The coven believed in the privileges of rank and for this reason the junior Trustees were usually made beautiful in the sight of the temple. Precious Cargo was an exception in that its junior Trustee was instead struck dumb, to mimic Zachariah. In his private life Roman DeMarco worked in a call centre; an eager Lauren Mays, then naturally beautiful, had long ago served her year in wondrous silence, a willing slave to one of the most respected elders in the coven.

This old man, now the First Proctor of the coven, had been with Precious Cargo since its creation, for Precious Cargo enjoyed another exception to temple convention. It was the practice of the temples to rotate its Trustees on a yearly basis, diffusing and sharing power in the manner of the Roman consuls, but while the junior Trustee served only a year, Precious Cargo's elder Trustee enjoyed a longer tenure. Continuity was regarded as essential to nurture the relationships with the children.

The limousine turned into the gravel drive of the Barrett-Danes' forecourt, neither Trustee making eye contact with Miles, who was already walking towards them. As the vehicle came to a halt the doctor studied the dials and instruments on her dashboard, as if something needed to be checked, forcing Miles to wait in his crouched position at her window. Shortly she turned, as if she was seeing him for the first time, and raised her pencil eyebrows in acknowledgement.

"Lauren, *wonderful* to see you again."

She didn't answer, but allowed him to open her door. Nothing was said until they were in the hall which was lined with roses in crystal urns, the only flowers his wife could find in bulk on such short notice. Years ago, when Gracie was only five, the then newly installed Lauren Mays had remarked that she liked the smell of flowers when she entered a house. Miles had never forgotten it.

"How long do you have before ... before you visit ... the sea?" he asked falteringly. He knew that every visit from the Trustees would result in a reciprocal visit to the sea; it always put him in a dark mood as he imagined that stupid black bitch playing on the Trustees' heartstrings; her wimp of a son beguiling them with his tricks.

"We're not visiting the sea this time," Dr Mays replied, resplendent in a jumpsuit of ermine fur, dyed beige at the collars and cuffs. "We've come straight here and we're going straight back."

Only a slight hesitation in Miles' step acknowledged this information, but he threw open the doors of the international room with delight.

"Look who's here to see you!" he declared.

He called his huge drawing room *the international room* because, with the care and patience of a cartographer, he had ensured that it referenced every country in the world: from the Spanish floor tiles to the Aboriginal animal carvings he defied anyone to tell him he had left an important nation out. He had designed the room three years ago when, on Gracie's thirteenth birthday, Dr Mays had predicted she might grow up to be a woman of international affairs, jetting around the globe with the world's chequebook in her despatch box.

International ... international, he had pondered for several evenings as he walked the room, until he had the Eureka moment.

There were four hide sofas in the centre of the room, one occupied by Gracie, her hair tied tightly back in her usual manner. The other sofas were empty; his wife consigned to the kitchen with the staff. Gracie rose cautiously, her hands behind her back, one hand stroking the index finger of the other.

"My Lady of the Manor," Dr Mays chimed, throwing out her arms with a display of affection reserved only for the children of Precious Cargo. When the girl approached, they closed slowly and mechanically around her like the claws of a carnivorous plant. "You become more beautiful every time I see you."

"Thank you, Aunt Lauren," Gracie whispered, stiff but yielding within the arms.

Roman signalled to repeat the compliment as he took his place on a sofa, noting with approval the bottle of Château

Lafite Rothschild uncorked on the ivory coffee table. Miles knew that the Trustees were always prepared to accept wine during their visits, though they would only savour the aroma, never drink it. Such was the quality of the wine that Miles was always tempted to pour their full glasses back into the bottle after they left, but could never manage it: the mere fact that the Trustees had breathed the wine's pulse established their dominion over it. No, the wine would be poured into the sink after they had gone, a glass in each hand as he cursed the waste and cursed the power they had over his only daughter. Even in the privacy of his kitchen his curses would be silent, communicated only through the fierce creases around his steel-grey eyes.

He was pouring three glasses of the wonderful 2005 vintage now, his poise relaxed and urbane at meeting welcome guests. On this occasion it was no act; his heart was thumping with pleasure and excitement.

"So beautiful," Dr Mays said, touching the girl's cheek before she took her seat next to Roman, beckoning father and daughter to sit down opposite. She considered her glass of wine awhile, then picked it up and closed her eyes appreciatively. In private life she was fond of red wine and she could rarely afford anything so expensive, but no food or liquid was ever consumed during the hours of service to the temple, hours that sometimes stretched into days. Their fasting bodies were in a state of grace at such times, the bounties of the earth worthless.

The offering of wine from the prosperous family was merely fitting, just as it was fitting for the poorer family to offer only water. With the Swansea experiment, which began in 1991 and was now reaching its fruition, the differential in wealth between the two families was particularly marked and so they always expected the very best offering from Miles Barrett-Danes; she had shown her disapproval when he had once tried to palm her off with a rather mediocre Barolo.

As she returned the wine glass to the table the doctor reflected that her Lady of the Manor had always been more astute than her father. The girl realised early on that her wealth conferred no advantages at all, that the temple would see to it that the balance sheet was always equal, that she needed to work harder than her counterpart by the sea.

But she had succeeded, as dramatically as the boy by the sea had failed, and in the glow of this moment it felt wholly right and fitting that the hill had triumphed. The doctor blinked with a sense of peace: there were no uneasy knots of uncertainty; the Father approved of this outcome.

"We decided a visit was overdue. Are you keeping well?"

"Very well, thank you Aunt," Gracie replied formally, as if she were in a job interview.

"And how is your friend, young … young…?"

"Jake?" Gracie asked.

"Yes, young Jake. Now how is he?"

Miles glanced up at the ceiling with annoyance, disapproving of his daughter's friendship with the young man who came around on weeknights for help with his homework. The lad was so stupid he seemed harmless enough, but boys – any boys – were an unwelcome distraction at this time. The fact that he hadn't been allowed to send his daughter to a single-sex school, that the Trustees had explained that she would acquire a fuller flavour of her world by mixing with children of the opposite sex, was an open wound for him.

"Jake is … fine," Gracie said cautiously. "I give him some help sometimes with mathematics and French, his two weakest subjects. His parents sent me a thankyou card on my birthday." She paused. "Would you rather I stopped him coming?"

Roman shook his head and remonstrated with his hands.

Good to have friends, Gracie heard.

"I don't really have friends," Gracie clarified carefully. Her father grunted his approval and tapped her hand.

The Trustees exchanged glances. "You shouldn't take everything we say quite so to heart," the doctor said. "Did we say it was important that you focus on your studies? Yes we did. Did we suggest that you think of all your classmates and teachers as colleagues, and be wary of building relationships that were too close, of sharing secrets they could use against you? Of course we did, and in this we were merely echoing the advice of any responsible parent." She paused, thoughtfully. "But sometimes … *sometimes* … friendships are important too."

Gracie nodded slowly in agreement, her eyes betraying a trace of mistrust.

"We know the young man," the doctor declared magnanimously, "and he appears a sensible kind of boy."

A bubble of silence expanded and popped, acknowledged by a confused frown on the part of Miles, puzzled at the Trustees' tolerance of the boy who was pestering his daughter. Gracie's response to this first vocal approval of Jake couldn't be read in her face.

"Did you like our birthday present?"

The Trustees always sent gifts on her birthday, and for her sixteenth had sent a set of gold suitcase tags. Gracie opened her mouth to answer but was cut short by her father who proceeded to praise the quality of the gift and explain how he had been compelled to find some suitcases worthy of them. Eventually he had found a boutique in Oxford Street where…

His monologue tailed off as Dr Mays turned to him with raised eyebrows. He shut up immediately.

"It was a thoughtful gift, Aunt," Gracie said, coming to her father's rescue.

"Thoughtful, how?" Dr Mays asked, her eyes switching back to Gracie.

"You're obviously telling me that I'm ready to travel. All your gifts carry instructions. The encyclopaedias, the histories and the gem globe were instructions to learn and understand. This is the first one which contains…" and Gracie stretched the fingers of her hands, which were resting on her thighs, to find the right word "…which contains a *promise*."

A promise…

The air seemed to be charged with current, such was the power, the sheer importance of the girl's remark.

"My beautiful little lady," Dr Mays whispered, enormously impressed. "My Lady of the Manor. You're so very clever and we have such hopes for you." Roman nodded thoughtfully and signed his agreement.

"There, you see," Miles muttered, his heart in flight. "And they're going straight back afterwards, Gracie. Straight back," he repeated meaningfully. Gracie turned her head slowly towards her father; he turned to meet her eyes and winked quickly and discreetly.

"The boy by the sea started well," Dr Mays conceded, pretending not to have noticed the private communication, "but in the last few years he's fallen behind. He foolishly attempted to follow his own interests, to find other talents, rather than accept the temple's gifts…"

Miles and Gracie turned to the doctor, struggling to conceal their astonishment. They had never heard the Trustees speak openly about the boy by the sea before.

"He's an accomplished musician," Dr Mays continued, "but at this point should have been turning his hand to composition. That was where he'd have been stretched." She dabbed at something in her eye. "He thinks of nothing but kissing empty-headed girls and running over walls."

"I blame the parents," Miles said gleefully, by which he meant Mercedes Tyde.

"Someone is certainly to blame," Dr Mays remarked, but she was thinking of someone else altogether: someone they would bury in the dead of night, next to the boy, silently shrieking for eternity to end. As the Father was generous, he was ruthless with failure.

"And when will he be sixteen?" Miles asked, tightening his grip on the armrest to contain his excitement. It was a rhetorical question, for he knew the date and time of the boy's birthday: he would be sixteen in exactly eight weeks, at three minutes past eleven am.

Roman wagged a disapproving finger, as if to say: eight weeks is a long time.

"Oh absolutely," Miles concurred in serious voice, heavy with emphasis. "We take nothing, nothing whatsoever for granted."

Eight weeks. When Gracie was born, he was told that when the youngest turned sixteen it would be over; at that meeting sixteen years seemed merely the moment between heartbeats, but now even eight weeks, fifty-six days, felt unbearably long.

"Does he kiss a lot of girls?" Gracie asked quietly.

Dr Mays considered the unexpected question with only the slightest measure of surprise. "They've always chased *him*," she conceded, "but he will go to places where there are such temptations."

Miles nodded with solemn disapproval.

"He *is* very sweet," Gracie admitted to her hands. "I can see why the girls like him." She stretched her fingers once more. "He has ... he has a helplessness, a raw naivety which is very appealing, I think." She shook her head with resignation. "It's caused him to make so many mistakes."

Her father's eyes had widened in alarm. The Trustees sat back, their manner cautiously inviting the girl to continue.

Gracie looked up, realising she had opened a door she had to walk through. "Yes, I've met him. It wasn't my fault, Aunt Lauren, honestly it wasn't. He approached me, waited for me outside school. It would be so much easier if we'd never met, if I hadn't come face to face with him ... if he was just a name..." She paused. "I see him outside sometimes. I think he worries about me; just as I worry about him."

"Gracie, be quiet," Miles whispered urgently. He knew about the oak tree, but he wasn't allowed to come into physical contact with the boy by the sea. The rules allowed him to remonstrate if his daughter was being spied on, but that was all.

Gracie armed herself with a breath. "Is it necessary, Aunt?" she asked.

"Is *what* necessary?" Dr Mays replied in cold voice.

Gracie swallowed. "Just for once, couldn't things be different? If I'm *very* good, if I make you so proud and I promise to dedicate my life to you and make you prouder still, couldn't...?"

"What?" Dr Mays asked, her eyes narrowing.

Gracie hesitated, then said, "Couldn't he be spared?"

Miles stood up with a bolt, desperate to find an excuse to

change the subject. The best he could manage was a remark that his wife was dawdling in the kitchen, that she should have brought out some cheese and grapes to go with the wine. Cheese and grapes they wouldn't eat, of course, in his anxiety slipping into an irrelevant observation. His eyes were darting in different directions around the room, but the camera in his mind had snapped and saved two distinct images.

The first was of his daughter, looking down at her hands, realising her mistake.

The second was of the Trustees, observing her with silent disapproval.

Gracie meanwhile was considering her father, seeing his face in her palms as she turned her hands over. She knew that she wouldn't look as well-preserved when she was in her seventies, that the years of worry and labour would have taken their toll. She suspected that something in her character would also be partly responsible; something bad that would creep in with time, as a promising wine is contaminated by its barrel.

In her palms, she saw herself as a wrinkled seventy-year-old, her looks battered by a lifetime of long nights in air-conditioned hotels. She recognised her face, but not the thoughts behind the severe mist of the eyes.

The face was no idle invention of a paranoid imagination. It was a true likeness, one that she had first glimpsed when she was five.

Gracie returned to her bedroom, confused at her father's protests now the Trustees had left. She didn't understand why they were all so angry; what had she done that was so very wrong? It was merely a question, a truthful question from the heart, posed in the most reasonable fashion. The question that had been gnawing at her since she had given her lecture on the Colosseum.

She heard her mother weakly attempting to placate her father, causing him to erupt into an even greater fury, as she quietly closed the door. Walking to her bed she stopped with a jolt, the air beaten from her lungs.

"No," she said. "No no no no no!"

The light of the chandelier in the doll's house had dimmed, its spotlight barely visible. As she approached she brought her hand to her mouth to stifle her scream, for her figurine was no longer in *the gallery*: it was in *the room with no windows*, next to Franklyn Tyde and it was turned to face the wall.

She shook her head, her hand still at her mouth. Whenever the figures in the doll's house were moved she could never quite remember if she had moved them herself. She was sure it must have been her own work: knowing the mistake she was planning to make with the Trustees she must have moved her figurine before she left the bedroom. Her dealings with the doll's house she believed created a sort of sleep trance, which fed on her own intuition; it was something so natural, ingrained in her subconscious from the moment she could walk, that it bypassed her memory.

She took another step forward and reached for her figurine, stretching into the room that reeked of damp and decay, the part of the doll's house that was totally evil and unforgiving: a quality she suspected all the baptism gifts possessed. Her hand hung in mid air, awaiting her mental command.

"Well, I'm sorry," she whispered. She glanced at *the roof attic*: the light was on, and stronger than usual, threatening to sear through the opaque glass of its solitary window. "I'm sorry," she repeated. "I won't ever do it again. I won't ever plead for him again."

She remained frozen, her attempt to reach into the room of danger and warning had failed. As she waited for the punishment to end she imagined tears running down the china face of her figurine, desperate for light and clean air.

"Well I hate him," she said at last. "The boy by the sea: I hate him, I do."

Her breath now came in heaves as proof of her sincerity, and shortly the light in the attic dimmed. She regained control of her hand, which snapped up her figurine and placed it on the faint circle of the spotlight in *the gallery*. As if the china figure had depressed a hidden button in the floor the chandelier glowed once more, the light enriching the coloured glass of the arched windows and the gold leaf in the wallpaper. Her father's tall figurine now emerged from the shadow.

She stepped back. "I'm sorry," she said once more, this time to her father, "it won't ever happen again." She pondered matters awhile, attempting to sweep her mind clear of fear. Nothing had changed. The house was as lustrous as ever, as wondrous as it had become after that time the boy from the sea had made that stupid mistake and waited for her outside school; when he had spoken to her.

We can take them on together. We don't have to be enemies…

She shook her head to exorcise his words from her memory.

You're so wonderful, so beautiful. I couldn't hurt you. Now that I've met you, I couldn't let anything happen to you … I'll kill myself, if it'll save you…

She squeezed her eyes shut, keeping them shut until the boy's words were banished. Opening them, she went to the wall's alcove and with two hands gently retrieved her egg. She placed it on her bed. A thumb depressed a switch, a finger of her other hand clicked and turned another, while her palm pressed at an exact point of pressure. The lid flipped open. It didn't always open, it wasn't some curiosity to be played with, some idle thumbnail; it could choose when to resist her fingers. Today however it was receptive, as if it understood and accepted her need to examine it.

Her finger walking methodically through the contents of the egg, as an auditor inspects financial entries. Her expression was impassive as she worked, the egg nestled at her knees, but shortly she sighed with relief, a silent *thank you* on her lips.

The silk-thin belt that unfolded held eighty-four glass compartments, of which only two were empty: the empty compartments were for her first year and eighty-fourth year, the first and last years of her life, but all the rest were present and correct. There were portraits of her as a toddler, with the shaggy hairstyle she recognised from photo albums; as a teenager as she appeared now; in middle age, looking very thin and striking, with the beginnings of worry lines. She didn't like to look too closely at the later pictures, glancing at them just long enough to know that they were there, and blinking in an attempt to erase the memory of grey and white, the melange germination of her skin and the collapse of her features.

The belt was just as she had seen it when she examined it on her sixteenth birthday, when to her delight, and as the best present she could ever receive, another face had slotted into position: this was the curious *thirty-one* face, which even in exceptional moments of triumph, when the belt rewarded her with a brief glimpse of the faces yet to be acquired, was one that always eluded her like some rare sports card. She was in her prime at thirty-one but it was not a face that the egg liked, hence it was among the last to arrive. For some reason thirty-one would be a bad year, she reasoned; almost as traumatic as the years of her birth and death. People would die during that year and she would change forever.

She briefly slid a finger across the belt, its sheen surface only finding a place of reality in her mind. All the pictures were oil paintings, with perfect strokes and texture notwithstanding their miniaturisation, and a magnifying glass would have revealed the signature of Master Zehngraf. She sighed as she looked at the eighty-four years of her life, aware from the strain in the lever of the lid that she was overstaying her welcome. She closed the egg, letting the catches slide into place to create an impossible lock.

XIV

Tour van

"THE TRUSTEES ARE here," Franklyn announced to no one in particular. His mother came rushing out of the kitchen, a tea cloth over her muscled forearm.

"Where? When?" she barked.

"They're up on the hill," Franklyn replied. He was sweating with exertion, having broken into a spontaneous free run down to the pier, finding every possible obstacle to negotiate to the jeers and protestations of pedestrians, in an attempt to shut out the screaming in his head. "They arrived about an hour ago. Saw their car."

His mother looked in horror at his clothes, which were scuffed and dirty. "We need to get to the shops," she said, her face full of numbed surprise. She looked up the stairs and shouted, "Jerreeeee!" It was answered by a groan in the bedroom, followed by some muttering. "Why are they coming, d'you think?" she pondered, going to the hall mirror and jabbing her hair with a fierce expression. "Perhaps they've got good news for us." She nodded as she tugged at her collar and winked at her reflection. "Good news, good news," she whispered to herself, the mantra helping to ease her hot flush.

"Mum, they ain't coming," Franklyn muttered.

"Coming? Course they're coming. They always come and see us when they visit the hill. They have to. That's rules."

She paused, then turned and shouted to her husband again. This time Jerry's response articulated a few words, most of them obscene.

Franklyn sighed and shook his head. "Mum, they always telephone. Always. They don't ever come here without word."

Mercedes shook her head firmly, only a slight twitch in her right nostril acknowledging the point. "Maybe they tried to call. I ain't been in all day, and your daddy's been asleep."

Franklyn bowed his head. "Mum, they always know when to call. You know that for sure, 'cos you've checked enough times with BT. They ain't *once* called this house when we weren't in."

Mercedes turned angrily from the mirror, knowing her son was right. "What are you saying?" she snapped irritably.

"That they ain't coming, Mum. If they were, they'd have called."

Her eyes narrowed. "But they can't visit the hill and ... not visit ... us."

He didn't reply.

"They can't do that!" she declared.

Still Franklyn didn't answer.

"What does this mean? Franklyn, tell me what this means. What have you done?"

"I ain't done nuthin'."

"Then tell me what it means!"

Franklyn looked up to see that his father had appeared on the turn of the stairs in his dressing gown. He was fully alert, having immediately detected the warnings in his son's defensive posture.

"Are you in trouble, son?" Jerry asked, ignoring the flash of hatred from his wife's eyes. Sixteen years of his wife blaming him for every setback had made him numb to her reproofs.

"Yes, Dad," Franklyn answered quietly.

"Shut up! Shut up!" Mercedes shouted.

"The Trustees ain't coming, Mum," Franklyn repeated in an even voice. "They don't even want to bother with us now." He put his hands in his pockets. "That means the girl on the hill has won. It's over."

Mercedes threw up her hands in hysterics. Franklyn ran to the stairs and tried to squeeze past his father, who caught him by the shoulder before he could dart up to his room. Jerry was a big man and he turned his son around effortlessly with one hand.

"Mercedes, look at him, woman. Look at him!" His Caribbean inflection was pronounced in his anger. He repeated his command until she locked a scream in her throat. "He's well," he said. "He be a fit, healthy young man. As healthy as any sixteen-year-old could be. Didn't the heart doctor say so? Eh? Didn't the man say *strong cardiac muscle,* and told you not to bother him again? Woman, you're insane."

Mercedes looked at her husband with a dumbfounded expression, as if he were trying to sell her dirt from the street.

"I never did believe it, y'know," Jerry continued, caught up in the moment. "For the peace and quiet I went along, because I know you had it in your head that those people had a hold over us, but I never did believe."

"Don't say that," Mercedes whispered. "They'll hear you…"

"They won't hear us, woman. They down the motorway, y'hear? It's all in your head."

"That's why we be in this situation, fool," Mercedes hissed. "You never were no help. You never were no help with nuthin'."

"Not when it came to *them*," Jerry agreed. He reordered his grip on his son's slender shoulders, feeling resistance. "And I don't believe any of their crazy talk. We got lucky and we had us a child, that's all. But we don't have to spend our lives paying for it." He closed his eyes briefly, summoning up the courage to venture into the realm of taboo. When he opened them he said, "Sixteen-year-olds don't just go to sleep and…"

"Don't say it, Jerry!" Mercedes warned him, horrified.

"…and don't wake up. Their hearts don't just stop."

He turned to his son and allowed him to shake free of his grip. "Isn't that right, Frank?" he asked. Mercedes, her expression still in a freeze frame of shock, looked at her son. "Isn't that right, Frank?" he repeated, his conviction faltering mid sentence.

"I wasn't supposed to be born," Franklyn answered quietly. "So I ain't got no right to be here."

"That's fool's talk, boy," his father said.

Franklyn allowed himself a sardonic chuckle. "Someone else said that to me recently, but all that really matters is what *I* believe, ain't it? And I believe what I've been taught from the time I could think. I believe my heart *can* just stop." He shook his head with resignation and walked up the rest of the stairs. "At least it will be painless," he remarked, with his back to his parents. "That's something, ain't it?"

His mother was screaming again by the time he opened his bedroom door but he barely heard her, sitting down on his bed and contemplating The Dead Pharaohs. They were silent and motionless, Sphinx looking up from the microphone expectantly. Franklyn's heart sank: the tiny orange wig had found some flecks of grey since he was last in the bedroom.

Franklyn considered the sheet music on his windowsill,

which contained the beginnings of a semi-orchestrated composition he had been working on for the last two years. The piece, which had a working title of *The Desert*, started promisingly with an intriguing rhythmic pulse working between bass and violin, but then became discordant. He had been unable to find the work's central theme.

The piece mirrored his own life: a promising start, tailing off into confusion.

"And finally, extinction," he sighed. He looked up, noting that Rivers wasn't tapping his foot to his bass, as he always did when he was thinking about music. His stomach turned as he considered the bass player, moribund and lifeless; it bothered him even more than the grey in the lead singer's hair.

"We're in trouble, ain't we?" Franklyn murmured.

The Dead Pharaohs didn't answer; the wooden puppets looked exhausted with grief and fear. Franklyn reached for his egg, three fingers of his right hand and the thumb of his left automatically going to their exact positions and applying precisely the right amount of pressure. The lid snapped abruptly open.

By the time he closed the lid, tears were streaming down his face. Only two oil portraits remained: his third year, the year he believed was always the last to go, and his twelfth. The egg had loved him when he was twelve. It had been the year he had started to channel his voracious appetite for music and had attempted his first compositions, when the world was falling at his feet. His face was impish in this portrait, his bone structure yet to find its elegance but his eyes shining as if the painter had found a white and grey so brilliant they radiated their own light.

"Help me," he said to the puppets. "You have to help

me. I don't know what to do." He waited, the silence buffeted only occasionally by the shouts of his parents from downstairs. "Don't you understand? I don't know what to do!" he repeated, with as much emphasis as he dared when addressing his baptism gift.

There was no response. For the first time in his life, The Dead Pharaohs seemed to have lost interest in him.

Maybe they're in mourning, he thought later, as he closed his eyes to welcome sleep. *Maybe they think I'm already dead.*

They didn't think he was dead at all, but tonight they let him sleep.

Franklyn woke with a jolt.

It took a moment, two beats of his eyelids, to realise that he was travelling at a great speed, a bump on the road having made him knock his head. He was seated high up in the cabin of a large van, the stained and ripped upholstery reeking of beer and cigarettes. The intense cold was a clamp around his chest, refrigerating the air with a clinical staleness.

The vehicle slowed, performed a turn, then accelerated away. He was travelling through a fog so dense and heavy it buffeted as it parted before him, thick wisps shooting past his passenger window with a ghostly howl. In the far distance, something dumb and solid waited. It was gradually becoming bigger.

A brown finger pointed at it. Franklyn saw it was a wall.

Sphinx was seated next to him. Life-size, in fact a little over six feet tall in his new dimensions, the carvings of his rudimentary, unfinished features now startlingly revealed: two slits for eyes, chiselled holes in their centres, a bump for a nose, no nostrils, and a mouth carved open, revealing two ragged buck teeth. His wood was dark and damp, like rotten bark, although the multi-coloured wig was iridescent with light, the green, gold and blue recreating themselves in wondrous shades.

Sphinx recalled his hand and leaned stiffly back, his upper torso a solid board. Franklyn saw the boot that belonged to Rivers, also life-size at the far end of the cabin, tapping the accelerator.

"Where are we going?" Franklyn asked. He jumped as something shook what he now believed to be The Dead Pharaohs' tour van. The disturbance felt like many hands beating at his window, quickly and violently making their presence known in their split second of opportunity upon the vehicle's passage.

Sphinx pointed at the wall again.

"We're gonna crash?" Franklyn asked helplessly of Sphinx, who was observing the howling fog road.

H-hippy spit.

"What can I do?" Franklyn muttered, the freezing, rancid air making him queasy. A creak was heard in the back and in the rear-view mirror he glimpsed a life-sized Sandy Tombes having sex with two groupies: wooden women with faces smeared with make-up and blonde wigs dark with perspiration. The drummer was snarling, each huge hand gripping the back of a neck as the women were wrestled face down to the floor with squeaks of pain.

The hands rapped at the window once more, snapping Franklyn away from the mirror. He considered Sphinx fearfully. "Can ya talk to me?" he asked. "Properly, like?"

The lead singer slowly shook his head, a finger slowly coming to his mouth.

192

"You're trapped, as what you are?" Franklyn asked, translating the movement. This was a dream, but even with The Dead Pharaohs animated, released from the limited movements of their design, they still had to play out the whim of their creator with whatever joke or black irony had conceived them.

Sphinx nodded, his hand moving out expressively.

"But you can show me this," Franklyn muttered thoughtfully, looking around him. "What *are* you trying to show me?"

Sphinx pressed his back further into the seat while Rivers' boot pressed down on the accelerator. Franklyn turned to see the wall racing towards them, filling their view though the windscreen; it was thick, jagged stone. The scream had barely managed to form in his throat before the collision, then fell from his mouth as the tour van continued crashing through the heavy fog, the wall left behind. Sphinx was considering him now with the slits that were his eyes.

"We can't die?" Franklyn asked breathlessly. "Is that what you're trying to tell me? That we can't die?"

H–hippy spit.

Franklyn shook his head, not understanding why the response was Sphinx's most negative pronouncement. A startled squeak from the back prompted him to check the rear-view mirror again. Tombes' hand was at the throat of one of the groupies as he applied his drumstick to her face. The drumstick ended with a rusted nail, which the drummer was using to score lines in her cheeks. The other groupie at her side, her face a web of scars, was crying silent tears.

The tour van shook suddenly. It was slowing down, Franklyn realised. It was stationary. The fog now encircled them greedily, like a stomach wall digesting food.

He fought back the urge to urinate. From an early age he had been programmed to do so when The Dead Pharaohs frightened him: they were trying to frighten him now, but they also wanted to tell him something and he knew he wouldn't wake up until they succeeded. Rivers, his friend and mentor, the purveyor of his talent, was staring patiently ahead: there would be no help from that quarter.

"Speak to me," Franklyn said to Sphinx. "Speak to me in your own way. Your own words. I'll understand ... I'm sure I'll understand."

Sphinx nodded slowly.

"Who are you?" Franklyn asked daringly. The question, with all its extraordinary presumption, prompted a short growl from Tombes, his shadow falling across the cabin like a sky of crows. The nail of his drumstick touched the inside of Franklyn's ear.

"I didn't mean to ask that, I'm sorry," Franklyn said hastily. "I didn't mean it!"

Sphinx replied in his distant baritone.

Going down a k-key.

I am one of the fallen...

J-jammin' with you.

Here to protect you...

"Just tell me why we've stopped," Franklyn said, his voice shrill. "Just tell me that."

Gig's d-done.

Your life is over...

Franklyn considered this. "And what if my life *is* over?" he whispered. "If my heart stops ... if I die... Then what?" He paused, terrified of asking his next question.

"Will I be free of you?"

He squeezed his eyes shut as the nail broke the skin.

When he opened them his expression showed defeat; he had wet himself at last.

Sphinx didn't answer but Rivers leaned forward and turned to him, mournfully shaking his head. The fog solidified to rock, which set against the glass, the tour van becoming a tomb. The cold intensified, the stench freezing the cabin air. Franklyn, careful not to move in case the drumstick might puncture his ear drum, groaned with his first ever experience of claustrophobia.

"Will we be *here*?" Franklyn wailed, blood running down his neck.

Sphinx's wooden fist was beating the dashboard, softly, but with a relentless method that communicated his anger.

B–big sustain.

Franklyn hadn't heard this phrase from Sphinx before. He considered the word *sustain,* being the length of time a note can ring on a musical instrument, then translated the musical notation with reference to the lead singer's incessant pounding on the dashboard.

His stomach came up to his throat.

"Big sustain," Franklyn whispered, his face dropping.

For eternity...

★

The Mumbles pier had a different sound at 4 am, the time when Franklyn had sneaked out of the house. The wind was circling the wide, uneven gaps between the narrow boards, the struggle of the wooden planks against their securing bolts audible in the silence of the morning.

He walked as if in a trance, just happy to be outside after the horror of his nightmare. He passed the joke electric chair, the dragon slide, the gorilla swing, all vaguely obscene in the half-light. Today he had jumped and swung round these obstacles but now he just drifted past, making his way to the end of the pier. He stopped at an area sectioned off with warning signs, where the boards were loose or missing.

Here, he thought, glancing at the Mumbles islands ahead of him. If he fell here they might not even think it was suicide. He had come out for some fresh air and wandered into the section under repair. It was a local tragedy; a young man with so much to live for...

They can't touch me if it's suicide. They won't have stopped my heart: they'll have no power over me.

He filled his lungs with the cold night air and it cleared his mind. He might be right, and he might be wrong. Who was to say they wouldn't stop his heart, put their brand on him, the moment before he drowned? Perhaps his punishment would be even greater.

He looked out at the lighthouse.

There must be hope, he reasoned, otherwise The Dead Pharaohs wouldn't have warned him of the consequences of failure: for him, and for them.

I won't just go to sleep. I'll wake up in the tour van, with the band, entombed, and we'll work out our punishment together.

The thought made him imagine a voice on the air. It was the muted sound of the wail of an animal, made with a wooden throat deep beneath the earth.

He turned curiously towards the sound. The hours passed while the fierce cold, carrying the wails of the buried and the damned, brought him the chrysalis of a plan.

X V

Howl

A PLANK CREAKED with the strain of its rusting nails; she smelt salt, heard the whistle of the cold morning air.

"Who's that then?" Jake asked cheerily.

"Just a boy I know," Gracie replied as she considered Franklyn Tyde's figurine, wondering at this sudden vignette of shared experience.

"He looks scared," Jake remarked.

She nodded slowly. "He's been looking out to sea. From a pier, I think." Her eyes narrowed. *He's calling to me … in his desperation. I must be strong…*

Jake's cautious chuckle prompted her to throw him a good-natured smile. The bedroom door was open, Gracie's mother making the occasional conspicuous noise in the corridor. Her father was out of course, otherwise he wouldn't have been allowed anywhere near the bedroom, school books in hand or not.

"So these are all people that you know and stuff?" Jake asked in a state of perplexed astonishment, having been shown his own figurine in *the gallery*. "D'you make them yourself?"

"Jake, as I told you, they all come out of *there*." Once more, she indicated *the servants' quarters*. "They've all been in there since the day I was born. I picked you out on the morning we first met, in grade four. I *told* you."

"Oh, okay," he murmured, realising that she wanted him

to play along with her fantasy. He supposed he was being tested in some way; after all, she had warned him in the sternest terms not to touch the doll's house. "And they come out … so…?"

"So I can understand them," she said wearily, for the third time.

"Understand, yeah. Okay."

She blinked to shut out the voice on the cold morning air and reached into *the gallery*, lifting out Jake's figurine. The chandelier dimmed with annoyance at the loss of one of the room's occupants.

"Your figurine is very heavy," she said, weighing it in her hands. "That means it belongs in the house."

"Okay."

"And its face is all polished and clear. Like a mirror. Look." As he leant forward she took an involuntary step back. She frowned, troubled by her own instinctive reflex.

"Did I scare you?" he asked.

She shook her head and held up the figurine. "The figurines give me clues. Your face is so clear because your thoughts are transparent; there's no guile in you."

He nodded, wanting to enjoy this moment with her rather than acknowledge how odd it all was. "So what am I thinking, Gracie?"

"That you love me," she whispered distractedly, hearing an object being moved in the corridor.

"I do, Gracie. I do love you. I'd do anything for you."

A trace of concern crossed her eyes, recalling the thrill when she had collected Jake's figurine from *the servants' quarters* to find that it belonged in *the gallery*. Her father had always shared *the gallery*, but only two other people had ever visited it and both their tenures were brief: a particularly eloquent history teacher who inspired her when she was in

198

junior school, and a favourite aunt who visited when she was very young. Her father distrusted both people accordingly, organising their transfer and estrangement respectively; he was now working on the latest intruder. "No one apart from my father has stayed this long in *the gallery* with me," she conceded.

Jake beamed. "What about your mother?"

Gracie shook her head. Her mother emerged from *the servants' quarters* occasionally but only in order to be read in *the library*. Sometimes she was hiding things and her father needed to be told.

"So does that mean that you … that you *like* me?" Jake dared. His neck sunk into his shoulders as if he was embarrassed to be so much taller than her.

"Well I suppose," she replied, but with puzzlement in her tone. This was an important moment for her: no one, not even her father, had ever been allowed to look inside the doll's house. The house would demand its walls be closed if there were visitors to her bedroom, and when the walls were opened again the house would be cold and dark with annoyance.

It had begun to dawn on her that Jake might be her life partner. He was certainly qualified: he had been in *the gallery* for more than a year now, but most importantly the doll's house was content for him to look inside its rooms. Perhaps this was an essential requirement for someone who was to share her bedroom, as necessary as his slave-like devotion. She returned the heavy figurine to *the gallery* and the chandelier brightened, iridescence briefly charging the Venetian glass windows.

"How does it do that?" Jake asked.

"Ssshh."

She considered him awhile, then closed her eyes and pursed her lips expectantly. His lips were on hers immediately, the tongue desperately trying to claw its way through, his large hands grasping her slender hips. She held them there for a few moments, feeling the weight of his erection, then pushed him gently away.

"Oh, Gracie," he groaned, his hand brushing his groin in embarrassment. It was the first time they had kissed.

Her smile was all encouragement as she turned to the doll's house to give him some privacy. It was important, she decided, that she mustn't hurt his feelings by losing her smile too quickly, yet her mind was rapidly turning over a conundrum. As she feared – as in hindsight she realised she had known all along – she hadn't felt anything when they kissed, just as she hadn't felt anything when they first met, in spite of the expectation that morning created by the appearance of his figurine. What was the house trying to tell her? Perhaps Jake would be her husband but she simply wasn't destined to fall in love. With this sombre revelation her eyes fell balefully upon the terrified figurine of the boy by the sea. Her nostrils breathed salt air.

Please, please come to me ... rescue me...

"D'you know him, then?" Jake asked, having recovered himself and following her eyes to the figurine. He experienced an odd shiver, as if a cold wind had blown through him.

"A little," she conceded, not noticing the shudder in his shoulders. "He's in *the room with no windows*. He's ... well he's not a friend."

"Oh, right," Jake reflected. *Good*, he thought, not liking the look of the black kid. He again experienced that cold wind, now with a distant, hollow howl on the morning air. This time he found the sensation bracing, making his thoughts cold: he fought the urge to reach for the figurine and snap it in two. "What's his name then?"

"His name? Uh … Franklyn … Franklyn Tyde." She broke the taboo of saying his name with both outrage and exhilaration, as if she were stripping off for the first time at an orgy. "This room is where I put the people who don't like me … when the house warns me about people. People who might want to hurt me."

Franklyn Tyde, Jake muttered silently to himself, storing the name away. "*I'd* never hurt you, Gracie."

"I know. But anyway, the house protects me." She sighed as she considered the room of danger and warning. "Lots of people have come to this room. I wait, and then I prune it."

"Prune?"

"That's what I call it. It's like when you have a plant and the leaves die and dry up." She lifted the figurine of the large man with the overcoat and the bible, found that he was as heavy as ever. The woman with the white skin and face of illness was also still heavy. Gracie felt a shudder in her fingers as she touched the figurine, the porcelain sending mixed signals.

She's in indecision. Perhaps she's resisting … the faithful husband may be losing the battle…

A quick trip to *the library* revealed nothing, the woman still defied a reading, and the figurine was returned to where she had found it. She still didn't understand what was so dangerous about her.

"And is that kid dangerous?" Jake asked, pointing to Franklyn's figurine.

"No, he just wants to talk to me, that's all."

"But you don't want to talk to him?"

"No. No, I don't."

She briefly closed her eyes. The call on the morning air had passed; whatever attempt the boy by the sea had made to reach out to her, it had failed.

But the voice kept travelling.

Alex held up her right fist, which grasped the key ring, in answer to the plaintive howl, inaudible to all but the wooden orphan that she now carried constantly.

She had stepped out of the court offices before the Monday possession hearings began, leaving her client in the waiting room on the false pretext that she wanted to see if the barrister was on his way. Drawn outside as if she were magnetised, her conscious mind reasoned that she simply needed a stretch and some fresh air to think. The internal discussion was, as always, Precious Cargo.

She took a long breath, the key ring swelling with excitement.

Perhaps she wanted to believe those people could perform the impossible; to believe it as earnestly as Lloyd. Perhaps she did...

With an unhappy sigh, she replayed her dark protocol. First, she pictured Cerys and envied the young woman her baby; second, she pictured Cerys' mother, Bethan, and envied her the bond with her teenage daughter; third, envy turned into resentment at how easy it had been for both women to get pregnant and, finally, a hideous part of her wished them both bad luck.

Her hand was still raised. She shook her head in an attempt to dispel her negativity.

It was such an easy thing, the task that Precious Cargo had set them, which the doctor had said would guarantee them a child.

Lloyd says it's all about the power of prayer...

She wondered if that was so wrong. That recent survey in the papers said that 40 per cent of the population prayed, believing that it did some good. Perhaps there was some cathartic energy the body released when in prayer.

But I prayed constantly during each IVF session. Prayed violently before each pregnancy test … for all the good it did me…

She brought her hand down in resignation.

Well, perhaps they were just the wrong prayers.

"It's soon now, isn't it?"

The minister was standing a few feet away, holding what appeared to be a hardback copy of Robert Harris' *Archangel*, but which was in fact his bible. The disguise allowed him to read it anywhere without attracting the attention of the curious and concerned; it was an odd feature of modern life that the sight of a bible outside a church was generally a cause for alarm.

Alex considered the book suspiciously, her stomach sores burning with annoyance, and he returned it to one of his roomy pockets. She glanced at two smokers by the court door and discreetly put the key ring in her jacket.

"I've got nothing to say to you," she said quietly. The triggers on her thinking – the headaches when at home, the stomach sores outside – now came completely naturally.

"The babies' gestation is always precisely nine months, you see; everything is perfect with these children." Honeyman attempted unsuccessfully to make eye contact. "And the baby has to be born this year, so I *know* you only have a few days left. The temple must make its final assault very soon."

She looked away, pretending not to hear him, but thinking of the last needle that awaited her tomorrow evening. Her heartbeat quickened.

"There's still time," he pleaded. "I can't even begin to

describe the torment awaiting you. If you could have seen Ray Matthews…"

"Leave me alone," she murmured, putting a protective hand to her jacket; she smiled reassuringly at the smokers, who had noticed the minister.

"You can't even speak to me, can you? Can't you feel their hooks in your flesh? Their locks in your head?"

"D'you want me to call security?" asked one of the smokers.

She shook her head and walked towards the door.

"You've met young Franklyn Tyde, then?" Honeyman called after her. "Did you sense it, when you saw him? When you touched him?"

Alex gave a misstep, but didn't stop, returning inside.

"That he was doomed," Honeyman finished, to himself.

★

Honeyman had slept only sporadically in the past few weeks, carrying out randomly desperate vigils of all the families in Precious Cargo's orbit in the vain hope that the Trustees would appear. Barred entry to all the houses, there was nothing else to do.

It had been easier with the previous temple … getting through the doors. The first temple had dealt with death estates and he merely had to contend with greedy or disinterested relatives when hunting for its artefacts. Not so with Precious Cargo, with its determined parents who were both frightened and radicalised.

Returning wearily to his Cardiff digs, a sharp ache attacked him in the process of removing his overcoat, then his shoes, and he realised he was exhausted. Still, he would resist sleep for as long as he was able: sleep now led to dreams of the alphabet abacus, the warning marker the coven had planted.

The coven liked to play games, punishing him whenever he ventured too far into uncovering their mysteries. The warning marker set by the first temple had been a premonition of being buried alive, an horrific experience that turned out to be all but true. He glumly massaged an elbow joint. Something terrible was also waiting for him with that abacus.

But I have no choice, he thought. There was nowhere left to go if he was to prevent the Morrows' sacrament: Margie Wight was prepared to admit him, to let him see her child and the guardian. It was a trap, of course, but perhaps the coven would make a mistake … let slip some vital piece of information… Too many people were relying on him: he had to take the opportunity to acquire knowledge of Precious Cargo, even at the most desperate price.

In his imagination the white keys turned with a terrible reveal.

He briefly closed his eyes, hearing the Mozart, then, with a shake of his head, reached for his notebook.

His latest entry, after the episode in the church, read:

The faithful parent imagines the child.

The 'character' imagines the baptism gift: the child's guardian and mentor.

What is the character?

The Shelby dice told me it's like a sketch of the guardian; its scout party into this world. They're kept by the faithful parents, but ANYONE can touch them.

So, is finding a character the key to confronting a guardian?

The key to the temple's destruction?

He nodded, the ritual of concentration with his notebook helping to ease his fears. He sat heavily back on his bed and replayed his meeting with Alex Morrow that morning.

He grunted as he pictured her hand going protectively to her jacket, and his eyes flickered towards his overcoat draped over the bedsit's chair. Something was in *his* inside pocket too: a cryptic note from the late Ray Matthews of Talybont.

He closed his eyes in concentration, then sat up abruptly, recalling something Ray had told him after the remembrance service, as he railed about his wife.

Somehow ... somehow ... *I'll find a way of hurting them...*

With a glimmer of understanding, Honeyman collected his notebook. With another glance at his overcoat, his moustache twisting into a smile, he wrote:

Alex Morrow has been given a character.

XIV

Sacrament

"IT'S TODAY, ISN'T it?" Margie said to Honeyman. She had opened her front door to its widest extreme and she now stepped back to put as much distance between herself and her visitor as possible. Her smile was subservient to her eyes, which were alive with hatred.

Honeyman quickly closed the door behind him, with a stab of pain as his elbow joint flexed too far, realising she must be referring to the Morrow's sacrament. Either the Trustees had given her this information, or it was a fuel-injected maternal instinct; he suspected the latter.

"Mrs Wight, there's still time to go back. Until both babies are conceived, there's still time."

Margie opened her mouth in mock surprise.

"You don't believe that?" he asked.

Her frozen expression invited him to continue.

"The second baby has to be born this year and the Trustees would have so little time to make alternate plans." Desperation strengthened his accent, throwing a long emphasis on the words *year* and *time*. "It's in your power to bring it all to an end."

"Now why would I want to do that? The temple has given me a daughter."

"But only one child will survive, Mrs Wight."

"*My* child," she confirmed acidly.

"Perhaps, perhaps not. Speak to Mrs Morrow, tell her what you know."

"And kill my Shelby?"

Honeyman was taken aback by the directness of the question. "I don't believe … I don't think…"

She gave a short, humourless laugh. "But you don't *know*, do you?"

He hesitated, the woman having found his weak spot: his fear that his interference was reckless and dangerous. The curse of profanity had already returned. Was there worse to come?

"No, I don't know," he admitted, his hands disappearing into his overcoat. "I shan't lie to you."

She considered him triumphantly for a few moments. "You'll forgive me if I choose my miracle over your faith; what I *know* over what *you believe*." She squeezed her S cube, as if to illustrate the reality in her hand. "Now, the Trustees told me that I should allow you into my home, so I have. I don't understand their reasons, and I don't ask, but I trust them. I know who you are, Baptist, and I despise you for it. And I despise *her* … the woman at the crossroads. She'll want my Shelby dead. She'll wish for it and pray for it. So why should I help her?"

"She's not the faithful parent… "

"But she'll do as she's told when her husband takes control. Just as Henry will do as *he's* told."

Honeyman grasped at the mention of her husband as he would a lifejacket. "You're already losing Henry," he persisted. "Doesn't that mean anything to you?"

Her eyes flickered but she didn't reply.

"There are no winners, Mrs Wight. All the marriages fail. The original crime demands that, you see. Henry is already watching you change before his eyes; think of all the years you've been together, everything you've meant to each other..."

"My marriage is my affair."

"It will fail. Mrs Wight..."

"I have no intention of discussing my marriage with *you*. The subject is beyond discussion." She turned towards the stairs, a twitch of her shoulder telling him he should follow.

The violins could be heard faintly on the stairs and the cello became audible on the landing, but there was a tidal wave of sound as the bedroom door was opened. He advanced to Margie's encouragements, trying to look straight ahead; her lips were moving though he couldn't hear her, the volume of the music being for his ears alone.

She was motioning to the cot and he tried to read her lips: he detected the words *My Shelby* but nothing else. From the centre of the room he considered the cot and the Fabergé egg, then took several deep breaths as he felt his attention being pulled to the left. As he turned the energy drained from his body; the loss of all his strength, his sudden physical helplessness, was like starvation.

Every block on the abacus, apart from the one that displayed an open eye, was spinning at a frantic speed. The blur found a heavy place in his brain and he clasped his head as he slumped to his knees under the weight.

"I am not kneeling!" he protested, the words lost to the music.

The pressure became pain, and his second hand went to his head. He closed his eyes in a grimace, until the pain retreated. When he opened them the blocks were still.

Aa Bb Cc Dd Ee Ff Gg
⬭ Ii Jj Kk Ll 🧍 Nn
Oo Pp Qq Rr Ss Tt Uu
Vv Ww Xx Yy Zz ! 👁

With a groan of understanding he considered the symbols. "Halo … man…" he muttered. The two blocks spun again, this time with irritation, and he winced as pain nibbled at his forehead. When he had seen these images before in his imagination, they had been merely pictures, but coming into the presence of the abacus brought understanding. "Holy man," he said hastily. "Priest?"

Priest…

The abacus turned once more.

Aa Bb Cc Dd Ee Ff Gg
Hh Ii Jj Kk Ll Mm Nn
Oo 🧍 Qq Rr Ss 🦷 Uu
Vv Ww Xx Yy Zz ! 👁

"Pirate … teeth…?" he muttered. The symbols turned with the blaring sweep of a chord change. "Thief … speak…" he said, with difficulty. They spun again, forcing him to concentrate through the pain.

"Thief, speak … steal, speak … deception, words…"

The symbols spun again, violently quickly.

"Lie … lie!"

The pirate and the teeth turned, followed by the halo and the man.

"Lying priest," he whispered with relief, as if he were setting down a heavy load.

The thing is satisfied now. It has given me a name and I have recognised it.

The music retreated and he stretched his back, assembling his strength. He noticed that Margie had deliberately turned away, ensuring she didn't look at the abacus, even by accident. "Can you talk to me?" he asked, the question directed to the abacus.

The abacus swiftly retrieved its images, while the exclamation mark turned slowly.

"Will you talk to me?" Honeyman repeated.

The quick sequence of symbols that signified *lying priest* turned once more, then three new symbols appeared.

"Factory, man, woman?" he groaned, touching his forehead in pain.

The exclamation mark became a question mark.

"Question. Factory. What does a factory produce…?" With the word 'produce' the pressure in his forehead vanished. He blinked. "What do a man and woman produce?"

He looked up.

Child…

"They create a child…"

The abacus paused with satisfaction, then turned to present two new symbols.

Aa Bb Cc Dd Ee Ff

[oval] Ji Jj Kk Ll Mm Nn

Oo Pp Qq Rr Ss Tt Uu

Vv Ww Xx Yy Zz ?

A gate…?
A halo…?
An entrance to the next world…
Death…

The question mark became an exclamation and he shook his head, perplexed. The abacus continued to offer its turning exclamation.

Death.

Death!

"Kill," he whispered, putting the exclamation mark into context.

The abacus again presented the man, the woman and the factory.

"*Child* killer," he clarified. "Who? Who is the child killer?"

The abacus paused salaciously, then showed *lying priest.* He reacted as if he had been punched.

"It won't lie, Baptist," Margie muttered, now pacing the room with the baby crying in her arms. "Lauren told me that they can never, ever lie."

"No, they never lie," Honeyman muttered, believing the woman and believing the abacus too. The music had returned, now unbearably loud, telling him this audience was over. He got up stiffly and without a glance back stumbled, defeated and desolate, out of the bedroom.

★

I've got an egg, Alex thought, as she looked miserably at her dressing table mirror. *One egg is all I need ... and I've seen it ... it's as big as Christmas, that's what Judy said...*

She was in her underwear, her thigh blushing from constant rubbing with antiseptic swabs. It had just turned 8.45 pm. Lloyd was in the living room, but from the stony silence she knew he wasn't watching television, wasn't even reading one of his diving magazines. She pictured him sitting stiffly on the settee, waiting patiently as Sheba dozed at his feet. He had said very little all evening, just smiled sympathetically whenever their eyes met, then looking away with concern as if he too pictured the agony that awaited her at 9 pm.

She had already filled the Pregnell needle, a fairly complicated procedure involving breaking and mixing bottles of saline solution. Infuriatingly it had taken less time than usual, the tiny necks of the bottles snapping easily, almost joyfully, to enable the needle to be armed. The Pregnell syringe rested in its orange case, the long, thick shaft of the needle cold and dry. In her mind, she measured it: it was three inches at least, three inches of agony through the hard muscle of her thigh.

You have to do it, girl. They can't collect the egg without the Pregnell. And it hasn't been so bad in the past, has it?

No, not so bad, but it was always the worst of the injections: the Puregon and Suprefact injections were mere scratches, while the Pregnell always smarted. Her paranoia, grown huge with logic and experience, told her that the pain would be amplified in direct proportion to the agonies discovered with the lesser injections.

A whimper escaped, stifled by her hand going to her mouth. She closed her eyes and heard words of reassurance. Oh, just to accept the promise of Precious Cargo; a wondrous, soothing balm that would spare her this torment.

The success rate is one hundred per cent ... that's a fact ... they only choose two families each year ... I should be honoured, grateful...

And she had seen her follicle. Was that not her baby? Wasn't Lloyd right when he said that positive thinking was everything: that they merely had to believe it to be true? How arrogant was she to say that you couldn't make children with prayers?

As she opened her eyes she knew that she was simply deceiving herself to avoid the inevitable. The sacrament that Dr Mays had described was indeed simple, but it was ... wrong. Unholy. It had made her storm out of the office, she reminded herself.

But the success rate is one hundred per cent ... even the crazy minister had admitted that... What does it matter if the prayer is ... is inappropriate? What matters more than having my baby?

She gloomily considered the needle, which seemed to have grown in length and girth. The roaring passage of a bus had it sparking red.

And perhaps I can't change things anyway. I saw my son when I was in Judy's office...

The large follicle was troubling her. After throwing away the Puregon she hadn't expected even one follicle, not with a chemical interruption to her pre-menopausal hormones, and especially one so big, one that seemed to be the product of many other follicles that it had greedily devoured. The odd notion had been playing on her mind; that the follicle wasn't hers at all, but some parasite that had eaten her meagre offerings to fertility.

That she had no right to it.

Wasn't that what the doctor said?

*We offer it, but you have no *right* to it...*

"You okay, Allie?" Lloyd called from downstairs. "You haven't forgotten? Nine o'clock."

She didn't answer. He didn't call again and she supposed he wasn't expecting any response. Her eyes settled on the needle once more, the steel had picked up some condensation. She saw the sting of a huge wasp, perhaps as big as a helicopter, the beat of its wings a low moan rather than a high buzz, its poisonous spine dripping with dirty, alien solution, its point hard but blunt, requiring an exertion to force it through the flesh, to push it, burrowing and winding, through the muscle...

She whimpered as her mobile alarm went off and she banged her hand down, frantically searching for the buttons that would squeeze the life out of the alarm.

It was nine o'clock.

It was silent again.

Her hand went to her mouth once more, as she tasted her stomach.

"I can't do it," she said.

She was still in her underwear and she smelt of mouthwash. Lloyd sprung up from the settee to kiss her, a long, passionate kiss that even Sheba took note of through the haze of her cataracts. Alex moaned with pleasure, her hand finding his bottom; she had forgotten that he had such kisses in him. Shortly, she pulled away.

"I can't do it," she repeated.

"It doesn't matter."

"But it's gone nine ... I have to..."

"It doesn't matter, Allie. It's all a waste of time. Can't you see that?"

She considered him with a blank expression, then nodded.

Only a mild expression of surprise crossed his face as he quickly undressed. When he was naked, she nodded again and removed her underwear. They sat down on the floor, cross-legged. Dr Mays had explained that they both had to be naked.

"Lloyd, I'm scared. It feels wrong … it feels…"

"It's just mind games, Allie. Don't even hear the words, if you don't want to. It's just positive realisation. That's all it is. We believe it will happen, so it *will* happen. But it's important that you believe. You have to *believe*. That's what Lauren … what Dr Mays said."

She closed her eyes and moaned as he reached over and kissed her nipples, his tongue turning them into points. As he sat back up she groaned, feeling more aroused than she had ever felt in her life. He looked so handsome, his features chiselled in the soft lighting, and she remembered why she had fallen in love with him. His erection was huge: she couldn't ever remember it being so big, but he gently brushed away her hand as she reached for it.

"Not yet," he whispered.

"Oh Lloyd, I was so frightened…"

"I know, sweetheart, but it's all over now. We're going to make a baby."

"Oh … Lloyd, do you really think so?"

"I know so. It's a promise we've been given. They don't lie, Allie. They *can't* lie."

From under the settee, he pulled out a bible. They had a bible in the house but this wasn't it: she didn't recognise it, the leather cover looked worn and old. He opened it to a page reserved by a purple lace marker; she closed her eyes again, feeling a delicious ecstasy of expectation surge through her.

"Look at me," he demanded.

She opened her eyes.

He waited a moment, then returned to the page. "Luke one, chapter thirteen," he announced. "'Do not be afraid, Zechariah; your prayer has been heard. Your wife Elizabeth will bear you a son, and you are to give him the name John.'"

Lloyd handed her the bible. In the passage the words *Zechariah, Elizabeth* and *John* had been crossed out, replaced with *Lloyd, Alex* and *Theo*.

"Read it, Allie," he urged. "You have to read it."

She turned to the passage and the words fell out of her mouth. "'Do not be afraid, Lloyd; your prayer has been heard. Your wife Alex will bear you a son, and you are to give him the name Theo.'" She shrugged uneasily and handed him back the bible.

"Now the prayer," he said, taking her hand. "Together, the prayer." He waited until they made full eye contact; they took a deep breath together.

"'We dedicate these names to you,'" they said in unison. He gripped her hand tightly. Once more, the words fell helplessly out of her mouth. "'To our Father Below.'"

Lloyd released a moan of relief and exultation. Alex opened her mouth to speak, but no words came. Her eyes registered her surprise and alarm, her hand instinctively going to her throat, her mouth and tongue moving desperately like warning flags in a high wind. Still, no sounds were heard.

"It's okay, it's okay," he whispered soothingly. "They told me this would happen: it won't last long, it's just the shock of your body pumping out all those hormones. Your voice will come back." He guided her hand towards his body, and her expression changed to one of confusion and dismay. "You turned on?" he asked.

She nodded dumbly, only a small beacon in her mind flashing a warning that she should be concerned over this development. Her lips and tongue were still moving as she touched his penis, the experience impossibly erotic; every nerve in her body was receptive, her mind a dervish of fantasies. She moaned, unable to speak, her invisible gag only taking her excitement to new heights. She was young and beautiful again, her body carrying the contours of ultimate desire. Her expression tightened with salacious determination.

They kissed; it was another long, deep kiss and their bodies shivered in the knowledge of what was to come. Lloyd pulled back and blinked, with a half smirk of surprise. Then his eyes widened and he vomited copiously over her breasts and shoulder. His entire stomach had come up, and it smelt of strawberries. They looked at each for a moment, readjusting their understanding of the moment, the smell of the vomit inflaming them. She ran her fingers along it, its very texture bringing her to the point of orgasm.

He grabbed her hair and pulled her over, pulling back her arm so that it was almost dislocated. Her screams were silent, lost in the howling echoes of her throat.

"I'm pregnant," she whispered.

It was three hours later and they were lying on the bed considering the ceiling, somehow having found their way up the stairs. Their traumatised bodies were riddled with bruises.

He nodded his agreement, exultation in his eyes.

"I don't know how I know," she murmured, "but I do." Her voice was unsteady, having returned just a few minutes ago as they reached their thirteenth agonising orgasm. She blinked, unable to see her oak kitchen table.

Lloyd tried to move his shoulder, but shuddered with pain where Alex had grabbed his shoulder socket. He chuckled mischievously.

"You okay?" he asked.

She nodded slowly then looked down at her breasts, which were smeared with vomit. Her eyes widened with shock as she smelled it for the first time; Lloyd muttered a 'fuck' as he smelled it too. She struggled out of bed and hobbled to the shower.

"Can I come too?" Lloyd asked of her back, which was red raw.

"Stay the fuck away from me," she muttered angrily, her mind gradually awakening from its erotic coma. "Don't ever come near me again."

Lloyd lay back and grinned as he heard the shower, though his eyes saw something unpleasant.

XVII

Named

THE DEAD PHARAOHS had emerged from a fatalistic inertia. They were turning restlessly in their limited arcs of movement with tiny insistent creaks.

"What is it?" Franklyn asked as he lay forlornly on his bed. It had been five weeks since the pier and the frail strands of hope he had glimpsed that morning remained elusive.

Sphinx came to the microphone.

T-top of the pops.

Franklyn immediately sat up: the phrase signified the height of good fortune. "Why, what's going to happen?" He heard the doorbell ring and his mother's rapid exit from the kitchen. She was still hoping, still believing that the Trustees would visit. He heard the door open, some muttered words he couldn't make out, then his mother's heavy tread on the stairs. The Dead Pharaohs were motionless as the door opened.

"Someone here to see you, Franklyn," Mercedes said warily. "He won't come in. He wants to speak to you outside."

"Who is it?" Franklyn asked, getting up.

Mercedes sneaked a look behind her, though the front door was out of sight. "He says he's a friend of…" she whispered excitedly, but unable to say the name, "a friend of *hers*." She stroked her chin several times. "Shall I come out with you? See what he wants?"

"No, Mum, let me handle this."

"But what does he want, Franklyn?"

Franklyn put on his shoes with a shrug.

"*She* couldn't have sent him, could she? That's against rules. Strictly against rules. You can't make contact through someone else. The Trustees always said…"

"I know, Mum, I know."

Mercedes nodded thoughtfully, her eyes ablaze.

The young man at the door was a good six inches taller than Franklyn and he was wearing a tight t-shirt to show off his physique. Franklyn thought he had a good-natured face that was doing its best to look fierce, but, he noticed, automatically found a homely smile when his mother crossed the hall on her way to the kitchen.

"Who are you?" Franklyn asked.

"I'm Jake Cassidy," the visitor replied. "I'm a friend of Gracie's."

Franklyn nodded slowly, his mind turning.

Jake, still smiling in case the mother should re-emerge from the kitchen, crooked his finger, then stepped back and walked out of view. Franklyn sighed and followed. When he was outside a large hand grabbed his collar and pushed him against the wall. Franklyn didn't resist, looking Jake directly in the eyes. Jake's resolve faltered, but the grip on the collar intensified.

"What the fuck do you want with Gracie Barrett-Danes?" Jake asked.

"What d'you mean?"

"I mean why are you camping outside her house? Up in that tree. I've seen you."

"She don't own the road. I like sitting in trees."

"Bollocks. You're spying on her."

Franklyn allowed himself a small smile. "If I'm spying, why's her father done nuthin'?" He paused to let this question find its mark. "You know her father, right?"

"Yeah," Jake conceded, unhappy with the riposte. It was true: if there was any hint that someone was peaking through Gracie's window her father would have cut him up into sausage meat. "Maybe her father doesn't know. Anyway, she's got this little model of you, in her doll's house. Says you represent danger or something. That's how much you've freaked her out."

"She's got a doll's house?" Franklyn asked, all alert. "And *I'm* in there?"

"Shut up." Jake was thinking that the little twat was far too pretty-looking for comfort. He had intended on just giving him some rough handling, at most some body bruising, but now he felt a maniacal urge to break his nose. The kid was also taking this far too calmly. Yeah, he was definitely going to break his nose.

Franklyn seemed oblivious to the hand at his collar. "Jake, tell me about this doll's house. What does it do? How does it work?"

"Don't call me Jake. Jake's for my friends." Jake was regretting having mentioning the doll's house; it felt as if he'd revealed an important and intimate secret. His right hand made a fist.

"What're you doing?" Franklyn whispered, noticing the fist. "I ain't allowed to get hurt."

"If you call for your mother I'll just get you some other time, and it'll be the worse for you. Take it now."

Franklyn's eyes were beginning to glaze over. "No, you don't understand," he said dreamily. "You can't do this, it ain't allowed."

"What?"

"They won't let you hurt me," he said, his voice trance-like. "Listen to me, Jake. Jake…"

Jake grinned, his shoulder tensing for the punch.

"J-jake."

Jake hesitated, blood rushing to his fist. It felt like he was holding a heavy ball of blood.

"J-jake. J-jake Michael C-cassidy."

A toneless voice was coming out of Franklyn's mouth, his lips barely in synch with the words. It was both quiet and loud, a booming voice from the sky.

"I have n-named you, J-jake Michael C-cassidy."

"You have named me," Jake groaned. All the blood in his body was now in his fist, in his offending right hand; his life only had relevance in the act that he was about to commit, for he was empty, merely the husk of a man. The name, his name, uttered in that dead voice had classified him and judged him: his life was without hope or meaning, his drives and passions senseless and comical. He was named.

"I am named," Jake murmured in a hollow voice. His arms were limp at his side.

Franklyn was breathing heavily, his mouth open, his unseeing eyes directed towards the sky.

"B-bum note, my man."

"Yes, I've made a mistake," Jake replied, life returning to his eyes.

"Ain't no b-backstage pass."

"Yes, I promise never to try to talk to you again. Never. Never."

And with that Jake turned and ran down to the sea front, running straight past the taxi that was parked and waiting for him at the pier. He kept running and when he reached the end of the Mumbles coastline he turned round and accelerated, running until he dropped from exhaustion.

Franklyn would think long and hard on Jake Cassidy and his surprise visit to his home.

He was wondering about the doll's house Jake had mentioned as he pulled at a stubborn fruit machine in the arcade on the Mumbles Mile, studiously ignoring the occasional glances of the three girls sitting near the bowling alley. He didn't want to have to deal with the boys who were with them, didn't want any repetition of his experience with Jake the day before.

He put his last few coins into the slot. The prettiest of the fifteen-year-old girls in the group had vowed she would be at least seventeen and in a steady relationship before she lost her virginity and she was having trouble understanding what had happened with the black boy from across the tracks. It couldn't be explained through lust: she simply hadn't been able to stop herself, just as she couldn't stop herself looking over now, openly burning with resentment.

Franklyn dared a quick, furtive smile in her direction as she gloomily followed the movement of his arm pulling the lever. He paused, then moved away from the machine as he saw a gleaming black Bentley pull up smoothly on the road outside. He considered the car for a few moments, then overcoming his surprise briskly left the arcade and walked towards it, stopping some distance away.

The driver had a chauffeur's hat and turned in his seat. The girl in the back shook her head, motioning him to stay put, then opened the door.

It was Gracie, looking furious. She marched up to him.

"Hello," Franklyn gasped as she approached, thinking she looked stern and wonderful with her hair tied back, in a plain shirt where everything was buttoned. He detected just the trace of make-up, a natural lipstick with some light grey eye shadow, and his heart leapt. Had she applied the make-up for his benefit?

"What have you done to my friend?" she snapped, her voice shaking with anger.

"Your friend? You mean Jake?"

"Don't play the innocent. He was in hospital overnight. Terrified. I know it was you. I know! No one else could have frightened him like that. You almost killed him."

Franklyn was shaking his head.

"Don't try to deny it!" she said, a little too loudly. Her attention switched to the arcade, noticing the three girls who were looking at her intently. Their suspicious, unfriendly expressions told her they were *his* girls and she pulled her eyes away, back to Franklyn, angrier still. She didn't like the idea of him being with them; of him being with *anyone*. With a note of alarm she cleared her mind.

"I ain't denying it, Gracie," Franklyn replied softly.

She opened her mouth in horror and pointed an unsteady finger at him. "Don't say my name. You don't say mine, I don't say yours. You know the rules. You KNOW!"

"But it's *their* rules. Ain't you tired of playing by their rules?"

"Shut up. Shut up. You're just saying that because you're losing."

Franklyn smiled sadly. "Losing? I've already lost. The Trustees don't even visit me anymore. I'm gonna be sixteen next week, and I'm gonna be dead."

A momentary relapse in her severe demeanour acknowledged this fact. "Don't hurt my friends," she said weakly.

"Jake came to *me*. Came to my house. He just wanted to protect you." He paused. "He's pretty cool, that friend of yours. Thinks the world of you."

She nodded uncertainly. "He's very sweet," she said.

"But he wanted to hurt me. I warned him, but he wouldn't listen." He let this information sink in. "You know they won't let us be touched. Don't your doll's house protect *you*?"

"How do you know about my doll's house?" she whispered, a shudder going through her. If Franklyn was speaking the truth, then he was blameless. That meant ... that meant she shouldn't be here ... shouldn't be speaking to him...

"Don't fret. I've got three puppets dressed up like a glam rock band, if you want to know."

"I don't," she murmured, stepping away, but the parting comment found its mark. She thought for a moment and crumpled her nose up. "Glam rock band?" she asked incredulously. "How on earth does *that* work?"

He chuckled. "I could ask the same about your doll's house."

She nodded thoughtfully, enjoying the moment of empathy. The objects that went with you through life, especially the things that nurtured you as a child, were always natural and obvious. All else was alien and nonsensical. To her, a doll's house that introduced and explained all the people in her life was the ultimate comfort and support; for him, a toy which no doubt encouraged his musical talent was the same. And for both of them, the fight for survival, the judgment at age sixteen, was natural too.

"You're very beautiful, Gracie."

She acknowledged the compliment with an embarrassed shrug. "Well, so are you. But they make us that way, don't they?"

"Why does it matter who makes us?"

She glanced at the arcade, making brief eye contact with the girls.

"No one else will ever be closer to you than me," he dared. "You've thought about me every day of your life, possibly every minute. I've thought about you too."

"That doesn't change things," she said in a voice that was barely audible.

"When I die you'll mourn me the rest of your life. You'll try and find me in others, but it'll be useless. Your life will be for shit, Gracie, because there'll be no one for you to love. The Trustees know this. They don't care."

"Frank, shut up…"

Franklyn shuddered with delight at hearing her call him *Frank*: somehow she knew he preferred the shortened version of his name. "It's just a big game to them. And a joke, of course. They built us for each other, then make us fight…"

"Don't…"

"I've worked it out, see. I worked it out on a pier the other night, when I was thinking of jumping into the water. We love each other because we're part of each other. We're the reason the other exists."

She put her hand to her ears and shook her head.

"My egg is almost empty. But you know that, don't you, because yours is almost full."

"Stop it!"

"Talk to me, Gracie. Talk to me, before it's too late."

"No, I can't. I can't! It will kill my father if I don't survive this."

"But no one's got to die. We can make our own rules: I know we can."

As she shook her head her hands slipped behind her back.

Franklyn instinctively knew that she was holding her left forefinger in her right hand. He had never seen her do that, just as she had never heard him being called *Frank* before.

He quickly reached out his hand and without thinking, her muscles responding purely by instinct, her hand released her index finger and took it. A moment of charged energy passed between them as they touched, before she pulled her hand back, making a fist which she placed at her chest.

"You don't know," she said, stepping away until she reached the road, her eyes never leaving him. The chauffeur had the back door open and she ran into the car.

The doll's house had an unusual air on her return. She had expected it to be angry, which would manifest itself with a sullen gloom and occasional flashes of garish light to give a fierce aspect to the figurines, but instead it was non-responsive. All the figurines were of equal weight, and the rooms seemed to have forgotten their functions. It was as if it were an ordinary doll's house.

"I'm sorry," she whispered. "I wouldn't have talked to him if I'd known. I thought I was protecting Jake." She sighed. "You *like* Jake. I thought you'd *want* me to protect him."

The light went off in the attic and her heart froze, for the house had never gone to sleep before she had. She felt a compulsion to close the doors; the house was apparently saying it wanted to be left alone, her lie being too much to bear. She closed the walls, feeling them move quickly and with strength, as if they were magnetised. She stood in front of the house awhile, her mind racing.

"Alright, I wasn't trying to protect Jake," she said at last. "I thought I was, but I wasn't. Not really. I just wanted … well, I just wanted to see *him*." Her breathing was laboured with the admission, drawn unwillingly from the depths of her being.

The light returned cautiously to *the roof attic*. Her hands reached for the walls, but they were unwelcoming. She left them closed and looked around desperately, finding the separation from her baptism gift distressing and frightening, as if she were a naughty little girl parked by her parents on the porch with her suitcase.

She realised what she had to do; the thing she dreaded most. She took the egg from its alcove and sat down on the edge of her bed. Her eyes on the doll's house, her hands worked the intricate lock that detached the lid.

She looked inside and with a groan of fear saw that a part of her future was missing. For the first time since her birthday that elusive thirty-first year was missing again. She replaced the lid and returned the egg hastily to its alcove. She opened the doll's house, the walls offering no resistance this time.

She scanned the rooms. The boy by the sea looked as terrified as ever: relief, as well as a conscious hardening of her resolve, helped rebury her feelings for him; it was merely a small mistake on her part after all, and she would now work more furiously than ever to correct it. Her debating team had made it to the quarter finals of a national competition, her articles in the local press were receiving comments from prominent businessmen and her father had managed to secure an appointment at Number 10 with media coverage for her lobby group. What was the boy by the sea doing? She was sure he wasn't composing. She briefly picked up his figurine, considered its weight and shook her head. No, he wasn't even playing; he'd given up.

"Well I don't care for him," she declared with a small voice. "I don't care for him at all."

As if to reinforce this statement she fondly picked up Jake's figurine from *the gallery*, but she was unable to maintain her smile. Jake's figurine was lighter than usual. She studied the figure awhile and wondered at the plans the Trustees had for him. Perhaps he was just someone strong and loyal they thought could protect her, although she had never needed any protection. The boy by the sea was right when he said that the baptism gifts would never allow them to come to any harm.

She blinked as it occurred to her that the house wanted Jake to be read. She ran the figure along *the library* floor and a book popped out. It was Dickens' *A Tale of Two Cities*.

Her hands went behind her back, one thoughtfully massaging the finger of the other.

"It is a far better thing that I do now…" she murmured.

Her teeth bit into her lower lip, wondering what it meant. *A Tale of Two Cities* was the book of noble sacrifice.

XVIII

Christmas baby

THE STAFF OF Millennium Fertility broke into applause as Judy rushed out from behind her workstation and gave Alex a big hug. "Oh I'm so happy for you, my darling," she declared.

"Even if you did get there by yourself!" one of her colleagues remarked dryly. The story of Alex Morrow, the woman who had eleven sessions and then became pregnant naturally, wouldn't be one they bandied around, but they were all delighted nonetheless. Alex raised a reluctant smile to acknowledge the attention as she followed Judy into the scan room. She didn't speak until the door was shut.

"I know this wasn't an IVF baby, Judy, but I'd still like your help and support as if it were. That's why I got in touch."

Judy tapped her hand reassuringly. "When you didn't turn up for egg retrieval, just left that message, then weren't contactable for two weeks…"

"We went on holiday. We thought it would be a good idea."

Judy nodded. "I'm sure it was. Good to see you with a sun tan. I'm just saying we were worried, that's all."

"I'm sorry, I shouldn't have just left a message. I should have spoken to you. Things were…"

"No need to apologise, my darling. Now, let's have a look at you…"

Judy took a scan, grinning like a Cheshire cat as she observed the embryo. "Five weeks, you say?" she asked.

"Five weeks, two days. I'm pretty certain."

The nurse did the sums in her head. "December. Late December, most likely."

Alex sat up without being prompted and casually started dressing. Judy was concealing her mounting surprise at Alex's apparent lack of enthusiasm.

"Does he look alright, Judy?" Alex asked, referring to the scan.

"Absolutely dandy…" The nurse hesitated. "*He?* You're sure it's going to be a *he?*"

Alex put a hand to her forehead. "Certain of it," she muttered.

"Headaches?" Judy asked. When Alex nodded she added, "Rotten luck, what with the nausea to boot."

Alex nodded again, thinking that she hadn't had any nausea at all. No cramps or flushes either. Her pregnancy so far had been something out of a fairy tale.

"Alex, can I ask you a question?"

Alex shrugged reluctantly, knowing what was to come.

"At six weeks it's too early to tell the sex of the baby: at around sixteen weeks you can arrange a gender scan. Why are you so sure the baby will be a boy?"

"I just know, Judy."

Judy leaned closer to her. "I sense your husband's involvement in all this."

"What do you mean?"

"Does your husband want a boy?"

"Yes," Alex conceded weakly.

"And you'll be letting him down somehow if you have a girl?"

Alex finished buttoning her shirt. "I know what you're thinking, but..." and she sighed, wearily "...look, I haven't told you everything, Judy." She looked at her buttons. "This is completely confidential, isn't it?"

"Of course, my darling."

"Lloyd would kill me if he knew I was telling you this. He swore me to secrecy."

Judy found her most serious face and pressed her hand. Alex waited awhile, gathering her strength, then blurted it out rapidly, barely pausing for breath.

"We've had help, Judy, from these people who say we can get a baby with prayers. Not babies, mind, but a baby. They gave Lloyd something in an envelope, told us not to open it unless we wanted their help. I thought Lloyd had thrown it away but this man, this minister, told me differently. I don't know. Anyway, they told us to say this verse from the bible, then repeat it using our names. Then told us this prayer we had to say. I stormed out when they told me that, thinking they were cranks, and that it was sacrilegious, but I started taking them seriously when I heard that they'd had all these other successes: we met some of the other families, they had beautiful kids. So I thought, why not? What have I got to lose? And the injections were getting so painful. More than painful, Judy. They were just terrifying. We said the verse and we had the most incredible, horrible sex ever. I can't even describe it, it was so disgusting. And afterwards I knew I was pregnant ... and I was."

She gulped for breath. Judy's expression was unchanged, though she had retrieved her hand. "My, you've been wanting to get *that* off your chest, haven't you?"

Alex nodded, with a smile of relief wiping a tear from her eye.

"What was the verse from the bible?"

"Luke one, the thirteenth verse. One thirteen," Alex clarified, her first configuration of the numbers leaving an unsatisfied taste on her tongue. "It's Zacharias visiting the temple. He was the husband of Elisabeth, the mother of John the Baptist. Elisabeth was barren, Judy. The angel Gabriel appeared to Zacharias and told him they'd have a son. Zacharias didn't believe it and Gabriel struck him dumb for his lack of faith."

Again she stopped breathlessly. For the first time it occurred to her there was a parallel during their night of passion, if passion was the right word. She had been struck dumb too.

She waited for Judy to say something.

"Judy?"

"Alex, I think you should go back and see that counsellor."

"The psychiatrist? No way. He'll just tell me it's all in my mind."

"It *is* in your mind, my darling. Can't you hear what you're saying?"

Alex looked at her aghast. "I thought that you of all people would believe me," she murmured, then sighed and looked down, realising how naïve she was being. Why should Judy believe her? Why should anyone?

Judy brought her hands together, slowly and decisively. "I don't think we can treat you, Alex," she said.

"What? Why not?"

"I don't think our insurance would cover us."

"Judy, what are you talking about?"

The nurse was maintaining a calm speaking voice, though she had become a little afraid. "Alex, you need help. Psychiatric help. I couldn't let Millennium even give routine follow-up unless I'm satisfied that you're psychologically fit to cope with your pregnancy."

Alex's face dropped.

"It's the insurance, as I said," Judy said uncomfortably.

"You think I'm a nut job, don't you?"

"No, not at all…"

"I really am alone in this, aren't I?"

Alex didn't give the nurse the opportunity to answer. She got up and walked out of Millennium Fertility, ignoring the well wishes that followed her.

The appointment card arrived on a Sunday and it was collected efficiently from the doormat by Cristabella.

"I'd have got it, Mam," Alex muttered irritably, having noticed that Cristabella had recently fallen into the habit of reacting whenever she took more than three steps in any direction. She and Lloyd had agreed that it was far too early to tell the family yet, although she suspected from the increasingly frequent visits of Mother Morrow that he had reneged on the deal.

Still, his mother wasn't quite the control freak that Lloyd had turned out to be: ready with a dozen answers if he didn't approve of something she wanted to do, eat or drink. He was monitoring her sleep pattern, limiting her television time; he had even contacted John Beere to ensure she was getting regular breaks and that her workspace was ergonomic, throwing health and safety directives down the phone. At first, with the novelty of it all, she had found Lloyd's energetic launch into parenthood endearing; six weeks on, it was beginning to wear.

"It's for you," Cristabella murmured thoughtfully to both of them as she returned to the kitchen, as if their ownership of a card on their own doormat was an unusual development. She handed it to Lloyd who had just come in from the shed. "What's the miracle?"

The gold card was from Precious Cargo. It read, simply: *On the subject of your miracle...* An appointment had been fixed in Brecon for the following Saturday. Lloyd showed no reaction as he passed it to Alex, who blanched when she read it.

"What's the miracle?" Cristabella asked again.

Lloyd sighed. With a glance at Alex, he said, "Look Mam, don't get all excited because it's early days and everything, but Alex is pregnant."

Cristabella opened her mouth a little to acknowledge this news.

As if you didn't know, Alex thought. "Lloyd, I'm not going," she murmured, handing back the card. Lloyd shrugged to say the matter was of little interest to him.

"Who are Precious Cargo?" Cristabella asked.

"Some people who helped us get pregnant," Lloyd answered immediately.

"They did *not* help us!" Alex exclaimed.

"Yes they did," he remarked quietly. "You *know* they did, Allie."

"Well who are they?" Cristabella persisted, annoyed behind her pretence of surprise.

"They're a registered charity," he said. "They're unconventional, but they mean well. And ... and this is all I really care about ... what they do ... *works.*"

"What *do* they do?"

He rotated the card between the palm of his hands, finding each sharp corner with a flicker of his eyes. "They're sort of faith healers. That's what they mean by *miracle.* There's no drugs or anything. It's a mental thing; you know, finding a state of mind."

Cristabella's suspicious, inquisitive expression hadn't changed.

"They helped me give up the booze," he said.

His mother softened on hearing this, immediately warming to the people who had helped her son. Alex turned to him accusingly.

"Yeah," he admitted uncomfortably.

"Why didn't you tell me?" Alex asked.

"You didn't trust them. Now can you understand why I was so willing to follow their advice?"

Alex thought about this. "If you'd told me, I might have had more of an open mind. Lloyd, why all these secrets?"

He didn't answer. Dr Mays had given him strict instructions not to mention the alcohol treatment until after the sacrament: Alex had to come to the sacrament by faith alone; there could be no demonstrations of their power. For Lloyd of course it was different because he had already proved his faith.

"So what did they do?" Alex asked.

"Just some mind suggestion stuff. Hypnosis, I suppose. I didn't contact them," he added defensively. "I met the doctor by accident when I was working."

"Well it's marvellous, whatever they did," Cristabella declared. "And what help did they give you with the pregnancy?"

Alex looked down and clenched her fingers.

"Same sort of stuff," Lloyd murmured. "Positive mental attitude, mind controlling the body … that sort of thing."

"Like yoga?" Cristabella asked.

Alex uttered a humourless chuckle, prompting a raising of Cristabella's eyebrows.

"Yeah, a bit like yoga," Lloyd said, throwing his wife an icy look.

"We're pregnant because of the zinc supplements," Alex said.

Now it was Lloyd's turn to laugh.

"And you being off the booze," she said petulantly.

He smiled. "Well, if that's true it's *still* down to Precious Cargo that you're pregnant, isn't it?"

"I don't care. I'm not going back there."

Cristabella considered the appointment card still rotating between her son's palm, then sighed and went to stir the gravy. "If you don't mind me saying so, Alex, it sounds a bit ungrateful. You should at least go back and thank them. And besides, maybe they can give you some more useful advice."

"Advice for what, Mam?" Alex snapped. "Against miscarrying?"

"I didn't say that, Alex," Cristabella replied calmly.

"But that's what you're thinking, isn't it? You're thinking that with my track record I'm probably not going to hold the term."

Cristabella gave close attention to the task in hand, stirring the gravy with rapid whirring motions. "I'm not going to argue with you, Alex," she said in a lilting voice. "Everything has to be nice and peaceful, that's what you need…"

"Absolutely," Lloyd agreed.

Alex was abashed, annoyed at herself for allowing her mother-in-law to become martyred in her own kitchen. "I'm not *trying* to argue with you, Mam, but there are things you don't know about these people."

"Really? What don't I know?"

"It doesn't matter." Alex turned to the window. "I'm not going back, and that's final."

The headache started that afternoon. It kept her up that night, then kept her in bed all day Monday. On Tuesday she struggled into work, but could only manage an hour before she went home. The pattern continued, with no amount of paracetamol, wet flannels or dark rooms able to deaden the trample of hooves in her brain.

On Thursday evening, out of exhausted desperation, she told Lloyd that if she was better, and only if she was better, then they would go to Brecon. The headache vanished within minutes.

In the early hours of the morning Alex crept out of bed and with a soapy bucket of water went to the box room with the sharpest flat tools she could find. Bit by bit, piece by piece, for the paper resisted like the skin on a living animal, the poster was slowly stripped from the wall. It was in countless paper strands on the floor, as if it had been shredded, for nothing had peeled off willingly, and it had taken her all night. In fact, she had eventually fallen asleep among the scraps, her hair soapy, a scraper still in her hand.

The nightmare she experienced on that floor concerned a square tunnel, shaped with black shadows, that appeared gradually in the wall. There was nothing but silence beyond the blackness, for she had the impression that wherever that tunnel led to it was so far away that it was beyond her imagination. She felt no sense of danger. Indeed, the tunnel had a soothing effect: it reminded her that this was her home and she had nothing to fear.

There was however a sense of intrusion. Something was here that emitted a disorientated isolation, as if it had taken a new form which had been assigned to it, like a stranger in a foreign land who wears the first clothes he finds.

When she woke the poster was still on the wall. There were no shreds on the floor; her soapy bucket was full, the water cold.

I must have dreamt it, she reasoned. *I've been so tired with the headaches … I must have just fallen asleep.*

She was holding the key ring with the rocking giraffe as she crawled into bed. She realised that she was still exhausted, as if she really had been up all night.

"You okay?" Lloyd murmured sleepily.

"Just some morning sickness," she lied, having taken the soapy water and tools back downstairs. She clutched the key ring tightly, wondering why she found this gift from a man she had never met such a comfort.

Perhaps it was simply because she had kept it secret from her husband, and on that count alone it was something to be treasured.

★

It was if a vital muscle in her mind had been cut. All the questions Alex intended to throw at Dr Mays, all of her own explanations for her pregnancy, vanished the moment she entered the Brecon house.

She was seated in one of the Chesterfields considering the computers, their screensavers gently rolling with red globs and liquid. The sight was hypnotic, anaesthetising her emotions, allowing her to believe it was only her imagination when she glimpsed something inappropriate: a tiny black eye … a partially formed hand…

The sparse furniture in the reception had been rearranged. The computer stations were pulled closer – she saw that they were in fact round tables with white cloths – while Dr Mays was addressing them from an ornamental plinth in the centre of the room. This held the clinic's Fabergé egg, which was somewhat smaller than the one she had seen at the Tyde house and looked much older, a brassy sheen on the gold casing.

"You're aware, both of you, that you're having a boy?" the doctor asked. As if it were the requirement for some exotic marriage ritual, her make-up was thicker even than usual: a mask that prevented her full smile.

Lloyd nodded enthusiastically, while Alex furrowed her forehead, unable to protest.

"He's called Theo," the doctor clarified.

Lloyd nodded again, his eyes alive with pleasure.

"That's the name we agreed upon, the two of us," Alex murmured. She managed a small weary sigh: that had been difficult to say.

The doctor raised her eyebrows. "*You* agreed upon?"

"That's right," Alex said quietly, almost in a whisper. "We both talked it over. Years ago."

Dr Mays looked at Roman waiting attentively at the foot of the stairs, and perhaps would have smiled if her face pack had allowed. "You mean, after the poster arrived?" she inquired, returning to the Morrows. "You started talking it all over after *The Night Before Christmas* arrived?"

Alex blinked, aware that Lloyd was casting evil glances in her direction. "The poster?" she asked uncertainly.

"The poster you're always trying to take down, Mrs Morrow."

Alex shook her head in confusion. "Only once … I only tried to take it down once … but that was a dream."

"No dream, Mrs Morrow. And you've tried more than once. Have you forgotten? When your poor husband has been out you've tried all manner of soaps and powders.

You've tried chemicals and rat poison. You've even used an industrial stripper."

Big noisy thing, Alex heard as Roman signed with dramatic splays of his hands. *Whole street heard…*

"Is this true?" Lloyd growled.

"No, no," Alex protested weakly, her hand over her eyes as she imagined yet another brutal migraine, sensing its presence just on the fringe of her consciousness. Had the headaches been so painful they had erased her memory? With a groan she experienced a sudden series of picture images, as if she were watching a photographic slide show in a mirror misty with condensation. She saw herself negotiating the poster with buckets, sponges, mops, hoses and, eventually, machinery. Banging the wall with her fists; collapsing to the floor in exhaustion.

She blinked once more, unsure whether any of it was true. The headaches reminded her that it was best not to think too hard when it came to certain matters. Yes, that was best. Then the pain would go away.

"What has the poster got to do with the naming of our son?" she asked slowly.

"Everything's been planned from the moment the poster arrived," the doctor explained. "From the moment Lloyd accepted it into your house," she clarified. "The correct name for the poster is a *character*. Just as your husband has imagined your child, the *character* imagines…" and she glanced briefly at the ceiling "…something else."

Lloyd nodded slowly. "Why *that* poster, Lauren? Why *The Night Before Christmas*?"

There was an exasperated sigh. "Can't you guess?"

"Because Theo will be born on Christmas Eve."

It was Alex who answered. She was thinking of Judy's

remark when they had looked at the huge follicle on the scan.

As big as Christmas…

"Bravo, Mrs Morrow."

Alex thought that it seemed natural that the doctor should address her formally as *Mrs Morrow,* while adopting a chummy first name for her husband. "What do you mean, our child is *imagined*?" she asked wearily.

"Just that, Mrs Morrow. We, the temple…" and the doctor extended both her arms to illustrate the qualification "…allowed you to imagine Theo, just as the *character* imagines his companion."

"Companion?"

"That's a discussion for a different day. And with your husband only. In fact, this is our only scheduled meeting with you, Mrs Morrow. We'll meet with you of course, when we come to your home, but all further instructions will be given to your husband."

Alex eyed the doctor cautiously; the explanation was perfectly reasonable but there was, perhaps, something a little too direct and inelegant about it. She couldn't quite put her finger on it: it was as if she had bitten into a delicious cake to find a hard seed or nut that left a coarse aftertaste. "So why am I here today?" she asked.

"Because we need to lay down some ground rules. There are only two." The doctor's eyes narrowed momentarily; to each side the computer screens continued to flicker their rolling, blood-coloured globs.

"Rules? Why do I have to follow *your* rules?" Alex muttered with the beginnings of a smile and the vague stirring of opposition.

"First rule," the doctor declared, ignoring her, "you will

never approach the family on the marina, whether directly or through someone else, or through any little device you might invent."

Lloyd shifted uncomfortably in his seat, attempting to disguise his irrepressible urge to spy on the Wights. He had turned over countless ideas as to how he could turn up at their house: disguised as a plumber; a stranger asking directions; as a concerned member of their neighbourhood watch…

"It is a reciprocal arrangement, you understand. They have been warned never to approach the family at the crossroads. It is important to the children's development that you are completely estranged, in spite of the ground you share." The doctor paused. "Second rule: you will never discuss our dealings with anyone, unless sanctioned by us. There is one notable instance where it *will* be sanctioned: in sixteen years time two families will visit you, seeking references. You will provide glowing references, reassuring the families while nevertheless uttering not one word of a lie. You will explain that your son was a miracle."

"Why do I have to follow your rules?" Alex repeated quietly and dreamily.

"Because the baby is not only yours, but ours."

"Yours? How is he *yours*?"

"Because we have helped you imagine it. That gives us … rights…"

Rights, Roman signalled with a raised finger, which he slowly crooked.

"…which we will exercise. And because we have helped you imagine the child, the child will be exceptional. Theo has the potential to live eighty-eight years and he will be both gifted and beautiful. What parent could ask for more?"

Alex blinked. "What do mean by … *potential*?"

"Talented, I knew he'd be talented," Lloyd muttered excitedly. "He's going to be a sportsman, like me, isn't he?" His eyes rolled. "Doesn't have to be diving or sailing; I'm not particular. He could be an athlete, who'll win a gold in the Olympics or something. Or a professional footballer, who'll be so good he'll take Wales to the World Cup. Fuck me. I know it. I just know it…"

The doctor was looking at Alex, not offering even a flicker of response to Lloyd's outburst.

"What do mean by *potential*?" Alex repeated.

"Your child belongs to both of us, or to neither of us. You're here in order to understand two basic rules that need to be followed, because breaking them will compromise the life of your child."

Alex put her hand protectively to her belly.

"Very good, Mrs Morrow," the doctor remarked approvingly. "Until Theo is baptised, he is vulnerable. He can be lost. And if he's lost, then so are we. This is a dangerous time, for we have no means of protecting him."

"I'll protect him," Lloyd gasped. "I'll *always* protect him."

Alex sat back in a daze. There was nothing in the air she could detect, no sedative or drug; her subconscious suggested she had been mesmerised by the screensavers. That must be the reason why on this occasion they hadn't been invited into the sandalwood office, why the doctor had instead positioned herself carefully between the two computers.

"What's so important about the child being baptised?"

"Alex, shut up," Lloyd whispered.

"I want to know," Alex replied, vaguely aware that her husband didn't seem to share her sense of peace. Were the screensavers intended only for her?

"Don't question them," Lloyd hissed.

Your wife is allowed to ask questions, Roman signed with irritated palms.

Lloyd glanced fearfully at the nurse. "Yeah, sorry," he muttered.

Dr Mays allowed the rebuke a few seconds of life before she spoke. A proud resonance enriched her voice. "We will answer all your questions. Understand that we are holy, Mrs Morrow…"

Holy, Roman chimed with outstretched hands.

"…and while we are Trustees of this temple we are in a state of grace." She paused a moment, then continued. "You ask why it's important the children are baptised. Baptism has no place in our religion, Mrs Morrow, in fact it's abhorrent to us, but Precious Cargo mirrors the birth of John the Baptist. You'll be aware of that from the sacrament you performed, from the verse you read, which forms the number of this temple. John the Baptist was a so-called miracle birth, issuing from an old, barren womb. And only one of his parents believed, while the other was struck dumb for his faithlessness. So John the Baptist is the means by which the children of Precious Cargo are able to be born: that is why when they are baptised, they are sanctified; that is when they come under our protection."

"How do they come under your protection?" Alex asked, thinking that the minister, Honeyman, had told her something along these lines. With the thought came the warning tremor of a headache, creating a crease in her forehead. Since the needle cramps had vanished, the reindeers had followed her outside the house.

"Because the gifts of Precious Cargo are indestructible," the doctor replied, turning to Roman who carefully took an ornamental egg from a box at the foot of the stairs: a replica of the egg on the plinth. He smiled and walked over to Lloyd.

From his vehicle, Honeyman watched the Morrows emerge from Precious Cargo. Lloyd Morrow's face was set with firm resolve, a bundle under his arm; his wife looked mystified.

"The egg is given on the second appointment," Honeyman remarked. Ray Matthews had given him this information, explaining that it was the last time the Trustees had discussed the rules of the temple, or that they had answered any of his questions. In the years that followed he would curse himself for not having asked more questions; countless questions they would have been obliged to answer.

Honeyman watched the Morrows drive away then collected his notebook. He turned to the page entitled 'Morrow' and wrote in today's date.

"Are you hungry?" he asked, turning to the passenger at his side.

"Suppose," came the answer.

The passenger was Franklyn Tyde.

XIX

Children of science

SITTING ON THE only chair in Honeyman's Brecon studio flat, Franklyn was flipping through a scrapbook. Honeyman peered out of the single window; the pages were stored in his memory.

A turn of the page told him that Franklyn was looking at a black-and-white photograph of a young woman working at a microscope. She had striking dark hair, a prominent nose and large baleful eyes. "Marie Stopes," Franklyn muttered, reading Honeyman's inscription: *Marie Stopes: as a student.* "I've heard of her." He shrugged. "Somewhere…" He considered the photograph. "Was she a scientist or somethin'?" he asked, noticing the microscope; the only piece of equipment he recognised amongst the gas-powered glass paraphernalia.

"She ended her life as a poet," came the answer, "but yes, she started out as a scientist, a university student. A hefty achievement for a woman in that day and age."

Franklyn turned the page to find more photographs. The first was a street view of a terrace house converted into a shop, with a sign in the window which read: *The mothers clinic … constructive birth control … open daily…* On the page opposite was a wooden caravan with a notice *Dr Marie Stopes … birth control clinic.* A nurse in large white headgear was posing happily. More nurses were in the photograph below, standing behind an older Marie Stopes.

"She revolutionised ideas of birth control and the sexual rights of women during marriage," Honeyman explained, his gaze still out over the town, "and she opened the first fertility clinic designed to prevent pregnancies." His finger scratched an itch at the shoulder of his green waistcoat. "She was a best-selling author on the subject."

A turn of the page displayed a publisher's advert for a book entitled *Radiant Motherhood* with a caption: *For those who are creating the future ... by Marie Stopes Dsc Phd, author of* Married Love.

"Wasn't that good?" Franklyn asked, as he turned the page.

"All good," Honeyman agreed wistfully. "She was a very fine, well-meaning lady: extraordinarily ahead of her time."

"But there's something bothering you about her, ain't there?"

Honeyman heard the page turn once more and he answered with a glance to the sky. He knew that the boy was looking at a photograph of a middle-aged Marie Stopes, sitting at a desk with a young couple standing over her; they both had enthusiastic smiles and each had a baby in their arms.

"Who are these people? Charles and Queenie Sobarth...?" Franklyn added, reading the inscription.

"Clients of Marie Stopes. Wealthy patrons and admirers."

"Who are the children?"

Honeyman uncomfortably shifted his weight from his right to his left leg. "Their twins. Alice and Maximillian."

Franklyn walked through a number of pages filled with print copies of faint, handwritten letters, all in the same rolling hand. Interspersed between the letters, in chronological order, were newspapers articles concerning Marie Stopes.

"The letters are written by Charles Sobarth to Marie

Stopes," Honeyman said, blinking as he heard each page turn. "They're the copies he made on carbon paper, together with his own newspaper clippings, because he followed the woman's progress intently. It doesn't appear as if Mrs Stopes ever replied."

"How did you get these?"

"They were introduced into evidence at a criminal trial in nineteen thirty-nine. The correspondence starts some ten years after the date of that photograph with the babies: I suspect Mrs Stopes was actively distancing herself from these particular admirers." Honeyman's sigh was charged with ironic humour. "Charles Sobarth was perhaps the first celebrity stalker."

Franklyn paused to read a newspaper article. It concerned Stopes objecting to her son Harry marrying a young woman called Mary Wallis on the ground that she wore glasses. She was quoted as saying it would be *'a crime against his country which increasingly needs fine and perfect people ... Mary has an inherited defect and morally should never bear children ... both Harry's father's line and mine are free from all defect. It is awful to both my husband and me that he should contaminate his splendid inheritance and make a mock of our life's work for eugenic breeding and the race ... it is cruel to burden children with defective sight and the handicap of goggles ... I will not in any way take part in or condone the planning of these crimes.'*

Franklyn looked up and mouthed the words *perfect people*, the phrase that was ringing in his head from the article. "Was this woman a Nazi or somethin'?" he asked.

Honeyman shook his head. "She did attend the Congress for Population Science in nineteen thirty-five, in Berlin," he conceded. "But you shouldn't judge her from that article."

"Why are you defending her?"

"In the early part of the twentieth century eugenics had a lot of support, my boy. The noblest minds are often deceived by misguided science."

"What's eugenics?"

Honeyman glanced over, pleasantly surprised by the boy's curiosity, then returned to his window. "It's a perceived improvement of the gene pool. In its most positive form it encourages reproduction among the genetically disadvantaged." His eyes narrowed as they found the Brecon house: the house which he watched from afar, but would never dare enter. "That would include in vitro fertilisation, of course: IVF treatment and fertility problems generally. The operating front, the *clinic*, for Precious Cargo."

"And ... and in its *negative*...?"

Honeyman smiled to himself, again impressed at such intellectual curiosity in one so young. "In its negative form it *removes* the genetically disadvantaged."

"Like the Nazis did?"

"Yes, but you mustn't think of Marie Stopes in that way. You must understand she saw eugenics as a force for good, for removing poverty and disease, as did many others. In an otherwise exemplary life it was her only flaw, and it was a private one. Her public work, the foundation for the women's clinic, still survives today."

Franklyn considered this. "You described it as *misguided* ... the science. What did you mean?"

Honeyman nodded. "A man somewhere has an idea, which he labels *scientific theory*. It is flawed in all its precepts, sterile in its application, yet ego and ignorance gives it wheels. In this case, the man was an Englishman called Francis Galton, someone else who led an otherwise productive and worthy life. The Devil loves misguided science, you see, because it casts mankind in its most absurd light: man stops looking at the stars and instead puts his head in the sand to count the grains. And illogical theory leads to illogical application. It leads to crimes, as with the Nazis of course, although the coven that Lauren Mays serves is interested in a crime far closer to home."

"You keep talking about a crime. What crime?"

Honeyman took his right elbow, briefly massaging the joint, before returning to his window observation. "Read on," he suggested.

On the same page as the Marie Stopes article was a letter from Charles Sobarth that began *Dear Mrs Stopes, I applaud both your wisdom and your courage! How right you were to cut your foolish, ungrateful son out of your will...* The letter opened by praising her public condemnation of her son's marriage choice, then went on to discuss the twins, now ten years of age. Sobarth expressed concern that Alice was clearly falling behind Maximilian in all intellectual activities and, unlike her brother, showed no inclination for any artistic pursuits. She seemed completely devoid of ambition.

Franklyn stopped reading as he recognised something uncomfortably familiar.

"Yes," Honeyman muttered. "You know where this is going, don't you?"

The next letter was dated a year later; Sobarth was now seeking Stopes' advice on how to motivate his daughter. He criticised his wife for suggesting that they just let Alice marry someone, that it was better that their boy be the achiever in any case. His wife clearly didn't understand the fundamental principles of eugenics, he remarked.

More letters followed. A letter explaining the importance of intuitive learning, describing a number of instructional toys he had commissioned when the twins were born. A letter reciting extracts from Alice's dismal school report, chequered with Sobarth's exclamation marks. A letter informing Stopes of some motivational experiments he had devised, to include forced memorisation of poems and mathematical theories on pain of food deprivation: the evening meal now began with Alice's ritual quiz. He sometimes had to discipline Maximilian when he whispered the answers to his sister, and his wife, when she protested.

Franklyn turned the page.

The later letters had Sobarth railing against Stopes for failing to answer his correspondence. Alice was getting worse as she was getting older; she was so withdrawn and unresponsive he had started to believe that she was actually retarded, although the quack doctors didn't agree. He had been forced to take matters in hand, stopping her going out and allowing no visitors or other distractions to her studies. He was in the habit of bursting into her bedroom to see whether he had caught her day dreaming again.

A newspaper article featured Stopes' attendance at the Congress for Population Science in Berlin; a letter recorded that Sobarth had tried to speak to her there, but had been kept away. The last letter reproved Stopes for having contacted the constabulary, who had warned him to end the correspondence. The dull-witted officers had even dared to question him about his dealings with his own daughter! This was his last letter; his disillusionment dripped from the page.

Franklyn hesitated before going further with the scrapbook, sensing what was to come.

"You'll recognise the photographs," Honeyman said.

The next pages contained a double-page article from *County Times*, Brecon's local paper. The lead photograph showed Precious Cargo's house on the rise of the hill, with the caption *the home of Charles and Queenie Sobarth*. The photograph on the opposite page showed a Fabergé egg with the lid open. It was in black and white but Franklyn recognised it immediately as the pelican egg. He frowned, then returned to the first photograph.

"The Sobarths lived in Precious Cargo's building? Up there?" He had been shown the house on his arrival, to mutter that it was the first time he had seen it. That was a half lie: he had seen it in his dreams.

"Where else would they have lived? As I said, the temple is built on the foundations of the crime."

Franklyn read the article, which was the story of the arrest and trial of Charles Sobarth. The man had gone into a fit of rage when he discovered that his daughter Alice had, on her sixteenth birthday, married in Gretna Green. He had tracked her down on the day of her marriage, bludgeoning her husband to death and driving her screaming back to Brecon. At some point she had been murdered. The crime came to light a few months later when her mother, who secretly knew about her daughter's elopement, became suspicious that she hadn't heard from her. The police searched the house and found the girl's remains, which were mostly ashes, some bone fragments, and her wedding ring. The remains were hidden inside a beautiful reproduction Fabergé egg.

"The egg," Franklyn whispered, going to its photograph.

"When I asked you what was inside it, you said *death*. I remember that very clearly. You were right, you see, it *does* contain death, just as it did in nineteen thirty-eight for poor Alice Sobarth."

"Is that why the temple uses it?" Franklyn muttered, his hand going to his chin. "I thought it was because it means fertility; an egg, I mean, and with the pelican feeding its young."

Honeyman was nodding. "You're right of course, but it's more than just an appropriate symbol. The thing on display in Precious Cargo is the original Sobarth egg, and is at the very heart of the eugenic crime, which is against God. It is an unholy relic."

Franklyn came to the end of the article, then quickly scanned it again. "What happened to the mother?" he asked when he'd finished.

"Her mind broke and she was committed shortly after her husband was hanged. I've checked the records of the institution, though they wouldn't let me copy anything. She committed suicide with a cutlery fork during the war."

"And what about the brother?"

"Maximillian was taken into care for a time, then went abroad. He didn't sell or even rent the house. He never returned."

Franklyn turned the page to find a copy of the death certificate of Maximilian Sobarth in late 1985. The recording hospital was in Cairo; the cause of death a medical scribble he couldn't understand. He closed the scrapbook. "Precious Cargo took over the house after he died?" he asked.

Honeyman nodded. "It was only a few months later that Precious Cargo opened their clinic. I've checked the Land Registry and the house was left by Charles Sobarth to Precious Cargo in his will. The coven probably got to him years before, but I suspect they didn't wish to set up the clinic until Maximillian died."

"Why not?"

Honeyman shrugged. "Sobarth's children were part of the crime, and so they needed to be dead. The crime is always a dead crime, you see. Anyway, nineteen eighty-five makes this a young temple, created three years before the first baby was born: the oldest Precious Cargo child is only twenty-two years of age."

"How's he doing?" Franklyn murmured gloomily.

"It's a she, in fact, and she's doing very well indeed. She's an actress." Honeyman sighed. "She refused to speak to me, of course."

"Everyone's frightened," Franklyn remarked, putting the scrapbook on the floor and looking at it with dejection. "You said you could help me," he murmured at length. "Can you? Can you really? Or was that just a lie, to get me to talk to you?"

Honeyman turned from the window with an uncomfortable smile. He didn't answer.

Franklyn looked up and waited, then returned to the closed scrapbook; his memory replayed the old images and dead news. "So is that it?" he sighed. "Lost a portrait to come here, the one when I was twelve. I got it back briefly after … it doesn't matter, it's gone now. I was happy in that picture; everything was going so sweet."

Honeyman nodded. Franklyn had told him about the Zehngraf portraits on their journey from the Mumbles pier to Brecon. "I have got one idea," he said, and smiled reassuringly as Franklyn looked up. "Let me talk to your baptism gift."

"The Pharaohs?" Franklyn returned incredulously. "Why?"

"They know the temple's secret."

"What secret?"

"To its destruction."

Franklyn laughed, the notion being so outrageous it didn't even warrant discussion. "You think the Pharaohs will tell you *that*?"

Honeyman hesitated, wondering whether he should continue.

"What?" Franklyn pressed.

"Maybe they *will* talk to me, my boy." He cleared his throat uncomfortably. "After all, Gracie Barrett-Danes is untouchable now: the Trustees have visited her, alone, which must surely have been to tell her the news."

"Yeah. So?"

"Nothing can stop it now, you see. You've lost. You're already dead in their eyes." He cleared his throat again, extremely uncomfortable with this line of dialogue. "So perhaps your baptism gift will help me. After all, the only way I can save you is by destroying Precious Cargo." He paused. "Let me try at least. What have you got to lose?"

Franklyn shook his head, unable to articulate his fears in words. "I'm done for if you do that," he said instead. "I won't even make it to sixteen." He considered the scrapbook awhile. "Letting you speak to the Pharaohs will be the death of me," he said eventually, "but I'm not ruling it out. Not if it will release Gracie and all the others. Maybe it's something I gotta do. As you said, I'm done for anyway."

Honeyman returned to the window with a shake of his head. "There'll be no sacrifices, my boy," he said firmly. The vision presented to him by the abacus, of the child murderer, flashed across his memory, sending a tremor down his spine. "If you tell me I can't have access, then that's that. I won't put you in danger." His last sentence was uttered with some passion.

"But the Pharaohs *hate* you. Maybe someone else could…"

"There *is* no one else. The temple has seen to that: they'll *always* see to that." Honeyman popped two sticks of chewing gum in his mouth as his gaze again wandered the length of the Sobarth house. "But I'm going to ensure you survive this, because we have a lifeline: Alex Morrow."

"How can *she* help? She ain't faithful."

"No, but the temple needs her cooperation none the less."

"So? That ain't stopped them before. They'll just drug her up and stuff. My dad told me he can hardly even remember the months leading up to me being born."

Honeyman nodded with an air of grim satisfaction. "True, but Ray Matthews might have helped us in that respect."

"Ray Matthews? Who's he?"

Honeyman turned from the window. With a reassuring squeeze of an eye he presented the handwritten note he had received from Ray Matthews' probate lawyer. Franklyn leaned forward and shrugged, for it read only:

Stolen.

Given.

Morrow.

Honeyman had also wondered at its brevity when he received it: after all, Ray had been perfectly lucid during their last discussion, and in their final weeks had freely discussed the Morrows when they appeared on the radar. Perhaps the explanation was not something difficult for him, but that he knew that every infraction would be a round of torment for his daughter. Honeyman couldn't be sure, but he was fairly certain that whatever was *stolen* had been *given* to *Mrs* Morrow, not the faithful parent.

And now he believed he knew what it was: the *character* of the Matthews' baptism gift. Ray had never mentioned it, but it would be something to do with a giraffe.

Honeyman attempted a confident air as he explained all his theories to Franklyn. Even if his assessment was correct, he still had no notion of how the *character* might help them. He suspected that the grieving father in Talybont had no notion either, other than it was *something*, one little act of rebellion for his daughter, even if it broke his wife's mind.

Ray Matthews had found his courage as a parent at last.

X X

Lock and key

THINGS HAD BECOME clearer for Alex in the days after her return visit to Precious Cargo. An important message had crystallised in her mind, as the tang of salt lingers after the wash of the sea.

The message was that it would be wholly inappropriate to visit the other Precious Cargo families, or indeed make any further inquiry into Precious Cargo's history. Dr Mays had put it so well during their meeting and while Alex was unable to recall her exact words, she was sure that the argument was unassailable. It was really very simple. Whenever she rejoiced in the fact of her pregnancy, when she unquestioningly accepted her good fortune, she was free of the pounding headaches.

Such was her state of mind as she checked in to Cardiff Central police station. Her smile hung uncertainly as she put her car keys on the counter and her briefcase on the floor.

"Alex Morrow to see the juvenile you're holding," she said. When her office had been called, the custody officer said the boy was refusing to give his name, but was insisting that his lawyer was Alex Morrow of Beere & Co and she was the only lawyer he would speak to. The kid wasn't in any great trouble, he had caused a little property damage but the owners weren't prosecuting: it sounded straightforward, just a quick interview followed by a caution.

She had considered letting the duty solicitor handle it, but it occurred to her that the juvenile might be Gary Holmes, the little thug who was the firm's best client. John was moaning about the slowdown in fees with criminal work and had even hinted that he might have to close the doors: she didn't relish the prospect of telling him that Gary Holmes now had a new solicitor because she hadn't fancied a trip to the police station.

On the drive down she convinced herself that it was definitely Gary Holmes, surely the only juvenile client who knew her because of his constant visits to the office. She stopped to pick up two packets of cigarettes – he smoked Marlboros and she bought the strong variety, hoping he'd choke on them – and as she was led to the cell by the custody officer she had a packet ready, together with her opening remarks designed to calm him down. He was hyperactive and she'd have to speak quickly.

The cell smelt of stale sweat and urine. The boy was huddled on the makeshift bed, his back to the door. "I'll leave you to it," the custody sergeant said, locking the door behind her. "Buzz me when you're ready."

"Hello?" she asked uncomfortably, listening to the retreating footsteps of the officer. She had realised immediately that the boy wasn't Gary Holmes: this boy was black. Franklyn Tyde turned around and smiled apologetically.

"Frank?" she asked, stepping away until her back touched the door.

"Hello Mrs Morrow."

She resisted making full eye contact. "What happened to you?" she whispered uncertainly.

Franklyn touched the right side of his face, which was cut

and swollen. Once again, she privately remarked how beautiful he was, the temporary disfigurement making him appear like a martyred saint. "Fell from a roof," he explained.

"You're a free runner," she murmured, recalling the poster on his bedroom wall.

He nodded. "It's not what I'm meant to be doing. *They* don't like me running."

"By *they* you mean your parents?"

"My normal Parkour group's in Swansea," he said, sidestepping the question, "but I wanted to see you." He looked up at her shyly, his hand going to his chin, the motion making her heart miss a beat. There was something more about him than just physical beauty: she shouldn't be drawn to a sixteen-year-old kid in this way, no matter how good-looking he was. "I didn't fall by accident, Mrs Morrow. The Pharaohs wouldn't allow me to fall by accident."

She frowned. "The Pharaohs…?"

"My baptism gift. The wooden toy you saw in my bedroom. The one your husband liked."

She wanted to leave the cell and she glanced at the buzzer. Franklyn sat up quickly as he noticed the moment of indecision.

"Please don't go yet, Mrs Morrow. I need to talk to you. I knew you wouldn't see me if I just telephoned or something, so I waited until I knew the man who works in your office was in court, then sorted it so I got arrested."

"I think you need the duty solicitor…"

"Honeyman told me you'd be in a daze now. Mr Matthews said that after his second trip to the clinic he wasn't thinking right until after his daughter was born. My own dad said the same. They've hypnotised you or something, though Honeyman says it's not really hypnotism, more of a power they have over you, because you've followed their instructions. It's all locks and keys. He said ... he said they have *rights* over you now."

"I ... I don't know what you're talking about," she muttered. The name *Matthews* chimed somewhere in her reasoning faculty and it prompted her to take her keys out of her jacket; she would need them for the drive home, to escape from this place. As her eyes once more went to the buzzer, Franklyn noticed the giraffe that dangled from the key ring. He made to say something, but changed his mind.

"Why do you need to talk to me?" she asked, the touch of the giraffe giving her the courage to take charge of this conversation. "Is it because you're scared? When I met you at your parents' house I knew something was wrong, that you were scared of something." She paused. "Have you been abused, Frank? Have your parents abused you?"

His attention was on her hand: everyone within the orbit of Precious Cargo immediately recognised its gifts. "I've been abused all my life, but not by my parents. Your kid will be abused too."

"What do you mean?"

"You have to help me. I met up with the minister, Honeyman, even though it made the Pharaohs furious. Honeyman says that there's something called an *imagined child*: your husband's got it and you need to find it, because now's the only time when it's vulnerable. That's why they've hypnotised you and stuff. When the hypnosis wears off it'll be too late."

"Imagined *what*?"

"Child. Your child. The boy your husband's been dreaming of for almost three years. There's an oil painting of him, as a three-year-old. I know, because I've got one myself.

You have to find it: when the child's born and baptised it'll be too late, 'cos the painting will go in the egg. The egg protects it, see, just like the envelope protected it when you left the clinic the first time. Honeyman's explained it all to me: that's why the last portrait in my egg is me at age three." He remembered a phrase his father had used when he had been made redundant a few years ago. "First in, last out."

She had opened her mouth to protest at this nonsense, but her words were hijacked by a mental image that she thought had been lost to her. The oak kitchen table was before her; she was alone in that kitchen, the voices and hands of her children unfulfilled promises.

"Visit the others …. the other families," Franklyn urged. "Speak to the parents who ain't faithful. Or speak to Jemmy Matthews' teachers: Jemmy's the girl Honeyman told you about, who died. Or go to Aberystwyth and speak with Carl Tyrone, who lives instead of Jemmy. They loved each other, Jemmy and Carl, just like I love Gracie." He swallowed. "I can say her name now, now that I admit it. She loves me too, though she don't admit it. We can't help it, see. We're closer than identical twins."

"I can't do it," Alex managed slowly. "I … I can't speak to … other families. It would be … wrong." She shook her head slowly and decisively. Her expression became one of firm resolve.

"Okay… I suppose you can't visit the families, that the Trustees won't let you."

"Yes…" she whispered, with relief.

"But you can return *that*." He was pointing at the hand which held the keys.

She opened her hand and looked at the giraffe. "This is just something that was given to me."

"By Jemmy's dad?"

She blinked painfully. "How do you know?"

"Because Honeyman told me about the giraffe. That thing's a *character*, Mrs Morrow. It allowed the guardian – all the kids have guardians, they look like toys – to imagine itself. You've got a *character* too, imagining your son's guardian, making a gate into your home."

"The poster," she murmured involuntarily, then pushed the buzzer. "I think you need the duty solicitor," she declared.

"The Trustees haven't told you what to do with the *character*," Franklyn insisted. "They don't know you have it, so there ain't no locks and keys." He stood up and gestured with both hands. "That's why Mr Matthews must have sent it to you. Don't you see? They don't know you got it."

He shook his head with frustration as the cell door opened. "They won't protect what they don't know you've got!"

Alex couldn't quite remember the explanation she had given to the custody sergeant, who seemed baffled and bemused. Her thoughts didn't find any focus until she got into her car and put the keys in the ignition.

Her palm settled around the wooden key ring; it had registered with her that she always did so, finding all manner of excuses to hold the little giraffe in her hand. Although it was but a minute's walk from home to the office, she had fallen into the habit of driving Lloyd to work and keeping the car, explaining that she needed it in case there was an emergency. Lloyd was fiercely territorial when it came to possession of their old people carrier, but with a delicate pat of her stomach she explained that having it close by would ease her mind.

Ten minutes passed, perhaps longer, before she turned the ignition over. She waited longer still, the engine running, her palm still around the giraffe.

The boy was right, she decided. It was inappropriate to contact the families, but nothing had been said about returning the key ring.

Her seatbelt was on and she was travelling, her senses locked in to the jangle of the keys; over the Gabalfa flyover, keeping left, then on the approach to Caerphilly Crossroads.

She didn't turn off for the crossroads. She accelerated and travelled straight on, joining the A470 that would begin her journey to Mid Wales.

It was early evening by the time Alex was standing at the grave of Jemmy Matthews. She had slowed, then parked, when the keys stopped jangling with excitement. As she stepped out of the car the weight of the giraffe had guided her to this spot like a lodestone.

She wasn't looking directly at the gravestone, but at a strip of earth that adjoined the grave. The earth here was dark and dense, as if it was soaked with peat. She became aware of something heavy in her hand.

It was her key ring. Suddenly, it became so heavy she was forced to drop the keys; in the split second that they slipped through her fingers she had the oddest sensation that even an articulated crane couldn't have held them. She watched them sink quickly into the earth with the force of their impossible weight. They were gone in seconds, only a small, traumatised section of crumpled earth attesting to their existence.

There was no thought to the loss of her car keys. Her

vision had found its way down, down into the earth to be with the large wooden giraffe, its legs and straps wrapped both protectively and hungrily around a beautiful girl with braided hair, fitful with dreams.

Alex was inside the giraffe. The animal told her that the return of its *character* was a thing of joy, that it would ease its tormented sleep. As the *character* was absorbed there would also be a few fleeting moments of waking experience and she could ask it any questions she wished. It was a fair trade: with the *character's* return it was no longer bound by the rules of the temple.

Through the bore holes that were the giraffe's eyes Alex saw the girl wince at something painful, feeling the wooden body rejoice in that pain. She shared its pleasure within the tremble of the wood. *She is trapped here for eternity,* the mind of the giraffe explained, *and her punishment is just.*

Ask me your questions…

I have no questions, Alex replied. *I am not allowed to ask questions.*

So be it. Then just lie here awhile with us.

The animal's casing was hurting her, as if she were a brain grown too large for its head. The girl now cried out at having seen something frightful, though her eyes remained closed. Shortly she began muttering a name: *Carl, Carl, Carl…*

The minutes passed as Alex considered the girl through the tunnel eyes: she had no questions, only a sense of satisfaction, sharing the psyche of the guardian.

Oh Carl … love me, please find me and love me…

She felt a sensation of movement in the slats: the giraffe was rocking with laughter.

Suddenly, she was above ground, looking down at the peat earth.

"Oh God," she muttered. Her hand went to her stomach, realising that the fate of that young, sweet, beautiful girl was the fate awaiting her own child.

She gasped as she felt a warning tug in her belly, her conversation with Frank in the cells now a lucid, uninterrupted memory. Instinctively she realised the rights of the temple were being asserted, that it had perceived her presence here. Another tug, this time giving her a cramp, told her that it was the beginning of a miscarriage. She felt the warm ooze of blood on the inside of her thighs.

"Come on then," she muttered fiercely, looking up at a grey and indifferent sky. "If that's what it takes to be rid of you, then come on!"

Blood rushed vengefully to her head, the pain putting sparks before her eyes as she lost consciousness.

★

Franklyn returned home that evening with his father in a police car. He slipped past his mother as she remonstrated about racial victimisation and police brutality, speaking so quickly, without pause and with circling repetition, that eventually the officers tired of reasoning with her. As they drove away, Mercedes looked accusingly to her left and right for witnesses, then slammed the front door shut.

Franklyn sat on his bed, ignoring his mother's screams and her occasional pounding on his locked door. Sphinx looked back at him mournfully. The singer was now completely grey and there was a stoop in his shoulders. His band mates were equally weary, although Tombes hadn't mellowed with age, his knotted snarl appearing fiercer than ever.

"I think it's time for you to talk to the Baptist," Franklyn muttered to Sphinx. He patiently absorbed a sharp crack of the snare with a blink of his eyes and waited. Shortly, Sphinx turned to the microphone; the singer paused, uncharacteristically, as if he needed to catch his breath.

D–don't know that lick.

We can't do that...

"I've worked out a way. If the temple ain't got no more hold on me, then it ain't got no hold on you. If I take out my last portrait, the one where I'm three, if I *empty* the egg..."

A manic drum roll followed until Sphinx again found the microphone. Rivers and Tombes waited expectantly for their mouthpiece to speak, but instead the singer simply bowed as the hinge in his hips was released. Rivers, balancing awkwardly on his remaining foot, followed suit, as did Tombes, after a final snap of the snare. The toy was asleep.

Franklyn's eyes narrowed in terror. The toy had never gone to sleep while he was awake; it was unthinkable. He felt hollowed out, without direction or purpose.

The Dead Pharaohs awoke, to the strain of his breathing, leaving him with a warning of what awaited him if he were to carry out his plan.

He felt as if were on the verge of having a stroke.

He felt dead already.

X X I

Visitors

S HE HAD WOKEN in such pain that they had pumped her
with morphine: she was unconscious for a full twenty-four
hours, she was told. Alex vaguely remembered resurfacing to
see Lloyd sitting, stony-faced, a distance away from the bed,
then being pulled back under into sleep to see the bloody
screensavers of the Precious Cargo computers: aborted
foetuses struggling to turn in their cramp positions, slowly
and with difficulty until their rudimentary eyes, black spots in
red holes, fixed on her accusingly.

"The baby is fine," the young attending surgeon
remarked in the waiting room of the Aberystwyth hospital.
Lloyd received this news without reaction. "We gave you
morphine because you were clearly in pain, but we couldn't
work out what was wrong with you." The surgeon smiled in
bewilderment. "You didn't even have a temperature…"

"But there was blood … between my thighs…?" she
murmured. The surgeon discreetly shook his head. Lloyd
looked at his hands, his eyes narrowing as he clenched and
unclenched his fists.

"You were found unconscious in a graveyard," the surgeon
said cautiously, glancing at his notes. "Had something upset
you? Is someone you know buried there?"

With the question she was back with the giraffe, wrapped
around the athletic-looking girl with the tight braids; shaking

with laughter as the girl repeatedly muttered a name. "No," Alex replied quietly, "no one that I know." She shrugged in embarrassment. "How long was I lying there?"

"Not long. Fortunately, the man who brought you to the hospital saw you collapse." The surgeon paused. "I'm obliged to ask you if you'd like to speak to someone. One of our resident counsellors perhaps?"

"You mean a psychiatrist," she said.

"She's already got one of those," Lloyd said, with venom.

They were the first words he had uttered and he was to say only a few more on the drive back to Cardiff: a remark that he had to catch a train to Aberystwyth so he could sit by the bed for four hours like a lemon.

"Like a fucking lemon."

In the car Alex rubbed her arm, it was aching from where Lloyd had pulled her as soon as they were out of the hospital. She didn't care, because she was remembering something: someone else sitting by her bed, his large hand on hers, his small, dark eyes watching every flicker of her eyelids. It was the minister, Honeyman...

I can't stay, Mrs Morrow. Your husband will be here soon...

A sneak memory had her travelling in Honeyman's speeding four by four, squirming on a blanket in the back seat. Had he been the one who had rescued her from the grave? If so, had he been watching her? He must have followed her from the moment she left the police station; that meant he was working with Frank Tyde.

What made you visit the grave, Mrs Morrow? Was it the thing Ray Matthews sent you? The thing he stole? Was it now? Yes, that's something the Trustees couldn't have predicted...

His accent was thick, formed solely in his throat, and a mental trigger told her that the accent was malicious and

271

evil. Her tongue tasted her anger, warning her that these outsiders, the boy and the minister, were attempting to ruin her pregnancy. The anger tasted bitter in her mouth; it tasted … not quite right. She tilted her head, wondering if they were really trying to help her. What an odd notion! She tilted her head the other way, as if to roll a thought ball in her mind, and realised that neither Honeyman nor his accent troubled her any longer. In fact, she wanted to hear more of it and she also wanted to bundle up poor Frank Tyde in her arms and protect him, just as she had wanted to when they first met. She couldn't understand why she hadn't done so when she encountered him in the police cell.

"Don't you want to know why I was there?" she asked quietly. Lloyd, uncharacteristically gripping the steering wheel with both hands, shook his head. He was livid but he wasn't speeding; he had negotiated every side turn and every traffic light as if he were taking his driving test. "Don't you want to know what happened?" she pressed.

"There's nothing to know. Stop talking. I've got nothing to say to you."

"But aren't you at least relieved the baby is okay?" Her voice was almost teasing, enjoying her husband's anger; she felt completely divorced from any notion that his good opinion was important to her. With a churn of her stomach she realised that he felt exactly the same and she knew in that moment that their marriage was over.

"Of *course* the baby's okay," he hissed. "Now shut the fuck up and let me drive." He said nothing further until he opened their front door, a *good dog* to Sheba as the German Shepherd bounded towards him. Alex, her arm aching again from being pulled out of the car, glanced suspiciously at the dog as she walked into the living room, ready to slump on the settee. The settee was already occupied by two people.

"Well, you *have* been busy, haven't you?" said Dr Mays.

Honeyman had managed to keep a healthy distance between himself and the Morrows' people carrier on the motorway, although he was sure Lloyd Morrow had spotted him long before. From Bronglais Hospital on Caradog Road it was an easy matter to pick up the roads out of the town but Lloyd had craftily selected a slow detour down the long, stormy sea front and Promenade, forcing him to slow to a crawl if he were not to come within eyeshot. Lloyd had even parked awhile, pretending to study his route map, outside a colourful townhouse near the pier.

"Yes, you know who lives there, don't you?" Honeyman muttered, with an impatient growl. "Play with me all you like. I'm still behind you."

The townhouse belonged to the Tyrone family; or at least, Honeyman had gathered from the gossip in the town, what was left of the family. The Tyrones were in the process of a divorce and Mrs Tyrone had moved out. Their son Carl, already a member of the Welsh literature body *Academi* and acclaimed in the national press for his poetry, had announced to his father that he was leaving for London, requiring a complete change of scene to write his first novel. His father, renowned with his neighbours on the Promenade for being the most protective and indulgent of parents, had been stunned to hear that he wanted to go alone.

Taking his puppet theatre with him, no doubt, Honeyman mused when he heard this news. Mr Tyrone had slammed the door in his face, but from an estranged school friend he learned of the toy in Carl's bedroom: a Georgian theatre that seemed to have an endless number of stick puppets that appeared from behind a velvet curtain.

Under the guise of a poetry critic, Honeyman had heard from concerned and talkative neighbours that Carl seemed very out of sorts, unlike his father who was boasting of the contract from a London publisher, to which was attached a cheque for five thousand pounds.

If my boy needs to be in London to work, then London is where we'll be, Mr Tyrone had declared. *He can do the writing and I'll handle all those literary sharks and parasites. We always did make a great team.*

But Carl was going alone. It was a pattern that Honeyman had identified with the five older Precious Cargo children: an actress, a mathematician, a doctor, an engineer and a painter. All of them had travelled as far from home as they were able, the actress making for Hollywood, the engineer discovering opportunities in New Zealand. The faithful parents, all divorced or separated, became withdrawn, rarely leaving their house.

Perhaps crusty Mr Tyrone would allow him into the house one day, Honeyman reflected. After all, the faithful parents of the older children had admitted him, refusing to speak but showing him their children's bedrooms, which without exception were kept immaculate. On each occasion Honeyman had immediately noticed the empty space where the baptism toy would have sat, the furniture and decor having been designed around it. The bedroom was a body without a head.

Once the bedroom had been shown he would have to leave, the front door shut wordlessly as he left the threshold.

Perhaps they welcomed his intrusion: while they hated him, he was nevertheless a reminder of the battle that had been their existence for sixteen years; they welcomed him in the same way as a war veteran embraces an enemy soldier.

There are no winners, he had recorded to his notebook, on a page entitled 'Rules'.

Everyone loses…

The unhappiness was not limited to the faithful parent. He had noticed from his observations that the five beautiful and successful children all carried a reserved sadness, a longing which nothing seemed to satisfy. None of them were in meaningful relationships.

He had raised this with Franklyn when they were in Brecon.

"It's because we're all in love," the boy said.

"In love? With who?"

"With the … *other* one. We try not to be. We spend our life trying to program ourselves not to be, but it's impossible. It don't even matter that we hardly see each other." He brought his hand to his chin. "Gracie's heart will break when I die. She won't ever get over it." He nodded mournfully; it was his sixteenth birthday in five days' time.

Honeyman reacted as if he had been punched. "You love each other…" he muttered, shaking his head in disbelief. "I had no idea. I turned everything inside out, looking in every corner, but I didn't see what was staring right at me."

Ray had mentioned how he was sure that Jemmy had a boyfriend, someone she was keeping secret, but they had both dismissed this as irrelevant. This was too obvious a reason why a sixteen-year-old might lose interest in a talent she had nurtured: far too simple for the intricate devices of the temple.

"They love each other, all of them," Honeyman muttered, after dropping Franklyn off one street from his home. Now on the motorway, following the Morrows, he was thinking about the bond between Franklyn and Gracie. "Perhaps they merely have to stop … stop being enemies … stop their parents *making* them enemies…"

He grunted, unsure whether his logic was watertight.

Temple 113, as with all the coven's temples, was built on a crime, and that crime had nothing to do with the love of the siblings: the crime concerned an obsessive parent's eugenic preference of one child over the other.

His mobile was ringing. He pressed the speakerphone on his dash. The volume was up high and Franklyn's sobs and gasps blasted out.

"Franklyn, what's wrong?"

The boy's breath was straining as if he had severe asthma.

"Franklyn?"

"I'm dying."

"What? What did you say?"

"I'm dying. I've taken the last portrait from my egg. It's empty."

A gurgle filled with fluid distorted the speakers.

"Franklyn, stay where you are!" Honeyman shouted. "I'm coming!" He anxiously checked a motorway sign; he was just passing Neath and Swansea would be the next exit. "Stay on the phone and talk to me." He moved out into the outside lane and accelerated. "Franklyn?"

But the connection was lost. He instinctively hunched down as he hurtled past the Morrows, but not really caring whether he was seen or not. Winding his window up, he realised he was shaking.

The alphabet abacus predicted he would become a murderer of children.

"Hold on, Franklyn," he whispered. "Hold on…"

"The Baptist overtook us on the motorway," Lloyd remarked to Dr Mays as he took a standing position behind the settee. The doctor gave no acknowledgement, her eyes fixed on Alex.

Alex was shaking as she found the armchair. It occurred to her to ask how the Trustees had got into her house, but the rumble of hooves within the blister of a headache would have accompanied such a question. She groaned, though there was no pain. Whatever had been clouding her judgment in the last few days had gone – gone from the moment she visited that grave – but with her mind clear the spectre of the headaches had returned. If only she could rip that damn poster off the wall.

"So what are we going to do with you?" the doctor asked thoughtfully.

The remark lit a spark of resistance, which twitched at the corners of Alex's mouth. "You're afraid I'll miscarry, aren't you?" she said.

Roman leaned forward with a curious expression. "Why would we be afraid of that, Mrs Morrow?" his colleague inquired.

"Because you need this baby to be born."

The doctor's tone hardened. "Mrs Morrow, your baby will be born with or without your cooperation. Nothing can prevent that now: your child's name is written. Written in the history of Precious Cargo."

"What do you mean nothing can prevent it…?"

Roman leaned closer still, one hand in the air as if his

palm were feeding off some unseen energy.

"When you took our sacrament," the doctor said, "you placed yourself in our hands. Don't pretend you didn't know *precisely* what you were doing. We have rights over this child and it can't miscarry. That's now a medical impossibility: in fact, it's the safest pregnancy in history. By the same token, you'd find it impossible to abort, if that notion were to enter your mind." Her eyes flicked to the ceiling. "There's a guardian assigned to this baby, and its *character* would prevent it: imagine the punishment it would inflict on you even if you think of it, let alone attempt it."

Alex swallowed, the hooves restless in the dust.

"But this is hardly satisfactory," the doctor remarked wearily, her tone prompting her assistant to sit back. "So we are here to warn you: warn that you will be judged for all your little disobediences."

"Judged...? What do you mean?"

The doctor's eyes narrowed as she ran two fingers along her forehead, creating a shallow trench in her foundation. Alex shuddered, seeing an earth grave being dug. "There will come a time when you will need us, Mrs Morrow. You will wish to please us ... to please us beyond all measure and reason. After all, the fate of your son will depend on it."

"She's talking about Theo," Lloyd hissed, unable to keep silent. He raised his chin and took an angry breath through his nose. "Don't you realise what you're doing, you stupid bitch? You're killing our son! Killing him, with every fucking move you fucking make."

Alex considered her husband, unmoved by his outburst, and her thoughts turned to Jemmy Matthews, sleeping fitfully in the earth. "I'm moving out. I'm going to the police."

The dog had chosen this moment to pad into the room;

she made her way to Roman's hand and gratefully accepted the attention he gave her.

"You're not going anywhere," Lloyd said. "Not until our son is born."

"Watch me," Alex said, getting up. She stepped back quickly, her back and elbows finding a wall. Sheba was growling at her, watching her intently through her cataracts. The animal's teeth were bared.

"I suggest you rest," Dr Mays snarled, presenting the fierce mask from Alex's dreams. "This stress can't be good for you."

"I've told Beere that you won't be coming in to work anymore," Lloyd said. "I'm the breadwinner, after all. This work nonsense has gone on long enough."

XXII

Backstage pass

HONEYMAN HEARD THE quiet chatter of a television as he walked into the house: the front door open. Peeping into the front room, he saw Mercedes and Jerry Tyde seated on the settee. They were sleeping with their eyes open, a shard of surprised excitement having sliced across Mercedes' face, her momentary last reaction to whatever had dared immobilise her. Honeyman closed the door of the room then, as an afterthought, the front door. He quietly went upstairs.

Franklyn was curled up on his bed in an embryonic huddle, his eyes also open but sightless, his breath coming in delayed but steady streams as if an oxygen mask was keeping him alive. His egg was open: it was empty, not even the supple portrait belt remaining.

With a hand on Franklyn's forehead Honeyman cautiously considered The Dead Pharaohs, then sat on the bed opposite the toy. He was telling himself that he mustn't panic, that he had to concentrate. He studied the stage, then the puppets; he was already aware of it from Franklyn's description but it was smaller than he had imagined. Perhaps it was the fact that the three figures were bending forward that made them seem innocuous; he wondered if the guardian was still in this thing or whether it was simply a husk, a shell left behind now that Franklyn was dying.

He wondered if he could touch it.

His experience with two guardians to date told him he couldn't. He had been shown the Matthews' giraffe within a very small window of opportunity, when Ray had smuggled him into the house. It was old and wretched, liable to break at the slightest movement, yet it resisted all his attempts to touch it: moving his hand towards it was like creating an opposing force in the mind.

He hadn't even dared attempt to touch the abacus: it was young and vital, eagerly rising to the challenge of a hostile intruder and delivering a delicious lance of warning that went directly to his subconscious fears.

Child killer.

He closed his eyes as he pictured Franklyn curled up behind him.

I'm useless to Franklyn if I don't concentrate. I must put aside my fears and my doubts.

He opened his eyes with grim determination. The idea that the abacus could be touched was impossible, preposterous, but he felt no such qualms with these innocent-looking puppets that called themselves The Dead Pharaohs. He reached out, then snatched his hand back with the snap of a snare drum that was so sharp, so loud, that he was sure he felt its impact on his knuckles. The drummer had risen with a snarl. He was followed by the singer, then the bass player, and Franklyn let out a long moan, the frequency of his breathing now following a regular, human pattern.

"How long can you do it?" Honeyman whispered, when he had recovered from the shock. "Keeping Franklyn alive, just as you're keeping his parents asleep? You won't allow him to die until he's sixteen, will you? Even though he's removed the *imagined child* from the egg."

The Dead Pharaohs didn't answer, but a shadow crossed the stage.

"Oh yes, I know about the *imagined child*. I have already destroyed one of your temples, you see, though I am wounded for it. Wound me again if you will, but this temple must also fall with the children spared."

Still the toy refused to respond.

"I am the Baptist," Honeyman announced formally, "and you must commune with me..."

He was cut short by another rap of the snare. Sphinx turned slowly towards the microphone, his neck knotted with pain.

You gotta b-backstage pass.

Honeyman frowned with non-understanding, concealing his inward shudder at the low, monotone voice that seemed to boom from far away. Sphinx painfully repeated the movement.

B-backstage p-pass!

With the exclamation the air in the room surged into Honeyman's mouth and was sucked down into his lungs. Perhaps he lost consciousness, or was frozen like the Tydes downstairs, but he stepped out of his body.

He was walking.

Walking along a corridor to the sound of rock music that was so loud, so impossibly loud, that the very bricks were throbbing. In his hand he held a card, which read *Backstage Pass: admit one*.

Up some steps, for a moment catching a glimpse of a huge stage and auditorium below, where thousands of fans were cheering impatiently. They were all smiling wooden puppets, all identical, only the wigs and discreet bumps in their chests differentiating male from female.

Through a door guarded by a barrel-chested puppet who

snatched the card from his hand, the music now only an echo. Life-sized versions of Sphinx and Rivers sat in chairs in the otherwise empty room, their instruments on their laps. Ripped tour posters were on the wall, the numerous venues listed as *the bedroom, the boy's bedroom, the stupid boy's bedroom, the stupid, snivelling boy's bedroom...*

A closed door led off from this room, labelled *Sandy Tombes' dressing room*. Some laughter, interspersed with female screams, could be heard in the room beyond.

"Who are you?" Honeyman asked, his pencil poised over his notebook as if he were playing the part of a reporter.

Sphinx tilted his head to signal he didn't understand the question.

"What do you want? What are you doing here?"

The puppets exchanged glances as if he was talking in a foreign language. Honeyman struggled to concentrate. Why was he in this setting? Were The Dead Pharaohs not only housed but *trapped* in the form of the baptism gift – a parody of a seventies glam rock band? If so, perhaps this was the only way in which they *could* communicate; perhaps this was why they had brought him here, with the backstage pass rock notation for the freedom they were allowing him. He looked down at himself and noticed that he was wearing flared jeans and a rather garish corduroy jacket.

"I ... I am from the music press?" he ventured.

Sphinx nodded slowly.

Y-you are the NME.

Honeyman had a photographic memory and while he had a limited knowledge of rock music he recalled news articles that mentioned the *NME*, the *New Musical Express*. The choice of publication must be relevant, he reasoned: Sphinx was attempting to understand him.

"Yes, I am the NME," Honeyman replied.

I am the Baptist … your enemy.

A high-pitched shriek reverberated from the adjoining room, then something banged Tombes' door. There were a few moments of stunned silence, followed by some quiet weeping. Both puppets looked at Honeyman, awaiting the next question as if this were the most natural thing in the world. He considered his question carefully, struggling with the role he had been assigned and attempting to block out the commotion in the other room.

"Your … your sound, Pharaohs. What are you trying to say?"

L-listen to the rhythm, man.

Rivers started to play and the bass notes walked effortlessly off the frets into Honeyman's mind, into his understanding. The notes were beautiful, perfectly formed and loaded with meaning. Rivers introduced himself first, explaining that he was the part of the guardian that nurtures and protects, for the *character* had created the baptism gift in three parts. Tombes was the part that is full of hatred, the part that punishes: for this meeting they had spared him an encounter with the drummer; indeed, it would be impossible if he were here. Sphinx was the guardian's mouthpiece; more than that, he was the thinking mind. He was the one who now informed them they were ruined.

The rolling bass tailed off.

"Your history, Pharaohs…" Honeyman said anxiously, desperate to keep this line of communication open. He shook his head in frustration. "Your musical roots," he clarified. "What are your influences?"

The bass returned. The true nature of the *characters* could not be explained here: he merely needed to understand that they were gates, allowing the guardian to imagine itself on this earth. For this temple they took form of an instructional toy, in the spirit of the perpetrator of the crime. They had no influence over the form the toy took, and within its restrictions the power and malice of the guardian was merely a fraction of its true state. Still, incapacitated or not, the Father did not tolerate failure. Their projection into this world was also a prison, potentially for all eternity.

Sphinx took this opportunity to interject.

Record c–contract's up. W–washed up man. P–playing the blues.

We are damned. We are doomed. We despair...

Honeyman wanted to ask a particular question, but struggled to find the appropriate rock metaphor. "How big are you on the hit parade?" he asked with a squirm of unease.

The bass answered. They were one of the Fallen, but of lower rank. Still, he could not begin to imagine the extent of their power. He was able to commune with them only because they were bound by the rules of this prison – the joke that was The Dead Pharaohs – and because Tombes was locked away.

"How do I destroy the temple? How do I save Franklyn?"

The two band members considered him in puzzled silence.

The silence continued, it seemed for an age, as Honeyman realised that he was exhausted, barely able to speak. A dead thump on Tombes' door startled him back to attention. Further thumps followed, each one heavier than the last. The door was shaking. Sphinx turned towards the sound; Rivers covered his face with his hands.

H–hippy spit. B–better split, man.

"Tell me how to save Franklyn!" Honeyman shouted,

summoning his last store of energy. He closed his eyes, scrambling to find the rock notation. "You say your contract's up. How do I get you a new ... a new record deal?"

The pounding continued, the door shaking on its hinges. Rivers had returned to his bass and was playing frantically, faster than before, the wooden blocks that were his hands moving like a machine across the frets. Sphinx, his attention still on the door, remarked:

G–go to the H–haight–Ashbury.

"The Haight–Ashbury," Honeyman murmured, recognising the name of the famous junction in San Francisco from the Sixties' Summer of Love. What did it mean?

Find the girl on the hill ... the one we hate and love...

The Precious Cargo children loved each other, the bass explained, but the stakes of the temple made them deny it. If they acknowledged it, as Franklyn had done, as Jemmy Matthews had before him, they lost their way. Franklyn started free running to get Gracie out of his head; Jemmy stopped training because she was pining for Carl Tyrone. That was the real test for the children: to deny their love for each other.

Honeyman nodded, urging the bass player to continue.

Gracie can save Franklyn, the bass continued. She simply has to acknowledge that she loves him.

But she already knows, Honeyman thought, his mind moving with the bass notes, in the groove of the rhythm released from the constricted dialogue with Sphinx.

She has to say it, the bass explained. To announce it, understanding what it means. She has to tell the egg ... the Precious Cargo egg that holds her future ... that she no longer desires the death of Franklyn Tyde.

It's as simple as that? Honeyman wondered.

The bass took a descending scale in reply.

We cannot lie, Baptist. You understand that, don't you?

Honeyman nodded wearily, then got up in alarm as the door flew off its hinges.

Leave now!

He was running down the corridor, past life-sized wooden mannequins who politely made way for him, their eyes turning fearfully towards the sound of the drummer in pursuit, his sticks cracking the walls. The roar of the crowd went up, the mighty opening chords of an electric anthem, and his hands went to his ears. He was back on the bed, drenched in sweat.

Franklyn was still asleep, and so were The Dead Pharaohs. Sphinx's hair was snow white, as if the puppet had seen something frightful. Rivers' left tapping leg and the right hand that plucked the bass strings were gone, completely dissolved.

"Gracie," Honeyman groaned.

His mobile was ringing. He frowned, not recognising the number. "Hello?" he asked quietly, for a weird moment thinking it might be Sphinx.

There was no response.

"Hello?" he repeated.

"Mr Honeyman," came the young female voice, which was struggling to remain steady. "Frank Tyde gave me your number. It's Gracie Barrett-Danes."

The doll's house had told Gracie that Franklyn was dying.

His figurine had toppled. It wasn't on the floor yet, but rather leaning precariously into one of the dank corners of *the room with no windows*. The Baptist and Mrs Morrow were facing him, but neither of them seemed to be actually looking at him. His true form was lost to them; he had wrapped the shadows of the corner around him like a blanket.

When she had allowed herself to imagine the moment when the boy by the sea would die it had always been in the middle of the night, mercifully when they were both asleep. There would be nothing she could do; she would hear the news the following day, when it was too late. It would be done.

It shouldn't be like this. This was torture.

With a hand to her mouth she stepped away from the house. It was confused, the chandelier dimming occasionally with inquiry, the books stubbornly refusing to budge when she tested them. Something was happening that the house didn't understand, something unforeseen over which it had no control; it was disabled with shock.

The sense of isolation made her concern over Franklyn even more acute. Without the house to guide her she felt almost like a normal person, no longer the superhuman the temple intended her to be: and if she was human, she reasoned, she was allowed to be weak.

"Frank," she whispered as she considered his figurine, glorying in her moment of bittersweet freedom as she experienced no beat of shock at saying his name. From a drawer she located Honeyman's card that Franklyn had planted in her hand on their last meeting, where he had written *If I'm in trouble, call this man. He'll help me.*

Even then, when she had rushed back into the car attempting to block out that dangerous encounter, she couldn't bring herself to throw the card away. Confronting Frank properly at last in her anger over Jake – or perhaps that was just an excuse, she now told herself – and speaking to him, really speaking … actually touching him … had left her shaken. She wasn't able to reject him now: the temple might take him, but she couldn't stand by and watch it happen.

"What's happened?" she asked Honeyman.

"Franklyn's dying, Gracie," the minister replied.

"I know. But something has happened. Why is Frank ill? He isn't sixteen until next week."

"His egg's empty. I think he removed the last portrait himself. He's accelerated the process, I suppose. His guardian's asleep."

"Asleep? How can it be asleep? That's impossible." The thought made her shudder, as had the notion of taking a portrait from the egg. It would be like removing one of your eyes.

They both considered the other's breath through the connection. Hers was quick and stilted.

"I communicated with his guardian," Honeyman said. "I asked it how I could save him."

Gracie was considering her doll's house. So, his guardian was asleep: no wonder the doll's house was confused. "What did it say?" she murmured.

"It said that *you* can save him, Gracie."

When she replied there was no surprise in her tone. She merely asked, "Do you believe it?"

Honeyman sighed. "The guardians can't lie, just as you or your parents weren't allowed to lie when you were visited by the Wights and the Morrows. That's a rule laid down by the temple."

She nodded, knowing this to be true, for her doll's house had never lied to her. From her first memory of contact, when she had fumbled in *the servants' quarters* to find her own figurine, age five, followed by her father's figure, through all the promises and warnings of the people who were to follow, the house had never deceived her.

"What do I have to do?" she asked quietly, but knowing the answer in her heart. Her blood was cold as she got up and collected her egg.

"You have to take the pelican egg," Honeyman whispered.

She sat back on the bed, and with a twist and press of her hand popped open the lid. "I know. I already have it open."

Her heart missed a beat. It had been some time since she looked inside and within the folds of the portrait belt she saw her face at age eighty-four, the last year of her life, the last but one portrait to be collected. She was … she was almost complete. Just the one–year-old remained. She knew that when she had that one, the year of her birth, that Frank would be dead.

"Tell the egg that you love Franklyn. That you no longer desire his death. It's important you tell the *egg*."

"Because the egg is my future," she muttered. She took a deep breath, then attempted to speak, but the air stubbornly refused to leave her lungs. An inquiry whispered in her subconscious: between them the eggs held eighty-four years; if Frank's egg was empty, where was the last portrait?

"Concentrate," Honeyman urged. "Remember it's the collection of your portraits that is killing Franklyn."

She took another breath. Out of the corner of her eye she noticed the chandelier in the gallery flickering urgently. She tried to speak once more, but only a sob emerged. One portrait was missing, floating in the ether… That wasn't right…

"Please, Gracie, *concentrate…*"

"Well I love him!" she shouted, tears streaming down her face. "Well I love him, well I love him," she repeated miserably. "And I want him to live. I want him to *live*."

She heaved a sigh of relief, wiping the tears from her face.

The seconds ticked by. She was staring at the mobile in her hand, not daring to look away; she felt cold and alone.

"He's awake," Honeyman announced at last, his voice thick with excitement and relief. "Gracie? Are you there?"

Exhausted, she switched the mobile off, unable to speak.

More time passed. At last she dared a look at her egg and pulled out the portrait belt, now very much incomplete. A few of the remaining portraits were years that had passed: a wonderful eighth year, when she entered a school debating competition that caused her confidence to soar; her fantastic fourteenth year, when she had fully uncovered the hidden resources of her intelligence; the majority were in the future, the promise of rewards to come, except for that uneventful third year, which had always been with her.

Many others had been lost, all of them portraits she had collected in the last two years. She counted them. There were forty-two: exactly half. A sudden compulsion came upon her, charged with foreboding like a frosty air of déjà vu: it told her that she had examined the portraits for too long. She closed the lid, aware without having to check that the lock was now impenetrable until the egg was again ready to admit her.

"Exactly half," she murmured curiously, as she turned to her doll's house. Franklyn's figurine was standing freely, without the support of the wall, and she sighed with relief. Then she stood up uneasily, noticing that the figure was different. She shook her head, unable to remember taking a new one from *the servants' quarters*. For all the memory blanks associated with her house, she *always* remembered collecting each figure for the first time: that signified her control; signified that it was for her benefit alone.

Franklyn's figurine had its electric guitar in clear view, posted at its side like a pike; the polished face betrayed a small, enigmatic smile.

"My parents will be waking up," Franklyn murmured, sitting up and greedily drinking the water Honeyman had fetched for him. "You better go."

Honeyman nodded. "I'll visit Alex Morrow now: just to make sure all the knots are unravelling."

Franklyn considered the empty glass and Honeyman noticed his quick glance at The Dead Pharaohs. The puppets were upright and looking younger. Rivers had regained his lost limbs.

As Honeyman stood up he reached for his overcoat, deliberately allowing the sweep of his hand to pass through the toy. His arm was knocked back to his stomach, as if repelled by a magnet.

"My parents … you have to *go*," Franklyn whispered urgently. "And thank you," he added.

Honeyman glared suspiciously at the toy as he left the bedroom. "It's not over yet, but it has to be close. What we've done here … bringing you back … has to make it close."

When he heard the front door close Franklyn reached for his egg. The lid opened gleefully, and he counted forty-two portraits. Sphinx came to the microphone.

The NME w-went to the H-haight-Ashbury.

Franklyn smiled.

The Baptist brought us the girl on the hill.

"And I brought the Baptist," Franklyn ruefully reminded the singer. He touched the stage and Rivers began to play, the bass ringing to the musician's left foot.

Franklyn nodded along, not having heard the bass metronome ring so clearly for a long time.

Shortly he turned to his unfinished composition on the window sill. He briefly studied the time signatures, then the key, then began to write.

XXIII

Behind the door

WITH A TIRED groan of relief, Honeyman observed Lloyd Morrow finally leave his house and walk to his car. Several loud attempts at the ignition were required before it responded with a gas bang and Lloyd drove off with a scowl.

Honeyman stretched painfully and found his toothbrush and lemon wipes to remove some of the vestiges of his long vigil, ignoring the odd curious look of a pedestrian. It was nine o'clock in the morning, the night having passed with the incessant tap of rain. He had spent many nights such as this. His Land Rover was his only permanent home, having sold his house in Flint, finally giving up the dream of ever returning to his parish. His suitcases, which now contained his life, were stored in the boot; one was reserved for the treasured possessions which held the memory of his wife and his marriage.

Believe me I know, it is possible to be happy without children, he had so wanted to say to the Morrows in the service station, but knew it would have fallen on deaf ears. The need to have children, even under the most appalling conditions, was in the DNA and brooked no argument.

The limp in his right leg was pronounced, the stiffness in his elbows more acute than usual as he walked to the Morrows' front door; the night had exacerbated the terrible wounds he had suffered at the hands of the coven. Nevertheless, his heart was soaring. While the beast that was Precious Cargo still growled – after all, The Dead Pharoahs still couldn't be touched – it had surely been fatally wounded. He had succeeded in saving Franklyn Tyde, in restoring his Zehngraf portraits: the death race had been derailed; there would be no repeat of the Sobarth crime in the year 2010.

He rang the Morrows' doorbell, then, realising it didn't work, he knocked heavily to the loud but distant barks of a dog. Eventually he glimpsed Alex's shadow through the opaque bubble glass of the door, slow-moving and hesitant. He stepped back a considerable way from the door.

Alex's expression of mild bewilderment turned to one of pained distraction as she saw Honeyman. She shook her head, struggling against an impulse to slam the door.

"I'm not coming in, Mrs Morrow," he said quickly. He stretched out his arms and looked at his feet. "I'm barely on the threshold."

"I can't speak to you," Alex said in a surprisingly calm and steady voice, her words in complete opposition to the distress in her face.

Her husband has given her a telephone voice, Honeyman thought: perhaps people were ringing, asking where she was. He noticed her wince as her hand went to her forehead. "I know this is painful for you, but I also know you want to hear what I have to say. After your experience, at the grave at Talybont, I know you're incapable of deceiving yourself anymore. The Trustees have been forced to use *the prayers that are keys* to hold you here; they'll continue to do so until you're weary of rebellion."

She armed herself with a breath.

He said, "I have, I believe, prevented Franklyn Tyde's

death. I communed with his guardian, you see, who told me how it could be done."

"Frank is safe?" she asked jovially, her eyes creases of pain.

He nodded. "The children love each other, though the faithful parents devote their lives to ensuring otherwise." He watched the door closing slowly. "The children's love for each other is the key to the temple's destruction."

"You think you can destroy it?" she laughed, torment in her eyes.

"Its destruction is laid out clearly before us. That's a rule, you see. The Trustees have to return to the Brecon house now, to examine the original egg, to see how Franklyn's escape has affected it. So I have to go too, but I wanted to speak to you first." He saw her hand tense on the door. "Leave the house if you can, Mrs Morrow. But if you can't, I'll come back for you once I've dealt with..."

The door slammed shut.

On the drive to Brecon his thoughts were happily occupied with Franklyn Tyde and Gracie Barrett-Danes, a smile forming as he replayed the girl's pained, reluctant declaration.

Well, I love him...

On arrival, turning at the bridge by the canal to drive to his studio flat, the Sobarth house briefly popped into view. As it did so, Gracie's lament was lost to him; instead, he saw the alphabet abacus.

And it told him, once again, that he was a child murderer.

Alex saw the turning blocks at exactly the same moment, for the toy had chosen this moment to visit all its enemies.

She knew about the Wight's alphabet abacus, the headaches leaving behind a residue of understanding.

She had been sitting on the settee for an hour since Honeyman left. The vision of the abacus, which the headaches told her was something dangerous, something to be feared, now spurred her with energy. She rose, her hands protectively on her stomach, suddenly afraid for her unborn child.

Yes, the abacus was hateful: a danger to Theo. With a peculiar moment of empathy with the sleigh rider she realised that the poster hated it even more than she did. The sleigh rider was the brain of the poster, the reindeers were its aggression: again, as with her knowledge of the abacus, she didn't know why she understood this. All she understood was that it had become clear to her after her visit to Jemmy Matthews' grave.

Fortunately, the drugs — there must have been drugs involved, because she was so sleepy — that the nice people from Precious Cargo had given her stopped her from worrying about it too much.

She walked into the kitchen, then looked thoughtfully at the garden shed. Perhaps something was in the shed that would help her beat back her enemies … the enemies coming to her home to kill her son. After all, the shed was where her smart and resourceful husband spent his time. It must be a place of strength and wisdom.

As she opened the back door Sheba rose from her sleeping position and growled. In that moment of stand off the dog performed an action that was completely non-canine: this was a long intake of air through its wet nose as it raised its muzzle.

"Sheba?" she said uncertainly. "Good dog?"

Shortly her expression changed.

Something's in the shed … something that will help me escape.

The dog snarled, then barked twice. She screamed and ran back into the house.

Not another step, Allie.

She considered the dog from the open kitchen window as it stared back, its hind legs tensing. The animal narrowed its right eye as a voice echoed in her brain.

And don't try the front door, either. I can run faster than you. And I'll rip your fucking throat out.

★

The Baptist has lost his way… Gracie thought. *He's back in his home, wherever that is. He's watching the temple, but no one comes and no one visits. He's lost his way.*

Honeyman's figurine was facing the wall to signal that he had no sight at present, and he was positioned away from the other figurines. One of these figurines was Alex Morrow, looking out but from a dark corner.

She's trapped. Imprisoned, somehow.

These were all idle observations for the girl who was now refusing to leave her bedroom: her meals left on a tray outside. Her parents were being patient and understanding; her father assumed she was sad for the boy by the sea. Well, that was natural, and it would pass.

She was startled by the three soft raps on the door; she knew it was her father. She bumped into the bed and sat down on it.

"Are you alright?"

"Yes Daddy."

There was a pause.

"It won't be long now, Gracie. Thirteenth of May. This Thursday. Then it's all over." He was referring to Franklyn

Tyde's sixteenth birthday, which he knew as well as his own.

She blinked and dared to look at Franklyn's confident new figurine: his back was straight and he was playing his guitar with a laughing smile. Three new figurines had been drawn from *the servants' quarters* in the last week; each one taken with mounting despair, as a plague victim discovers boils.

"Don't be too sad," her father crooned. "You don't really know him, after all."

She nodded slowly. Something had happened to reset the eggs. At first she had dared to hope that the resetting meant they would both live, that they would have a life together, and for those few wonderful days she had been happier than she had ever thought it was possible to be. But she watched the road and the oak tree, and Franklyn didn't come. Then her egg started to lose her portraits and her life force went cold. Franklyn was composing again.

"Unfair, so unfair," she whispered. Franklyn had his work, his compositions and his music, things to accomplish, things to *do*. There was nothing she could actually do, for her achievement was her own persona: the people she influenced and the knowledge she acquired. It had taken her years to become that person.

She pictured Franklyn running across roofs.

Yes, he was a sprinter, she a long-distance runner. It was unfair.

"Someone's here to see you," her father added with a note of annoyed resignation.

The doll's house also recognised that it was unfair, but it had anticipated this contingency. The boy by the sea had cheated, it had explained in *the library* with its most angry and terrible books, so she was allowed to cheat too. There was a shortcut she could take that would give her that much-needed burst of speed; in fact, it would make her impossible to beat.

"Who is it?" she asked her father.

"That big stupid boy, from school. He says you rang him and asked him to come over."

"I did," she confirmed in a flat voice. "Could you send him up, Daddy?"

"I'm here, Gracie," Jake called, apparently unperturbed by her father's description of him.

She smiled in spite of herself. "Hello Jake."

"Hi Gracie. Where've you been? You're never ill. Everyone in school's worried sick about you."

She walked to the door. "Could you give us a few minutes, Daddy?" She heard a reflective grumble and then retreating footsteps. She waited until she heard something slam downstairs.

"Is everything okay?" Jake whispered.

"No," she whispered back. She had tears in her eyes as she put her head to the door; she perceived a tremor in the wood as she imagined Jake put one of his large hands flatly against it in an attempt to touch her.

"Tell me what to do, Gracie. I'll do anything." Though all confusion, he sensed that something both terrible and important had happened. "Anything. Anything at all."

"I know," she muttered tearfully.

The doll's house had offered her Jake as her contingency plan, devised out of a calculated prediction that she would try to save the boy by the sea. That was why the house had permitted the boy to be her friend; it was why even the Trustees, to the complete bewilderment of her father, had encouraged it.

"Would you die for me?" she asked miserably.

"Yes I would," he answered immediately.

"It's a serious question, Jake. If I was drowning, and you knew that if you were to rescue me, you'd die: would you do it?"

"Of course. I love you, Gracie."

The house hadn't told her what she needed to do because the details were unimportant. She knew that all she had to do was accept what the house was offering: Jake's figurine, now so light that it didn't belong in *the gallery* anymore, yearned to be returned to *the servants' quarters*. When he came into the room, perhaps he would have a heart attack. Perhaps there was a thin membrane in his brain waiting to snap: the doctors would remark that he was a walking time bomb; how distressing for the young girl to have witnessed it. It was as simple and as easy as that, and she would be safe.

In the last twenty-four hours Jake's figurine had activated a book in addition to Dickens' *A Tale of Two Cities*, the book of noble sacrifice, which she now understand was Jake's sacrifice. She had only seen this book once before, when she was seven years old and about to lose her first pet, a rabbit which lived in a hutch at the far end of the garden. The animal was placed in a shoebox in the ground and her father said some words of regret; afterwards he had remarked that it was important that she understand that animals died. Everyone died, eventually.

She still remembered the rough thud of the earth on the shoebox lid as her father worked, just as she remembered the book that had warned her of this calamity the night before. It wasn't a novel, but a play: it was *Hamlet,* the book of tragic death. It told her not to have regrets; that everything was as it should be.

"Gracie, please let me in."

As she reached for the door handle she felt the bedroom brighten, as if she had just swept open the curtains on a glorious summer morning. The doll's house chandelier was delirious with excitement. Her palm pressed against the lock; all she had to do was depress the button to make the handle turn.

"Gracie, open the door. Speak to me."

She remembered how helpless and wretched the rabbit had looked when they found it that morning. Some kids had opened the hutch door and it had been mauled by a cat. It wasn't dead, but stiff, its legs twitching. Her father had made her turn away so he could give the rabbit some medicine, and when she turned back her pet was dead, its head at a different angle.

With a crease in her forehead she realised she couldn't remember the rabbit's name. She had often asked her father, who would mumble something in response, but the words found no place in her mind. It was just a dead rabbit: it was painful to remember it, so the house didn't allow her to remember it.

"I won't even remember you," she murmured to the door.

"Gracie?"

"Well you deserve to be remembered," she declared, wiping away her tears. She waited, gathering her strength. "Go away," she said eventually.

"Gracie?"

"Go away, Jake. I don't want to see you again."

"Please, Gracie, I…"

"I'm in love with someone else. Okay? The black boy you've met. I called you here just to tell you that … to stop you pestering me. I won't see you again."

In the silence she still felt the weight of Jake's hand on the door.

"Go! Go! Go!" she screamed, and she heard him running in shock and distress. She crumpled to the floor.

It's not hopeless, she thought. *Franklyn wouldn't do this to me. He must have something planned. Another cheat to let us both live. Yes, that's it. That's it...*

She looked up hopefully, but there was no light coming from the doll's house; it was drawing to it all available energy, as a dying man gasps for air. Her bedroom was falling into darkness.

Jake barely noticed Gracie's father watching him with a curious air as he thumped down the stairs and ran past him in the hall. Miles took a moment to reflect, then strolled to the front door to watch the boy's progress across the gravel drive, then out onto the road. He closed the door with satisfaction.

Good girl, he thought. *I've been waiting for you to give that fool his marching orders.*

★

As Alex opened the door Cristabella brushed past her like a rogue gust of wind. "What's this I hear about you not wanting me to come round anymore?" she asked.

The growls of the dog could be heard from the rear of the house. "What are you talking about?" Alex muttered, following her into the living room.

"Lloyd said I wasn't to bother you, that you needed peace and quiet." Cristabella sat down with her erect posture, her expression impassive except for a widening of her eyes. "Was that your idea? Don't you want to see me anymore? Am I that terrible?"

Alex shook her head slowly and sat down.

"Why aren't your phones working?" Cristabella asked.

"Lloyd disconnected them today. He's taken my mobile. Cancelled our internet connection too."

Cristabella hesitated, unsure what to do with this information. "You sound different. When I spoke to you on the phone yesterday you were full of the joys of spring."

"I know." Alex's voice was all weariness: the animated, chirpy voice she had acquired for visitors had vanished.

"So what's wrong? Lloyd said you've given up your job. And you look awful. Aren't you eating?"

Alex managed a smile; in fact, she was feeling better by the minute. Something had happened after Honeyman's visit this morning: perhaps it was her sudden fear of the dog, or possibly simply having the strength to keep the door open as Honeyman spoke from the garden path. Whatever it was she no longer felt as if she were walking through a cloud, although the headaches still battered her when she thought about the things that were forbidden.

"I'm not leaving until I get some answers, my girl," Cristabella declared, defiantly clicking open her handbag. The action made Alex wince as a migraine threatened a fresh attack on her skull. "What's wrong?" Cristabella asked suspiciously.

Alex put a hand to her forehead. "Mam ... Cristabella..." she whispered to the carpet, "...you have to listen to me now. Please, please ... just listen. Talking is very difficult for me ... on certain subjects. And when I tell you what I want to tell you, I'll be in a great amount of pain. So will you listen?"

"I don't know what you're talking about," her mother-in-law remarked, taking a frilly handkerchief out of her handbag and dabbing the corners of her eyes for effect. "First I hear you've given up your job, even though you haven't got two brass farthings to rub together, then you all but tell me you don't want to see me anymore…"

Cristabella continued with her lengthy monologue, reciting various examples of financial, domestic and emotional support she had given to her son and his wife. Eventually, her voice tailed off as she realised there would be no reaction from Alex, who remained poised with her hand on her forehead, waiting to speak. Unnerved by this response, she put her handkerchief back in her handbag and looked at Alex, inviting her to speak. Alex's sentences were short and abrupt, pumped out of her mouth as if she were spitting stones.

"Your son is keeping me here. Against my will. I don't love him anymore. He doesn't love me. Evil forces surround us. Surround our child. Help me escape."

A long, painful silence followed as Cristabella attempted to absorb this information. "Is there another woman involved?" she asked at length, her lips pursed. Alex slowly shook her head. "Another *man*?" She shook her head again.

Cristabella took some time to consider her daughter-in-law, looking wretched with pain. The minutes passed in silence, a grim sparkle of resolve gradually charging her expression. "Leave him then," she decided at length. "I mean it Alex: leave him."

"What…?"

"I never dreamed my son could make anyone so unhappy. That you've actually come to believe he's evil."

"No, not evil," Alex muttered. "He's not a bad man. He just wanted a baby … so much…"

"No baby is worth this. Leave him." Cristabella got up and gave Alex a half hug; as an afterthought she also gave her a peck on her head.

Alex was almost laughing at this show of affection. "And I

thought you disliked me," she said, all confusion and relief.

"My son was always wayward, Alex. You changed him and that was more important to me than a hundred grandchildren; but I won't see you unhappy. Now, listen to me. I'm ninety-nine per cent positive you're having a nervous breakdown: you need to get help, and get it fast. Put all this nonsense behind you." She paused. "Why do you think you can't leave the house?"

"It's the dog."

Cristabella shook her head ruefully. "Sheba is *Lloyd's* dog, isn't she? Are you *that* afraid of my son?"

Alex sighed. "I know what you're thinking, that I'm just crazy or something, but please, Mam, please be careful. Sheba's dangerous now. Some people came to the house … and did something to her." She clutched her forehead once more, her migraine becoming more fierce. "This morning I heard Lloyd's voice … through the dog."

Cristabella tapped her handbag with a long, perfectly manicured fingernail. "If I take the dog away," she suggested reasonably, "will you be able to leave?"

"You'll need help. The dog's dangerous."

Cristabella smiled sympathetically. "I'm going to take Sheba with me. Then you can go. See a doctor. Get in touch when you feel strong enough."

"Please Mam…"

Her mother-in-law gave her another quick hug then marched into the kitchen and out through the back door. Sheba sprang to her feet. Cristabella snapped her fingers and pointed at the dog. "Come on girl," she said.

The dog defiantly lifted her muzzle with a long breath through her nose.

"None of your nonsense, now," Cristabella said firmly,

only a glint of uncertainty in her eyes acknowledging the incongruous, almost human response of the dog. A manner which she recognised. "None of your nonsense," she repeated slowly, holding out her hand. "You're not going to try and scare *me* now, are you?"

With a small whine, for between her short-term memory and store of instinct the dog was confused over how she could have behaved in such a fashion, Sheba blindly ambled up towards the hand and let herself be led away.

XXIV

Imagining Theo

Despite her eagerness to escape, Alex had fortunately remembered her handbag: it contained her purse and, for a few pounds, she borrowed the taxi driver's mobile. After searching through her business cards, she called Honeyman: he didn't answer so she left a message. With a sigh of thanks she passed the mobile back to the driver.

Sitting back, she was shaking with the memory of something else she had taken from the house. Secreted in an old air compressor, she had found something she knew her husband was hiding; that his dog was guarding.

She took it now from the inside pocket of her jacket. It was the envelope he had pretended to throw away in the service station. Her eyes narrowed and she tried to rip the envelope as she had attempted to do in the shed, only to find once again that it resisted all her efforts. It was made of something that reminded her of the appointment card she had tried to rip before she threw it into the canal. No... she recalled with a frown ... before Lloyd snatched it from her hand and threw it in.

She unfolded the little boy, the highly realistic oil portrait on paper she had discovered inside the envelope. The face meant nothing to her. Once again, she tried to rip that too, and failed. The boy looked back at her resiliently from the fragile-looking paper.

The taxi driver considered her in the rear-view mirror. "Want a hand?" he asked with a smirk.

She quickly returned the painting to the envelope and the envelope to her jacket, giving the driver a destination that cancelled her instruction to drive around the city. She asked him to take her to Penarth Marina, to an address she had found scribbled by Lloyd on a notepad in the shed, accompanied by an obscene sketch of a rather ugly, naked, middle-aged woman giving head.

If this was Lloyd's attempt to capture the likeness and spirit of Margie Wight, then it was quite unlike the bejewelled and elaborately dressed woman who opened the front door with the debonair smile of an experienced hostess, revealing a house crammed with smartly dressed people eating canapés to the quiet rumble of disco and soul. Margie didn't lose her expression; in her surprise it simply froze, in those few startled moments becoming a waxwork of pleasant welcome.

"I'm sorry, I can see this is a bad time," Alex muttered, "but I know who you are, and you're the only person I know who'll understand; I mean you've been through what I'm going through…"

"What's happened?" Margie asked quietly.

"You know who I am?"

Margie nodded quickly.

Alex sighed with relief. "I was trapped. Kept prisoner by my husband. I've escaped, but he'll be looking for me. I've rung the minister, Honeyman, but he's not answering." She glanced with resignation at the throng of people. "I'll come back again, another time."

"No … wait…" Margie whispered, her mind ticking over. She pulled Alex inside, shut the door, then squeezing past the guests took her quickly up to the next floor. They stepped over a cord rope tied halfway up the stairs, with a notice saying *baby sleeping, toilet on ground floor.* "Henry's got his haulier and vehicle breakdown friends here. You'll recognise them because they aren't comfortable in their suits. The insurance people and bankers are the ones who *are.*"

Alex smiled gratefully at this demonstration of intimacy. "I'm really sorry to intrude. I should have called first."

Margie indicated a French chair on the landing and Alex sat down; she would have preferred to stand, but was anxious to defuse the tension. She looked around, her attention settling on the closed bedroom door at the end of the landing. "Lovely house," she remarked.

"Thank you," Margie replied in a distant voice, looking up at the next flight of stairs.

"The Precious Cargo people said we should never meet, but they're evil, Mrs Wight. I was in a sort of trance for a while, and I couldn't see it, but I visited the grave of this young girl and … and … something snapped. Then they kept me prisoner by changing our dog. But my mother-in-law…"

Margie was nodding without listening. "You've left your husband?" she interrupted.

Alex mouthed the word *yes*, no sound coming. She looked up as she saw Henry Wight coming down the stairs from the main bedroom, to the sound of a toilet flush.

"Hello there," he said, holding out his hand. "Are you allowed past the cord too?"

"This is … Alex Morrow," Margie muttered to the floor, the name distasteful to her. "The woman who lives at Caerphilly Crossroads," she clarified, this description a little easier on her tongue.

Alex felt the hesitation in Henry's palm at the word

Crossroads. It brought a reluctant smile to her lips as she wondered whether she and Lloyd would have one day come to refer to the Wights as *the family on the marina*. Henry, still smiling, stalled in confusion.

"She's left her husband," Margie explained in a distracted voice.

Henry nodded solemnly and Alex detected just a trace of empathy in his expression. "My husband's gone crazy, Mr Wight. It's these people he's mixed up with. And there's a poster he brought to the house, which seems to have a life of its own. I don't know. I'm pregnant, but I'm scared. Terrified, in fact. I don't know what of, I just know that something horrible is waiting for me … and for my baby."

"Call me Henry. And you'll be fine, my dear," he added, at a loss. He turned to Margie.

"Keep her here," Margie said to the wall. She quickly shook her head. "I mean, look after her, Henry. I'm just going to pop downstairs to make sure our guests are alright, then I'll come back up and we'll talk. We'll see if … we'll see if we can get to the bottom of this."

"You're a mother, Mrs Wight," Alex said hopefully. "You're a mother who's also at the mercy of these people. That's why I came. I thought if anyone would understand, then you would."

"Absolutely," Henry declared in a reassuring voice. Margie nodded thoughtfully, but as she turned to go downstairs she wore a deadpan face that said there were no comparisons to be drawn.

Margie showed no interest in talking to her guests as she wandered down to the ground floor, merely smiling as people attempted to divert her with compliments and small talk. Then she stepped out of the kitchen and walked onto the deck, where she found the quietest and most secluded place available under the wooden stairs. It required her to stoop, but she didn't mind. She took out her mobile and tapped in the number of a diving business she had found in Yellow Pages; she hadn't dare store the number in her mobile, but it was stored in her memory.

"Lloyd Morrow?" she asked coldly as the call was answered. "This is Margie Wight. I think you should know that your wife is here."

Alex was sure that she recognised a famous Mozart piece, *Eine Kleine Natchtmusic*, somewhere beyond the jungle of voices and bass rhythms. Fixing on the melody and following it briefly by nodding along, she turned to the bedroom door.

"Shelby's music," Henry said, with an uneasy shrug. "It comes on by itself sometimes." He made a resigned but unhappy noise in his throat as he also turned to consider the door.

"I know you're going to think I'm crazy, Mr Wight, but could I see your baby?"

"Shelby?" he answered uncomfortably. "She's sleeping."

"Just a peak. I don't know; it would put my mind at rest…"

He chuckled. "I know what you're thinking. The same thing went through my mind."

She turned to him with an urgent expression. "What? What are you thinking?"

He hesitated, realising he had said something that would risk *Margie displeasure*. "Your baby's going be beautiful, my dear. Perfect, really. Don't be fooled by the way it was made."

Alex nodded slowly. "You too? The prayer ... the ... the...?"

"The sacrament. Margie calls it the sacrament." He shrugged unhappily. "We don't talk about it." He wanted to say *We don't really talk at all, anymore,* but put the compulsion aside.

"Please let me see your daughter, Mr Wight."

He moved from one foot to the other, not caring for her use of his name and wishing she would stop it, then glanced down the stairs. "Quickly then," he muttered and led her into the bedroom, straight to the cot. "There, you see? A perfect little person."

Alex agreed with a smile, noticing the cute birthmark just above the baby's mouth. Shortly she frowned, realising that something inside her, something wholly unnatural, almost inhuman, was rebelling. She hated this baby. Her natural maternal urge was to rip it out from under the blankets, take it by its neck and...

She gasped and turned away.

"Are you okay? Do you want to sit down?" Henry asked.

She composed herself. "Beautiful baby," she said. She was aware that the Mozart had increased in volume. "What's that?" she asked, indicating the alphabet abacus spinning violently at the far end of the bedroom. She had the oddest sensation that it was looking directly at her. Henry moved towards the door, beckoning her to leave.

"What *is* that?" she insisted, sure that she had seen it in her dreams.

"Shelby's toy," he muttered warily. "The abacus will help her when she's older, with her grammar and things." He looked away, having never looked at the abacus face on since that first encounter in this bedroom, when it had warned him what it was: a demon that would snap his brain in two if he dared look on it again. The malevolent block code still jangled in his memory, though he attempted to shut it out. The halo, dog and king … the x-ray and teeth… "Good job too," he continued, finding a hopeful smile. "I'm a duffer with that sort of stuff. Margie always wrote my correspondence; I always had too much grease on my hands."

Alex nodded slowly, becoming mesmerised by the spinning blocks. Two of them came to an abrupt stop.

"Shelby," Alex muttered, the strings of the music sharpening and channelling her understanding.

The two blocks were immediately followed by another; the slight quiver in this block as it was positioned betrayed the toy's excitement.

"Shelby when she's grown up," Alex muttered. Suddenly from within the music she was struck with the image of a willowy girl of about sixteen, with a beautiful heart-shaped face framed within a cascade of Titian curls. A brown birthmark complimented the rich, sensual lips. Alex momentarily tasted her stomach: she hated this girl so much the face made her physically sick.

The abacus was spinning again.

"Make it stop," she whispered fearfully.

"I can't," Henry answered, with a resigned voice. He turned further away.

Three blocks clunked angrily into place.

"Crossroads woman," Alex whispered, her mind lost in the swirl of the music. She was struggling towards the door.

That's me. I'm the woman at the crossroads.

The abacus collected up the three blocks and slammed a new one into place.

Alex frowned and shook her head. The abacus spun again, quickly and heavily. This time the exclamation mark turned for effect.

!

"Anchor," she said.

Anchor ... don't move ... don't move!

"What do you want of me?" she said in a small voice, coming to a stop. She still felt nauseous from the vision of the sixteen-year-old girl.

The abacus waited gleefully.

"What do you want of me?" she repeated, and the blocks spun once more. They spun for what seemed like an age before dropping into place like bombs, detonating with her voice.

"Crossroads woman…"

"Man … egg." She blinked, the music lifting her. "My male offspring … my *son*…?"

And now she was shown an image of Theo, age sixteen. Yet while Shelby Wight had been an image from a nightmare, Theo filled her with irrepressible yearning. She recognised his eyes, which were blue and watery, though his ears no longer stuck out. He was as handsome as Shelby was beautiful, with cropped blond hair and the strong, even features of an Olympian statue.

"Theo," she whispered, her hand going to her chest, to the pocket of her jacket. The face in the envelope, that lovely little boy – yes he *was* lovely, she now realised – with the chalk-white hair and sticking-out ears was … was her son…

She blinked in reflection, mesmerised by the abacus, all its blocks spinning once more.

Was it so wrong for Lloyd to be obsessed with the image of their son? Was Theo not, after all, perfect? And he was theirs. What was she doing here, trying to bring it all to an end?

Only two blocks were spinning now and she watching the abacus with the fascination of a roulette player who had gambled everything on the last roll of the wheel. They came to a stop with a sudden violence.

"Death," she whispered to the music, the gate and the halo having immediately translated in her mind. She shook her head and made for the door.

She stopped, the command now grafted into her subconscious, commanding her muscles. The abacus waited impatiently, its blocks ready and quivering, then spun once more.

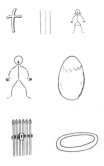

Another image presented by the spinning blocks made her as nauseous as she had been when she had seen the girl, but for a different reason. She saw her son, the sixteen-year-old Theo, with his eyes closed, his skin drained of colour.

It was the day of his funeral and he was dead...

As she staggered back it occurred to her that this was what

the abacus intended in communicating with her: to plant an image in her mind that would haunt her like a song with a forgotten melody or as a distant cloud that would gradually darken with its approach. The abacus was a fighter that steps into the ring and psychologically taunts his enemy.

My son's death...

She turned to see Margie at the door.

"You shouldn't be in here," Margie said, with an infuriated glance at her husband.

Henry raised his hands in a conciliatory fashion. "Margie, she just wanted to sneak a look at Shelby..."

The abacus went into a spiral of confusion at this interruption and Alex used the moment to brush past Margie. Henry followed, leaving the bedroom just in time before Margie closed the door. "Mrs Wight," Alex gasped, "we have to try and help each other. We can't be enemies: that's what they want, I'm sure of it." When Margie didn't answer, Alex considered the mobile in Margie's hand. "Have you rung someone?" she asked.

A thin smile of contempt appeared on Margie's face. She at last gave in to the urge to look the woman at the crossroads up and down in an aloof, critical fashion.

"I'm going," Alex announced uncomfortably.

"Stay here," Margie insisted, with a hand going firmly to Alex's shoulder. Alex found herself being pushed towards the French chair in the corner of the landing. "Someone's coming to pick up you up. You're not well." Margie turned to Henry, preparing to issue a series of instruction, but staggered back at a hard slap to her chin. Alex delivered her second blow as a fist, into the woman's left eye. Margie swooned backwards, into Henry's arms. In shocked disbelief the man laid his wife gently on the floor, where she immediately wrapped up into a ball, clutching at her face in horror. She made the pain appear worse than it was, rather than get up and receive more of the same treatment.

Alex retreated to the chair. Henry Wight was a large man and she would have no chance of escaping him.

"Your son *will* be born," Margie muttered from behind her hands. "There's nothing you can do that will change it." Her tone changed slightly, became introspective, as if her words were now only intended for her benefit; as if she had said them to herself before. "Life's one long tragedy, you know. We're born to death and disease, to loss and disappointment. Life gives us rules, and we do the best we can." Her tone hardened. "Accept the rules. Go back to your husband."

"You're wrong," Alex said. "Honeyman has stopped the deaths. The children all love each other: that's the secret to making all this end."

Margie looked up at her from between her fingers. Her face was red and swollen. "The Baptist is wrong. He couldn't *be* more wrong."

"What do you mean?" Alex whispered, with a wary glance at Henry; he was holding Margie's head, awaiting her instructions.

"Why do you think I hate you as much as do? I'll make sure Shelby hates you too; and that rat spawn you'll eject from between your legs."

"Okay, I'm going now," Alex suggested gently to Henry, raising her hands in a conciliatory manner. From his poised crouch he returned her gaze.

"You'll stay here," Margie snarled. "Your husband's coming and the temple will be grateful to me. Henry, get her into that chair."

Alex looked at Henry imploringly. He hesitated, then

mouthed the word *go!* She slowly backed down three steps of the stairs then turned and broke into a run. She was out of the front door, down the steps onto the marina, to the cries and screams of Margie Wight. The hostess no longer cared about her guests, those uncomfortable in their suits or otherwise, all of whom were quietly listening to the tantrum on the floor above.

As Alex returned to her waiting taxi the driver handed her his mobile: Honeyman had returned her call. When she called him back he explained he had been sleeping, sleeping more than he should have. His observations of the Sobarth house were exhausting him; he suspected that the temple was making it so. She recounted how she had escaped from her house, then her experience with the Wights, all to the occasional worried glance of the driver in his rear-view mirror.

"The woman on the marina said you were wrong about Frank and Gracie," Alex said, feeling uncomfortable now about calling Margie by her real name. The taxi came to a stop opposite the numerous car showrooms on Penarth Road, where she intended to buy the cheapest car on a forecourt and get out of the city.

"Wrong?" Honeyman murmured.

"About their love for each other solving their … their problem," she clarified, briefly meeting the eyes of the taxi driver in the rear-view mirror. With a quick smile she pressed a lot of cash into his hand and stepped out onto the long, windy stretch of road, the mobile still to her ear. She signalled to the driver that she'd be one minute. "She said you couldn't *be* more wrong." she whispered.

Honeyman didn't answer; she could hear his uneasy breath.

"Honeyman?"

"I think perhaps I should come back," he said, his voice rich with concern. "Franklyn Tyde is sixteen today," he added, attempting to make the observation sound coincidental.

Alex looked down the road, wondering where she should walk first. She realised she was trembling, traumatised by her experience in the Wight household.

"Yes, come back," she agreed. "Where shall I meet you?"

"I'm going to Swansea."

She could hear some mild commotion in the background; he was already starting to pack.

"The Mumbles?"

"The Mumbles, yes. I have to move quickly now: get yourself a mobile and stay in touch."

As he terminated the connection her hand went to her breast pocket. She handed the mobile back to the driver with a smile of thanks and realised she hadn't told Honeyman about the envelope and painting. She considered ringing him back, but the driver was making to leave and anyway Honeyman was clearly in a rush. It could wait, she reasoned, although something in the pit of her stomach inquired if she really wanted to tell him. Whether she wanted to tell anyone.

With a sigh she braced herself against the wind, experiencing a delicious shock of freedom in the cold moving air.

X X V

The father's tale

ONCE AGAIN, THE Tydes' front door was open.
"In here, in here," came an excited female voice
from the front room as Honeyman warily entered the house.
Mercedes Tyde was sharing the settee with an array of musical
instruments, which she was stroking affectionately. She didn't
look up. "Franklyn just played all of them, one after another,"
she declared proudly.

The curtains were drawn, the room lit starkly by a table lamp
with a powerful bulb. With a look that was a mix of anguish
and relief, Jerry Tyde turned the page of his newspaper. He
didn't know that damn spoilt white girl on the hill. He didn't
know her...

"Played them? For who?" Honeyman asked from the
doorway.

Mercedes now looked at the ceiling. "They said you'd
come. They were right, always right." She jubilantly shook the
violin she was holding halfway down its neck, chewing her lip
in her impulse to laugh. "They said we should let you in, so we
have, to see my boy. *My* boy."

Honeyman nodded with a confused smile. "So he's ... he's
well? He's safe?"

Jerry roughly turned his page.

"My boy's sixteen today, but the heart don't stop until the
night after," Mercedes clarified. "It's always in the night that

the heart stops. But yes, he's safe, the Trustees told me so." She stood up to the jangle of strings. "Franklyn!" she called in a voice so loud the room seemed to recoil.

Honeyman looked to the stairs and saw Franklyn standing at its turn. "The Trustees told you that?" Honeyman asked slowly. "They've *been* here?"

"Yeah, they've been," Franklyn said.

Honeyman's hesitated, a blind falling from his mind. In his concern and anxiety for the boy by the sea he hadn't even considered the possibility that girl on the hill might be in danger. The Trustees' favourite was unassailable; as strong and as safe as America. "We should go and help Gracie," he suggested cautiously to Franklyn.

"I can't help."

"He can't help, can't help," Mercedes confirmed.

Honeyman felt as if his heart stopped momentarily with the dawning realisation of incalculable error. "Franklyn, have you declared your love for Gracie, as she did for you? Declared it to your egg and portraits?"

"I can't do that," Franklyn replied.

Honeyman's expression darkened. "You can, and you must. I'm not leaving here until you do."

The silence was punctuated by a cautiously slow turn of the newspaper.

"Franklyn only loves his mother," Mercedes said eventually.

Franklyn's hand went to his chin; the picture created was so artistic and graceful it seemed as if his hand formed a plinth for his face. "She was always going to win the long race," he mused, to acknowledge the statement, but without sharing his thoughts. "I'm a sprinter. Suppose that's what the free running was always telling me. That and getting *her* out of my head."

"Franklyn, you *love* Gracie," Honeyman insisted.

"Yeah, I do," the boy replied with a shudder, feeling the cold stale air of the tour van.

But I love her, he had muttered to Sphinx.

Honeyman moved towards the stairs. "If you won't come willingly…"

Franklyn's eyes quickly misted over.

"N-no encore, NME."

That's enough, Baptist.

Honeyman gasped. He glanced at Mercedes, then at Jerry, wondering if they had also heard the booming, hollow words coming from their son's mouth. They seemed oblivious; Jerry was reading the paper, Mercedes having returned to examine the musical instruments. He recalled how The Dead Pharaohs had put them to sleep before.

"Please, Franklyn…" he pleaded.

"The H-haight-Ashbury is off the ch-charts."

The girl on the hill is lost…

"No!" Honeyman's large hands became fists as he advanced towards the stairs. He stopped on the second step: this time Franklyn didn't speak in code.

"I n-name you."

I name you…

"Don't," Honeyman whispered.

"T-tristyn H-honeyman."

Tristyn Honeyman…

Honeyman staggered back, his face contorted as if he were having a stroke.

It was the most terrible of names.

It was the name he would be given at his judgment: the name that defined his life. It was *his* name.

Tristyn Honeyman.

The name told him with a fluent and unassailable logic that existence was meaningless. Human beings and all their achievements and creations, together with everything that nature had made impossibly beautiful, the outline of a tree, the colour of a red sunset, the form of a woman, the inexplicable compulsion of laughter, all products of a random, disinterested evolution.

Honeyman retreated through the front door pursued by his logic. There was no God and there was no salvation; the Bible was a collection of fictional stories, devised by madmen, sponsored by ambitious politicians, perpetuated by the ignorant. The wonder he experienced when he was saved was merely a pleasant form of indigestion. The sights he had witnessed were merely delusions. There were no such things as temples or *prayers that are keys*; his obscenity in church wasn't a curse at all, but a product of his own depraved imagination: for he was a vulgar man; a vulgar, deluded man, hiding in his religion. And he was also a child murderer.

Back in his Land Rover, Honeyman sat back in panic. He concentrated, willing the tumour in his mind to shrink and disappear, until eventually he found the lost outposts of reason and faith.

With his eyes closed he murmured a prayer; it emerged as an obscenity but it helped nonetheless. When he opened his eyes his watch told him that several hours had passed since he had pulled up on this road.

"Gracie..." he whispered urgently, putting his vehicle into gear.

★

The tour van had shown Franklyn his punishment, the doom that would be his eternity, and it had showed it because there was still hope.

Rivers had collected his bass guitar from under his seat, waited for Franklyn to collect his semi-acoustic guitar, then they played together. The music told him that something had happened, something unexpected that had derailed the machinery of the temple. A *character* had been lost: a guardian that had been buried was animated and a window of opportunity had opened.

What window? he strummed back.

The *character* needed to be held by the faithful parent if the temple's locks were to remain in place, the bass explained. A guardian had broken silence, so they could too. He should make contact with the Baptist, using him to widen the breach in the temple's defences, the mischief caused by the loss of the *character*. Then, when the Baptist was blind to everything but his need to save him, they would talk to him.

Is that all? Franklyn replied, picking with his plectrum.

No: the hardest part was something they couldn't help him with. They also needed the Haight-Ashbury, the girl on the hill. She had to come to *him*. And when she did, he had to say her name. He had to *touch* her. The bond between them was stronger than she released: when her guard dropped, she would fall.

How? She won't speak to me…

Rivers sound a final chord, two bass strings pulled in grim harmony.

A *character* has been lost. Treachery is on the wind. Anything is possible now.

Franklyn didn't understand what a *character* was, and The Dead Pharaohs wouldn't tell him, but that morning on the pier he heard the howl coming from that wooden throat under the earth. He called back to it and it carried his lament to the girl on the hill; she resisted his entreaties but it found her friend, Jake Cassidy. Rivers had been right: with the voice on the air, anything *was* possible. The locks of the temple had been picked.

When you speak to the Baptist, will you tell him how to save us both? Franklyn had asked.

It was Sphinx who answered.

Only one n–number one s–slot.

But I love her, Franklyn muttered.

The puppet motioned to the stone that entombed them, set like concrete against the windows of the van; behind him, the drummer once more brought the nail to his ear. Sphinx didn't need to ask the question:

Do you love the girl on the hill … more than you *fear this?*

★

Miles Barrett-Danes had been standing in the large bay window of the international room since the early hours of the morning, watching the road. It was a winding incline but from the right position, standing on his Turkish trunk, he could spot the gold limousine when it was just joining the road, about five minutes away.

He always waited here when the Trustees were coming, the international room immaculate, barred to his wife and the home help, the carefully selected bottle of wine uncorked and breathing. He had often wondered how he would feel today, on this, the last day: the day of the boy by the sea's sixteenth birthday.

It wasn't jubilation, as he had expected. The game was

won, the Trustees had virtually told them so on their last visit, but he wanted it to be over. To be sure. To be safe.

It was early evening, the streetlights just flicking on, when he saw the limousine snaking its way up the road. Gracie was still locking herself in her room, but it didn't matter. The old Trustee had explained a long time ago that the final interview would be with the faithful parent only.

This will be your time, to grieve or to rejoice, the old man with the rather obvious red wig had said. *The instructions will be for your ears alone.*

Miles nodded grimly as he recalled the scene, the moment his blood turned to ice as he realised that it was too late to go back, that he had no alternative but to dedicate his live to saving his little girl.

"Well here we are then," he muttered to himself. As always he waited at the bay window until the vehicle dipped out of sight then walked briskly to the front door, stepping out onto the porch with a broad smile just in time to catch the vehicle's approach on the gravel drive.

The Trustees' faces couldn't be read as they entered the house but they carried uncharacteristic expressions of weariness. Miles poured the wine, a very old Rioja, and handed each of them a half-filled glass. His breath stopped in his throat as he watched them both drink appreciatively. They held out their glasses, which he refilled eagerly but in confusion.

"Today we can drink with you," the doctor explained, reading the question in his head. "It's fitting."

Roman lifting his glass in a manner of both appreciation and farewell.

"We've already visited the family by the sea," the doctor added quietly to her glass.

Miles smiled, his mind rapidly sorting this new information into a manner that was favourable. They were drinking with him because this was obviously a celebration. There must be a reason why they visited the sea first: the loser would have to be told first. Now they were here, to give Gracie her salvation…

"We have only bad news, Miles," Dr Mays remarked sadly.

Miles hesitated, then broke out in a toothy smile to acknowledge the joke.

"In the end, the boy by the sea proved more resourceful."

Miles awkwardly shifted his stance, his left leg having gone numb with shock. He retained his smile. "Lauren, what are you *talking* about? My girl has performed brilliantly."

Dr Mays finished her wine and returned the glass to the coffee table. "But she failed in love," she said, looking forlornly at the empty glass. Roman placed his glass next to hers with an exaggerated face of sympathy.

Miles' guard dropped momentarily, allowing the visitors to glimpse his animal desperation. "Love?" he asked, gathering up his smile again, his heart pounding. "What's *love* got to do with anything? She's done everything you asked, she's won prizes for…"

"Miles, did you never understand our purpose in this? Yes, we prize accomplishment and duty, but only as far as it focuses the child's mind away from the other child. The children love each other with a passion, and that obstacle, that *scourge,* is their true challenge. They have all been given beauty, and they have been given talent; their only duty is not to squander it. In this my Lady of the Manor has failed, just as others have failed before her."

"Gracie doesn't love the boy by the sea…" Miles protested in a choking voice.

"But she does, and she's declared it: declared it in a way that makes it impossible for her guardian to protect her."

Roman pointed to the sea and tapped his head thoughtfully.

"Yes indeed," the doctor agreed. "He's been clever." She cast a glance at the bay window as she imagined the arrival of the hateful green Land Rover driven by the Baptist, now horror-struck. "In fact," she said to herself, "his guardian broke a few rules, for reasons I won't explain here. I don't know what the consequence of that will be." She returned to Miles and cleared her thoughts. "But that isn't a matter which concerns you. Miles, you need to be aware that your role as faithful parent doesn't end here."

Miles slumped into a chair.

"No indeed," she continued gently. "Your daughter will need you now. In fact, she will need you more than ever…"

Gracie's door surrendered to the third heavy assault from her father's shoulder. Sitting on the end of the bed, she looked on without surprise or alarm as the door fell away.

He entered in a rage of grief: words lost to him. His eyes switched to the doll's house; he saw that the wall doors were open and he approached it with a deep groan of anger and surprise. In the limited time available to him before he was forced to look away, his anger having made him reckless, he saw Gracie's figurine in *the gallery*, her head bowed in anguish, and his own figurine a little distance away, both hands on his head in despair. The rest of the house was empty, cast in brown shadows. The chandelier had only the faintest twinge of light in its tiny crystals; what appeared to be mud was smeared on part of the walls.

"It's dying," Gracie murmured.

Inside the roof, cowering in one of the attic's corners, he detected the red glow. It was growing steadily fainter.

"By tonight the light will be out completely," she said. "There's just the two of us now, Daddy…"

Her father swung around and grabbed her wrist; he pulled her to her feet, then out of the room. She followed with neither enthusiasm nor resistance. Her mother came out of the kitchen, her eyes wide with alarm.

"Leave us alone!" Miles growled before she could speak.

"Miles, what's wrong? What did they say?"

"Shut up! Shut up!"

He pulled Gracie into the international room and locked the door. He jammed a heavy French writing bureau and an African hide chest against the door, the door handle being shaken by his wife. Then he hurried across the long room to the bay window and pulled the curtains. Standing in the bay once more he found his will and determination; he managed a smile as he composed himself and turned, the sound of his wife's palms on the door panels no more than the irritating patter of rain on a stormy night.

"This is *our* room," he declared to his daughter. "No one … *no one* gets in."

Gracie had sat down calmly on a sofa. She cast an occasional glance at the door.

"I built this room for you, Gracie. This is where your future is, with me." Miles began to pace. "You know, I saw to it that there's something here from every part of the world. I did that because I know it's your destiny to travel the world. Not only to travel it, but to hold it: hold it in your hands. D'you understand, Gracie?"

"Yes, Daddy," Gracie answered dutifully. A blink of her eyes briefly revealed some fatigue, which she camouflaged with a big smile.

"No one can touch you in here," he said, his heart lifting as he saw her brighten. "It's our world, Gracie. *Ours.*" He continued pacing. "You're not tired, are you?"

She shook her head, a twist of fear sending a chill down her spine.

"You mustn't sleep," he said urgently. He stopped to consider a coffee table where a tray held a kettle, a cafetiére and a large mosaic jar. "I've got the strongest Javan coffee on the planet. It'll keep you awake for days." He took a steadying breath. "And I'm going to tell you stories."

"Yes, tell me some stories, Daddy. I always loved your stories."

In her imagination she felt the first cloudy wave of sleep. It was warm and comforting, blown with a hint of sandalwood. The odd wood smell took her somewhere else, to a dark office, and she returned only with a forceful blink of her eyes.

"Gracie?" her father asked.

"I'm fine, Daddy." In spite of her mother's persistent banging and protestations she felt as if it were very quiet, that she was wrapped in the warmest of duvets.

"Stories from all over the world," he continued. "One from every country, from every culture, every nation in the world. This room is your future. D'you understand, Gracie? Your *future.*"

A dense cloud of sleep washed through the wall of her waking mind; she suppressed the urge to yawn.

"I'll have some coffee, Daddy," she suggested.

"Yes, yes," he muttered, switching on the kettle then tapping his foot impatiently as the expensive machine boiled rapidly. He had ten other full kettles of water, and ten more jars of coffee, secreted away for just such an emergency.

"I love you Daddy," she said, the words coming out as *I lud you Addy* because of a numb sensation creeping up her tongue.

"None of that," he murmured, his eyes ferocious with concentration. "We're going to keep you awake."

His hands were steady with resolve as he quickly filled the cafetiére, leaving the coffee the shortest possible time before pressing down the plunger. He poured Gracie her first cup of the evening, waited until she had taken her first sip, then started telling his stories. He began with their recent trip to Rome, listing all the places they had seen together. Then he moved on to some of his more memorable business trips, each of which through fact or fiction threw up an interesting local character. A drunken Mexican taxi driver who didn't have words in any language for *left* or *stop*. An Australian shark fisherman with a four-foot scar and a penchant for lucky amulets. A French onion seller with a lisp; a Canadian Mountie whose horse went crazy at the sight of carrots; a Greek surgeon who chain-smoked during his operations.

She managed a smile as she pictured each of these characters in her imagination.

An eccentric African chief, a vocally talented Indian monk, an alien-abducted Scot; a Spaniard, a Chinaman, an Afghan and a Russian. Gradually the protestations of his wife became fainter, then stopped altogether as she slumped into an unhappy vigil on the floor outside. Before long, his wife slept, unaccountably sleepy as her face felt the carpet. And

Miles slept too, but never letting up with his task, still telling his stories in his dreams.

Eventually he ran out of business trips, and went on to mythological folk tales from around the world. Shortly he found frightening stories locked in dark memories, and as he slept he muttered the tale of the Caribbean vampire that shed its skin when it searched for its prey, then of the Phoenician god that required child sacrifice. The altar of the pagan god was heated, the baby placed in one of the altar's compartments...

He woke with a start in the middle of the night, instinctively rising from his chair, his knee knocking over the half-empty cafetiére of cold coffee. He put his hand to the cheek of his daughter, her head gently positioned on a cushion. She had a peaceful, almost playful expression.

Her cheek was cold, and she was dead.

XXVI

The book of sacrifice

THE LAND ROVER sat awkwardly on the rise opposite the Barrett-Danes house, the vehicle a few feet away from the edge that would take it plummeting down into a valley of trees. The front wheels were twisted to their full extremes in a skid of mud, the signature of a sudden turn that was part of an urgent braking manoeuvre.

Alex tapped several times on the passenger window before Honeyman opened the door.

"I know what's happened," she said immediately. "Neighbours saw the funeral directors taking her away this morning." She got into the vehicle with a sigh. "Poor little thing. Her school's closed. They say her father's sedated to the nines."

Honeyman was gazing at the Barrett-Danes house with a look of dumb exhaustion.

"Are you alright?" she asked cautiously.

"It's funny, but I can feel her," he said at length in a wistful voice. "It's is as if she isn't gone at all."

Alex nodded, choosing her words carefully. "That's good. Your faith, after all…"

He shook his head. "No, no, it's not that. I can actually *feel* her, you see. Feel her as if she were sitting in here with us." He closed his eyes; they were moist and they each pressed out a tear, the first tears he had given to the world since the death of his wife, five years before. Alex tapped his forearm with concern.

He grunted to acknowledge the gesture and at the same time indicate it was unnecessary. "I can't talk a great deal," he admitted. He took his hands from the steering wheel, unlocking his fingers as if they had been soldered together, and opened his mouth in pain as he sat back. "The abacus predicted I'd become a child murderer," he murmured, calling on all his reserves of strength to maintain his composure. "Franklyn's guardian tricked me, you see. The guardians can't lie, but I heard what I wanted to hear. Yes, what I wanted to hear. And the temple blinded me to the danger to Gracie: perhaps with the abacus' prediction; or perhaps Franklyn achieved it himself. He's very charismatic. You've met him, so you understand, don't you?"

She shrugged with a degree of scepticism, not caring for this criticism of her lovely Frank.

"The guardian only told me what I needed to do to save Franklyn," Honeyman murmured. "I was so desperate to save him, you see. I would have done anything."

"But you *did* save him. *He'd* be dead now if it wasn't for you."

Honeyman didn't reply.

"That doesn't help, does it?" she said sadly.

He sat in silent reflection for a few moments. Shortly he said, "Now, tell me everything."

Alex told him nearly everything, leaving out only the details of the sexual atrocity with her husband and any reference to the envelope she had found in his shed. When she had finished, Honeyman collected the scrapbook and his lever arch files from the back seat, with a shudder from his screaming joints, and handed them to her. His gaze switched forlornly between the house and the oak tree opposite as she studied his photographs and articles. "Uncovering the history is easy," he said when she had finished, "but I shouldn't have interfered: the coven allowed me to play God and Gracie's death is my punishment." He glumly massaged an elbow. "Another wound the coven has given me. The worst possible wound."

Alex was shaking her head in disagreement. "But you *have* to interfere. How else will you bring all this to an end? There'll be more children who need you…"

"I'm merely an observer, I can't bring anything to an end. Only those chosen by the temple, those poor souls drawn into its orbit, can do that."

"Do it how?"

At last he pulled his attention away from the house and considered his knees. "The children's love for each other isn't a danger to the temple, as the guardian made me believe. In fact it rejoices in that bond, for it creates nothing but pain, separation and regret. No, we must look to the thing that the temple *fears*." He nodded to himself. "The *imagined child*."

Alex frowned. "Franklyn mentioned something about that…"

"Yes, it's a painting of a three-year-old. A portrait, painted in the style of Zehngraf. Zehngraf painted the original miniatures in the Fabergé eggs, you see." His voice was still muted, his expression downcast. "The temple protects it, first in the envelope, then in the egg following baptism, but in between … it's vulnerable."

"What do you mean by *vulnerable*?"

"It can be destroyed. Everything spawned by the temple is indestructible, because it comes from Hell, but the clue was always in the temple's name: Precious Cargo. Alex, it's not the unborn baby but the *imagined child,* the painting itself, that's the precious cargo."

She had invited the use of her first name in their taxi conversation; she now considered how she had concealed during that conversation the thing she was hiding in her jacket. "No, you're wrong," she said, in spite of herself.

He turned to her in inquiry.

"The painting of the three-year-old is indestructible too," she declared. She hesitated, then reluctantly produced the envelope.

"You have the envelope? Why didn't you say?"

"My husband was hiding it," she answered, fudging the question. She tried to tear a corner of the envelope and her face went red with the attempt. "Must be made of metal or something." She removed and unfolded the painting. "Anyway, I tried to rip the painting when I took it from the shed. It won't rip either. Must be made of the same stuff." She looked at the painting with loving eyes, unaware of time passing.

"Alex!"

She snapped out of her trance. Honeyman was looking with puzzled surprise at the painting. "Try again," he suggested.

"Why?" she asked uncomfortably. "I told you…"

"You also told me the abacus showed you your son."

"So?"

"You've seen your son, Alex, and you're protecting the *imagined child.* Don't you see? You've effectively taken over your husband's role. That makes you … it makes you *faithful.*"

She shook her head in bemusement. "These things aren't indestructible, they're just … well, they're specially coated or something. Some sort of industrial resin. I don't know."

"Just try to rip it," he repeated.

"Why?" There was a trace of anger in her voice.

"If you believe, as your husband does, that the painting is the promise of your son, then you won't be able to do it."

"I don't believe anything of the sort!" she protested.

He grunted his disagreement. "The temple has a hold over you now, Alex. Why else do you think the abacus showed you your son? The temple is scared, you see: it knows you broke free of its grip. It also knows you're resourceful, while your husband is weak. Perhaps in its survival instinct it feels safer making *you* the faithful parent." He scowled grimly. "Perhaps you'll be Precious Cargo's first *single* parent."

At this challenge she prepared herself to apply the necessary pressure to rip the painting in two. Her breath quickened as her son stared back at her imploringly.

Or perhaps she would rip just a corner, she decided: yes, a small, harmless corner. She eased the pressure being applied by her finger and made the smallest attempt at a tear.

Somewhere in her imagination she heard a child's scream. The top right-hand corner of the paper was ripped: it was small and barely noticeable, but it was there. She quickly folded the piece of paper, stuffed it back into the envelope, and returned it to her inside pocket. She sat back in confusion and distress.

"The *imagined child* can be destroyed," Honeyman explained slowly. "It can be destroyed because it is the one part of this whole ghastly parody of life that the temple is unable to create. A perfect human being, that is. The temple can't create a child any more than a monkey dressed in collar and tails can direct an orchestra. So as the parent imagines the child, the parent ... and only the parent ... can also destroy it."

"But why is this … this *imagined child* three years old? What's so important about being three?"

"Because it mirrors the *character*. The *character* imagines the baptism gift and that takes three years; I don't know why, but that's how long it takes. And I don't know what the *character* actually is, other than it's some sort of gate into this world for the guardian. But I do know that the temple takes great trouble to keep the baptism gift and the *character* apart. And it's the faithful parent who is charged with its safe keeping."

She remembered the giraffe key ring in her hand. "The key ring brought the giraffe to life." Her face darkened with the memory and she looked at Honeyman, who was considering her with a sudden intensity.

"So you said," he murmured, a thought occurring. "So you said…"

"For a short while," she clarified uncomfortably. She had been reluctant to fully recount her experience in the ground. "Just a few minutes. And it was different after that. Happier, perhaps. I don't know."

He turned to the Barrett-Danes house.

"Do you have an idea?" she asked.

He grunted. "Possibly, but I'm going to need your help." His hand went to his door handle but he paused when he saw she wasn't moving.

"Alex?"

She looked away. "I'll do what I can for the others," she murmured, "God knows I will. But not at any risk to my son. To Theo." She shook her head. "I know this sounds stupid, but it's as if he's already been born. Born inside my head." Her smile was a mix of pleasure and anguish. "You know, I used to have this image of a kitchen table. It was made of oak, big and strong, built to last. It's a silly thing. My children were there but I couldn't see them. I couldn't see them because I never really believed they were mine." She paused. "But I believe Theo will be born. No, I don't just believe it ... I *know* it, just like I know what he'll look like, and how much I'll love him." She gave a weary smile. "Does all this sound ridiculous?"

"No, not at all..." Honeyman said, glancing thoughtfully at the house and wondering at the untapped dimensions of parental instinct. Could it come to their rescue now? "Not ridiculous at all," he repeated, opening the door.

A heavily sedated Miles Barrett-Danes opened the front door. It took a little while for him to recognise the large man with too much hair; when he did, he had the vague notion that he had cause to be angry with him. He also recognised the pale-skinned woman, but couldn't quite place her.

"Don't you remember me?" the woman asked. "I'm Alex Morrow. I came to your house with my husband. On Precious Cargo business."

He had a blank expression. "If you're looking for my wife ... she's gone out..." he droned.

"We need to speak to *you*, Mr Barrett-Danes," Honeyman said. "You can help us to help your daughter."

"My wife's gone to stay with her sister. They always hated me..."

"Your daughter has a toy, Mr Barrett-Danes," Honeyman persisted, "Precious Cargo's baptism gift. We need to see it."

Miles chuckled darkly. "It's all slime and shit," he slurred with a grain of satisfaction. "Slime and shit. No use to anyone. Trustees said they'd be taking it away after the funeral."

"The Trustees will bury it," Honeyman said slowly. "They'll bury it next to your daughter, so that they suffer together. So that they serve out their punishment together."

Miles rested his weight on the doorframe, his eyes turning in an attempt to focus. "Trustees said I have to cooperate. That she'll be safe if I cooperate … safe…"

Alex shook her head. "They lie."

"They never lie," he replied gloomily.

"Perhaps not," Honeyman conceded, "but they deceive you nonetheless. This lady has seen a girl just like your daughter, and she's not at peace, Mr Barrett-Danes. Quite the opposite…"

Miles blinked painfully but didn't reply.

"You have something," Honeyman said carefully, "something that might help us break their hold over your daughter. You know the thing I'm speaking of: it's linked to the baptism gift but it's yours."

Miles slowly made to shut the door, a faint note of alarm ringing through the sedation.

"I know you loved your little girl," Alex said quickly. "Loved her more than anything in the world." She waited until he made a sort of wary eye contact. "I also know how strong you are," she added thoughtfully. "I understand how powerful the brainwashing can be, really I do, but you can fight it. Fight it for Gracie's sake."

"But they told me…" he began.

"What? What did they tell you?" she asked.

He stretched out his face in the manner of an agonised yawn. "That the guardian would watch over her. So long as I remained faithful, and kept the crayon house safe. The drawing was my new mission, for Gracie." His expression became more distorted. "I want her to be safe. I don't want her to be alone."

"Your daughter will be in torment," Alex said. "I've seen it. I've *seen* it!"

Miles' head drooped. The instructions issued by Dr Mays yesterday had found fertile ground after sixteen years of service, but his deepest parental instincts had him picturing his daughter trapped in the earth with the decaying doll's house. His face contorted again in the ghastly parody of a yawn, as the drugs stopped him from screaming. Alex's hand went to his arm but he shrugged her off. He fumbled in his pocket and brought out a crumpled piece of paper. It was a crayon drawing of a house.

Honeyman sighed with relief. "Did Gracie show anyone how the doll's house worked? Alex has explained that we can ask the guardian anything, but we'll have so little time, you see. Minutes perhaps. Any information will be invaluable."

With one of the prison bars of his mind broken, Miles' tone became more assertive. "I saw the doll's house open sometimes, and I knew it helped her with people … helped her understand people. But I never looked at it and she didn't explain it to me."

"Will you show us?" Honeyman asked.

Miles weakly shook his head. The thought of watching the doll's house at work was as outrageously inappropriate as spying on his daughter naked. She would have had the same compunctions over examining his crayon drawing: the two things were linked but meant to be kept apart; this imperative had found its way into their psyches.

"Anyone else then?" Honeyman pressed.

Miles turned his drawing around in his hands with the

occasional smile as it triggered old memories. The two visitors waited patiently for him to work through the sedation.

"There's this boy she liked, from school," he said at length.

★

Honeyman had his hand supportively on Jake's shoulder as the young man replayed their last meeting. "She was trying to protect you, I think," Honeyman remarked. "Perhaps she cared for you more than you believe."

With a wink of encouragement he asked Jake if he would favour them with a sketch diagram of the doll's house, then got up and walked mournfully to the kitchen window, to observe the gazebo where Miles was hiding. The man had staggered out when Jake had started to describe the doll's house, unable to listen.

"What are you hoping to find?" Alex quietly asked Honeyman, as Jake finished his sketch.

Honeyman came back to the kitchen table and tapped the sketch with his finger. "You said the guardian offered to answer any of your questions in that brief moment when its *character* was returned. Perhaps we can reactivate the doll's house too." He grumbled thoughtfully. "Jemmy and Franklyn's guardians broke silence; why shouldn't Gracie's guardian break silence too?"

A pungent soup of mud and decomposition wafted from the remains of the doll's house. The chandelier was dead and a watery film of darkness had seeped like condensation into the walls and floors, apart from in *the library*, where a dust that resembled a grey fungus had consumed the books. There was a creaking air of imminent collapse in the walls; the house was empty.

"It was different before," Jake muttered fearfully. "And there were these china figures."

Honeyman nodded, quickly examining the egg in the alcove. Its lid was open and it was completely empty. It might have been an ordinary reproduction, except that it wouldn't scratch when he made a quick test to determine whether it was perishable.

He turned his attention to the doll's house, leaning forward with his arms stretched out behind him. An attempt to read the names of the books failed because they were obscured by the grey fungus; instead, he explored the trap door of *the servants' quarters*. "Is that where Gracie found the figurines?" he asked Jake.

"Yeah, she put her hand in and pulled them out."

The trap door was open and Honeyman brought an eye close to the hole. He saw only darkness, but whatever lay beyond was rank with slime. He blinked, believing he heard the distant, discordant whistle of countless voices, then turned to Alex with an apologetic expression.

"Your hands are too big, aren't they?" she muttered. She reached for the hole but snatched her hand back without making contact. The reflex wasn't her own.

"No, wait." Honeyman hastily produced Miles' crayon drawing and he approached the house cautiously, as if it were a fevered animal he intended to stroke and calm. It accepted his touch as he pressed out the drawing on *the gallery* floor, the drawing taking the form of the marble flagstones, the mud washing away as if the house had a supercharged drainage system. The crayon lines fused with the floor and disappeared. A strong red glow now appeared in *the roof attic* and the house was ablaze with light as the chandelier surged with energy.

"We bring you your *character*," he announced formally

to the doll's house, "and request information in return. Tell us how to destroy Temple One Thirteen, which is called Precious Cargo." The chandelier dimmed resentfully for a few moments, then blazed once more. He turned to Alex and nodded quickly. She stuffed her hand down the hole and produced a figurine of a young woman with red hair pinned back. Her hands were linked behind her back, her expression showing resigned despair.

"It's Gracie," Alex whispered. "What shall I do with it?"

"Put it in the house," he suggested.

"Where?"

"Anywhere. See where it's comfortable."

She first offered the figurine to *the library*, but shook her head. Shortly, Gracie ended up directly under the chandelier.

"It's Gracie's house," Honeyman said, considering the figurine and hardening his heart to contain his grief. "I think it had to show us Gracie. There must be another figurine."

Alex's hand was in *the servants' quarters* once more. It was a surreal experience: her hand seemed detached, as if it was travelling through space, the figurines floating pieces of debris finding her probing fingers against all laws of probability. This time the figurine she collected was of a boy about three years old with chalk-white hair and sticking-out ears. She gasped as she saw it, almost dropping it.

"Alex, what's wrong?"

To avoid having to answer the question, with her free hand she immediately reached back into *the servants' quarters*. She shook her head, her hand emerging empty.

"Place the figurine," Honeyman suggested gently.

Theo's figurine settled in *the library*. Honeyman slid it slowly across the floor as Jake had described; a book, free of the grey fungus, popped out. It was *A Tale of Two Cities*.

Honeyman stared at the book in silence.

"Honeyman?" she whispered.

"I don't … don't understand…" he admitted miserably. "This was Gracie's house. Only she knew how to read it." He shook his head with resignation. "I was foolish to think otherwise. The guardian was part of Gracie's psyche: things that would be obvious to her will be incomprehensible to us."

He stepped away and the chandelier flashed angrily, the light momentarily so intense that Gracie's figurine was clothed in radiant white. Honeyman frowned thoughtfully, then picked up Gracie's figurine. He clasped it tightly inside his large hand.

"*A Tale of Two Cities*," he muttered, the figurine a pulse of understanding energising his mind. "The book of sacrifice: a noble sacrifice of the heart's desire."

He discreetly examined Theo's figurine. On its base, carved thickly and deeply, he saw the number 113, but he kept the discovery to himself. "Why show Theo at age three?" he murmured. He stepped back, startled, for Theo's figurine chose that moment to crumble into dust. "The *imagined child* has to be destroyed," he muttered at this exhibition of destruction. "That's what the doll's house is telling us." He turned cautiously to Alex. "That *was* Theo, wasn't it?"

She was looking at his hand in distress: the dust was weightless and dissolving in the air. It was already gone. "But I can't…"

"I know," he said, beckoning to her to reach once more through the trap door. The figurine she produced was of a man in late middle age with a high forehead and a hook nose. "I recognise that face," she said, turning the figurine in her hand. "The scrapbook…?"

"It's Charles Sobarth," Honeyman confirmed. He examined the figurine and saw that it was holding a Fabergé pelican egg. Again, on its base was carved the number 113. This time he shared the discovery.

"What does the number mean?" she asked.

"It's the number of the temple. It means it belongs to the temple: that the temple has ... *rights* over it."

Alex put the Sobarth figurine in *the library* and slid it across the floor. *The Murder of Roger Ackroyd* popped out.

"Agatha Christie?" she asked.

"Her masterpiece," Honeyman clarified, his hand tightening around Gracie's figurine as he reached for understanding. "The book of cheats; of grand deception." He frowned. "Alex, place the figurine in the house. See where it settles."

It settled in *the room with no windows*.

"What does it mean?" she asked.

"That room's about warning and danger," Jake reminded them.

"Thank you, Jake," Honeyman muttered. "Charles Sobarth, with his Fabergé egg: the house is telling us to look at the egg. Not any egg, you see, but the Sobarth egg. The original." He hesitated. "The one in the temple."

And with that the Sobarth figurine dissolved. The lights in the doll's house flicked out, the rooms retreating into darkness, but the mud and fungus didn't return; the house now resembled some old toy that hadn't been particularly well cared for. Bemused, Honeyman tried to touch it, but snatched his hand back.

"So we're going to the clinic?" Alex said. "To the house in Brecon?" Honeyman nodded cautiously. "What's the matter?" she asked.

"That will be a trespass, Alex."

"What do you mean?"

He chose not to answer, instead summoning the Sobarth house in his mind's eye. Armed with the descriptions Alex had given him he went inside, up the stairs and into the sandalwood office, where he touched the Egyptian bureau; examined the Sobarth family pictures. Even in his imagination he experienced the house's outrage.

He had trespassed on temple premises before: the first time he had been cursed, the second time nearly buried alive, his arms and legs broken.

"Honeyman?"

His eyes remarked on an odd development as he registered what he was holding in his right hand. It rallied his courage and he made a protective fist. "Yes, Brecon," he said. "We have to visit Precious Cargo, and find whatever's waiting for us."

XXVII

The book of cheats

THE FRONT DOOR of the Sobarth house was fitted with two heavy bolts. While strong in their day they were now loose with fatigue; neither maintenance nor repair had been carried out since Charles Sobarth gifted his house to the concerned eugenicists who had coached him in the rearing of his children.

In prison, awaiting the rope, they arranged the transfer of the property with a promise to carry on his work once his son was dead: the son who would always mourn the loss of his sister, but would never return to Britain because his father had breathed its air.

Aside from a few modern installations to create the rudimentary appearance of a working office, the only innovation of the eugenic charity was a pit that had been dug under the stairs. The Sobarth family pictures were designed to one day house the souls of its serving Trustees, while the pit would hold its trespassers in the countless years to come. The coven's temples were created with the future in mind, as with the pyramids built with an organised, industrious fervour that had no reference to worldly considerations.

Yet sometimes they foundered early. Temple 113 was designed to be the most enduring temple of all because the Father's servants were part of its apparatus, but careful checks were needed to keep those servants in place. The loss of a *character* was the moment of distraction in the lion tamer's eyes; the shortness of breath in the snake charmer's throat.

As the door was forced the temple was unable to react, its defences collapsing.

Alex moved purposefully to the ornamental plinth, taking careful hold of the clinic's egg in both hands. The plinth was tall and she looked down on it without having to stoop.

She had been silent on the drive to Brecon, mentally rehearsing this series of movements. The lid flipped up and she threw Honeyman an inviting glance, but he remained at a respectful distance.

"The temple egg is for the parents only," he murmured.

"Why?"

"This is the original Sobarth egg: it contains the remains of Alice Sobarth and records the eugenic crime. The *parental* crime. I suspect even the Trustees aren't allowed access to it." He grumbled his private distress at having allowed himself to believe that the children, as opposed to the parents, would have the means of destruction before them. "The egg would always be available to the parents if they simply thought to look."

Alex nodded slowly, recalling how Dr Mays had drawn her attention to the egg as she was leaving.

Your son's name … is written here…

"But why can only the parents look inside?" she repeated.

"Because if Gracie's doll's house is correct the egg contains something that will allow you to reject your child." Alex stiffened in alarm. "To make the heart's sacrifice," he clarified sadly. "I'm sorry Alex, but that's what the doll's house was telling us, when Theo's figurine crumbled."

"I won't do anything to hurt Theo," she said, her tone cold.

"Look inside," he suggested.

With a suspicious glance at the minister she brought her face closer to the egg. Inside, it was bigger than it should have been, the revolving belt showing every crease of the skin in the oil portraits within its glass compartments. The faces were passing quickly across her vision as the belt stretched and flexed, presenting men and women, boys and girls, the newly born and people at the limits of old age.

From Honeyman's research she recognised Carl Tyrone, the belt snapping into a rigid position as if her gaze had pushed a button of command. The compartment produced the faces of his life and she shuddered as she saw him as a middle-aged man, his gaunt beauty tarred with a merciless expression, the promise of his future character.

"Is Jemmy here?" she asked.

"No," Honeyman replied, his right hand in a fist. "She was once, of course, but you'll find no trace of Jemmy Matthews now. For Precious Cargo, she no longer exists. She *never* existed."

Alex gasped as she saw Theo's three-year-old face, identical to the face in her jacket, and the belt snapped into a rigid position in response to her subconscious wishes and fears. Within the same compartment, Theo's image dissolved into a girl of the same age. She had a brown birthmark above her mouth.

"They share the same space," Honeyman explained, unsure how he knew what Alex was seeing. His fist tightened. "They'll continue to share it until they reach sixteen, like twins in the womb."

Alex put a hand to her mouth as she saw her son as

an older child, as a young teenager, then as the handsome sixteen-year-old she had glimpsed through the abacus.

"Theo…" she whispered.

The compartment glistened at the longing in her voice, pausing awhile then gleefully providing her with a snapshot of Shelby Wight's life. Shortly Alex frowned, for there were far more pictures of Shelby than there were of Theo. She saw Shelby as a radiant young woman, then, still striking, advancing to middle age and, finally, lined and exhausted in old age. Again, there was a heartlessness in the later portraits, from around the early thirties onward; a tremor of acquired evil. When the face was very old the portraits reverted to Shelby as a baby and once more charted the advance of her life. The glass compartment seemed to have forgotten Theo, save for the occasional glimpse of him through the parade of Shelby's life, never older than sixteen and very much an afterthought, only there to flag moments of importance in Shelby's life.

"What was that book again?" Alex murmured. "The Agatha Christie one. What did it mean?"

"I don't know what it means, Alex, but Gracie told me it was the book of cheats: the grand deception. It was triggered by Sobarth's egg."

With a look of disgust, Alex took her hands from the egg and pulled the Precious Cargo envelope out of her jacket. She removed the painting then discarded the envelope, letting it drift to the floor. The egg snapped shut with fury and offence.

"Give it to me, Allie."

She turned to see Lloyd at the door, his hand outstretched. The Trustees were behind him with blank faces.

"You have to destroy it, Alex," Honeyman said gently, coming to her side.

Alex blinked, attempting to order her thoughts. "And if I destroy it... Does all this end? Will that poor girl in Talybont be released from her suffering? Will Theo be safe?"

A short laugh echoed across the reception. "On that note, Baptist," Dr Mays said, "Roman and I will leave you with the parents. We trust you well enough to tell this poor deluded woman the truth: that if she rips that painting, she loses her child."

"You're leaving?" Honeyman murmured suspiciously, a hand going protectively to his elbow joint.

The doctor tapped her cheeks and forehead: her make-up was without flaw, and she kept her expression neutral. "You've already received your punishment for your trespass. And we're content, whatever happens now. If the *imagined child* is destroyed then the temple ends; but then perhaps it's the temple's *time* to end."

"And that's of no consequence to you?"

The doctor considered the question awhile. "Precious Cargo will have achieved its purpose."

"Its purpose? How?"

"With your help, I might add," she said, enjoying his discomfort. Roman took his hand from Lloyd's shoulder; Lloyd nodded, as if the movement communicated a message.

"I think I preferred it when your people broke my limbs," Honeyman grumbled. "At least I *understood* that."

"That was an older temple," the doctor remarked coldly, "with a clear, finite objective." Her voice hardened. "Years of patient, dedicated work, ruined." She paused, to collect herself. "But Temple One Thirteen is far more .... experimental. It is the parents who imagine the child, after all; we simply spin the wheel."

Roman was twirling his finger high in the air as he opened the front door, which was hanging lopsided on its hinges.

And Franklyn Tyde has now been imagined, Honeyman heard. He glanced at Alex, who was staring at the painting of her son, then at Lloyd, who was staring at his wife. Both seemed oblivious to this exchange. "Franklyn?" he muttered.

"Your creation, Baptist," the doctor said. "You created him, just as you murdered my Lady of the Manor." She nodded slowly with reflection. "You might even call it an *evolution*, for isn't that what Mr Darwin taught us, that the strongest emerge from adversity in any form necessary? And this is, after all, a temple built on a eugenic crime." She watched with satisfaction as Honeyman closed his eyes. "You've already witnessed the boy's power, I believe. Franklyn's guardian has entered him, both in punishment and in protection, because it's confused over whether he has succeeded or failed. *That* is the price of the cheat they perpetrated together." She turned to leave. "We'll have to see how that plays out, but we thank you, Baptist, for making it possible."

"Dr Mays, a word before you go," Honeyman said. With a twitch of surprise she stopped at the door, leaving her assistant to walk to the limousine. "Have you considered why all the children are beautiful and talented?" he inquired grimly.

The doctor's eyes shone with delight. "Because the Father is powerful and gracious. Because he holds in contempt the ugly, useless beings your god has spawned."

"You think Satan makes the children that way?" Honeyman asked reasonably.

The doctor hesitated. "Of course. Every child born to this temple is His miracle, so of *course* they're perfect. The Father wouldn't tolerate anything else. That's why I love them, Baptist: all of them, whether they live or die."

For the first time today, a smile was figured by the shift of Honeyman's moustache. "I believe you're mistaken. The parents imagine these children, and *all* parents imagine their children beautiful and talented, do they not?" He sighed, to let the statement find its mark. "The miracles you speak of are the miracles of the imperfect beings, you see, not your god."

Dr Mays considered this with a touch of her cheek, her eyes darkening with uncertainty, before being summoned by the revving of the limousine.

Time passed in silence, no one in the old reception of the Sobarth house speaking.

Eventually Alex looked up. "We have to destroy it, Lloyd," she whispered. She positioned her fingers at the tiny rip already started in the paper; Theo looked back at her, his expression pondering on the sort of mother who would destroy her own child. She hesitated.

"Allie, this is our child," Lloyd gasped. "It's our dream."

She shook her head. "It's *your* dream, Lloyd. I wasn't a part of it … would never have been a part of it."

"That's not true!"

"Just to give birth, that's all, then stand in a corner somewhere while you raised him, with those people, and whatever thing that awful poster would have brought in to the house. Just so he could die at sixteen."

"We don't know that! We've got a fifty-fifty chance, Allie. Maybe more. We'll be good parents, we'll be *great* parents. He'll make it, I know he will."

She smiled ironically. "No, he won't. The egg knows his future, and he won't survive. The girl on the marina's going to win. It's predestined."

"Rubbish!"

"It's true, Lloyd. The game's rigged. What they say about us being faithful, it's all a big cheat, just to make us raise him the way they want him to be raised and to keep us in line. We'll spend the next sixteen years thinking of ways we can bring him on, desperately finding things to please the Trustees, but it will all be a complete waste of time."

He had a face of mistrust, and she glanced at the egg. "Look for yourself," she said. As if in a trance, he wandered slowly to the plinth. The lid opened as he approached and he studied the inside for a long while, until his eyes showed his horror. Shortly his expression hardened. The lid snapped shut as he turned to his wife.

"Alright, then it's sixteen years," he declared.

"What?" she said, in disbelief.

"At least we'll have those sixteen years."

Her jaw dropped. "Those sixteen years are for *you*, Lloyd. Not for him."

"What are you talking about?" he laughed.

"You care so much about the idea of being a father that you'd see his death, knowing he'll be in torment after that." She stepped away from him. "You're just in love with the idea of *being* a parent: you'd make the worst kind of parent there is."

Lloyd lifted his chin and took a long breath through his nose. "Allie…" he warned.

"Don't call me that. Ever. I don't love you anymore, Lloyd. Whatever happens now, I don't love you. This place has seen to that."

Lloyd reached out his hand. "I don't give a fuck whether you…" He composed himself. "Look. Lauren said I couldn't interfere, that you had to give me the painting back of your own free will, but I swear … swear on my boy that I'll kill you if you damage the painting." He retrieved his arm and made a fist. "Give me my boy. You're not fit to look after him. You could never be faithful the way *I* am."

"Rip it, Alex!" Honeyman implored.

"Shut up, both of you," she said distractedly, holding up the portrait. She let out a long, painful sigh. "I reject my son," she said, "because I love my son." Her fingers tensed, the veins in her hands visible, the squeeze of her eyes showing the exertion.

"You … you can't do it," Lloyd said gleefully.

She screamed, then closed her eyes and screamed louder, as she ripped. The portrait ripped cleanly, directly along the middle contours of Theo's head, precisely down the centre of his forehead, making a road through his pug nose, his philtrum, mouth and dimple chin. She threw the pieces of paper on the floor in anguish; Lloyd raced to scrabble them up, but they had already vanished.

"Mr Morrow, listen to me," Honeyman said. "Their hold over you is broken, you…" He didn't finish his sentence, but staggered back, his hand against his forehead, then slumped to the floor. A trace of his blood was on the egg in Lloyd's hand, which Lloyd now opened, the frail original lock giving way easily. With disgust he tipped out the contents: some ashes, a hair ribbon and a wedding ring.

"It's over," Lloyd groaned, feeling the bones of the temple snapping, the baptism gifts becoming mere objects of wood and metal, the eggs emptying, the buried children at last allowed to sleep. He held the egg as a rugby ball, weighing it in his hand and moulding his hand to its shape, then lifted it slowly above his head. His face came alive with hatred as he lunged towards Alex.

"N–no encore."

Lloyd stopped, bewildered, barely a footstep away from his wife. He looked up to see Franklyn Tyde, who had appeared on the stairs, eyes rolled back white. His movements were stiff and abrupt, his face completely without expression. The image created was of a walking mannequin.

"I n–name you. L–lloyd M–morrow."

The egg dropped to the floor. With a groan, Lloyd followed. He hid his face in his arms, his screams muffled against his hands as his legs thrashed out in agony. Franklyn closed his eyes; when he opened them he was himself again.

"Franklyn, come with us," Honeyman muttered groggily as he struggled to his feet. "The temple's power is broken."

"He's right, Frank," Alex said, helping the minister. "You're safe with us." She had a glorious flash image of adopting the sweet, beautiful boy; of making him her own.

Franklyn was looking around the house with curiosity and interest. "You haven't destroyed the temple, Baptist, you've *completed* it. Just as Lauren Mays predicted. This is *my* home now." He finished his walk down the stairs, his movements supple and graceful. "You have to leave, before the Pharaohs return." He considered the man writhing on the floor, picked him up under one arm and marched to the door. Outside, Alex and Honeyman dragged the incoherent Lloyd into the back of the Land Rover.

"Frank, come with us," Alex repeated. "I don't care what you've done."

Franklyn smiled in response. "You would if you knew, Mrs Morrow." He nodded to Honeyman. "The Baptist knows."

"There is forgiveness, Franklyn," Honeyman murmured.

The boy threw him a rueful smile before he returned inside and closed the door. "There's only one person who can bring me forgiveness..." were his parting words "...and it's not you ... or your god."

Alex looked back at the Sobarth house as they drove away, expecting to see Franklyn at a window. She was disappointed: the drawn blinds looked lifelessly back at her. When the house out of view, she reached behind her in an attempt to comfort Lloyd, who shook violently at her touch.

"What's the *matter* with him?" she asked.

"He's been *named*," Honeyman replied.

"Named?"

He sighed reflectively as she turned back round. "We all face judgment, Alex, when we come before the throne: when our lives come under the harshest spotlight, as we see ourselves for who we really are. We need to see all of our vanities, conceits and sins, before we can set them down. We are *named*." He glanced in the rear-view mirror. "Franklyn's guardian is from Hell, and Hell understands all our fears. But Lloyd will be fine, I think: the glimpse of judgment is so traumatic that his memory will simply block it out. He won't remember anything."

They travelled awhile in silence. "So is it over?" she muttered, as her hand went to her stomach.

Honeyman raised his eyebrows in dismay and confusion. The finale of his last encounter with a temple had been all violence and destruction; Temple 113 was finished, the proof lying in the contents of the original Fabergé egg, but it didn't feel like success. "How are *you*?" he asked cautiously, noticing her hand.

"I'm not sure," she said, with a pained expression as Lloyd started to mutter from the back. She put her mind elsewhere, recalling the images of Franklyn and Gracie summoned by the Sobarth egg. That compartment had been different from the others: both the children were sixteen, the egg offering neither younger nor earlier representations. The portrait belt presented them only briefly, and with anger, fear and … and with something else, something that was almost akin to embarrassment, as if they shouldn't be there. Both portraits were in black and white. And both were upside down.

Honeyman was also lost in his thoughts. His hand went to the pocket of his overcoat, where his fingers once again touched the figurine of Gracie Barrett-Danes, which had somehow survived the destruction of the doll's house and shown him the contents of the Sobarth egg. His fingernail scratched the figurine's base; he was sure the marking 113 was gone.

"So I've lost my baby," Alex whispered, her tears coming. "I've lost him…?" she repeated at length, but this time in inquiry. Shortly she frowned as her hand again settled on her stomach, gently and protectively. Honeyman noticed the gesture and with a mystified expression slowed down, deciding to pay more attention to his driving.

With a cautious smile she registered the action, recognising its meaning.

He smiled back, thinking that perhaps there had been a small success after all.

EPILOGUE

I T WAS A short circuit in the Gracie/Franklyn portrait compartment: neither had won, neither had lost, so they both shared a measure of existence.

This was Honeyman's reasoning.

This was why Alex gave birth to twins.

When Mother Morrow visited the hospital on Christmas Day, the morning after they were born, Alex handed her the boy first. The boy was instantly recognisable as Theo, the perfect person glimpsed through the temple, although Alex knew the girl would be beautiful and talented too. After all, Millie was *her* imagined child.

"Lloyd wants to know when he can come," Cristabella said, her face contorting as she pursed her lips for a kiss.

"He can come whenever he likes, Mam. They're his children too."

Cristabella's expression held an inquiry. After Lloyd had spent a few months in hospital for what the doctors termed as acute exhaustion, he had made a valiant attempt to rebuild his life, his therapy including contacting the people connected with the Brecon clinic. The Wights didn't recognise him. They were in the process of moving when he turned up at their house, to be given a fifteen seconds window before Margie Wight dismissed him in order that she could remonstrate with a workman. As he wandered off he saw the alphabet abacus, broken, in a skip.

It's just the two of us, Allie. Only the two of us can remember anything – maybe because we were there, at the end. You've got to take me back, if only for that reason...

That was a conversation one morning when he had come to the office. The stale smell of alcohol was on his breath.

"I don't know Mam," Alex whispered apologetically in response to her mother-in-law's look. In the glow of her children she wanted to be generous and kind, but trust was gone.

"At least you have options," Cristabella suggested as she paced the ward with Theo. "I'm here, whatever happens."

As always when something warmed her heart, Alex pictured her oak kitchen table. Theo and Millie were sitting there, and she imagined them at every age as if she were Charles Sobarth's egg. Before, she had only been able to differentiate them as *oldest* and *youngest* and it was now a source of wry amusement that the difference in age was less than five minutes, that even her one clear perception of her future in those dark times had been inaccurate.

The oak table still held its secrets. In this symbol of home, of family unity, she was sure she could sense a man lurking somewhere in the background. She couldn't hear his voice or see his face.

Perhaps I should imagine a husband, she wondered. She smiled for a moment, picturing this glorious man, then supposed a perfect husband might just imagine a perfect wife in his turn.

"Nothing's impossible, Mam," she admitted, "and I know he wasn't himself. But some wounds run deep. Time will tell if they're just too deep to heal."

Honeyman would have echoed that truth as he watched the workmen walk the boards between the scaffolding erected around the Sobarth house. He wondered if he had the strength or the will to go on. Franklyn Tyde hadn't returned in the months he had kept a vigil at the Brecon studio flat, notwithstanding that before it was dissolved the charity called Precious Cargo transferred the house into Franklyn's name.

"Where is he?" Honeyman wondered. "Where will he go?"

Well he'll be looking for me, won't he? Just as I'm looking for him...

Honeyman shrugged in reluctant agreement and opened his hand, where the figurine of Gracie Barrett-Danes lay warm against his palm. He put it down next to a new notebook, an expensive one bound in leather upon which he had written in fine script: *Gracie's Book.* This was more than just sentiment, for he believed that the figurine of the forlorn girl with the hands behind her back was indeed the author of many of his thoughts; that it wasn't just a fantasy he had devised to live with his grief and his guilt.

She had helped him with his depression: the feeling of despair in his battle against the coven. His two encounters with the temples shared one unsettling common denominator: their defences were unassailable, the subtle locks and keys unbreakable; only fool's luck had carried the day.

In the front of the book was written:

With temple 1331 it was the folly of one of their servants.

With temple 113 it was the unexpected actions of a grieving father.

Luck, nothing more.

These were most definitely *his* thoughts. He had the notion that he could work from the front while Grace worked from the back, creating the illusion that they were engaged in the process together. The last page, Gracie's page, read:

Perhaps it is more than luck.

Perhaps God is with us.

364

There was a smiley squiggled underneath, a circle with two dot eyes and a smile. He traced it with his finger, then carefully placed the figurine on his tiny window sill. As an afterthought, he turned it so she faced the house, to await Franklyn's return.

But Franklyn wouldn't return: he was missing and not even his mother knew where he was. All she knew was that he'd be home soon; if he was sleeping rough it wouldn't be long before he missed his mother's cooking.

She was repeatedly telling herself this on his seventeenth birthday, as she played with something she was sure had once been very important to her, its significance now lost. It was a ticket to see a 70s rock band, *The Dead Pharaohs*; the price was £1.13p, though the date and venue weren't given. She must have seen them once, she supposed. Maybe it was nostalgia that made her keep it.

She heard the front door. "Jerry, is that you?" she called, then stiffened as she recognised the footstep. "Franklyn?" she whispered. Her son appeared at the door of the front room; she stood up in ecstatic surprise and advanced towards him, the ticket falling from her fingers.

Franklyn calmly pushed her back, propelling her onto the settee. All the while his eyes stayed on the ticket as it floated slowly and gently to the floor, as if it was made of insect wings.

"Franklyn? What are you doing son? What's wrong?"

He hesitated, then collected the ticket. His body shuddered with shock and outrage as his hand closed around it.

"Franklyn!" Mercedes called as she put a hand to her forehead in dismay, but he was already leaving. "Come back! Where are you going?" She ran out onto the steep road and looked around urgently: it was late and the one working streetlight at the corner couldn't penetrate the gloom. She screamed and threw her hands up dramatically as a 70s' sports car came racing down the road, catching her in its beam and narrowly avoiding her.

The car, which was an E-Type Jaguar, was driven by Franklyn, a present for his seventeenth birthday from Dr Lauren Mays, who was in the passenger seat.

"That's my Little Lord B," she announced, considering the band ticket that had appeared like a bright tattoo on the back of Franklyn's left hand. The garish red tattoo was identical to the ticket that had been held by Mercedes Tyde, except that it now had a venue: a residential address in London.

Franklyn glanced at the tattoo and saw an announcement appear in the centre of the ticket: *Presenting Carl Tyrone.* "Carl Tyrone. Is he first?" he asked. He blinked to acknowledge and accept his sudden disfigurement; a leather glove, yes he'd wear a leather glove, like those guys in those old shows on *Top of the Pops*...

She answered with a wide smile and touched the stereo with an air of satisfaction. The car swirled with the rapid scales of a fractured piano.

Watching him dash away ... swinging an old bouquet...

"I don't like ... this music..." Franklyn muttered, tentatively eyeing a cassette case on the dashboard which showed a glam rock star with a lightening bolt down his face. He had been given that LP as a birthday present by the Trustees when he was six: he was told that the lightening bolt was the mark of schizophrenia.

He winced. The piano notes were scampering around his head like rats in a sewer, infesting his brain.

"Look at you," the doctor whispered. "My Lad Insane."

His rueful smile acknowledged the doctor's pet name for him that dated from that birthday, devised by the album that was called *Aladdin Sane;* he was nameless for the Trustees before that. It was the name his mother had always hated, the one he had always found confusing, notwithstanding its connection with the baptism gift, which indeed the doctor always used with a quizzical air as if she too queried why fate had chosen it.

He turned sharply onto the coast road, the music blaring, and accelerated into the night.

Who ... will love Aladdin Sane...?

"Am I two people now?" he said, feeling the burn of the tattoo on his hand. "Is that it? Is that what it means?"

Her mouth opened widely in wonder and understanding. "You were *always* two people, my beautiful Lad Insane."

The answer made Franklyn think of the girl on the hill, prompting the instructions on the ticket to fade. They were replaced by the face of Gracie Barrett-Danes obscured by a red muss, as if someone had tried to scribble her out with a felt pen.

The doctor pretended not to notice the boy guiltily retrieve his hand, hiding it in his pocket. She was thinking how much she was looking forward to seeing her Little Lord B again, for she hadn't lied to the Baptist, she loved all the children with a passion. The Father had given her many children in exchange for the child she had lost, and her service had been blessed with the countless tears of joy and sorrow that accompany parenthood.

"D'you want to change the record now?" Franklyn asked.

She settled back into the old leather seat. "No, let it play out."

With a shiver her gaze wandered out to sea, searching for her lost children in the cold, angry water.

Precious Cargo is just one of a whole range of publications from Y Lolfa. For a full list of books currently in print, send now for your free copy of our new full-colour catalogue. Or simply surf into our website

www.ylolfa.com

for secure on-line ordering.

TALYBONT CEREDIGION CYMRU SY24 5HE
e-mail ylolfa@ylolfa.com
website www.ylolfa.com
phone (01970) 832 304
fax 832 782